AMBUSHED

Susan told herself that there really was nothing she could have done to avoid what happened.

David Wiggins was too swift, too skillful for anyone as inexperienced as she to stop from doing exactly as he pleased.

He did not even have to exert any force—he was so big and strong. And Susan had no time to react when he pressed her against the stable wall and brought his lips down on hers.

But one thing still puzzled her.

Why had her hands gone around his neck? Why had her lips parted beneath his? And why had she returned his kiss so fervently?

The questions were disturbing, and the answers Susan was able to come up with were more disturbing still. But most troubling of all was the thought of what might well happen when this man, who knew so much about passion and cared so little about propriety, decided that a mere kiss was not enough. . . .

D0756870

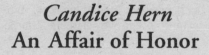

The Lady's Companion

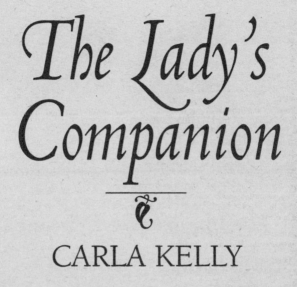

CARLA KELLY

A SIGNET BOOK

SIGNET
Published by the Penguin Group
Penguin Books USA Inc., 375 Hudson Street,
New York, New York 10014, U.S.A.
Penguin Books Ltd, 27 Wrights Lane,
London W8 5TZ, England
Penguin Books Australia Ltd, Ringwood,
Victoria, Australia
Penguin Books Canada Ltd, 10 Alcorn Avenue,
Toronto, Ontario, Canada M4V 3B2
Penguin Books (N.Z.) Ltd, 182–190 Wairau Road,
Auckland 10, New Zealand

Penguin Books Ltd, Registered Offices:
Harmondsworth, Middlesex, England

First published by Signet, an imprint of Dutton Signet,
a division of Penguin Books USA Inc.

First Printing, June, 1996
10 9 8 7 6 5 4 3 2 1

*To Metta Lieb and Laurie Sampson,
good friends and readers*

To every thing there is a season, and a time for every purpose under the heaven: . . . a time to die . . . a time to plant . . . a time to kill and a time to heal . . . a time to laugh; a time to mourn . . . a time to keep silence, and a time to speak . . . a time to love, and a time to hate; a time of war and a time of peace.

ECCLESIASTES

Chapter One

It takes a birthday to bring out the worst in a woman, Susan Hampton decided as she propped herself up on one elbow and watched the maid of all work ration out the morning coal. Already I am wearing my father's socks to bed, and goodness knows that is an old-maid thing to do, she thought. But it was warmer that way, considering that this was January, money was tight, and coal dear.

"Jane, do you know that I am twenty-five today?" she asked the maid.

Jane straightened up from the hearth and stared at her in honest amazement. "Gor, miss, you can't be that old!"

Susan winced, then collapsed onto her back, giggling in spite of herself.

"Oh, miss, I didn't mean . . ."

"It doesn't matter, Jane!"

It really didn't, she told herself after Jane left the room in a blush of apology. She pulled the covers back, then thought better of it, because the room was so cold she could see her breath. She huddled herself into a ball and remembered summer, and luncheon alfresco beside the lake.

Except that there won't be any more lazy times sitting on a blanket, eating strawberries. Hampton Hill was gone now, swallowed up in Papa's debts and sold at auction to a raw-faced industrialist from somewhere north, and his overdressed wife.

With a sigh, Susan snuggled down deeper into her pillow. The pillow slip wasn't ironed, because the laundress had been let go two years back, along with the downstairs maid, the upstairs maid, both footmen, and the stable hands. Papa's last horse found itself under scrutiny at Tattersall's, and the butler's wages were reduced, thanks to Sir Rodney Hampton's run of bad luck at faro. Jane, the maid of all work, did most of the household tasks now.

She used to pull on a frilly apron when the doorbell rang, but Susan couldn't remember when she had stopped doing that. Ironing pillowcases had gone from the necessary to the frivolous category. And besides all that, the doorbell didn't ring often anymore.

"At least we have this house," Susan spoke into the pillow. There was less furniture in it now, after Papa's disastrous weeks at Newmarket last fall, but that meant less dusting. She sighed again and flopped onto her stomach. If only Papa hadn't sold the iron-bound leather trunk that was new during Elizabeth's reign. It had been Mama's and Papa had promised he would always keep it for her. "I forgot, my dear," he had told her after the carters removed it. He gave her his most charming smile, as if that made things right.

It used to, she thought as she sat up and hugged the pillow to her. Charming Sir Rodney could woo the bark off the trees, Mama used to say. Susan lay down again, wishing, as she did with more frequency these days, that Papa had other skills. Nothing vulgar, mind, she assured herself. Papa was a gentleman and couldn't be expected to work, but what a pity he had never learned how to manage his resources. Too bad he could never look farther ahead than tomorrow's appointment with the tailor.

Susan sat up and draped a blanket around her shoulders, the pleasure of sleeping late gone with each new reminder of Papa's misdeeds. She was being unfair; he hadn't been to the tailor in over a year. At least, not since that much-tried tradesman had sent letter after letter that Papa only allowed to pile up on the bookroom desk. She had worried about the other mounting piles of bills on Papa's desk, going out of her way sometimes to detour into the bookroom and just stand there, looking at the desk, willing them all to disappear. Then she did not go in the bookroom anymore; the sight was too painful. Papa wore last year's clothing and shined his boots himself, his valet having fled to greener pastures.

The feeble ration of coal was no good against a January colder than any Susan could recall. She would dress herself and hurry downstairs. They kept the little salon warm with a cheery fire, in case someone should chance to call. Few did anymore, and never any young gentlemen. Sir Rodney Hampton had seen enough bad luck in clubs up and down St. James Place to discourage any bachelor interested in Susan Hampton. True, her face was as pretty as any seen in recent years. And while there were some generous of pocket who could have overlooked her lack of dowry, there was no one in pants foolish enough to take on the present and future liability of Sir Rodney himself. A husband with such a father-in-law would be wooing his own financial disaster, no matter how lovely the wife who hung upon his arm and warmed his bed.

It had taken several years for Susan to bring herself to face that bit of pain. When she was eighteen, anything had seemed possible. Papa had promised her a Season, and beautiful clothes, and what remained of Mama's portion. When the Season was at its height, and she was still not part of it, Papa had come to her, contrite, but smiling his charming smile, and assuring her that next year would be her turn.

So she had waited, and had made a few plans—fewer than the year before, but still plans. Next Season's beauties were already primping and pouting in the foyer, ready for their turn to dance and flirt and marry. She had reason to hope; Papa had promised that her nineteenth year would see her presented and suitably wed.

Susan took a deep breath and leaped from the bed, tugging on her clothes and standing close to the hearth and its paltry fire, which gave off no more warmth than colored-paper flames. Shoes in hand, she snatched up the hairbrush on her dressing table and hurried downstairs. She would return and make her bed later.

It almost happened during her twentieth year. Papa had a wonderful two-year-old named, oddly enough, Hampton's Promise, that should have won at Newmarket. That he did not, Sir Rodney blamed on the rainy weather ("Ah, Susan, you should see Promise on a dry stretch!"); his groom ("Dear me, how could the man have left all that grain around for Promise to gorge upon?"); and even Waterloo ("My dear, I never suspected that all those officers would come home and set up their stables!"). And always there was Papa's charming smile to make things right.

That Newmarket year, and the selling of the estate ("Oh, I'll win it back, my dear, just you wait."), had marked the end of Susan Hampton's plans. If her smile was no more than automatic now when Sir Rodney spun his cobweb schemes, he did not notice. Perspicacity was never a strong suit of the Hamptons. If she was quieter now, contemplating the marriage of her former friends and rejoicing with them in their increasing waistlines and the anticipation of babies, Papa did not notice. He barbered his own hair now, shaved his own face, brushed his own clothes, and assured her that everything would come out fine.

Breakfast was everlasting porridge, eaten off Mama's beautiful china, to be sure, but tiresome day after week after month after year. She ate thoughtfully, skimping on the cream and wondering if anyone would call today. Aunt Louisa would remember that it was her birthday. Last year she had sent around gloves, and followed them with an afternoon visit, breathless with news of Amanda's own comeout. ("Of course, dear Susan, I wish I could do the same for you, but this is Amanda's moment to shine, and I know you would not begrudge her.")

Susan poured herself some tea. She missed the oolong, but gunpowder was not as bad as she had feared. It warmed her middle and sat sturdily on top of the oatmeal. Amanda's Season last year had been rewarded at the eleventh hour with a proposal of marriage from a second son with a Northumberland estate. Aunt Louisa had swallowed her pride and given her permission. If she was secretly grateful that Amanda, who had freckles and gap teeth, had found a man at all, Aunt Louisa did not admit it.

Susan rested her elbows on the table and contemplated her cup. "And now, dear Aunt, you are avoiding me," she murmured, watching her breath ruffle the smooth surface of the tea. "You know you do not wish the expense of bringing me out this year, and Papa will only promise and forget. I have become an obligation."

It pained her that Louisa was avoiding her. She had so few relatives, that the defection of one—even an imperfect specimen like Aunt Louisa—brought its own discomfort. As she sat blowing on her tea, it never occurred to Susan to wish for improvement in their character. What she saw was what she got, and she was used to the uncertainty that accompanied being a Hampton.

Still, she considered as she left the breakfast room, brushing her hair, how novel it would be to have relations that could be depended upon. Her friends had parents, aunts, and uncles who were almost boring in their dependability. She stopped in front of the mirror to part her hair. Susan eyed herself, smiling to notice that twenty-five years didn't seem to set any heavier on her shoulders than twenty-four had. "For my birthday, I would like someone, anyone, to rely on."

Susan had finished braiding her hair into two neat plaits when she heard Papa's quick footsteps. He whistled as he hurried down the stairs, and she smiled in spite of her mood, knowing that he was probably giving his neckcloth one last twitch, and tugging at his waistcoat, impatient to be off—where? She knew that Papa's friends all crossed the street when they saw him coming, hoping to avoid being touched for a loan. Sir Rodney dressed with a flourish every afternoon and left the house with some importance, but where he went, he never said, and she had not the courage to ask.

But it was still morning, and here he was now, smiling at her from the doorway of the little salon. He surprised her by pulling a long, comical face. "Susan, why so glum? It's your birthday!"

"My twenty-fifth," she reminded him, amused that he actually noticed her sobriety. It was so unlike him to be aware of others, unless they sat across from him at a gaming table. Then they had his full attention, or so said one of her former suitors when she asked him what Papa did, night after night, in White's.

Papa came to her and leaned across the back of the sofa, rubbing his cheek against hers. She breathed in the familiar smell of bay rum, content for a brief moment, and crossing her fingers that he would not spoil the moment with any of his extravagant promises. She hoped in vain.

He struck a pose and gave her his elegant profile. "My dear, this very day will see the end of any discomfort you may have endured over the last few years. How fortunate that good luck should come on your birthday."

He was in such a good mood that Susan hoped he did not notice her little sigh. He came around the sofa and sat down beside her, looking around the room.

"We'll have new draperies before the week is out, and I'll get the plasterer in to do something about the ceiling. Just see if I will, Susan." He kissed her cheek. "Happy birthday, my dear."

She smiled at him, but said nothing, knowing well that Papa would supply the text, if she was reluctant.

"Susan, I have been invited to such a card game at White's!" he said when she continued her silence.

"Papa, no . . ." she began, but he cut her off with one elegantly shaped finger to her lips.

"Susan, trust me to know what's best. There now. He is an industrialist from somewhere to the north," he explained, gesturing vaguely in the direction of Scotland. "Lord Kinsey tells me that he is ripe to pluck, has a face as easy to read as a mirror, and a hammy hand with wagers."

"No, Papa," she cautioned more urgently, but she might have addressed the fireplace for all the attention he paid her. Sir Rodney Hampton was on his feet now, pausing in front of the mirror for one final prink at his collar points. She started toward him, but Wilde stood in the doorway now, extending Sir Rodney's coat to him.

He allowed the butler to help him into the coat, and accepted his hat before turning to his daughter again. "Susan, sometimes I wonder if you are really a Hampton," he scolded, his voice light and teasing. "One could almost call you stodgy."

"One could almost call me sensible," she said to the window glass a moment later as she watched her father pick his way down the icy sidewalk. The glass fogged over, and by the time she had wiped it clear, Papa had settled himself into a hackney. She sighed. He would ride it to within a block of his destination, then get out and walk the rest of the way, so no gentleman looking out of White's big bay window would suspect that Sir Rodney Hampton had sold his carriage horses. But if she could believe the arch looks that she endured when they were out in public, the only one fooled by his charade was Sir Rodney himself.

Her heart burned for him, but she did not know what to do, beyond saying a little prayer that he would not be fleeced beyond his means, and that he would remember to come home in time to share her birthday dinner. Cook had promised Georgiana pudding with fruit sauce, one of her particular favorites. She grinned at the windowpane, fogging it again. At least I need not fret and starve myself like my cousin Amanda, she thought. We Hamptons may not be blessed with too many coins of the realm, but we do have slender figures.

"Even if I am now facing the perils of my twenty-sixth year, I can do it with a little waist," she said out loud, then hurried upstairs to make her bed.

She ate her Georgiana pudding alone, her ears pricked for the sound of Papa's key in the lock. It didn't taste as good as she remembered, but she knew better than to allow Jane to take even a stray spoonful belowstairs. Cook would mope and stew and create scenes that would require all of Wilde's patience, so Susan forced herself to eat it all, even though her mind and her heart were on Papa.

He did not come in at bedtime, and she allowed herself the luxury of a little hope. If he was having a successful run of cards, she reasoned, he would stay. When she finished the last of her mending, she lingered a few minutes more in the sitting room, soaking in warmth to carry upstairs to her cold bedroom. I am too old for a comeout now, she thought, spreading her fingers over the cooling fire. But if there is a respectable dowry, even a small one, perhaps I could attract a widower.

And that, she concluded, would be better than no man at all. Susan hurried into her nightclothes and leaped into bed, blessing Jane for providing a rare warming pan in honor of her birthday. I would like it if he were not bald, or paunchy, or lacking teeth, she thought, after she said her prayers in bed (The Lord would under-

stand how cold the floor was, she was sure, and it was her birthday). If he liked to carry on conversations about books, and didn't
mind her sketches, that would be so much leaven in the loaf.

And that was as far as her fancy ever took her anymore. "I suppose I am stodgy, for a Hampton," she told the ceiling as she
hugged her pillow to her. "Oh, Papa, even a little dowry would
make such a difference!"

She was just about asleep when she heard Wilde open the front
door. She lay there smiling into the dark, then got up and padded
on stockinged feet to the stairway landing that looked down on
the front hall.

Papa stood there in his coat. He held out his arms automatically
for Wilde to remove it, then shook his head and said good night to
his butler.

Susan got no farther than the first step down. She was about to
call a greeting to her father, but something in his stillness stopped
the words in her throat. Scarcely breathing, she lowered herself to
the top step and sat crouched in the shadows of the chilly upper
landing.

She held her breath and watched him standing so motionless,
his eyes riveted to the floor as though he searched for something
he had dropped. She let her breath out slowly and put her hands to
her mouth as he sank to his knees, pitched forward onto his elbows, then rested his forehead against the cold parquet flooring.

He didn't cry so much as moan. It was a ghastly sound, worse
than Mama's last, long breath that had gone on and on until it
seemed to blend with the breeze of a long-ago summer. That was
death, and it comes to all. This was worse: it was the sound of
hope gone.

Susan closed her eyes against the sight of her father groveling
on the floor below. There was a pain in her as though someone
had slit open her chest, ripped out her heart, wrung every drop
from it, then crammed it back into her body. She opened her eyes
and calmly observed her father. She rose to her feet, more steady
of motion than she felt, and climbed the one step to the landing.
She would not stomp on his dignity by rushing below to join her
tears to his, but would wait until morning.

Bad news always keeps, she thought as she dragged herself into
bed and closed her eyes again. Papa will have to tell me tomorrow, but we will deal with it. She pulled the covers up to her chin.
But as for me, I will not trust another's promises every again.
And when I get up in the morning, I will have turned a page in
my book of life.

Chapter Two

ℰ

As it turned out, there wasn't time to mourn the evaporation of social repute, town manor, household effects, and servants on the turn of a card; the matter came to a head too quickly. Papa's disgrace crashed down around him on a Tuesday night; by Friday evening, that most enterprising young Lancastershire weaver was sitting, with a sigh of satisfaction, in Papa's favorite chair, snapping out Papa's newspaper, and waiting for Wilde's summons to dinner.

Susan and her father followed the carter in a hackney to Aunt Louisa's house six blocks over on the corner of Timothy and Quayle streets. Susan would have walked to save the pence, but Sir Rodney wouldn't hear of it.

"Tush, my dear," he said with a wave of his hand, "how would it look?"

She could only close her eyes and turn toward the window, biting back angry words that she would only have regretted later. In the three days since his ruin and their expulsion, she saw her father quite clearly for the child he was, and would always be. As long as Sir Rodney possessed two groats to rub together in his pocket, he would always choose to flick one at a beggar, squander the other on a bunch of violets, and look around for someone to provide him with two more.

"Besides, Susan, you know that we will come about again," he said, taking her clenched fist between his two hands and trying to smooth out her fingers. He leaned closer, speaking confidentially. "And I have heard of a wonderful game tonight at Lord Crutchley's."

She opened her eyes and jerked her hand away. "Papa! We have lost everything! How can you speak of gaming!"

The hurt look came into his eyes and he pouted, leaning back against the dusty cushions. "I had thought . . . your mother's pearls," he said finally, his voice heavy with misuse.

"No, Papa. That is all I have," she said quietly.

He was silent then for the rest of the brief journey. I will not permit you to shame me into giving you my last treasure from Mama, she told herself as she wrapped her cloak tighter about her. She was so tired, worn out with the hurried packing of her clothes and what household items the estate agent had allowed her to keep. She burned with the humiliation of having to fight for the taken-for-granted treasures of her life that could have had no possible meaning for the new landlord. "What can he possibly want with a portrait of my mother?" she had finally shouted in frustration at the agent, weak-kneed almost at the humiliation of having to dicker.

"He's a brash man from the weavers' district," the man explained. "He's got an indecent lot of cash, but no background. These paintings will give him countenance, or so he told me. Instant ancestors," he concluded, chuckling at the absurdity of his client.

"But this is my mother's picture!" Susan had pleaded. "Can you help me?"

To answer her, the agent had patted her cheek, sidled a little closer, and suggested to her a service she could provide him, in order to retain her paintings and some of the furniture besides.

Nothing shocks me now, she had thought grimly as the man folded his arms and leaned even closer to her. He knows there is no one beyond an aging butler to come to my defense. He knows how useless my father is. I have no champion.

From somewhere, she had pulled the tatters of her dignity around her shoulders and looked the agent in the eye. "I think not, sir," she had informed him serenely. "You may keep the paintings and the furniture and go to hell on the next mail coach."

She stared through the dirty pane of glass as the jarvey picked his practiced way through London traffic. "Do you know, Papa, the real estate agent told me I could keep the paintings and furniture if I let him lay with me," she commented, keeping her voice normal and conversational.

Sir Rodney sighed and shook his head. "I know I can come about again, daughter, I know it! I need your help."

"Papa, did you hear what I just said?" Susan asked quietly.

He looked at her, really looked at her, for the first time. "Something about paintings, wasn't it? Don't know why you gave them all up without a fight, but then, no one ever said Hamptons were any good at dickering for this or that like fishmongers."

"Papa . . ."

He put a hand to his head and smiled at her in that brave way of his that made her want to grind her teeth. "I have such a headache, my dear. I do hope Louisa isn't entertaining tonight. Do you think she will feel obligated to give a party for us? I sincerely hope not. My waistcoats have all seen too much duty lately; everyone knows them. It's such a worry."

I think we will be lucky if Aunt Louisa does not direct us to the nearest workhouse, Susan thought, and smiled sourly to herself. Well, at least Papa and I could learn a trade there.

"Papa, do you think you could ever get a job?" she asked suddenly, her mind on the poorhouse.

Sir Rodney's shocked stare said more than words ever could. "Dear me, what was I thinking?" she murmured and settled herself lower into her cloak, drawing the folds around her.

"I cannot imagine," he replied and ignored her for the rest of the ride.

The carter, arriving before them at Timothy and Quayle streets, had deposited their few boxes and luggage on the steps leading up to the front door. He left without lingering about for a tip to augment the agreed-upon fare that Sir Rodney had carefully counted into his mitten at the other house. How perspicacious he is, Susan thought. The carter knows there is nothing extra from such threadbare shabby-genteels as we.

"Well, Papa, knock," she said a few minutes later as they stood together, facing the closed door. It was beginning to sleet again, the icy rain scouring them.

He only stood there, as though unable to raise his hand to his sister's overly impressive door knocker. He stared at the thing—a somewhat dyspeptic-looking gilt lion—as though he expected it to roar and lunge at him. "My dear, do you recall how we used to laugh about Louisa's vulgar door knocker?" he said, not taking his eyes from the thing.

He glanced at her then, wincing as the sleet drove into his eyes, and for the smallest moment she could see the pain that he had contrived so earnestly to hide for the last three days. "My dear, Louisa is Louisa, even if she did marry a purchased baronet who smelled ever so slightly of the shop." He took her arm. "I trust this will not distress you."

We are destitute, without a home, it is sleeting again, and you wonder if I mind a little vulgarity? she asked herself, amazement edging out contempt by only the slightest margin. She opened her mouth to pour out her distress, then closed it again, stopped in time by the sight of her father's anxious face. Unbidden from nowhere like an additional dousing of cold water came her mother's last words to her: "My love, do take care of your father," Mama had said. Susan had been fourteen at the time, but as she shivered on those steps with Sir Rodney Hampton, she understood them finally. She swallowed the great lump lodged in her throat and touched his arm.

"I do not mind, Papa. Let me knock.."

And so they found themselves rescued by Lady Louisa Sanderson, relict of Sir William Sanderson, a man with distant Yorkshire mill connections who had indulged himself in life with a purchased title and did not object to vulgar door knockers. With a pang, Susan watched as her father allowed himself to be rescued, clucked over, and folded into the depths of his sister's obligation and disdain, dished out in equal parts to her little brother.

They were treated well enough, better than Susan would have suspected, considering the nature of the burden Sir Rodney represented to his older sister. True, their rooms were at the back of the house, when there were larger chambers to spare elsewhere. And was it her imagination that the servants only turned away to chuckle when Sir Rodney, dressed impeccably if shabbily, passed them as he made his stately progress from room to room? Never mind; he did not notice, not would he ever. It was Susan's misfortune to writhe inside, bite her lip, and overlook that which she was powerless to control.

For all that she was unhappy, it was a quiet week. Families were only just now straggling back from Christmas celebrated on their country estates, and the Season was yet an anticipation. Few came calling, and it was just as well. To hear Louisa tell it, breakfast room tables all over London were littered with pattern cards and modistes' drawings as mothers and daughters conspired over swatches of spring fabric and dreamed of grand entrances.

In the Sanderson household, Louisa's youngest daughter, book on head, practiced her own entrances and exits while her mother frowned at the dressmaker's news that jonquil would be all the rage this year.

"Emily will completely vanish in that shade of yellow," Louisa protested as she pushed away the fabric pieces.

"It is the high kick of fashion, my lady," said the dressmaker, obviously not a stranger to the pale-eyed, pale-haired daughters of the Sanderson household.

"But she will disappear!" Louisa lamented, careful not to disturb Emily's gliding progress up and down the room. "I ask you,

how will she find a husband if no one can *see* her? Show me
some blue fabric, Madam Soileau," she insisted.

"It is *not* à la mode," said the dressmaker, gathering up her
swatches. She glanced at Susan, who was watching the pageant
before her as she worked her way through Louisa's darning.
"Now this one, with her dark hair, would fairly glow in jonquil."
She took Susan's chin in practiced hands and turned her head this
way and that. "And with brown eyes! Madame, hearts will
break!"

"They will mend with amazing speed when their owners discover I have no dowry," Susan said, her amusement genuine.

The dressmaker let out a great gust of a sigh and released
Susan. "Men are pigs," she declared. With her martyr's air, well
developed through some twenty Seasons, she shook her head at
Emily's wispy blondness. "I shall find some blue from somewhere, but I do not think you can hope for more than a second
son."

Louisa did not flinch from the dressmaker's hard-eyed pronouncement. "I would even settle for a clergyman for that one,"
she whispered, her eyes on her daughter, "although I am sure
Emily does not know Genesis from Ecclesiastes."

"Most clergymen don't either," Susan added, her eyes lively.

The dressmaker put her hand to her bosom. "La, my dear, what
a treasure this one is! Her face is this Season's face, and she has a
sense of humor, and her figure is just enough without being too
much—although, my dear, I think you should lace tighter. I
would say an earl at least. Perhaps a marquis."

"And she is quite twenty-five," stated Louisa, delivering the
final blow. "Madam Soileau, we will concentrate on Emily.
Susan, you may put away that darning now."

I know when I've been dismissed, Susan told herself as she du-
tifully folded up the darning, dodged around Emily and her
books, and made her own graceful exit from the room. I do not
think Aunt Louisa will want me tagging along at any of this Season's events. It was not a reflection that caused her any pain, but
she did pause in front of the mirror at the top of the landing to admire herself for a moment. How nice to know that I have this Season's face, she told herself. Some eligible marquis will never
know what he is missing.

The thought made her giggle. She was still smiling over the absurdity of it during dinner. Her amusement lasted into the drawing
room as Aunt Louisa signaled for the footman to set up her embroidery frame. Sir Rodney, hands clasped behind him, traveled

to and from the windows, peering out, looked back at Susan, and repeated the circuit.

Susan watched him, her good cheer gone. I know the signs, she thought as she threaded her darning needle. If he had any money, he would tell me now that he is going to White's, and give me that pugnacious stare, daring me to say no.

But he had no money. With a sigh, Sir Rodney collapsed onto the sofa next to his sister, who looked at him over the spectacles she wore for close work.

"Rodney, you are a flibbertigibbet," she said, her tone querulous. Obviously the afternoon's plain speaking from the modiste about Emily's prospects still rankled. Susan tried to make herself small in her corner of the sofa, wondering already how soon she could decently say good night to them both.

"I suppose I am, sister," he agreed, ever the complacent one.

Susan jabbed at the darning in her hand, embarrassed for her father.

"Rodney, I want you to know that there is no way I can finance a comeout for Susan," Louisa said, her eyes on the canvas before her.

"Oh, Aunt, I never . . ."

"I know you have not, my dear," she said to Susan, all the while keeping her eyes fixed on her brother. "I want your father to understand my situation. Rodney, Susan is your responsibility. If you have some little fraction remaining of your dear wife's expectancies, it might be enough to find Susan a clergyman, or perhaps a widower who is not disgusted by her age. Rodney, speak to me plainly: can you provide anything for your daughter?"

Sir Rodney stared back at his sister, the astonishment evident in his face. "Of course I can!" he declared, glaring at his sister with indignation.

"When?"

It was a little word, but it hung on the heated air of the drawing room like a vulture over carrion. Louisa was looking at her brother now, her hands idle in her lap. "When?" she repeated, more softly this time.

Sir Rodney leaped to his feet, his face red. "As soon as I can, Louisa!" He looked at Susan. "Just ask Susan! She knows that I have great plans for her comeout. Tell her, Susan."

I wish I could, Papa, she thought as she stared back at him, then lowered her eyes to her darning again.

"Susan!"

"It is much as I thought, Rodney," Louisa said as she selected a skein of thread. "More shame to you."

He went to the doorway and stood staring from one to the other. Susan looked at him once and cringed at the pleading expression in his eyes.

"Susan, can you get my embroidery scissors from the breakfast room?" Louisa said.

"Of course, Aunt." She rose and went to the door. "Is there anything else you would like?"

It was a simple sentence, but when she said it, Susan knew that their relationship had changed. From now on, if she stayed in that house, she would be the one to fetch and carry. Papa could do nothing for her, and his sister would not, beyond providing for her and using her for errands, interventions with the cook, contact with the tradesmen. The years would pass and she would gradually become Louisa's almost-maid.

"Just the scissors, my dear."

"Very well."

Papa followed her into the hall. His face was white now, his eyes more desperate than she could remember. He tugged at her sleeve like a child. "Susan, this one last time, trust me with Mama's pearls. I can win and you will have your season!"

"No, Papa."

He did not ask a second time. She gently removed her arm from his grasp and went to the breakfast room. When she returned with the scissors, he was moving slowly up the stairs. From her seat on the sofa close to Aunt Louisa, she heard him leave the house an hour later.

She remained where she was, even though she wanted to run upstairs, throw herself on her knees in front of the lowest drawer in her bureau, and feel the reassurance of Mama's pearls in their red velvet bag. He would never, she thought as she darned socks. Yes, he would, she amended.

Grimly she stuck at her task, nodding and saying "Um," and "Indeed," to her aunt's numerous comments on friends, enemies, neighbors, the government, and stray dogs. These will be my evenings from now on, she told herself. I had better get used to them.

To her relief, Aunt Louisa finally pushed back the embroidery frame with a sigh and called for tea, drinking it slowly, thoughtfully, while Susan chafed to go upstairs.

"Good night, Susan," Aunt Louisa said at last. "Do you think you could return a book to the lending library for me tomorrow morning? It's long overdue."

"I surely can."

Louisa made a face. "I cannot spare a maid to walk with you, but you don't mind, do you?"

"Of course I do not, Aunt."

"Very well then." She took Susan's hand as she passed by. "We will get along famously, I am sure."

"Of course, Aunt," said Susan as she bent to kiss her.

In her room, Susan stood for a long time before the bureau, her hands clasped in front of her. Everything looked in order. If Papa meant to deceive, he had done better than usual this time. She knelt by the drawer finally and opened it.

Her neatly folded petticoats and chemises were turned back. I could have done that, she thought as she reached underneath them. She sighed with relief as she touched the velvet bag, then bit her lip as she felt for the familiar shape of Mama's beautiful pearls, a gift from her father. The bag was empty.

Susan was still awake hours later when she heard her father climbing the stairs. A week ago, she would have felt some hope, some anticipation that he would burst into her room with good news, the best news. He paused outside the door a moment, and she almost held her breath.

The moment passed; he moved on slowly. She turned her face to the wall and closed her eyes.

Chapter Three

She did not expect her father to say anything to her over break-fast, and he did not. After selecting from the sideboard, he sat qui-etly in his chair, his gaze going more often to the icy window than to the eggs on his plate. If he was chastising himself, Susan knew that it would pass soon enough. In a week, or maybe even a few days, he would be casting about for something else to stake on the flip of a card. I hope you do not take to stealing from your sister, Susan thought as she ignored her own breakfast. You have stolen everything from me now, and I have nothing left to lose.

She applied herself to the porridge in front of her, patting down the mush and watching the cream swell inside, then seek a lower level. She created a series of connecting terraces before she looked up at her father.

"I am going to seek employment."

It was not a question, nor was it spoken with any heat or blame. It was the most matter-of-fact sentence she had ever uttered in her life. She put down her spoon and took a deep breath as Aunt Louisa gasped.

Sir Rodney said nothing. Aunt Louisa looked at him, her face a study in stupefaction. "Can't you say anything?" she asked finally.

He could not. She turned to her niece, her words coming out as brisk and cold as sleet on window glass. "No Hampton has ever worked, Susan. How can you forget that?"

Susan let her breath out slowly. Either I continue now or I fold for good, she thought. "Then perhaps it is time one of them did, Aunt," she said, each syllable distinct. "I cannot continue to be a charge on you, and you will be the first to remind me that I am getting old. My mind is quite made up, Aunt."

"You can't meant that!" Louisa burst out. "What will our circle think when they learn that you have hired yourself out as . . . as . . . what? Think what this will do to Emily's chances!"

"It will do nothing to Emily's chances, Aunt," Susan said quietly. "The only one affected will be me."

Aunt Louisa leaned back in her chair. "I forbid you to even think of such a thing!" She put her hand to her forehead. "Now I have a headache, and there is so much to do today!" She rose, cast another scathing look at her brother, and swept from the room.

Susan finished her breakfast, wiped her lips, and rose to go while Sir Rodney still sat staring at his plate. She went to the door, but turned back when he cleared his throat.

"Don't do anything rash, daughter," he begged, raising his eyes to hers for the first time.

And how many times did Mama and I plead so with you? she wanted to scream at him. Instead, she took another deep breath until she felt calm enough to speak. "Papa, I am taking charge of my life now," she said, her voice rising with emotion, despite her efforts to control it. "I am long of legal age, and I have such a grievance against you, you know I have!"

He said nothing more. She went upstairs and stood for a long time staring out the window in her bedroom. It was snowing lightly, and her determination wavered. Perhaps there will be no snow tomorrow, and all the walkways will be swept, she considered. In another day or two, the snow could be entirely gone. She leaned her forehead against the windowpane. And in another year or two of days, I will be too old to make this attempt. I will be biddable and do whatever Aunt wishes of me, as if I never had plans of my own.

Well, perhaps I don't, she thought as she pulled on her boots and wound her muffler tight around her throat. I wanted to marry and have children, but unless some miracle happens, that plan is gone. I cannot depend upon a man to make my way safe or smooth. I must learn to do that for myself.

It was a daunting thought, and not one that she had entertained much in her life. All the women that she knew were taken care of by men, or at least in Aunt Louisa's case, were left pots of money to keep the coal flowing freely into grates, and excessive dinners on the table. I wonder, can I do it? she asked herself as she pulled on her mittens and picked up Aunt Louisa's book for the lending library.

"Susan!"

She looked up, startled and a little guilty as Aunt Louisa bore down on her from the front salon. With a gulp, Susan held up the book. "You wanted me to return this, Aunt?"

Louisa stopped and eyed her. "You're not planning anything foolish, are you, my dear?"

It's not foolish to want to provide for myself, Susan reasoned. "No, Aunt, nothing foolish," she said. "I'll be back before you know I'm gone." And with any luck, you and Emily will be out trying on hats or gloves, or taking measurements or umbrage, and won't have any idea when I return.

Aunt Louisa smiled at her, and Susan owned to a prickle of conscience. "I'll overlook your nonsensical little comments this morning, Susan," her aunt said generously.

"Very well, Aunt," she replied, standing aside for the footman to open the door. That was noncommittal enough, Susan thought as the door closed behind her. I could become an accomplished liar, if I worked at it.

Her determination wavered as the wind tugged at her skirts and spat snow into her face. I could return this book tomorrow, she thought as she stood, indecisive, on the front step. But it was beautiful outside, with a skiff of snow covering muck on the road and muffling the sound of horses' hooves. She shrugged at the particles of snow that trickled down her neck and started off at a brisk pace.

The lending library was busier than she expected, considering the blustery nature of the day. Obviously she was not the only person on the planet who enjoyed stretching out on the sofa with a good book, especially on a raw day. But now what? Susan returned the book and stood looking out at the snow, panicked suddenly by the realization that she had no idea how to look for employment. Her mind in turmoil, she watched a young matron with her small daughter, their heads together over a book. The sight, a familiar one from her own experience, calmed her and gave her an idea. She remembered earlier, more plentiful days when she had a governess.

Well, here I go, she thought as she made her graceful way through the stacks toward the woman.

"Excuse me, madam," she said, smiling and extending her hand. "My name is Susan Hampton. I am new to London, and I am looking for both an abigail and a nursemaid. Do you know . . . can you tell me of employment agencies in town?"

The woman smiled back and handed the book to her daughter. "It's hard to find good servants!" she said, taking in Susan's modish pelisse and smart bonnet.

Yes, I am one of your kind, Susan thought as she dimpled and smiled back. You can speak to me, for I am, as of ten-thirty this morning, still respectable. "It is so hard to find help?" she asked, her eyes wide with what she hoped was country naiveté. How excellent for my chances, she considered. Perhaps I will be lucky today, if good servants form a distinct minority.

"Let me suggest the Steinman Agency four blocks toward the Strand," the woman replied, gesturing toward the window. She leaned close to Susan then. "That's where I found our treasure of a governess. Of course, Steinman is Jewish, but a good businessman."

The woman giggled behind her hand, and Susan joined in. My, we are superior Christians, she thought. Enjoy the hypocrisy while you can, Susan. When you're earning a living, you'll be fair game, too. She thanked the woman for her advice and left the bookstore. It was snowing in good earnest now, but she bowed her head against the wind and hurried on.

Susan almost walked past the agency, but STEINMAN in modest letters on an iron plaque caught the edge of her vision. She stopped and stared at the door, wishing that an earthquake would suddenly swallow it. I could always pretend to myself that I couldn't find the place, she considered. Maybe in a year or two, I would even believe that I had done the right thing by winding myself back into Aunt Louisa's web.

But there it was, a substantial door with two neatly curtained windows to the side. A discreet sign in the window closer to the door said NOW HIRING. Susan took a deep breath and opened the door.

A young man looked up from the desk as a blast of wind came in with her. He grabbed at the paper he was writing on, leaning on it with his body and trying to clutch other papers now fluttering to the floor. Susan closed the door quickly behind her, wondering briefly why he did not just grab the papers, and then noting that he had only one arm. Oh, this is a good beginning, she thought as she knelt on the floor and began to gather up the papers.

"There you are, sir," she said a moment later. "I'm sorry for the commotion."

"Well, until I reach such a lame disposition that I have to blame a young lady for the wind, I thank you."

She smiled at him and held out her hand. "I am Susan Hampton," she said simply.

He had lost his right arm, so he held out his left. She shook it and sat in the chair he indicated. "I'm Joel Steinman, he with too many papers and not enough fingers anymore to subdue them all. Are you interested in hiring a maid or a governess? I might warn you that this is a difficult time of year to hire. What can I do for you?"

He was impossible not to smile at, with his rumpled black hair and lopsided grin. There was no question that he was a son of Abraham, as the lady in the library had mentioned. His nose was long and high-bridged, his warm olive complexion a striking contrast to the average pallid Londoner adrift in a gloomy English winter.

She smiled back, struck by the fact that this was the first man she had ever spoken to who was unknown to her father or aunt. I have never spoken of business matters to anyone before, she considered. And if I keep on grinning, he will think I am an idiot. The thought only widened her smile.

And he smiled back, as unconcerned as she was bemused. "What can I do for you?" he asked again.

"You can offer me some tea," she suggested as she pulled off her gloves and wondered if she had taken complete leave of her senses. "It's cold out there and I need to talk business."

Nothing seemed to surprise him. He leaned back in his chair. "Mama! Do put on some tea."

In a few minutes a lady who, other than being a foot shorter, was almost a duplicate of Joel Steinman came into the room carrying a tray. She nodded to Susan, set the tray on the desk, and settled herself into the chair at the other desk.

"Miss Hampton, this is my mother. We are equal partners in this business."

Enchanted, Susan held out her hand for the cup and saucer. "You run a business together?"

"Since my husband died, Miss Hampton," said the woman as she stirred two lumps of sugar into her tea. The glance she gave to her son was almost as warm as the tea Susan sipped. "If you could wait a few months, I am sure we will have a better selection of servants for you to select from. As it is now . . ." She shrugged her shoulders in an eloquent way that Aunt Louisa would have found uncouth, but which delighted Susan.

I cannot dupe these kind people, Susan thought as she set down her cup on Joel's desk. "You do not precisely understand. I want to hire myself out as a governess."

The Steinmans looked at each other and frowned. This is going to be more difficult than I thought, Susan considered. "I am proficient in French, piano, and needlework, and know the rudiments of grammar, math, and composition," she offered, stammering in her desire to please.

Mrs. Steinman shook her head, while Joel Steinman frowned at her. "It won't do, Miss Hampton," he said, and his tone was decisive. "There's not a married woman in the whole country who would hire you."

"But . . . you just told me how hard it is to find good servants, and here I am offering . . ."

The Steinmans exchanged glances again and sighed. "Mother, you tell her," Joel said. "She might think I'm being forward."

Mrs. Steinman folded her arms in front of her and leaned toward Susan across the desk. "Miss Hampton, when was the last time you looked in a mirror?"

"Why . . . only this morning. I don't understand," Susan protested.

"Ladies come here for abigails and governesses, my dear, and most particularly they do not hire pretty women with tiny waists, dimples, and curly hair. You can't be over twenty."

"I am twenty-five," Susan asserted. "But I am qualified in every way for such a position!" And you cannot imagine how badly I need it, she thought, leaning forward, too.

"Ladies do not want women in the house that look like you," Joel explained, his face a dull red. "They have husbands and older sons who would consider you too much temptation." He held up his hand against the militant look on her face. "I'm telling you this for your own good, Miss Hampton. I assure you it's nothing personal. I mean, I think you're charming." He blushed some more, and Susan laughed in spite of herself.

"Well, thank you, I think," she said, rising to go. Now what, she asked herself as she looked outside. It was snowing harder. "No," she said, and sat down again. "I need a job. My father Sir Rodney Hampton is a gambling fool, my aunt wants to turn me into her footstool, I am twenty-five with no dowry, and I need a job." I could cry without too much effort, she thought as she looked from one Steinman to the other. She wondered briefly which one would yield the faster to tears, then rejected the notion. This is business, she told herself. Tears are out.

"You're making this difficult," Joel said after a moment, but there was more regret than dismissal in his tone.

She took heart and hitched her chair closer to both desks. "I suppose I am," she began, "but I . . ."

". . . still need a job," he finished for her, his eyes merry in spite of her dilemma.

"Oh, I do," she sighed. "Please, help me, sir."

Steinman looked at his mother for a long moment and then

drummed his fingers on his desk. The rat-a-tat sound had a definite military cadence, and Susan wondered again where he had lost his arm.

Her attention was broken by the postman's whistle and the *whush* of letters shoved through the opening in the door. Without thinking, Susan got up and gathered the mail together, brushing off the snow. She handed it to the man in front of her. He glanced at the letters, then slapped one of them.

"*Oy gevalt*, Mamele, here's another one from Lady Bushnell." Forgetting her presence for a moment, he made a face at it, then took the envelope in his teeth and carefully slit it open with the letter opener. He took out the letter and shook it open, looking over it at Susan again. "You'd appreciate this lady, Miss Hampton. I think she is almost as persistent as you."

He was about to toss it into a wire basket when he stopped and read it through again, looking over the letter at her when he finished. He put it down then with scarcely concealed excitement, and glanced at his mother. "Mamele, I have an idea," he said finally, triumph in his voice as he looked at Susan. "Miss Hampton, I have an offer for you."

"Joel! You can't be thinking . . ."

He swiveled in his chair to watch his mother. "And why not, Mamele? Everyone we've sent, she's rejected. 'Too old, too slow, too stupid, too vulgar, too this, too that' until I want to smack her!"

Susan grinned in spite of herself. Joel Steinman, you are irresistible, she thought. "She sounds like a dragon."

"Most certainly. And Lady Bushnell is only the dog guarding the entrance to the underworld. What *was* his name?"

"Cerberus," she said automatically, wondering what he would say next.

"Ah ha!" he exclaimed, kissing his long fingers at her. "Exactly. I have here a letter from Lady Bushnell, widow of Lord Bushnell, late colonel of the Fifth Regiment of Foot, the Cotswolds Guards. I have been trying for months to please her with a lady's companion for her mother-in-law, the dowager Lady Bushnell." He leaned across the table until he was quite close to her face. "Miss Hampton, do you have any objection to old ladies?"

Captivated by him, she shook her head.

"Strong-willed, stubborn, drive-you-crazy martinets?"

Again she shook her head. "I've been living with them for years, sir," she said.

His smile was beatific. She thought for one amazed moment that he was going to kiss her, but he sat down again, slapped the desk in triumph, and nodded to his mother. "Miss Hampton is going to put us all out of our misery."

Mrs. Steinman considered the matter a while longer, then slowly nodded her head. "There's no one there beyond the bailiff ever to be tempted by Miss Hampton," she considered, working through the matter out loud. "Not that he isn't a nice man, but after all, a bailiff. We needn't worry about her there, Joel."

"Done, then," Steinman exclaimed. He leaped to his feet and grabbed for his overcoat on the rack behind him, shrugging one-handed into it, and then reaching for his muffler. "Don't just sit there," he insisted. "I'm going to see you employed before the morning is over."

"Not until your muffler is wound tighter," Susan said. She stood before him, and he stooped obligingly for her to perform this little service. She tucked the ends inside his overcoat. "Very well, sir, lead on."

He took her hand in the street, hurrying along sidewalks empty of pedestrians, but full of drifting snow. After several blocks of concentrated walking, he slowed down when he noticed that she was breathing heavily and almost skipping to keep up with him.

"I'm sorry, Miss Hampton," he said, smiling at her in such a way that she could never be out of sorts with him. "It will be such a treat to lift this burden from my shoulders and put it on yours!"

She laughed, and he joined in, standing still for a moment while she tucked in his muffler again. "Lady Bushnell—widowed since Waterloo—is about to remarry the colonel of her late husband's regiment. She has been wanting to find a lady's companion for her old mother-in-law, but she is a high stickler, indeed."

"The old woman, too?"

Joel made a face, and managed to look contrite, all in the same expression. "If you survive the younger Lady Bushnell's interview, that's your second hurdle. Old Lady Bushnell insists that she wants nothing to do with a companion. She insists that between her and David Wiggins . . ."

"David Wiggins?"

". . . the bailiff . . . they can get along quite fine," he concluded, taking her arm more firmly and pulling her back as a carter splashed through the intersection. He sighed. "She declares that companions are only for old ladies with one foot in the grave." He raised his hand and made a spitting sound onto his mittens. He looked sideways at her, apologetic. "Never tempt the devil with death, Miss Hampton," he said solemnly as he started her across the street.

"I wouldn't dream of it," she said, wondering with a smile on her face what kind of Hebrew charm Joel Steinman was working on her.

"So it stands. She tried other agencies without success, then turned to us. One or two of our companions got beyond the first scrutiny, but failed after a week in the Cotswolds with the dowager." He paused to consider the matter, and she had to tug him out of the street. "Sorry."

"Since then, Lady B the Younger has found fault with everyone we've brought over," he said as they turned onto a quieter street off St. James Park. "It may be that you'll do. Our other potential employees have been capable, but not particularly genteel. That you are, Miss Hampton."

"Why, thank you," she said, trying to keep the amusement from her voice.

He chuckled. "I do sound a bit managing, don't I, Miss Hampton?"

"You do, sir. I will overlook it, if this gets me a job."

They paused in front of an elegant town house not two blocks from Aunt Louisa's residence. "Oh, I know this place," she exclaimed. "And I do remember the windows draped in black and the black wreath on the door after Waterloo. And straw on the street to muffle the passing traffic."

"Ah, yes. No, no, Miss Hampton!"

She had started up the front steps, but he tugged her back. "We use the servants' entrance." He indicated the flight of steps behind an iron grating. When she did not move, he touched her elbow lightly and spoke closer into her ear, his voice sympathetic. "Miss Hampton, I think that only the first step down is difficult. I'll help you."

So it is, she thought as she swallowed the lump in her throat and allowed him to help her down the shallow flight to the servants' door. Her eyes filled with tears and she wanted him to wait a moment before knocking. He did, fumbling inside his overcoat to draw out a handkerchief and dab at her eyes, his own eyes kind.

"Forward, Miss Hampton," he said as he raised his hand to the door. "If Daniel can survive a discussion with lions, you can stare down Lady Bushnell."

He was well known belowstairs, everyone from the scullery maid to the footman greeting him as they made their way to the butler's parlor, where they left their coats. The butler led them up-stairs to a small parlor, where he suggested they make themselves comfortable.

It wasn't a long wait. While her heart may have sunk to her boots during that longest journey down the servants' stairs, it bounced back into her throat when the door opened. Joel was on his feet at once, shifting his feet to compensate for the overbal-ance of his missing arm. She rose, too, her hands clasped behind her to keep them from shaking in plain view.

Lady Bushnell nodded to them both, seated herself, and indi-cated that they sit, too. Joel accepted her offer of tea, but Susan declined politely, imagining the disaster that would occur if she dropped the cup in her nervousness. The maid withdrew for the tea.

There was silence for the longest moment, then Lady Bushnell directed her clear, unblinking gaze at Susan, even as she spoke to the employment agent. "Mr. Steinman, I do believe you are bring-ing me the infantry now," she protested, her voice cultured but tinged faintly with resignation.

"My lady, I am quite twenty-five," Susan said, her voice stead-ier than her hands.

To her relief, Lady Bushnell smiled at her. "I wish I were," she said, the humor subdued, but evident in her voice. Susan relaxed slightly and began, unaccountably, to hope. "It's obvious that you have more breeding than the usual scaff and raff Mr. Steinman brings to me," she continued. "Who are your parents?"

"My mother was Maria Endicott of the Marling, Kent Endicotts and my father is Sir Rodney Hampton." Susan looked Lady Bush-nell in the eye and politely dared her to make something of it.

"Oh." It was concise and said "I know who you are," as loudly as if Lady Bushnell had spoken it. She hadn't needed to; Sir Rod-ney's tattered reputation hung between them like a flag of surren-der.

"You will understand why I need a position, my lady," Susan continued.

"Is it that bad with him?" Lady Bushnell asked, her inquiry still polite, but not withdrawn.

Susan nodded, and gave herself a moment to reply. "There is very little between me and ruin, my lady," she managed finally. "My father may mean well, but he cannot provide."

"You have an aunt, I believe?"

"I do. She would like me to be available to fetch and carry for her."

"That's what you will be doing for my mother-in-law, if I select you," Lady Bushnell said, her words reasonable. "Why not
stay under the protection of your family?"

It was a good question, quietly put and extremely apt. In a way
that no words could express, Susan knew that her acceptance
hinged on her answer. Joel Steinman felt it, too, and she was
grateful. He stirred in his chair, his leg touching her dress briefly.
She felt the movement of the material and took heart. It was as
though he had taken her hand for support.

"I could, of course, my lady," she said. "I am sure there are
those who say I should, but it wouldn't be any time at all before I
vanished."

Lady Bushnell cocked her head to one side, intrigued, but she
did not interrupt. She only nodded when the maid entered quietly
with the tea.

"She means well," Susan went on when the door closed again,
"but I would become Aunt Louisa's unfortunate niece, and not a
person in my own right." She managed a smile with no mirth in it.
"I am already Sir Rodney's daughter, my lady, and that is difficult
enough to bear."

"Running away to the Cotswolds won't change that," Lady
Bushnell interjected, her voice mild.

"It might," Susan disagreed. "There I would be Susan Hampton, and I might discover that that is a nice thing."

"My mother-in-law does not want a companion, and has told
me this on numerous occasions. She is sixty-five and has buried a
husband, a daughter, and a son. She was a follower of the drum
through India and the Peninsula, and a legend in the army." Lady
Bushnell paused for the briefest moment, then continued in her
masterfully calm voice. "She is independent, stubborn, and dear
to me beyond all reckoning. I want great care to be taken of her
without her knowing it. Do you think you could do that? Her
bailiff does it, but he is busy with the estate. She will try you and
exasperate you." Lady Bushnell sighed. "I fear she does not wish
to give up even one inch of her independence." She regarded
Susan. "Something in your face tells me that you sympathize,"
she said in amusement. Her voice turned serious again. "Still, it
will be difficult. Are you equal to it?"

I must be, Susan thought. This is all the chance I have. "I do
not fold easily, my lady."

Lady Bushnell smiled. "Susan Hampton, I do not think you
fold at all. Pour tea for us, won't you?"

Susan eyed the teapot. "I think my hands are shaking too badly, my lady."

"And you are an honest body, Miss Hampton," Lady Bushnell noted. "That will suit Lady B's bailiff. Pour it anyway."

She did, picking up cup and saucer, and taking a firm grip on the teapot. She kept her back straight, as Mama had taught her, and even managed an artful splash at the end that sent a little geyser of tea evenly creating its cultured wave to the edge of the cup. Head high, she held out the cup to Lady Bushnell, who accepted it with a twinkle in her eye.

"You are made of sterner stuff."

Sterner than what was unspoken. I will spend a lifetime living down my father, she thought as she poured a cup for Joel Steinman.

"The position is yours, if you want it," Lady Bushnell offered after a sip of tea. "Can you leave right away?"

"Tomorrow, if that's soon enough." Heaven knows Aunt Louisa will wash her hands of me.

Lady Bushnell smiled. "I think that will be soon enough, my dear! Now you have to see if you can please a woman who doesn't need you, and a bailiff who feels the same. I don't know which will be more difficult."

Chapter Four

c

The job was Susan's, but even Lady Bushnell was hard put to explain why. "I have tried many," she said companionably over tea, and smiled when Joel Steinman nodded in agreement. "You're forty years her junior, and I can think of little you might have in common. And yet . . . oh, well. Only take good care of her."

"If she will allow me," Susan interjected.

"Yes, if she will allow you." Lady Bushnell hesitated then, as though she wondered if what she requested would be agreeable to Susan. "Miss Hampton, I wish to do all I can to give my mother-in-law a free hand, but if she falls ill, or suffers an injury, I expect you to tell me. I will spare no effort to see that she is removed from that remote valley and cared for, no matter what my other responsibilities."

"I will do as you ask, my lady," Susan said.

"I hope you will," Lady Bushnell replied.

It was a sobering reflection, Susan decided as they left the mansion in early afternoon. I am setting out for a place I have never been, to do something I have never done before, and among people who probably don't want me. More than typically silent, she allowed Joel Steinman to walk her home the few blocks from the Bushnell residence.

"I will see that a message to Quilling Manor goes on the mail coach tonight," he promised. "There'll be someone waiting for you in Quilling tomorrow night."

They paused in front of Aunt Louisa's town house. Steinman stood, hand in pocket, observing the impeccably swept front steps and the door knocker. "You know, if you change your mind about leaving all this, I will certainly understand," he commented.

She shook her head. "Don't give me any outs, Mr. Steinman," she said. "For all that this is an impressive house, it has a way of absorbing one."

He chuckled. "Well, I am certain many of your friends will wonder if you have taken total leave of your senses."

"Do you think I have?" she asked frankly.

He shrugged. "Who of us really knows anything about the lives of others?"

"That's no answer," she said, amused.

"It's a very good answer," he declared, then winked at her. "Besides all that, Miss Hampton, a good Jew always answers a question with a question. Good day." He looked up at the house again. "And good luck?"

"Do I need it?" she questioned back, quizzing him with her eyes. He laughed out loud and started back toward the employment agency, head down against the wind that was picking up again as the afternoon lengthened.

I will tell them over dinner, she decided, so I will only have to tell the news once. She wanted to begin packing, but that would have required her trunk from the attic, and she did not wish to alert the servants to her plans. Instead, she spent the little time until dinner sorting through her clothing, searching for the serviceable, winnowing out the frivolous. There was soon a respectable pile of sober clothing ready to be folded and packed into her trunk. She sighed and put her evening dresses and ball gowns in cloves and a sturdy box. She hesitated over her silk drawers and chemises, then added them to the pile. No sense in abandoning all pleasure for duty. When I am frumpily proper in serge and wool, she decided, I will enjoy my silk all the more.

It was a small victory in an afternoon of reflection and was swallowed up totally by the sound of the dinner bell. "I cannot face them," she said out loud, clutching a shawl of Norwich silk to her like a breastplate of steel. What had seemed so sensible and realistic before the dinner bell now felt foolish and desperate. If I say nothing at dinner, I can send round a note to the Steinmans in the morning, she thought as she prinked at her hair in the mirror and tried to squeeze a little color back into her cheeks. I can stay here and let Aunt Louisa throw me the occasional bone.

She stared at her own anxious face, closing her eyes against her own eyes so wide and frightened in the glass. Everyone knew that Sir Rodney Hampton had never kept a promise in his life; why should his daughter? "But I have promised I would go tomorrow," she said and opened her eyes cautiously. The fright was still there in her reflection, but something more, too, a curious kind of resolution more felt than visible, but real all the same. "I promised," she repeated. "I promised."

Susan saved her news until after the fish course had been removed by the breast of mutton. At least they cannot accuse me of springing horrible news on an empty stomach, she thought as she speared a slice of mutton with more intensity than usual. And I do not much care for mutton in the first place. She put down her fork.

"I have something to tell you."

They looked at her, and some instinct told her that even years from now, these would be the faces she remembered—Emily, her air of vague distraction made more pronounced by the burden of being a violet female in a daffodil year; Aunt Louisa, faintly annoyed to be disturbed from her mutton's path from fork to mouth; and Papa, wary and eager-eyed at the same time, desperate for good news from some source. And what had Susan ever been to him but pleasant company?

"I have accepted a position as companion to an elderly lady living in the Cotswolds. I leave tomorrow morning."

It sounded bald, even to her. The silence that followed her quiet pronouncement was the silence of disapproval so profound that there were no words. "I will be paid thirty pounds a year, plus my room and board," she added, wanting to fill that enormous silence, even if it was only with puny words that sounded like chicken peeps.

Papa spoke first, and this startled her. She glanced at Aunt Louisa, wondering if the news had rendered her speechless, and angry at her father for throwing her off balance.

"I spent more than that on gloves last year," he said, his tone oddly placating, which only brought her own anger to a high boil.

"I know, Papa!" she said, her voice big in the room. It was almost a relief to shout at him, to cow him in his chair and watch him shrink before her eyes. "I am tired of your endless, silly promises and your spendthrift ways! They have quite ruined me!"

He winced at her words as though she had lashed him with a whip. "Hamptons don't behave like this, daughter . . ." he began, but she would not let him continue.

"Oh, I know that," she raged. "They smile and simper and look big-eyed at the world, and hope for charm to help them over life's little trials! No, I am not like you," she finished, each word a slap in his face. "And I thank God for that!"

"That is quite enough, Susan."

Aunt Louisa was on her feet now, the fork with its bit of mutton still in her hand. "You will apologize to your father."

Susan leaped to her feet and flung down her napkin like a guantlet. "I will not! You cannot make me!"

Aunt Louisa seemed to tower over her, a patient expression on her face that made Susan grit her teeth. "You will apologize to your father, and we will forget this conversation ever took place."

"I will not revoke a word of it," Susan said with a calm now to match her aunt's. "It is enough that I have to earn my bread and spend a lifetime living down my father's sorry reputation."

Sir Rodney closed his eyes as if she had slapped him. Susan looked at him, suddenly aghast at herself because she felt nothing, no pity, no sorrow, no remorse. Pathetic man, she thought. Why should a body feel anything for you? She looked up from her contemplation of her father. Aunt Louisa was speaking again.

"You will apologize or you will not return to this house, once having left it."

"If that is your choice, Aunt," Susan said as she started from the dining room.

"No, Susan. It is yours."

She lay awake long after her trunk was packed, corded, and downstairs waiting for the carter who would take it, and her, to the Hound and Hare to catch the morning coach. Don't they understand what they have done to me? she asked herself over and over, until the words lost any sense or meaning. And when she had ground that subject down to hash, she thought about David Wiggins. Oh, I hope you are of a mind to be helpful, she thought. I am so weary of difficult men.

Before sunrise, she let herself out of a quiet house, permitted the carter to hand her up onto the high seat, and congratulated herself on saving the cost of a hackney. The morning was bitter cold, the air still and heartless. This is a discouraging time of day, she thought as she settled her chin into her muffler. She thought she would turn around for a last look at the town house, but she did not. If someone is looking out a window, she told herself grimly, they will not have the pleasure of thinking that I cared enough to glance around.

Muffled by snow, the streets were oddly silent. The further they drove toward the city, the more carts she saw, until there was the Hound and Hare, brightly lit, with a queue of passengers already waiting to scramble for the best seats.

To her relief, Joel Steinman stood in the inn door, stamping his feet to keep the cold at bay. He nodded to her and indicated a bench in front of the inn where two mugs of tea waited for them. She took one gratefully, holding the cup to her cheek.

"I won't have you laboring under the fiction that the Steinman

Employment Agency sees off all its clients," he said as he took her ticket from her and handed it to the coachman. "It's just that I suspect this is your first ride on the mail coach."

She nodded. "You know it is. Do you have any good advice?"

"What do you think?" he asked, a smile on his face. "Although I fear you are out of luck for this first stage of the journey, when you get back on after the first rest stop, try to get a seat facing the coachman."

"That's it?" she asked after a moment watching the ostler stow her trunk on top and knot it down.

"That's it. Let's get you in line, Miss Hampton."

She set down her tea and took the arm he offered, clutching it rather tighter than she meant to. He looked down at the pressure on his arm.

"Steinman has another service I forgot to mention," he said as they shuffled closer to the coach. "We let our clients know of other openings more suited to them, if some come our way. And we also don't mind getting letters from clients, if they get lonely."

She didn't have any more time than to give him a grateful smile, before the coachman was helping her inside the conveyance. Steinman leaned in after her. "One thing more: get on David Wiggins's good side and he will be your ally. He has a most excellent side."

Intrigued, Susan leaned across the clergyman squashed in next to her. "Excuse me, sir. Mr. Steinman, do you know him? Why didn't you tell me?"

Joel Steinman only grinned and waved his empty coat sleeve at her as the coachman blew his horn to warn bystanders. Susan sat back, her elbows close into her sides, warned from further exhibition by the *harumph* of the vicar on one side of her, and the warning stare of an overfleshed woman mashed next to her. They left London as the sky lightened.

Nightfall found Susan only just beyond Oxford, and with a huge headache. I have learned so much today, she thought as she leaned her forehead against the cool glass, smudged from a day of travel through snow three parts mud. I can jostle for a window seat with the best of them, eat standing up, and entertain three-year-olds with the oddest bits of things from my reticule. I have listened to Waterloo stories and Trafalgar stories, and grievances of master and worker, and traded recipes. I know remedies for morning sickness and how to keep fleas off cats. Travel by post chaise was never this enlightening.

She longed for her bed, ached for the comfort of a familiar mattress, and a maid to bring her a tisane. I suppose I will be fetching those for someone else, she reflected as she rubbed her temple. Oh, I wonder what a lady's companion does?

A nursemaid dozed beside her. Her head tilted farther and farther forward, then snapped up when the coach hit icy patches and slid sideways. I could ask her, Susan thought, then reconsidered. She would only wonder what planet I had dropped down from, that I was so ill-equipped.

The headache was a stubborn one and she knew it would not go away without a good night's sleep and something to eat. Food was out, no matter how many more times the weather forced them to stop tonight. She had spent her last few pennies on tea and a hard roll at the inn before Oxford, and even that was hard to come by, with the crush of travelers. Her stomach growled, and she could only chafe at her own pride that refused to ask a penny beyond the coach fare from Lady Bushnell, or a modest loan from Joel Steinman. Her reflection in the coach window hardened. She would starve the length and breadth of England before asking Aunt Louisa or Papa for a groat.

No, what we must do is arrive at Quilling, and I must figure out how to charm David Wiggins. Lady Bushnell had said he was one of her late husband's regimental sergeants, and before that, her father-in-law's sergeant, too. Susan tried to picture him in her tired brain, but all she came up with was someone old and forbidding, and used to strict obedience. Perhaps his wife is more easily worked upon, she considered. I can ask her advice on domestic matters, and work my flattery on her husband that way. And if he is convinced of my worth and value, perhaps he will convey it to Lady Bushnell.

About her future employer, she had no clue. "I only know that I simply must succeed," she said out loud.

"Wot, miss? Begging your pardon."

Susan glanced at the nursemaid, who was sitting up wide awake now, trying to pull down the bow of her bonnet from under her nose, where it had ridden up and curled like a mustache. She hesitated. Aunt Louisa would no more speak to this inferior than pack snuff in her lip. Susan looked at her seatmate—the coach was nearly empty now—and was struck with the fact that talking to her was going to be like taking that first step down to the servants' entrance.

"I am to be lady's companion to Lady Bushnell at Quilling

Manor," she confided, her unease overcoming her scruples after all these miles. "And I must tell you, it frightens me."

The nursemaid had wrestled herself out of her bonnet. She turned big eyes on Susan. "Coo, love, it would worrit me some, too. I hear she's a high stickler." She leaned closer, her voice low and confidential, even though the sailor sitting across from them snored. "I hear she sleepwalks and prowls about the place at all hours and ends up outside the family mausoleum, joost sittin' there. Keep your door locked, miss."

"Oh, I shall!" Susan declared. "This is grim indeed."

The nursemaid retied the bow under her chin and glanced out the window as the coach began to slow. " 'Tis what my uncle heard from the gardener's cousin, who had it from the laundry maid."

"Apocryphal, then," Susan murmured.

"No, miss. The apothecary ain't had nothing to do with it!"

"My mistake," Susan replied, careful not to smile. "But tell me something of David Wiggins. Do you know him?"

"Nobody knows him, miss, for all that he's lived here five years or so. He came back from Waterloo with Lord Bushnell's body, and he never left. I call that strange."

"He's not friendly then?" Susan asked, feeling her hopes dribble away.

" 'Oo knows? He could be shy or queer as Dick's hatband." The nursemaid smiled when the coachman blew his horn. "And here we are, miss, and I don't mind saying it's high time!"

It was high time, and then some, Susan agreed as she left the mail coach, stiff in all her joints and with a head so huge she felt like turning sideways to get out of the door. The coachman unstrapped her trunk and dropped it into the snow. Shaking her head at the ostler, who would only expect coins she did not have, Susan tugged the trunk close to the inn door. She glanced briefly at her reflection in the window, thankful to discover her bonnet straight and her hair still smoothed in place. Aunt Louisa always did say I had a knack for that, she thought. At least I will not frighten the shy, retiring, and elusive David Wiggins, be he ever so queer.

He was also the nonexistent David Wiggins. When Susan worked up her courage to enter the taproom and inquire of the innkeep, he only shook his head. "Haven't seen him today, miss. Not at all." The innkeep sighed and stacked away the last of the glasses. "Of course, it's been a rum day for the hostelry business.

I misdoubt he can get off the place, what with all this snow. Can I speak you a room, miss?"

She shook her head. "Thank you, no. I am to be Lady Bushnell's companion, and a letter was sent for someone to meet me. I can wait for conveyance."

"That'd be David Wiggins, then. Some tea, miss?"

She shook her head again. "I would like a glass of water, if you please."

The innkeep eyed her more closely. You are wondering why I am dressed so well, and such a nipfarthing, she thought, her humiliation complete. Her eyes were beginning to fill up and she wanted to look away, but she raised her chin higher instead. After another moment's appraisal, the innkeep turned away, then came back with tea.

"Oh, I can't," she protested.

"Take it, miss," he said, his voice kind. "We all end up at low tide sometimes." As she sniffed back her tears, he looked under the counter. "And Lord bless us, here's a pasty left from supper. Let me stick it on the hob a moment, and you'll never know it wasn't fresh."

"Oh, I mustn't," she began.

"You must and will, or I'll get ugly," he said, his tone firm.

Something tells me you have daughters, Susan thought as she sipped the welcome tea and then followed him a moment later to a table as he brought the meat pie. "And look at this, I even found a bit of soup all sad and lonely," he said, setting it down with a flourish beside the pasty.

She couldn't speak, but he didn't seem to expect her to. He gazed around the room while she blew her nose hard, and then he began to stack chairs on tables. "It's not a big village, miss, is Quilling, but we're good enough for most," he said at last.

Her headache was gone by the time she finished eating. The innkeep had busied himself in a back room somewhere, and she had the taproom to herself. She ached for sleep, but there wasn't anything she could do but sit there, back straight, like a lady, and wait for David Wiggins to show up.

As anxious as she was to meet him and take his measure, Susan felt no qualms about his nonappearance. I am used to dealing with men who do not keep promises or deliver what is promised, she thought. A woman unfamiliar with Sir Rodney's frippery ways would probably have worn the floorboards through to the ground, pacing back and forth. If one has no expectations, one is seldom disappointed, she told herself as her eyes grew blurry and midnight turned into one o'clock. The innkeep had given up trying to give her a room upstairs, and said good night an hour before.

It was nearly two o'clock when she realized with a prickle down her back that someone was standing in the taproom doorway, looking at her. She hadn't heard anyone come in, but there was a subtle difference in the air of the room, as if it had rearranged itself to accommodate another body. Intruding on stale tobacco was the fragrance of hay, remembered just vaguely from the years before Papa sold the estate.

I should be jumping out of my skin, she thought as she breathed the tiny odor and felt the intensity of someone's eyes on her. I wonder if the landlord has any ax murderers in Quilling, or Caribbean conjurers left over from market circuses. She smiled to herself. I think it must be David Wiggins.

Just as she turned around, the man in the doorway gave an enormous yawn, the epitome of all yawns. "Sorry," he said when he could speak. "It's been a day, Miss Hampton." He straightened up from the doorframe, where he had been leaning. "I'm David Wiggins and I've come to fetch you."

His voice had the lilt of the Welsh in it, and he had the look of dark folk beyond the Dee, Wye, and Severn rivers, for all that his name was so plainly English. If he was a little taller than some, and blockier of build, she considered, that would account for the Wiggins side. His dark hair and eyes and a certain intensity of observation about him told the Welsh side. And his lovely speech. But he was much too young to fit her fiction of a retired sergeant from the Regulars. Oh, dear me, she thought. I shall have to change my strategies.

"You're David Wiggins?" she said, wondering instantly at her stupid question.

"Said I was," he commented. "And you're our latest lady's companion, pain in the side, burr in the balbriggans?"

Double dear me, she thought. "I'm Susan Hampton," she said, sidestepping the question. "And I don't know what balbriggans are, sir."

He didn't reply right away, but he turned his head a little away from her and smiled into the dark, as though someone else were there. "I'll tell it this way," he began in his musical voice. "I hope you're wearing woolen balbriggans under all those skirts, because we have to walk partway."

He looked at her again and raised one eyebrow. You're hoping I back out, she thought, returning his gaze, even though her cheeks flamed. Her anger blew in and out like a spring wind through an open door. She shrugged into her coat again, and pulled on her gloves, nourishing herself with an honest reply.

"I'll manage," she said. "And you can mind your manners."

Again he turned his head away for that surreptitious grin, and he chose not to rise to the bait. "Come along then. I'll send someone to fetch your trunk in the morning."

She followed him into the inn yard, understanding why she had not heard him approach, with the snow muffling all sounds. The deep winter silence made her want to speak in whispers, had she possessed any desire to address David Wiggins, which she did not. Still, he had come a long way through the snow. She could at least follow with good enough grace and not let him know her legs were already cold.

The snow was deep. He set a brisk pace and she floundered behind him, her lips set tight against any word of complaint. She focused her attention on his perfectly disreputable hat, a wide-brimmed, squashed-in felt monstrosity. He wouldn't dare ever set that thing on the floor, she thought. A dog would commit misdemeanors on it. She chuckled in spite of herself. He looked over his shoulder, one eyebrow raised.

"You're a rare one, Miss Hampton," was all he said. "Too bad you will not last."

He talks as though he has murdered and buried a row of lady's companions in the shubbery somewhere, Susan thought as she labored on. Probably killed by his devastating wit. She suppressed most of her laughter, but still he looked back, and this time took her arm, tucking it close to his side.

"Big drifts," was all he said as he tugged her along.

She opened her mouth to protest his ill usage, then closed it again. He didn't seem so much impatient with her, as he was eager to get somewhere. How can I protest, she thought, giving him a small glance, when you look so tired?

"You know, you didn't really have to get me tonight," she said, out of breath from hurrying.

"This morning," he said. "I told Lady Bushnell I would."

And that was it, apparently. He had nothing else to say and it was pointless to waste her breath. This is a man with tight words, she realized as she grimly hung on to his arm and let him help her over the deepest drifts.

After another silent stretch, in which they seemed to be steadily climbing, they broke through the last of the deep snow. David Wiggins let go of her arm, but she did not follow him toward the gig and blanketed horse tethered to a tree. Instead, she clasped her hands together and looked around, enchanted by what lay before her.

They stood at the head of a valley all tucked in tidy and protected from the deepest snows behind them. The moon was up now, and it cast a brittle light on the snow that illuminated the valley as though it were day. She could clearly make out the dark coil of a river and a fringe of woods offering some shelter to fields asleep now, but still rectangles outlined by fence and furrow only partly snow-covered. She could not see Quilling Manor itself; it must be beyond the trees.

Lovely, she thought, stamping her feet. She cast a guilty glance at Wiggins, who tossed the blanket in the back of the gig and climbed onto the seat. She started toward him then, waiting for a scold to hurry up. He surprised her. Reins slack in his hands, he nodded in her direction. "It's beyond beautiful in the summer," he said, his voice warm.

Like all his few words, these were quietly spoken. She hurried to the gig now, buoyed up by his obvious affection. Someone who has a fellow feeling for his land can't be all prickles and rabbit pebbles, she decided as he tucked a lap robe around her and said something to the horse in a language she did not know.

"Welsh pony," he allowed, and that was all the conversation between them as they crossed the sheltered valley on a better road.

Lord, I am weary, she thought as she sat so firmly upright on the seat beside the bailiff. She tried hard not to touch him, but it was a narrow seat, and he was the kind of man who overlapped. He sat easy, his eyes on the road in front of him, almost as though she were not there. He seemed relaxed, except that he kept tapping his feet, as though he could speed the passage. I suppose there is a sleepy wife somewhere and a warm bed, she considered.

"I don't think the world would end if you leaned back and rested yourself."

She shook her head, surprised that he had noticed. Hamptons don't lean or lounge about, she thought. He shrugged and turned his full attention to the road again. Or he seemed to, at any rate; she couldn't tell.

Susan closed her eyes once or twice as they moved slowly across the valley, always opening them before she felt herself leaning toward the bailiff. She must have had them closed longer than usual, because the next time she opened them they were stopped in the barnyard.

How did that get here? she thought stupidly, staring wide-eyed at the stone barn that looked as though it had been there since the Romans. Her mind was sluggish and starved for sleep, and she waited for the bailiff to help her down. To her dismay, he knotted the reins, climbed from the gig and hurried on a half run into the barn without a look over his shoulder at her. "Worse-than-useless man," Susan muttered out loud as she helped herself from the gig.

She wouldn't have followed him into the barn, except that the wind was teasing her ankles again and lifting her skirts. She followed him inside, careful to watch where she walked. She sniffed the air and looked around her. They were in a cattle byre, pungent of cow and timothy grass. So this is where you were before you came for me, Susan reflected as she moved quietly down the stalls toward a lamp hanging on the far wall.

David Wiggins was sitting cross-legged on the hay-covered floor, a calf of ravishing beauty across his legs. He was rubbing her down with a piece of sacking, and speaking low in Welsh. He looked up at Susan and motioned her to join him. He nodded toward the fawnlike creature before him.

"This is why I was late, discounting the snow, Miss Hampton," he explained. "I had to blow into her mouth to get her going, so I figured you could wait."

Susan came inside the loose box and sat down on an overturned bucket, her eyes on the cow, a Jersey who gazed back mildly without missing any rhythm as she chewed her cud. Susan looked at the slimy rope on the hay beside the cow. "You had a hard tug of it," she commented, leaning forward and resting her chin on her hands.

"I did," he agreed. He lifted the little thing off his lap, smiling as it raised up on back legs and pitched nose first into the hay. "You come to a hard, cold world, lass," he said, his voice soft. He leaned back against the partition, content to watch the animal struggle, fall, struggle, and rise, wobbly but on all fours.

David got up, too, wincing as though he ached from everywhere, and prodded the cow to her feet. "Cush, lass, cush," he crooned, "there's work afoot."

The calf knew what to do. In another moment, she had found her way to the udder, nudged it, and settled to business. David sighed and rubbed his back.

"Now to you, miss," he said, turning to Susan.

"I'm tired, not hungry," she said. It was only a very little joke, but he smiled and held out his hand. She allowed him to haul her to her feet. Her eyelids felt weighted down with lead shot, and grainy in the bargain.

"There's a place in the house for you," he said, pulling her along the passageway. He chuckled. "I misdoubt it's still warm from the last lady's companion!"

She looked at him, her eyes narrowed, but his face was bland and smooth again and his dark eyes completely unreadable.

The wind braced her and woke her up again as they crossed the barnyard and came to the back entrance of the manor, solid stone and hunkered down to outlast any kind of winter thrown at it. I can admire it in the morning, she considered as her mind turned to porridge.

David Wiggins took off his boots inside the back door, put his finger to his lips, and took her hand. He led her up the stairs and paused outside a door. "I'll have your trunk here by noon," he whispered as he opened the door, "provided you're of a mind to stay."

She stood up straighter and glanced over his shoulder at the welcome bed beyond. "I have to stay, Mr. Wiggins," she said, not bothering to pull hairs with this man. "I don't have a penny to return to London on."

"So we're stuck with you?" he asked, and it didn't sound unkind. But how was she to know, with her mind already telling her how good the pillow was going to feel, if only she could get to it?

"I think so, Mr. Wiggins. Do forgive me for being rag-mannered, but you stand between me and that bed right now, and I wish you would move."

He gave another of his oblique smiles, stepped out of her way, and closed the door after him. She didn't hear him on the stairs, but as she sat in the window seat to remove her boots, she watched him head across the barnyard again. She could see a modest two-story house beyond the barn, but he made for a long building that looked like a succession house. She watched closely; in another moment, a lamp began to glow.

Don't you sleep? she thought as she let her dress fall to the floor, and crawled between the comforting weight of heavy blankets. The only reflections of any coherence that crossed her tired brain before sleep took over was the odd notion that David Wiggins had been her last thought the night before, too, as he was now.

Chapter Five

℮

To her continuing amazement, she woke to the thought of David Wiggins. She wiggled her chemise down around her knees where it belonged, wished for the comfort of her flannel nightgown in the trunk beside the inn, and wondered if the bailiff had slept beyond his usual waking, too.

She looked at the clock, and sat up quickly. "This will never do, Susan," she said out loud as she looked around her. Lady Bushnell will think I am a dreadful slug-a-bed. She allowed herself to lean back against the headboard, considering whether Lady Bushnell would seriously have a spare thought for her newest lady's companion.

Apparently I am only one of many, Susan thought, hugging her knees to her. She stared into the small but sturdy fire in the grate which some kind soul must have lit for her earlier. Lady Bushnell will likely ignore me and wait for me to go away. I shall not. I cannot, for I have no place else to go.

It was an uncomfortable thought, as soon followed by another one. I have to convince Lady Bushnell that she needs me, and I haven't the slightest notion how to go about doing that, she reflected as she got out of bed and rummaged around in the mound of clothes she had stepped out of last night as soon as David Wiggins closed the door. She shook out her petticoat and wrapped it around her shoulders.

The room was warm enough, so she moved to the window seat, tucking herself into its compact recess and grateful for her own small size. She gazed out the window at a white world clenched tight in the fist of winter. This was no London brown snow, but a white so intense that she had to look away after a minute's observation. The sky was the cold blue of the bottom of a pond, and the trees skeletal, but overshadowing all was the smooth undulation of low hills that protected the valley. No traffic moved on the road they had traveled last night. They might have been the only manor on the planet, so complete was the isolation.

But I am warm, she thought, fingering the hem of the petticoat about her shoulders. Whatever her reluctance about a lady's companion, Lady Bushnell did not allow anyone to stint on coal in her household. It was a pleasant room, too, low-ceilinged, with two chairs drawn up companionably by the fireplace, and a footstool. A sampler hung by the door that must lead into a dressing room. Her eyes still dazzled by the snow, she squinted at the writing.

"For he shall give his angels charge over thee, to keep thee in all thy ways," she read, wondering what young daughter or granddaughter had labored over the work, and remembering her own purgatory with thread and needle. Susan rested her chin on her knees. "I could use an angel," she said. Someone knocked on the door and she smiled. My angel, she thought as she called "Come" from her window seat perch.

If the young woman who came into the room carrying a brass can was an angel, then the Lord had a good eye for competence. She was round and solid like the buildings on the holding itself, firmly planted to remain. She set the can by the washstand and placed the dress draped over her arm on the bed.

"I'm Cora," she said and took a deep breath. "Mr. Wiggins isn't so sure that he can get through to Quilling to fetch your trunk, what with the new snow, and he told my mum to find you a dress for a day or two. My mum's the housekeeper," she finished in a rush of words. She looked at the dress doubtfully. "But I don't think it will fit. Mr. Wiggins said he thought you had a waist small enough to span with his hands, and begging your pardon, ma'am, there's nobody but Lady Bushnell who has a waist that size and she isn't loaning out clothes to any lady's companion."

"I shouldn't imagine," Susan murmured, coming out of the window seat and wondering what else Mr. Wiggins thought. She held up the dress. "I'm certain it will do, if you can find me a sash of some sort." She smiled then, and held out her hand. "I'm Susan Hampton, the *final* lady's companion."

Cora giggled. "No one's ever said that before!"

"Perhaps it's time someone did." Oh, brave words, she thought, and here I stand with my knees practically knocking. "How many have there been?"

"Lots," Cora replied, ticking them off her fingers. "There was the one who cried all the time because she was homesick, the one who ran off with the tinkers, the one who put Bible verses about hell and brimstone all around the place, the one who stole the spoons, the one . . ."

"Goodness, I think that's enough," Susan said. She sat down on the bed. "Stole spoons?"

"Lady Bushnell's very own apostle spoons," Cora said, and giggled again. "Tucked them right up her sleeves and in other places Mum says I shouldn't mention."

"Heavens!"

"I haven't even told you about the others. There was . . ."

"Perhaps it can wait," Susan broke in, eager to change the subject. "Cora, am I too late for breakfast? I really didn't mean to sleep so long."

"We keep early hours here, but Mr. Wiggins told Mum you needed to sleep and not to wake you."

"And I suppose he's been up for hours."

"Mum doesn't think he sleeps ever. But when you're dressed, follow your nose to the kitchen. Mum saved some breakfast for you." Cora went to the door. "There's lavender soap by the basin, and if you're needing it, I can find you a hairbrush."

"I have one, thank you."

"I can brush it sometime, if you like," she offered, her face shy with the suggestion, her eyes bright to please. "I disremember when I've seen hair so black before, and thick."

It *is* nice hair, Susan told herself after Cora left. She hadn't taken the time to braid it last night, and it was all tangled around her shoulders. Mama used to brush it until it crackled, she remembered. I would sit between her knees. . . . Oh, that was nice. She took her hairbrush from her reticule and began to brush her hair in front of the mirror. Truth, I would have liked a little daughter with long black hair to brush. Damn you, Papa, for spending away my husband, sons, and daughters.

But I am not to think of Papa, she told herself as she braided her hair and twisted it into a low knot on the back of her neck. It hung heavy that way, but did wonders for her posture. She thought briefly of Emily and her constant parading about the drawing room with a book on her head, and all for the purpose of snaring some vicar or second son who needed a bride's portion, no matter how poor her carriage. And Aunt Louisa? "Well, I have likely exchanged one tyranny for another, but it is my own choice," she told the mirror.

Cora's dress hung many times too large on her slender frame, so she stepped out of it, and tried to shake out the worst of the wrinkles from her traveling dress. The material had the virtue of being well cut, but there wasn't much she could do about it, not after trudging through mud and snow at midnight. She resigned herself to Cora's dress. The sash Cora brought helped, but couldn't shrink it four sizes. She tucked and pleated the extra fabric under the sash, her hands lingering for a moment at her waist. So you think you could span my waist with your hands, Mr. Wiggins, she considered. I'd like to see you try.

She couldn't find her boots, so she went downstairs in her stockinged feet, treading quietly on the stairs and looking around her with some pleasure. I wonder how old this house is, she thought, warm with pleasure from inside out at seeing it in daylight. The ceilings were low and the walls wainscoted, the oak mellowing and darkening through the years. Mullioned windows on the first floor sparkled with the snow's reflection, each little pane rubbed and cleaned and soberly outlined in its lead frame. She looked up at the open beams and decided that Queen Elizabeth would have been quite at home here. Two hundred years of wind, storm, and winter, she marveled, and hopes and dreams. "What is it you hope for, Lady Bushnell?" she whispered as she glided down the hall, following her nose. "Or are all your dreams done?" She stood still a moment, hugging her arms about her. "Mine are," she said. "Now I must please others."

The kitchen was at the back of the house, instead of belowstairs, and unaccountably her spirits began to rise. It was a small matter, but a fact that cheered her, all out of proportion to its relative importance. She opened the door and breathed deep of kitchen smells that must have been trapped in the overhead beams for two centuries. Bunches of dried spices hung in orderly clumps from ceiling hooks, conveniently at hand. Her eyes went to the huge fireplace at the end of the kitchen, then she smiled to see that it had been bricked over and replaced by a Rumford stove. And there were her boots, polished to a shine that reflected the lamplight overhead. Everything gleamed of order, well-being, and stability, and it was balm to Susan's soul. Cora, she thought, I believe your mother is a force to be reckoned with.

The force to be reckoned with was watching her from the depths of an overstuffed chair, a cat in her lap, and a cup of tea close to her hand. She was on her feet as soon as Susan looked her way, pouring the cat down her dress, and holding out her hand. There was no disguising the look of surprise on her face.

"Lord love us, and I thought Davey Wiggins was joking, except that he seldom jokes," she said as she came closer to Susan.

"You *are* scarcely more than a babe! But welcome and let us clap hands. I am Kate Skerlong, the housekeeper. Susan Hampton?"

Susan stepped forward gladly and shook hands. "Yes, ma'am, and thank you for letting me sleep."

Mrs. Skerlong nodded. "Davey insisted. He said he hauled you up and down hills and through snow half the night, and it wouldn't do to send you back to London in a box." She went to the stove and lifted a saucepan from the warming shelf. "That's the one thing that hasn't happened to our lady's companions yet."

Susan smiled at her, fascinated. "I'm sure it's not because some have not wished it!" she said.

Mrs. Skerlong only smiled. "Come now, sit and have some porridge." She chuckled behind her hand. "You'll have to eat a prodigious amount to fill out that dress!"

They laughed together, and Susan tucked into the porridge, marveling as she ate and tried not to exclaim like an idiot over the tastiness of it, just how it was that something familiar should taste better in these surroundings.

"That was so good I must have some more," she said when she finished, and held out her bowl.

"You'll still never fill out that dress, no matter how much you eat."

Susan glanced around. David Wiggins stood in the doorway, blinking his eyes after the amazing brightness of the snow outside. He nodded to Mrs. Skerlong, who reached for another bowl, shook the snow off his coat, and tossed it expertly over the coat tree. He sat down at the table across from her and watched her face in silence until Susan wanted to look away.

"What, sir?" she asked finally, hoping the exasperation didn't show in her voice, but half hoping that it would. For all that he was across the table from her, he seemed uncomfortably close.

"Thank you, Mrs. Skerlong," he said as she set a bowl of porridge already thick with cream in front of him. "You look a little fragile in the morning light, Miss Hampton. I was just wondering what I would have done if you had pegged out last night during our walk."

Silly man, she thought as she smiled at Mrs. Skerlong, and picked up her spoon again. "Well, if I had broken my leg, you could have shot me," she said, her tone conversational.

He grinned down into his bowl, but didn't say anything.

"Looks are sometimes deceiving, sir," she continued after a few mouthfuls more of porridge. "I could probably eat you under the table and outlast you on any march."

"We'll try it sometime," he said when he finished, and he reached for the coffee cup that Mrs. Skerlong handed him. "Coffee, Miss Hampton?" he offered.

She indicated her cup. "I prefer tea."

"Of course you do. Coffee's for old campaigners." He regarded her another moment, then turned his attention to the housekeeper. "Mrs. Skerlong, there's yet another new calf in the byre and another threatening. Tell me what possesses cows to drop their calves when it's colder than a well digger's arse outside?"

Susan choked over her tea and resisted the urge to laugh. I must have left the land of well-bred, boring conversationalists, she thought. The bailiff is a genuine article. She regarded Wiggins with more interest, admiring his face in profile as he looked at the housekeeper. Nose a trifle long, she thought, but straight. Chins like that usually mean stubbornness. Aunt Louisa's modiste would say that cheekbones so prominent show character, but that can't be, because he's a dark Welshman. I wonder how he came by a name like Wiggins?

Mrs. Skerlong was obviously no stranger to the bailiff's kitchen chat. "It's the same logic that compels women to reach their confinement in the middle of the night," she said. "All my babies came at night."

"I call it damned inconsiderate," he said frankly. He leaned back in the chair and the exhaustion seemed to ooze off him. He pushed the coffee cup toward the housekeeper. "Another of those, if you please, and I might stay awake for a few hours longer." He directed his attention to Susan again. "Well, now that you've scrutinized me, are there any questions about myself that need answers?"

"My, but you're blunt," Susan said before she thought. "How on earth does your wife manage?"

He did laugh then, with a sidelong glance at Mrs. Skerlong. "That's easy, Miss Hampton. I'm not married. Wives take time and money; I have neither."

She blushed and returned her attention to her teacup.

"Reading the leaves?" he inquired, the amusement showing in his dark eyes.

"No!" She finished her tea thoughtfully, then decided it would do no harm to speak. "Tell me this, Mr. Wiggins: what do you reckon are my chances of remaining here as a lady's companion?"

He considered the question. "Small, I would think." Elbows on the table, he rested his chin in his hands, regarded her with that unwavering gaze. "Nobody really needs you here, Miss Hampton, and that's the hard and cold of it. If you could make yourself in-dispensable, now, that might be a different wedge of cheese."

"And how do I do that?" she asked, returning him gaze for gaze, amazed at her own boldness. "I like it here, and I want to stay."

"That's for you to discover." He got up from the table and stretched, before starting toward the coat tree. "Mrs. Skerlong, do you think I should keep stalling, or try to fetch this little one's trunk?"

Susan laughed. "So that's how it is! Seriously, Mr. Wiggins, it can wait, if the snow is too deep."

"I'll get it today," he said as he buttoned his coat. "Promised I would last night, as I recall."

Promises don't mean much, she thought. "Suit yourself, sir," she said.

Again that look. "I always do, Miss Hampton," he said as he nodded to the housekeeper and left the kitchen.

Mrs. Skerlong gazed a long moment at the space he had occu-pied by the door, then turned back to the stove. "I disremember a time when he has said so much at once," she commented, careful not to look at Susan. "He likes you."

Susan shook her head. "If that's liking, I wonder why he didn't give me any good advice on how to deal with Lady Bushnell."

"Why should he? That's your domain. You're the lady's com-panion."

I am indeed, Susan thought. Now what? She pursed her lips and watched Mrs. Skerlong's efficiency over the stove. The cat twined itself around her ankles, purring and offering her advice on where to scratch next by gently butting her fingers with his head. "Oh, you are a spoiled gentleman," she said as she obliged him. Would that people were so easily managed, she considered, but that is another cup of tea.

"Mrs. Skerlong," she asked suddenly, "does Lady Bushnell take midmorning tea?"

"She does. Cora usually carries it in."

"Let me do it this morning. I have to meet her sooner or later, and it may as well be sooner. She must know I am here."

Mrs. Skerlong looked doubtful. "Lady B does like order and tidiness, and you could fit three lady's companions in that dress. You might wait until Davey returns with your trunk."

"That could be days!" she protested. "And each day I will grow more afraid."

"He said he would have your trunk today," Mrs. Skerlong reminded her. "Don't you trust people's word?"

"No, I suppose I don't," Susan said quietly. "But if you please, I would like to meet Lady Bushnell."

"Very well, then," the housekeeper replied. "If you're sure. Lady Bushnell usually spends the mornings in her room."

She felt less sure as she stood outside Lady Bushnell's door and knocked. This dress is a fright, but I know my hair is neat, she thought as she waited and knocked again.

"For heaven's sake, just come in!"

Oh, dear. Susan took a deep breath and opened the door. Lady Bushnell sat at a small desk by the window, with a ledger open before her. She was hard to see, because the strong light from the window was behind her, but Susan had no trouble recognizing posture as uncompromising and well-bred as her own, and the profile of a chin that looked even more stubborn than the bailiff's. I have stumbled into a nest of strong characters, she thought as she hesitated at the door.

"Come closer," said the woman, setting down her writing pen. "Over there, please, then tell me who you are." She spoke crisply, the voice of command.

Susan did as she was bid, then approached Lady Bushnell, who had clasped her hands in front of her on the desk. What she saw was a woman no bigger than herself, with a wealth of white hair pulled back and arranged much as her own. There any resemblance ended with all the finality of a slammed door. The woman before her was immaculate, with snapping green eyes that almost glittered under hooded eyelids and a gentle rose complexion that young women would perish for. The set of her lips was formidable, and Susan felt her stomach quiver. This was not a woman who would take easily to the reality of old age, and its attendant frailties.

"Well?"

Susan never knew a one-word sentence to have such a nuance. Aristotle could have written a treatise on it. "I'm Susan Hampton, your companion," she said simply. "I would like to know what I can do for you."

Susan could see a hundred cutting remarks cross Lady Bushnell's expressive face. I wonder where you will begin, she thought.

"I suggest that you pour me some tea," she said.

Susan did as she asked. Mrs. Skerlong had put two cups and saucers in the tray, obviously in the forlorn hope that Lady Bushnell would like to share a cup with her newest employee. She did not. Susan poured the tea, handed it to Lady Bushnell, and stood before her with her hands behind her back, her fingers clenched tight together.

Lady Bushnell sipped her tea, never taking her eyes from Susan's face. She set down the cup and cleared her throat. Susan could feel the hair rising on the back of her neck.

"Joel Steinman has taken complete leave of his senses. When my pea-brained daughter-in-law searches for your replacement, I will suggest to her that she try another agency."

Susan blinked. Do I say "Yes, mum" and hang my head, burst into tears, or do I look her in the eye and tell her what I think? "You won't need another agency," she heard herself say. "I have come here to stay, Lady Bushnell."

There was a long pause. It gave her cold comfort to see that Lady Bushnell had not expected that answer, or the well-bred cadence of diction that matched her own.

"Even if I do not want or need you?"

"You'll need me, ma'am, particularly if you do not wish to be visited by other lady's companions who won't be as good for you as I will be," Susan said, wondering where the words were coming from. Only please, please don't ask me what a companion does, because I am sure I could not tell you.

"And what will you do for me?"

Oh, no. Susan felt her mind go blank, except for one thought.

"I will never, ever steal your spoons," she said, her voice firm.

There. Susan let out the breath she had been saving, and dug her stockinged feet into the thick carpet. She probably mistook it, but for the smallest moment, there was a different glimmer in Lady Bushnell's eyes. It was quickly gone, but Susan hoped.

"Have you ever stolen anything, Miss Hampton?" The question was as frosty as the air outside.

Susan considered the question. "Why, yes, I have," she replied, smiling at the memory. "When I was ten I stole my perfectly odious cousin's marzipan Father Christmas and ate it. I considered it my duty, because my cousin was quite fat."

Lady Bushnell looked down at her desk and pushed the ledger away before she turned her gaze on Susan again. "Did someone steal your clothes, Miss Hampton?"

Susan thought there was the slightest quaver in her voice. She felt some of the strain go out of her shoulders. "No, Lady Bushnell. This is a loan from Cora Skerlong. Unless Mr. Wiggins can engineer a road through the snow, my trunk is destined to remain at the inn in Quilling for the present, I fear."

"David will fetch it," Lady Bushnell said. "Unlike you, he has the virtue of being useful about this place."

"I can be useful, too, Lady Bushnell," Susan said.

"I cannot imagine how." Lady Bushnell turned in her chair to face Susan and folded her hands in her lap. "Estimable woman that she is, my daughter-in-law has so much time on her hands that she feels obliged to meddle in my affairs. I had a trifling accident on the stairs eight months ago, and must use a cane now." She indicated the delicately carved stick beside the desk. "What will Emmeline do but send me lady's companions." Lady Bushnell made a face as though the words were distasteful. "If I cough, the companions tattle on me and bring all manner of solicitations and unwanted advice from Emmeline! What do you think of that, Miss Hampton?"

"I think you are fortunate that someone loves you as much as that," Susan replied. "It has been my experience that people who are ignored are not held in much affection."

"Your experience!" Lady Bushnell snapped. "Oh, please! You can't be a day over eighteen."

"I am twenty-five," Susan said, her voice even. "My father is Sir Rodney Hampton, England's worst gambler. He has frittered away the family estate, our house in London, and my entire dowry, until I am obliged to earn my own way. I have no place to go if you turn me off here, so I am determined that you will find me entirely satisfactory."

"Do you wish me to feel sorry for you because your improvident family has sent you into the ranks of the lower class?"

I did not think a slap would hurt that much, Susan thought, taking a step back as though the widow had struck her. This is a poisonous old woman. She tried to regard Lady Bushnell calmly, even as the last bit of her own pride dribbled away. Or it is a proud woman who has lost children and husband, and sees her independence slipping through her fingers.

Lady Bushnell was silent then, sipping her tea. When she finished, she turned her attention back to the ledger on her desk. Susan stood there in the middle of the room until it became obvious to her that she had been dismissed. Her face burning, she gathered up the tea tray and went to the door, her heart so low in her toes that she felt as though she were kicking it with every step.

"I intend to write Joel Steinman and tell him that I am turning you off. There will be no more lady's companions, and so I will tell Emmeline, face-to-face, if I have to. What do you think of that, Miss Hampton?"

For the first time since her father stole her pearls, Susan felt tears prickle the back of her eyelids. It is all I should have expected, she told herself as she stood there with her hand on the doorknob. No one wants me here. I was defeated before I came.

"Well?"

"That is your right, Lady Bushnell," she replied, struggling to keep her voice even. "It frightens me a little, but I expect I'll manage." She opened the door. "The innkeep in Quilling told me last night that there are good people around here. I suppose he was only referring to the village. Good day, Lady Bushnell. I'm sorry you'll never know how well I would have suited."

To her immense relief, the kitchen was empty when she brought back the tray. She sat down because her legs wouldn't hold her anymore. She put her arms on the table and rested her head on them, her mind turning like a whirligig. There's nothing I can sell to get me some cash for a ride back to London. And even if I get to London, I can't knock on Aunt Louisa's door. I just can't.

She sighed and waited for the tears to come, but they did not. I suppose I have finally gone beyond tears, she thought, and what a relief that is. She rested her chin on her hands. Well, I was right when I told Cora that I was going to be the final lady's companion.

The cat nudged her ankles and she sat up, looking about her to make sure that no one had seen her sprawled all over the table like a barmaid. She got to her feet and stood there a moment until she felt entirely steady. Her boots were still by the stove, so she retrieved them and put them on, enjoying their warmth. I can at least spare Mr. Wiggins a trip for nothing, if I'm not too late, she thought as she snatched a shawl from the coat tree.

It was going to be a chilly walk back to Quilling, she thought as she left the house and went to the cattle byre. The barnyard was muddy, and she hated to think what was happening to her beautifully polished boots. She pushed open the door, smiling in spite of her misery at the pleasant odor of hay and cows. Who can be too unhappy around cows? she asked herself as she hurried down the central passageway, looking for the bailiff.

He was sitting in one of the loose boxes, regarding a cow in labor. He looked up at her and then returned his attention to the cow. Susan leaned on the railing.

"I'm so glad you haven't gone to Quilling for my trunk yet!" she said. "I can spare you the trip."

"Change your mind, Miss Hampton?"

She shook her head. "No, but it's been changed for me. Lady Bushnell . . . Lady Bushnell says I won't suit. She turned me off. I'll leave in the morning." She didn't trust herself to say anything else just then, and truly, he didn't seem too interested. She looked at him a moment more, remembering a time in her life when everyone was interested in her. "Thank you for whatever you did, Mr. Wiggins. I'll not trouble you any further."

She turned to leave, but paused when the bailiff stood up, brushing the hay off his leather breeches.

"Where will you go?"

"I don't know."

He came to the railing and rested his elbows on it, looking directly at her again with that unwavering gaze of his that she was familiar with, in spite of their brief acquaintance.

"Miss Hampton, I could loan you the fare back to London." He smiled. "I have that much, at least."

She shook her head. "That's kind, but I have no way of repaying you, Mr. Wiggins."

"Marry me, then."

Chapter Six

Susan couldn't have heard him right, but she was suddenly too shy to ask him to repeat himself. She swallowed, and stared at him. *Maybe if I do not say anything, I'll discover that I was just hearing things. He looks perfectly rational, except that he has hay on his shirt.* Absently, she reached out and plucked it off.

"God knows I can't afford a special license," he continued, "but I know a family you could stay with in Quilling until after the banns are cried. My house isn't big, but it's big enough."

He stopped talking then, waiting for her to say something. Susan tried to remember everything her mother and aunt had told her about proposals, but she couldn't think beyond the fact that this was the nicest offer anyone had ever made her. It was impossible, of course, but she was moved past words. She just patted his arm, resting so close to her shoulder on the railing.

"Mr. Wiggins, yours is the very first proposal I ever had and I do not think anyone will ever make me a kinder offer . . ." she began finally, unable then to look him in the eye.

"But no, thank you," he concluded for her.

She nodded, embarrassed.

"It was a foolish notion," he murmured, "but I thought to help you. I suppose I overstepped my bounds. I do that, sometimes."

"Oh, no!" she said, putting her hand on his arm again. "That is not my objection! Mr. Wiggins, you don't know anything about me! Suppose I turned out to be a . . . a thief, or a wine bibber, or . . ."

He laughed softly and moved away from the railing, away from her hand. "You're nothing of the sort, and I have never been safer, Miss Hampton!" He scuffed his boot in the hay and looked down at the cow, who was regarding him with mild interest as her insides heaved. "I've never been so impulsive." He shook his head at his own temerity.

He chose a light tone, and she matched it. "I didn't think you were given to sudden starts, Mr. Wiggins. Please don't worry about me. Perhaps I could accept that loan from you. I . . . I think Mr. Steinman would make it good."

"Joel will do me right," Wiggins said, coming to the railing again.

"You know him, don't you?" she said, forgetting her own troubles for a moment.

"Quite well. I remember that arm of his . . ." He shook his head. "You don't need to hear those stories. Yes, I know him, and he owes me a debt beyond payment. I'll get my shillings back, if you need to borrow them, Miss Hampton."

"I do, sir. Let us shake on it."

They shook hands over the railing. Susan hitched the borrowed shawl higher on her shoulders and turned to leave the bailiff to his business.

"But what will you do in London?"

She looked back at Wiggins, who still regarded her over the railing. "I will have to crawl back to my aunt and my father and give up any hopes I had of a future of my own." She spoke softly, but she knew he heard her.

"Then my offer still stands, if you ever need it, Miss Hampton. I know what it's like to be in bondage," he said just as quietly, then squatted on his heels again, facing the cow.

Such a day this has been, and it is not yet afternoon, Susan thought as she left the cattle byre. I've been turned off a job, offered marriage, then forced to swallow huge lumps of pride. I suppose I can swallow more and return to Aunt Louisa. She turned her face up to the sun and smiled. And if things get too onerous in London, I can nourish myself with the knowledge that someone in the Cotswolds will always come to my rescue, even if it's just a bailiff. At least I've been asked.

She ate a quiet lunch in the kitchen with Cora and Mrs. Skerlong, accepting their condolences over the briefness of her employment with a degree of equanimity that surprised her. Perhaps I do long for the safety of Aunt Louisa's tyranny, where everything will be done for me, if I surrender my personality, she admitted to herself as she drank the last of her tea. And according to these hardworking people, what is so terrible about a fashionable roof over my head, food cooked by a French chef, and warm surroundings? In time, I might believe them, too.

Mrs. Skerlong warned her that Lady Bushnell had taken up her usual afternoon haunt in the south-facing sitting room, so Susan did not slow her steps as she passed that room. She went thought-fully up the stairs, ready to compose a letter to Joel Steinman that she could send to him, once she was back in London. By the time I am back in London, she reasoned, I should have so little pride left that I can throw myself on his mercy without a qualm. It is a theory I shall likely have to test, at any rate.

She went into her room and admired its compact, comforting utility, sorry that she would be leaving it so soon. She stopped and frowned at the bed. There was another dress, this one of blue so deep at first she mistook it for black. She picked it up, admir-ing the mother-of-pearl buttons and rows of little tucks all across the bodice, and the deep flounce from knee to ankle that spoke of another decade. She held the dress up to her, knowing that it couldn't ever have belonged to Cora Skerlong. She laid the dress back onto the bed and picked up the shawl of Norwich silk lying next to it. A note fell out of the rich blue and yellow folds.

It was one sentence only: "In the interest of fairness, I will give you a probationary period, as I gave all the others." Clutching the note, Susan spread out her arms and flopped back on the bed. "Yes!" she told the ceiling with fierce exultation. "Will anyone want to work so hard for thirty pounds a year as I shall?" she asked. "Surely not my father!"

She made herself comfortable on the bed, thinking of the bailiff again. He seemed to rub along well enough with Lady Bushnell. He will have to tell me something about her, Susan told herself. I will bother him until he gives me some idea of how to please her.

She knew she should devote her mind to the matter at hand, but the mutton stew and brown bread from lunch was nicely mud-dling up her insides and making her drowsy. She was still tired from last night's trip through the snow, for all that the bailiff had declared that she was tougher than she looked. She undid the sash and let Cora's big dress sprawl around her. I could turn over in-side this dress, she thought, and closed her eyes. I wonder if Mr. Wiggins is still sitting on his heels beside that cow. He is a patient man. I wonder why it is that I always seem to think of him before I go to sleep? I will *not* think of him first when I wake up.

Susan knew she wouldn't have thought of Mr. Wiggins first when she opened her eyes, except that she had the oddest dream of trudging behind him as they climbed up and down hills, bal-ancing her trunk on the back of a cow. I must not eat so much mutton, she told herself as she lay in bed, her hands pressed to her middle. The softness of the light outside told her that the afternoon had already taken that turn into evening.

She exchanged Cora's dress for Lady's Bushnell's, exclaiming over the excellence of the fit as she viewed herself in the mirror. This dress looks better than I do at the moment, Susan decided as she pulled from her hair the few remaining pins which had survived her nap. She brushed her hair and soon had it tamed into submission and wound neatly about her head again. I will do, she told herself as Cora tapped on the door to announce that dinner was ready. She was still in her stockinged feet, but the dress was long enough to cover that minor deficiency.

Susan dined in the kitchen with the Skerlongs, content to let the cat curl up at her toes as she ate oyster soup and fricassee and wondered where Mr. Wiggins was. She must have looked toward the door once too often, because Mrs. Skerlong smiled at her.

"He's with the cows, Miss Hampton," she said.

"I was afraid he might have gone to Quilling for my trunk this evening," Susan explained.

The housekeeper shook her head. "I did take the liberty of telling him your good news when he came in to eat before milking." She laughed and began to gather up the dishes. "He said he'd get your trunk tomorrow, and put it on rollers, in case he had to take it back in a few days!"

"No, Mama," Cora said decisively, shaking her head. "Miss Hampton told me that she is to be the final lady's companion. You're here to stay, aren't you, Miss Hampton?"

"I do hope so," Susan said. "And I wish that you would please call me Susan."

"We couldn't possibly," the housekeeper declared. "None of the other lady's companions went so far."

"And they're not here, are they?" Susan countered. "Please call me Susan, and give me some good advice on Lady's Bushnell's likes and dislikes."

Mrs. Skerlong went to her chair by the stove, and Susan followed, sitting on her footstool. The cat leaped onto her lap and nudged her fingers to remind her of her duty. Absently, she rubbed the animal behind the ears.

"You want to talk to David Wiggins, my dear," said the housekeeper as she threaded her darning needle. "Cora and I only came here this last year ourselves when the old housekeeper died. What I learned, I learned from David. The bailiff's known her for years, from back when they soldiered together on the Peninsula."

"Oh, surely not," Susan said, picking up a skein of yarn at Mrs.

Skerlong's indication and starting to roll it into a ball. "Ladies don't soldier."

"I guess they do if they want something more exciting from their husbands than letters, my dear!" said the housekeeper, smiling as Susan blushed. "Old Lord Bushnell was quite a man, from every indication. Lady B stuck to his side like a burr up hill and down dale through all of Spain and Portugal." She shook her head. "And when the old man and their daughter died in that last trip over the mountains to France . . ."

"I'm wearing her daughter's dress?" she whispered, her eyes big.

"You are—and don't think it doesn't surprise me!" The housekeeper focused her attention on the sock in her lap for a moment. "Lady B took the bodies home, and gave up following the drum. The new Lord Bushnell had served in another regiment. He took over the family title and the Fifth Foot." Mrs. Skerlong rested the darning egg and sock in her lap. "He insisted that she stay in England with her daughter-in-law at the family estate about twenty miles from here, towards Bath. And there it stood. I don't think there was a battlefield in Spain or Portugal that Lady Bushnell didn't know."

"I wouldn't have imagined it," Susan murmured, putting down the ball of yarn. "She looks so refined and elegant."

"And probably did on the back of a donkey, too," Mrs. Skerlong said. "The aristocracy ain't like the rest of us. Begging your pardon, Miss Hampton . . ."

"Never mind," Susan said. "I'm certainly not in Lady Bushnell's class. But to travel like that . . ."

"You wouldn't follow your husband from bivouac to bivouac?" Susan looked around, startled. "You are much too quiet, sir," she protested to the bailiff as he stood behind her, milk pails in hand. She regarded him, wondering if she should feel disconcerted, especially since she had turned down his amazing proposal only hours ago. There was nothing in his face of embarrassment, so obviously his impulsive offer was not a concern to him now. I will take a light tone, she decided. "How can we gossip, if you sneak up like a Mohican?"

"Quite easily, I think," he replied, handing the pails to Emma, who apparently had been waiting for them. The girl took them to the room off the kitchen, and Susan heard the sound of milk being poured into a larger container. "I could have rolled a cannonball in here, and you wouldn't have heard me, the two of you sitting there like conspirators!"

Mrs. Skerlong expressed her opinion cheerfully in pungent words that made Susan blink, then smiled at the bailiff, obviously used to him. "Susan wants to know about Lady Bushnell."

"She's keeping me on sufferance for a little while longer, and I must discover how to please her," Susan explained. "Oh, sir, can you help?"

The bailiff nodded. "If you don't mind discussing this in the cattle byre." He looked at Mrs. Skerlong and rolled his eyes. "I disremember why I told Tim the cowman he could spend the month with his old mam in Bristol. I haven't squeezed so many tits since I left off soldiering."

Susan coughed and looked long at the stove, held her breath and tried not to laugh out loud. Aunt Louisa, if you could hear these two, she thought, remembering her aunt harrumphing and "my wording" when Papa unleashed the occasional vulgarity.

"You're kind to old Tim 'cause you're such a good-hearted bastard, David Wiggins," Mrs. Skerlong replied as she threaded her needle again.

"Only don't let it get about," he replied, unruffled by the housekeeper's commentary on his parenthood. "Those your boots, Miss Hampton?"

She nodded, hoping that her eyes didn't look as merry as she felt. "Yes, sir."

"Kate, loan her your coat. Let's see if her curiosity extends beyond the cattle byre and into the dread succession house. If I have to talk, she has to work, too."

When her boots were on, he helped her into Mrs. Skerlong's coat and took her hand as they crossed the barnyard. "Wind's picking up," he explained when she drew back in surprise at first. "You'd blow over in a strong gust, I'm thinking." He stopped and put his face up to the wind, breathing deep. "It's coming from the west; I'm also thinking the snow will be melting tomorrow." He took a firmer hold on her hand. "Just remember to look out for east winds, Miss Hampton."

"Yes, sir," she replied dubiously.

"And for God's sake quit sirring me," he said. "Call me Mr. Wiggins if you must—although that makes me feel forty . . ."

"Aren't you?" she interrupted, suddenly quite pleased with herself. I have not felt like making a joke for ever so long, she thought as he stopped again.

"Miss Hampton, do you see that mound of cow muck over there?" He pointed with her hand in his.

"Yes, s . . . Wiggins."

"Another remark like that and Wiggins will see that you're the first lady's companion in it! I am thirty-three. It may seem like forty to you, but let's keep that straight."

She laughed, then shrieked as he steered her toward the mound. "You wouldn't!"

"Well, no," he agreed, turning her into the cattle byre. "Mrs. Skerlong would probably make me clean your boots." He released her hand and she followed him down the corridor between the stalls, thinking to herself what a pleasant walk he had. You look like someone who knows how to walk and walk, she thought.

"Were you infantry?" she asked, wanting confirmation.

"Yes. Do you like to walk?" He smiled. "Well, certain you do."

Susan nodded. "It used to irritate my cousins. They went walking in Hyde Park to see and be seen, but I liked to walk."

"No flirting?" he asked as he took off his coat and reached for the hay fork.

"Of course! But not with some sprite whose pantaloons were too tight to move fast," she said, sitting herself on the same bucket from yesterday. "Some men are slaves of fashion."

"Not around here," he said as he pulled down straw from the loft overhead and spread it around the loose box where the newest bovine arrival was lying. "Or in Spain." He leaned on the hay fork a moment, remembering, then looked at her. "Up you get, Miss Hampton, if you will earn your thirty pounds. Take that sacking over there and wipe down this heifer. She's a bit delicate yet, and a good rubbing will do wonders for her circulation. I didn't have time while I was milking."

She did as he asked, gingerly at first, and then vigorously as the fawnlike Jersey struggled to rise.

"Good girl!" Wiggins said, and Susan didn't know if he meant her or the heifer. "Let up now, Susan."

She sat back on the newly mounded straw and watched with satisfaction as the calf struggled to rise. The cow, who still appeared to be nursing her own grievances at the irritation of birth, looked around and lowed her encouragement.

"And there we go," the bailiff said as the calf wobbled to all fours, swayed back and forth a moment, then moved stiff-legged, to her mother's side. "They do have an instinct, do little ones."

He put down the hay fork and sat beside Susan, just watching mother and daughter, a slight smile on his face. "I never get tired of it!" He laughed. "Except when it's too cold, or I'm feeling forty."

"I promise not to tease you about that again," Susan said. "Now tell me about Lady Bushnell."

He hesitated. "I've always made it a point to respect her privacy."

"You promised! If I can find out what she's like, perhaps I can please her. Surely you will help me. After all, you did ask me to marry you . . ." she wheedled, well aware of the growing look of stubbornness on his face.

He got up and brushed off the straw. "I have a feeling that this is going to come before many a negotiation with you," he told the cattle byre in general.

"Probably," she allowed. "You did offer your help."

"But you didn't accept," he pointed out, even as he looked away from her and smiled.

"True," she agreed, her tone reasonable, "but that doesn't mean I won't use you."

He laughed out loud and helped her to her feet. "Well, you're an honest piece," he admitted, reaching for his coat and putting it on again. "Come on, I'm not through yet."

Neither am I, she thought as he took her hand again and they faced into the wind. I have a lot of information to pry out of you tonight.

She thought they were going back to the kitchen, but the bailiff led her instead to the long, many-windowed succession house that stood apart from the other outbuildings, away from the shade of trees. The building was dark inside, but there was sufficient light through the windows for David to light a lamp and set it by a draftsman's desk, and then light other lamps.

Susan looked about her with interest, removing Mrs. Skerlong's coat because the long room was warm. There along the south-facing wall were several mounds of cucumbers and cantaloupe with large, healthy leaves and blossoms indicating fruit to come.

Catching her attention were the long rows of grain in full growth on the tables down the middle of the succession house. She didn't know what kind it was—one grain was much like the next to her, and always had been—but the renewal of coal in the furnaces had set off more warm current of air that stirred the greenery in front of her fascinated eyes. "It's beautiful," she said softly, and found her heart aching for spring and summer and warmth again. And all from rows of grain. She wondered why Lady Bushnell would want grain in her succession house, when she could have hothouse fruits and flowers.

"Nice," she said to David Wiggins, who walked past her carrying a coal shuttle.

"I think so," he agreed.

She watched the bailiff shovel coal into the small furnaces at opposite ends to the succession house, then admired the white and yellow-middled strawberry blossoms blooming in their own bed.

"Strawberries in winter." She sighed. "How I should like some dipped in sugar and cream." She looked down at the cat at her feet and patted the tall draftsman's stool beside her. The cat meowed and paced back and forth, but did not leap up. "Oh, goodness, you're a lazy creature," she said as she picked up the cat and set it on the table.

"No, she's just in the family way, and not given to leaping about," the bailiff said as he joined her. "I'm sure you would feel the same." He patted the animal's bulging sides. "Thank goodness cats do not require the attention of cows." He rubbed the cat under the chin, set her gently back on the floor, and pulled out a ledger. "She's a good mouser and that's why I keep her in here, but she does like the toms."

Susan smiled, wondering what Aunt Louisa would make of such a conversation. She looked over his shoulder at the rows and rows of careful entries. "What do you have there?"

"Something to occupy you while you pummel me for information about a rather private lady I would just as soon not discuss."

Wiggins took off his coat and picked up a ruler on the desk. "I'm going to call out numbers. I want you to locate the number, then look for a, b, c, or d. I'll call out inches to you, which I want you to record next to the date. What is today?" he asked, more to himself than to her.

"January 15th, 1820," she said promptly."

"I know the year!" He nudged her over to get the pencil out of the drawer under the drafting table. "Pencil in the date by each number group."

"Very well. The things I must do to get information," she grumbled as she tried to find a ladylike way to climb onto the stool.

Without a word he picked her up and set her squarely in the middle of it, then looked over her shoulder at the neat entries of dates and inches before starting down the row. As he approached the first row of grain, she noticed that it had been subdivided into smaller boxes. A, b, c, and d, she decided as she took up the pencil and carefully wrote in the date.

"Fifty-nine a," he said, then stood the ruler next to the grain shoot. "One quarter inch."

She recorded the measurement, then put the pencil on the b entry.

"Fifty-nine b. One quarter inch and a plus." He looked up at her. "It's not quite half and I don't have a better ruler right now."

She wrote in the inches he dictated to her as he went efficiently down the row, wanting to know what he was doing, but mindful of breaking his concentration. When he finished the row, he looked up at her.

"This is such a help to me. Usually I get Matthew Beverage—he's my underbailiff—but he got married at Christmas and can't get the bed off his wife's back."

Susan grinned over the figures, wondering what else he would say. No subject seemed too sensitive for the bailiff. "And you assured him you could do all his work, too?" she said when she knew she wouldn't laugh.

"Why not?" he countered. "It's winter, and Matthew's got to keep his wife's stomach warm. He and his bride will be back in a few weeks. She usually helps Cora with the milk and the laundry."

He came around to the other side of the wooden tables and began to go up, calling out numbers and inches as she recorded them in the right slots. "Eighty-three d, one inch. Damn, that's good."

He was back at the draftsman's desk again, looking over her shoulder at the entries, putting his arm around her to run his finger down the columns. She would have been offended, except that he was not mindful of her presence at all. He kept nodding, chuckling to himself, and nodding again, his eyes on the page, and then down the rows of grain in front of them. He put his arms down finally, and she felt free to breathe again. Not that such nearness to the bailiff was unpleasant; far from it. She found that she enjoyed that smell of hay always about him, and the clean honest scent of lye soap. I am a long way from ballroom pomades and gagging colognes, she thought as she sat quietly, the pen still in her hand.

He took the pen from her and then lifted her from the stool. "Now let us each take a side and pluck out any weeds. I just want the grain shoots. You can ask me about Lady Bushnell now, if you choose." He hung two more lamps over the tables, then began to weed silently and efficiently, as he did everything.

"What *is* this grain?" she asked. "Why are you doing this?" She weeded slower, her eyes on the tender, fragile stalks before her, force-grown in winter.

He looked over at her. "Didn't I say?"

"No! And I've been wanting to ask."

"It's my Waterloo wheat, Susan," he said, his eyes unfocusing for the briefest moment and looking beyond her to a place she had never been. "A detachment from my regiment helped fortify Hougoumont and I swiped a handful of grain from a storage bin that night. I intended to eat it, but never got the time. And when the battle was over, there it was in my pocket."

He continued his work, then he reached across his row of grain to weed hers, too, and speed her along. "It was growing on the hillside above the chateau. You can't imagine how tall it was, before it was trampled by both armies." He touched a sprout, and the touch was almost a caress. "I'm growing it with English grain to get a good seed. This is the third growth and so far, my best combination."

"My goodness," Susan said, for want of anything better.

"Waterloo tall and English tough. I'll call it Waterloo Harvest." He returned his attention to his own row when Susan caught up with him. "Now what do you want to know about Lady Bushnell?"

"How did you meet? Mrs. Skerlong said you soldiered together in Spain, but I hardly . . ."

"So we did," he agreed, his eyes unfocusing again for a moment. "And harken. I'll only tell this once, because it's no kind reflection on David Wiggins. She saved a thief from a three-hundred-lash flogging."

"Who?"

"Me."

Chapter Seven

Susan couldn't say anything for a moment. She stopped weeding and stared at the bailiff across the row from her. When he started weeding her row, too, she remembered what she should be doing and shook her head at him to stop. She weeded in silence for a moment, then her curiosity was bigger than her amazement.

"How can someone survive three-hundred lashes? My God, Mr. Wiggins, what did you *do* to earn such a punishment?"

"I thieved. I was a sergeant in a Welsh border guard called up when Sir John Moore went to Portugal. You seldom saw a regiment so poorly commanded. We were all starving and I stole a box of hard tack for me and my men. The colonel wanted to make an example of me." He stopped then, looked at her intently. "You really want to hear this?"

She nodded, unable to speak, her eyes wide.

"I think they were about halfway to three hundred. I quit counting after one hundred. All I remember was that my blood was dripping on the ground and I was grunting like a pig."

She shuddered. "I can't even imagine such a thing!"

As she watched, horrified, he turned around and pulled up his shirt. His back was crisscrossed with scars from his neck to his waistband. "They go lower, but you don't need to see those, too." He tucked his shirt in and continued weeding as calmly as though he had shown her a hangnail that was troubling him. "It was a hard army, Susan."

"Yes, but . . ." she began, then dabbed her fingers across her eyes.

"I don't remember hearing Lady Bushnell say anything, but the next thing I knew, the flogging had stopped and she was standing between me and the punishment sergeant." He finished the row and waited for her to catch up. "Apparently she and Lord Bush-

nell had been riding by the regiment. I wish I could have appreci-
ated it, but I was a bit fine drawn by then."

It was masterful understatement. "She just leaped off her horse
and threw herself in the middle of all that?" Susan asked when
she could speak.

"So Lord Bushnell told me later. She refused to move until that
colonel, goddamn him, agreed to stop. I think she gave him a real
tongue-lashing, but it all sounded like a swarm of bees to me. I
can't remember it." He grinned at her. "Old Lord Bushnell told
me later that he learned some new words that morning."

When Susan finished weeding, he walked with her to the fur-
nace and put in more coal, then upturned a bucket for her to sit on
while he perched on the edge of an empty table. "I don't know
how she did it, but I was moved from my regiment to the Fighting
Fifth. It was regular army and a dandy outfit."

"Why didn't you die?"

He shrugged. "I wanted to. You know on Good Friday services
when the vicar usually talks about Christ on the cross?" He shook
his head. "I have some small idea . . . and I can appreciate the
thieves on either side."

"Were you in hospital?" she said, almost fearful of intruding on
his thoughts.

"No. It was just after Vimeiro and were on our way back to
Torres Vedras. And you know, Lady Bushnell came to me that
night when I couldn't do anything but lie on my stomach and cry
from the pain. She washed my back and told me that if I ever
thieved again, she would be the first to flog me. I believed her."

Susan nodded, remembering her sharp words.

"In the morning I put on my clothes again and marched with
the Fifth." He looked down at his feet. "I was crying again by the
afternoon, but by God, I marched."

"You owe her your life," Susan said finally, when the silence
was too big to ignore.

"Yes. There wasn't anything I wouldn't do for her or the
colonel," he said simply. "He made me a regimental master
sergeant a year later before Talavera, and I always kept him in
sight in all our battles together." He sighed. "But I couldn't help
him on the march across the Pyrenees, and it pains me to this
day."

"Was that when he died, he and his daughter?"

The bailiff left his perch on the table, as though only by walking back and forth could he finish the story. "It happened so fast.
It was raining, pouring, more like. Lady Elizabeth's horse slipped

off the trail and down a gorge." He snapped his fingers, and Susan jumped. "Just like that she was gone. I was on the far side of the colonel, and he beat me to the edge of the path. It was deadly slick, and he went over, too." The bailiff shook his head as though he still could not believe it, after all that time. "We went through so many years of danger, and there we were, on the road to Paris . . ." His voice trailed off and he looked into that far distance again.

"And Lady Bushnell?"

"She saw it all." Wiggins turned his back to her, his hands on his hips, staring out at the moon on the snow. "She sent me down the gorge with a rope and two pistols. Told me to make sure they were not suffering." He tightened his lips and looked at Susan over his shoulder.

"The horses or the people?" Susan asked quietly.

He shrugged. "I never asked her. And don't ask me. Not now, not ever."

Susan was silent then, her chin in her hands. The only sound was the purring of the cat at her feet as it wriggled around to find a comfortable spot. Absently, she rubbed its swollen abdomen. And I have the effrontery to think that I can be Lady Bushnell's companion? she asked herself. A woman so strong has no need of my puny efforts. She is right, after all.

"I took the three of them home to Bushnell—it's about twenty miles from here—then rejoined the regiment, and served with the next Lord Bushnell. And after Waterloo, I brought his body back and stayed," Wiggins said as he extinguished the lamps. "I don't know that it was anybody's idea that I remain, but it happened that way." He smiled at her. "Another story for another day."

Susan followed him down the row. "She lost everyone to the wars."

"Yes. The Bushnells—father and son—may have earned the gratitude of a nation, but that's cold comfort to the widow." He was at the draftsman's desk again, where he looked at the ledger one more time, an expression of satisfaction on his face.

"What on earth can I do for someone like Lady Bushnell?" she asked, voicing her fear. She looked back at the long rows of Waterloo wheat, the green sprouts motionless now, as the furnaces cooled. The color was gone, too, with the light from the lamps, changed to gray. "I wish it were spring," she murmured, more to herself than to the bailiff. And now you will think I am whining, she thought. Well, I am.

"It will be spring soon enough," he said, his voice gentle, as though he were advising a grumpy child. "Then I will be too busy to come here so often. You ask what you can do for Lady Bushnell. Well, what would you like someone to do for you?"

Susan looked at the bailiff. He had extinguished the last lamp, and the color was gone from him, too. "You're as trying as Joel Steinman, exchanging question for question!" she exclaimed, then remembered the employment agent's last words to her. "And tell me how you know him," she demanded.

He laughed. "That can keep for another day. Seriously, what would you like someone to do for you?"

Susan leaned against the stool and considered his question. I would like someone to love me, she thought, but knew she could never say that out loud. "When I was a little girl, I liked someone to read to me, and brush my hair, and make sure I was tucked in at night." That was true enough. No matter how old I get, a part of me will always long for my mother, Susan thought. It was a foolish notion. She was afraid to look at the bailiff. You must think me an idiot, she thought. "You know, those things mothers do. It can't be far different from a lady's companion, do you think?"

"I wouldn't know," he said as he finished buttoning his coat. "My mother either died when I was born, or just abandoned me at a workhouse. That's where I grew up, and I don't remember anyone reading to me."

"Oh, I'm sorry," she said automatically. How strong you must be to have survived that, she considered as he carefully lifted the cat into a box lined with soft rags. And then the army, and war. I wonder you are not out of patience with my silly problem.

"Why be sorry? What you never have you can't miss." He laughed, but she couldn't hear much humor in it. "And the matron shaved our heads, so she wouldn't be bothered with lice. I think we had very different upbringings, Miss Hampton."

"I suppose we did," she agreed.

He took her by the elbow and steered her from the dark succession house. The cold made her gasp out loud. The bailiff tightened his hold on her as he walked her to the kitchen, then released her when they were inside. Susan took off Mrs. Skerlong's coat and hung it on the coat tree, her mind full of Spain and soldiering.

"And yet reading—it's not a bad notion," he said, his hand on the doorknob. "You might try that. I've come in on her several times and seen her staring down at a book in her lap."

"She likes to read?"

"She did once, I'm thinking. More and more now, I'll see her

with the same book in her lap, but no pages turned. Could it be
that her eyes are not what they once were?"

"It *is* a good idea," Susan agreed, "but what should I read to
her? I feel as though I know her better, but that I am no closer to
solving my problems. And would she ever let me read to her?"

He opened the door. "I suggest that you read to her whatever it
is that you . . ."

"I know, I know!" she interrupted, exasperated with the bailiff.
"Whatever I would like someone to read to me!"

The bailiff closed the door and she heard him laugh as his footsteps crunched on the icy path. "You are remarkably shortsighted
yourself," she told the closed door. "Anyone can see that Lady
Bushnell and I are nothing alike. How will I know what she
likes?" These people are giants, she thought, sitting in Mrs. Skerlong's chair and breathing in the fragrance of spices overhead and
tomorrow's yeast bread, a lump of covered dough on the table. I
feel young and foolish and out of my sphere, and yet, I have to
try, because I have been given a chance.

Mrs. Skerlong's tom jumped into her lap, startling her. He
turned about several times, as if testing her lap for solidity, then
settled down to purr and groom himself. Absently, she scratched
around his ears, smiling a little when he turned to oblige her fingers. "And I suppose you are the father of that forthcoming litter
in the succession house?" she murmured, her fingers gentle now
on his back. "I trust you'll do right by your family."

She leaned back in the chair and closed her eyes, thinking of
her father. And don't disgust your little ones, or make extravagant
promises you have no way of fulfilling. If you promise them a
mouse, give them a mouse. And for God's sake, teach them how
to hunt for themselves. She settled lower in the chair, unmindful
of her posture for once, and propped her feet on the footstool. The
cat was warm, and his purring created a pleasant vibration against
her stomach.

She must have dozed off, but for how long she had no idea. She
snapped her eyes open and tightened her hand on the cat, which
tensed to spring. David Wiggins stood looking down at her. He
shook his head. "Miss Hampton, go to bed!"

She relaxed again and regarded him out of sleepy eyes. "What
are you doing still up, Mr. Wiggins?" Her accusation was blunted
by a yawn that she could not stifle.

He looked down at his boots as though she had caught him at
mischief. "Oh, I just had to take another look at the Waterloo
wheat." He squatted down beside her chair until he was on her

eye level, his enthusiasm balancing the exhaustion in his face. "I'm going to sow an entire field of it this spring. It's a good blend of wheat, Susan. You'll see."

She nodded and closed her eyes again, but opened them wide when the bailiff picked her up, cat and all. With a hiss, the tom jumped off.

"Do I have to carry you upstairs to bed?" he asked.

"No . . . no," she stammered. "I'll go."

"When?"

"Now! Only let me down." He did as she asked and she straightened her skirts around her. I should be so indignant, she told herself as she frowned at him. How odd that I am not.

"You won't get anywhere staying up late to worry about things, Susan," he said as he went to the door again. He observed the frown on her face. "But maybe you weren't worrying about Lady Bushnell. Homesick?" he asked, his voice sympathetic.

"Not at all," she said too quickly. "There is nothing to miss there."

He watched her face another moment, his own expressionless. "So that's how it is," he said finally. "Well, life is short, Miss Hampton. Don't hate them too long. Go to bed."

She waited until she heard his footsteps on the path again, then took up a candle and holder on the table beside the lamp, lit it from the lamp, then extinguished the greater light. She went carefully upstairs and set the candlestick on her bedside table.

The curtains were still open, so she went to close them, and stood there instead, watching the bailiff make his progress to his own house. She inclined her head against the window frame, enjoying the simple pleasure of watching the man in motion. He had a competent stride, and she could only marvel at the miles he must have walked, and under what circumstances. No wonder both Lord Bushnells had relied on him, she thought as she stood at the window watching him and slowly unbuttoning Lady Elizabeth Bushnell's dress. He looks enormously capable, even from a second-story window. I can sleep now.

She did sleep well, to her gratification, and woke with Jane Austen on her mind—more specifically, Emma Woodhouse, she of the sharp tongue and strong will. Susan had nearly finished *Emma* on the long journey from London to Quilling, but she knew she could begin it again with no loss of interest. She got up from bed and wadded her nightgown—a loan from the generously endowed Mrs. Skerlong—around her as she padded on bare feet to the dressing room for her reticule. When she picked it up, she knew it was too light to contain the book, and then she remembered stuffing it into her trunk before walking to Quilling Manor. "Drat!" she said as she plumped herself down on her bed again, and she flopped onto her back with her arms out. There was a knock on the door.

"Come," she said, trying to keep the dismal note out of her voice. No sense in troubling Cora with her woes.

It was the bailiff; he stood there with her trunk on his shoulder, surprised at first, and then smiling as she lay there and stared at him, too startled to move.

"Miss Hampton, such a dramatic pose," he said finally.

She scrambled under the covers. "I . . . I thought you were Cora," she stammered. "I mean, when did you retrieve my trunk? Is it later than I think? How's the weather?" She had the good sense to stop and grin at him. "Am I babbling?"

He hesitated a moment, then came into the room and lowered the trunk carefully to the floor. "I woke up really early and made the trip to Quilling in no time. The road is clear now, and yes, you're babbling." He looked at her and winked. "Now you can probably locate a nightgown built on a less gargantuan scale."

Her smile was sunny. No sense in being embarrassed in front of a man who had already bared his back to her. "Well, excuse my drama, please." She crossed her legs under the covers and tucked the blanket around her. "It's just that you are an answer to a prayer, Mr. Wiggins."

He shook his head at her. "I never thought I would live to the day when I would be an answer to a maiden's prayers!"

"Don't give yourself too much credit, sir," she said, then stopped. "See here, Mr. Wiggins. I know I am not to call you sir, on threat of being thrown into a muck heap, but Mr. Wiggins sounds endlessly formal, and you have, after all, proposed to me, and shown me your back . . ."

He burst out laughing before she could finish, and she blushed. "And I have called you Miss Hampton and Susan, and why don't we both just call each other Susan and David? Is that what you are attempting to tell me? Considering the nature of our employment here, I think it would be entirely appropriate."

"That's one thing settled then," she said, folding her hands in her lap and wishing her hair were not tumbled around her shoulders, but neatly in place. "I fear I do not look too much like a lady at the moment," she apologized. "But then, I did not expect you with my trunk. For such, si . . . David, I thank you."

He took his cue and went to the door, turning back for a last smile. "Susan, you would look like a lady if you were simmering in a cannibal's iron pot in deepest Africa!" He leaned against the door, closing it with his weight. "Lady Bushnell always looked like a lady, even on our worst campaigns." He touched his chest. "I'm neither an authority nor a gentleman, but I suspect that being a lady comes from within."

She nodded. "My mother was that way."

He opened the door again. "You are, too, Susan," he said softly as he left the room without looking back.

She watched the door, pleased with herself. *Mama, you would be pleased to know that a bailiff in the Cotswolds thinks I am a lady.* The whole idea was so amusing that she laughed out loud, then bounded out of bed and threw herself on her knees by the trunk. The book was there on top of her underthings, just where she had left it. She leaned against the trunk and leafed through the pages, smiling over favorite passages.

"Lady B, if you are not amused by *Emma,* then you are a hard case indeed," she declared as she pulled off Mrs. Skerlong's nightgown, and dug down to a nightgown of her own. *Much better,* she thought as she put it on. *David Wiggins could have no objection to this, and may the Lord smite me if I think of him again, when I should be concerned with weightier matters.*

Although her own dresses were here now and hung in the dressing room, Susan wore Lady Elizabeth's blue wool dress down to breakfast. *I want her to see me in this,* she thought as she opened the kitchen door and sniffed deep of bread baking. *She needs to know that I am appreciative.*

The bailiff was just taking his dishes to the sink when she sat down at the table and thanked Mrs. Skerlong for the porridge the housekeeper set in front of her. David passed her the cream as he came to the table again, and sat down beside her, straddling the chair so he could face her.

"Could you do me a favor when you finish breakfast?" he asked as she poured on the cream and sprinkled in some sugar.

Susan nodded as she took a bite. He indicated a ledger in the middle of the table. "Lady Bushnell and I go over the accounts at the beginning of each month," he explained. "Would you check my math? Sometimes it's a bit creative."

She took another bite, then glanced at him, unable to resist. "What? Not enough fingers and toes, David?"

Mrs. Skerlong laughed and quickly turned her attention to something bubbling on the range.

The bailiff grinned. "Now that you mention it, I am missing a couple of toes—that's what happens when you try to stop a cannonball with your foot." He leaned down as if to remove his boot. "Do you want to verify my more honorable scars?"

Susan blushed and applied herself to her porridge, after a warning look at Mrs. Skerlong's back. "I have seen enough of your army trophies, sir! But yes, I will check your math."

The porridge done, Susan sipped her tea and looked at the columns of figures under the January 1820 heading. She worked through the entries on a piece of scrap paper, mindful of the bailiff's proximity as he leaned over the ledger, too. The hay fragrance was more prominent than the soap this morning. "See here," she pointed out, "you forgot to borrow here on this hemp and cording entry, so all the rest of these entries are incorrect." She ticked them off with the pencil.

"At least it was at the end of the month, so I don't have to redo it all," David temporized as he took a wad of rubber from his pocket and erased the faulty entries. "There."

Susan smiled over the ledger as she inserted the correct figures. "Am I to gather that schools on the Welsh side of the border are less than effective, or that you were a truant?" she teased.

He shrugged. "I never saw the inside of one. Learned my ciphering in the army. And how to read and write." He closed the ledger and stood up. "Thank you. It will be nice not to have Lady Bushnell twit me about my subtraction this once."

"I can check your figures whenever you want," Susan said, suddenly shy when he nodded in agreement and lightly touched her shoulder as he passed.

She waited in the kitchen all morning, polishing silverware for Mrs. Skerlong, but Lady Bushnell didn't release the bailiff until luncheon. He took a cheese and bread sandwich from Mrs. Skerlong and worked into his coat, muttering something about cows and the trouble with underbailiffs who think they are lovers. He looked back at Susan before he left the kitchen.

"I think she's in as sweet a mood as ever," he informed her. "And by the way, she asked me what I thought of you."

Susan put down the polishing cloth and held her breath. "Well, sir?" she asked finally, when he just grinned at her.

"I told her you were something out of the ordinary and that her apostle spoons were entirely safe." He laughed and caught the polishing cloth that she wadded up and threw at him, and tossed it back. "Charge, Susan."

Chapter Eight

⸙

Courage, Susan, she told herself as she paused outside the sitting room door. She missed the security of the heavy tea tray, but it was too early after luncheon for tea. And while *Emma* had seemed such a brilliant idea in her bedroom, the book was small protection now, even hugged to her chest. As she raised her hand to knock, she thought about praying, then dismissed the idea. God had not heard from her lately; Susan chose not to add hypocrisy to her faults. She knocked.

"Come."

Was there a longish pause between the knock and the acknowl-edgment? Was it too quick? Had she knocked firmly enough, or would Lady Bushnell think she was a forward piece? Susan took a deep breath. You are an idiot if you read malice in every word, she scolded herself. She opened the door and found herself imme-diately under Lady Bushnell's scrutiny. She dropped what she hoped was a graceful curtsy and started on her journey across the room, which seemed miles deep. She thought briefly of Emily balancing books on her head in the hopes of achieving some dig-nity, and thanked God for good posture and gentle bearing.

Then she stood in front of her employer, much closer than the day before. If she had not been so terrified, she would have taken a long look. As it was, she could only see those marvelous, hooded eyes and a firm mouth. Everything about the woman seated before her spoke of a person who did not suffer fools gladly. And she already knows I am a Hampton, a family name synonymous with fools, Susan thought in a panic. For one wild moment she considered picking up her borrowed skirt and run-ning from the room. I could be in Quilling in an hour, she thought as she managed what must have looked like a ghastly smile and even bunched the material of the skirt in her hand.

She didn't run. As she quaked inwardly before her employer,

she pressed the book against her stomach to stop its quivering and released her death grip on her skirt. She knew her appearance was nothing to disgust her employer; now if only her voice would not tremble, or her words would not come out in a breathless rush.

"Good afternoon, Lady Bushnell." That was easy enough. Her voice did not sound strange to her ears.

Lady Bushnell nodded, and her eyes went from Susan's face to the dress. "It fits?" she asked.

"Pretty well, my lady," Susan replied. "It is a trifle long, but then, I am a trifle short."

It was the smallest of jokes. It may have been Susan's imagination, but Lady Bushnell appeared to smile slightly in return. It came and went so quickly that Susan decided it must have been a trick of the light.

"You are more deep-breasted than my daughter," Lady Bushnell commented, "so you may wish to set the buttons over to give yourself more room. Certainly you may hem the dress, if you think you will be around for at least the length of a probation."

"I shall, my lady," Susan replied, gratified.

Exhausted, the subject wilted. Silence settled around the room like dust motes in a shaft of sunlight. Lady Bushnell looked out the window for a lengthy time, sighed, and then turned to face Susan again. She seemed chagrined that Susan was still there.

"What is it that you wish of me, Miss Hampton?" she asked, and there was resignation in her tones. "What do you propose to do?"

"Why, earn my salary, ma'am," Susan said, unable to keep all the surprise from her voice.

There was another brief flicker of amusement in Lady Bushnell's eyes. Green eyes, Susan observed, and such a wonderful, unfaded green.

"Then you will be the first one." Lady B said, with just a touch of asperity.

"I have already told Cora that I am to be the last one, Lady Bushnell," Susan said with a firmness she did not feel.

Lady Bushnell directed her gaze out the window again. Susan's heart sank, and she mentally kicked herself. Why can I not just say "Yes, my lady," or "No, my lady"? and leave the windy treatises to others. She waited to be dismissed again.

"How do you propose to do this?" came the question. Lady Bushnell continued to regard the view beyond the window. "If you plan to cheer me up, it's already been tried. If it is to be a needlework project, don't bother. I have a drawer full of unfinished doilies and china paintings. If you wish to chat, I doubt we have much in common."

"Mr. Wiggins allows that we do," Susan said suddenly, then hesitated. "Although I cannot see it, either," she concluded in a rush when Lady Bushnell turned quickly to look at her.

"I have never questioned my bailiff's skills of observation," Lady Bushnell commented, "but I do not think he is overacquainted with the gentry. We share this room and we are women, but I do not think our similarities extend much beyond that. What do you propose to do with me?" she asked, her voice heavy with irony.

"I intend to read to you."

"Read to me?" the widow repeated, and her voice rose for the first time. "Read to me like a bedridden pensioner whose wits are too twaddled for anything else?"

Susan winced but did not falter. "No! I do not see it that way." Without an invitation, she sat in the chair opposite the dowager. "David . . . Mr. Wiggins asked me what I used to like to have done to me, and the second thing was to have someone read to me. It's a pleasure."

Again there was that twitch of the lip and slight flicker of the eye that lasted no more than a millisecond. "Do enlighten me what the first thing was on your list?" she asked, but it sounded more like a command.

"Mama brushed my hair. I liked the way it felt," she said simply. Lady Bushnell was not someone to bamboozle with an elaborate answer. "I did not think you wanted me to brush your hair."

"No. I'm quite capable of that; always have been. You do not think I have the wits left to read to myself?" she asked, indicating the open book on her lap.

"You misunderstand me, my lady," Susan said, her voice earnest now. "I always thought it the height of comfort to have someone read to me. I could close my eyes and just let the words wander through my mind. I . . ." She paused. I am making a fool of myself, she thought miserably. Please, Lady Bushnell.

"If you must, you must," the woman said finally. "I suppose if I do not allow you to read to me, then I will be forced into needlework, or some other project for my own good."

Susan smiled. "Never that! I'm an indifferent needlewoman myself, so you need not fear that I will trap you in a daisy chain, or force a French knot on you."

Lady Bushnell put her hand to her mouth and coughed, or at least it sounded like a cough to Susan. "What a relief to know that

I am safe from the dreaded feather stitch. Now, set my mind at rest and assure me that I will not be forced to tat against my will."

"Never!" Susan replied, unable to keep the laughter from her voice. "And I will never inflict crewel punishment."

Lady Bushnell coughed again. Susan wondered if she should suggest a seat farther from the window, then decided that her courage did not extend that far. The widow closed the book in her lap, not even marking the page, and set it aside. Perhaps David is right, Susan thought. Perhaps she would like to read, but cannot anymore. You are a proud old thing, Lady Bushnell, and I hope I am just like you when I reach sixty-five. I doubt I will have any more family around me than you do, she considered. She took heart and opened the book.

"I would like to read *Emma*, my lady," she said. "It's rather modern, but it makes me laugh." She leaned forward. "Emma is not exactly a pattern card of perfection, such as one finds in some novels, my lady."

"I wouldn't know," Lady Bushnell cut in. "I never read novels."

"Oh, I do!" Susan said, choosing not to accept the rebuff. "Sometimes nothing is better than a romance where events resolve themselves to everyone's satisfaction." She noticed the set look return to the widow's eyes. "I know it seldom happens in real life, but there is nothing wrong with the occasional happy ending," Susan added gently.

"I wouldn't know," the widow repeated, but her voice was softer this time.

There was nothing in Lady Bushnell's demeanor that encouraged it, but Susan leaned forward impulsively and just touched the woman's knee. She regretted the gesture almost the moment she made it, but Lady Bushnell did not draw away. Instead, she sighed and folded her hands in her lap. "Well, then, if you must read, let us get on with it," she said, as though humoring a puppy leaping about and growling at the hem of her dress.

This is one fool you are forced to suffer, Lady Bushnell, Susan thought, at least until I have failed whatever probation you permit me. And I fear it will not be long. She turned to the first chapter and cleared her throat. "'Volume One, Chapter One. Emma Woodhouse, handsome, clever, and rich, with a comfortable home and happy disposition, seemed to unite some of the best blessings of existence, and had lived nearly twenty-one years in the world with very little to vex or distress her.'"

The afternoon sun was changing the look of the sitting room when Cora Skerlong came in with a tea tray. Susan looked up from the book with a quick glance at Lady Bushnell, one of a series of darting glances she had made all afternoon. Early in the first chapter, Lady Bushnell had closed her eyes, which made Susan open her own eyes wider and wonder if she was listening at all, or merely suffering her presence until some interruption like a tea tray could relieve her.

Susan marked her place and put aside the book. I wonder if I should have chosen something more serious, like *The Decline and Fall of the Roman Empire,* or Fox's *Book of Martyrs,* she thought, then shook her head slightly. Then *I* would have trouble staying awake. She smiled at the thought of falling asleep until the book tumbled from her hands and she pitched forward to lie snoring in Lady Bushell's lap. No, she decided, no *Book of Martyrs* for me. She looked at Lady Bushnell, who was indicating that Cora set down the heavy tray. I think there have been too many martyrs for Lady Bushnell's peace of mind, as it is.

Cora left the room, pausing just out of Lady Bushnell's vision to blow a quick kiss to Susan, her eyes merry. Susan found herself wishing for escape, too, and a return to the kitchen and the comfort of soup, or stew, or whatever it was she had been smelling this past hour and more. She picked up a cup and saucer and poured tea for Lady Bushnell.

"Thank you."

That was all. There was no offer that Susan take up the other cup and pour for herself, too, so she did not, even though she was as dry as a hay sprig from reading.

Cora had left the day's mail on the tray. As soon as Lady Bushnell had taken several sips, Susan handed the letters and a small package to her.

"There is a letter opener on my desk."

Susan rose, grateful to move again, and went to the desk, which was covered with letters brittle and yellow, the ink faded. The dates were two decades gone now. She moved the letters aside, but not before her eyes caught several of the salutations. "Beloved Lydia." "My darling wife." "Sweetheart." Susan sighed, marveling how it must feel to receive letters addressed like that. She returned to her seat by the window and took the letters which Lady Bushnell extended to her, slitting them open. The widow took them back and indicated with her head the package on the tray.

"That is for Mr. Wiggins. See that he gets it."

"Very well, my lady." Susan picked up the items. Should I offer to read her correspondence to her? she questioned herself. Can she manage? Do I dare attempt to remove such autonomy from her? A moment's reflection told her that she did not dare. She picked up her book. "Will you be needing . . ."

"No," the widow interrupted. There was no disguising her eagerness to see Susan gone. "That will be quite all."

Susan hesitated at the door. "I could return after din . . ."

"No need."

She was absurdly close to tears but she forced them back and squared her shoulders. "I will return tomorrow for chapter seven," she said, hoping she sounded confident.

"You will not," Lady Bushnell contradicted as she reached for a macaroon. She took a good look at Susan, one that measured her up and down. "I believe we were on chapter six, Miss Hampton, and not seven. Tomorrow then. Don't forget Mr. Wiggins's package."

Susan paused outside the sitting room door and leaned against it. I have survived one afternoon, she told herself. I refuse to allow myself any wild flights of fancy, such as are common to Hamptons, but I will permit myself the luxury of hope. She looked down at the book she clutched so tightly. "Thank you, Jane Austen," she whispered, and never meant anything more.

She went down the hall to the kitchen, where she surprised Mrs. Skerlong, dozing in her chair. The cat leaped off the housekeeper's lap, twined itself around Susan's ankles, then returned to the housekeeper, satisfied with ownership in the newest human. Another leap, this one more dignified, landed him back in Mrs. Skerlong's lap.

Susan set the book and package on the table. "Is Mr. Wiggins about?" she asked. "There is this package for him."

"He has gone to choir practice," the housekeeper replied. "Would you mind stirring that pot on the stove?"

"With pleasure, provided I can lick the spoon. Choir practice?"

Mrs. Skerlong settled herself more comfortably in the chair. "You don't think any self-respecting curate would permit a Welsh bass to live unmolested within parish boundaries, do you?"

Susan laughed as she stirred the stew. "I wasn't aware of Mr. Wiggins's considerable talents before."

"Then you'll be the first lady's companion who isn't!" Mrs. Skerlong replied, amusement evident in her voice.

"Really, Mrs. Skerlong!" Susan protested as she felt herself blushing.

"Yes, really!" The housekeeper smiled and turned her attention to the cat, who was kneading her stomach. "They've all looked him over, but I don't know that it did any of them much good. Of course, I suppose your being of the gentry yourself will make you less liable."

"Of course," Susan agreed as she poured herself some tea and sat down to resume polishing silverware from her morning task. She looked around for Mrs. Skerlong's daughter. "Did Cora go to choir practice, too?"

"She did. There is a tenor she is fond of."

"Tell me, Mrs. Skerlong, if David is a Welshman, how did he come by a name like Wiggins?" Susan asked, concentrating on the intricate pattern of Lady Bushnell's best table knives.

"I think it had something to do with what hurried him from Wales in the first place, Susan." She leaned closer and lowered her voice some more. "Poaching."

Susan's eyes widened. "My goodness, but he's a resourceful man. So he thought it best to revise his name?"

"Happens there is a village name of Wiggins just this side of the border," Mrs. Skerlong explained. She shook her head. "I expect he's not the first Welshman to decide on a name change, considering what hotheaded, impulsive works of nature most of them are. And it was probably one of those silly names with loads of l's and y's that decent folk can't pronounce."

"And then he took the king's shilling and went to war?"

"It would appeal to a Welshman," Mrs. Skerlong said. "When you're done polishing, there's plenty of nice warm water on the Rumford for rinsing."

When the last piece of silverware was polished, washed, and returned to its felt-lined case, Susan sat down with Mrs. Skerlong for a bowl of mutton stew and brown bread good enough to exclaim over.

"On Thursday nights, I just leave the pot on the hob and everyone helps himself," she said as they pushed away from the table. "Cora always seems to find the longest way home, usually dragging a tenor behind her."

Susan went to the sink to help with dishes. "I should want a shortcut, on these cold winter nights!"

"Well, then, you're not in love, are you now?" The housekeeper said as she handed Susan a bowl to dry.

No, I am not, Susan thought, and felt a momentary pang for Cora and her singer. I think I would like to be, however. It was a pleasant notion, and one that nourished her through another slice of bread and cup of tea. She listened to the clock tick and the cat purr, and felt content. Last week I was stewing and fretting at Aunt Louisa's, Susan reflected as she picked up her book and Mr.

Wiggins's package. Now I am happy enough to polish silver and eat in a kitchen. I am thinking that good breeding may be just a veneer among the Hamptons. Aunt Louisa would be flabbergasted. Susan nodded to the housekeeper, who was preparing Lady Bushnell's dinner tray, and went upstairs.

There was another dress on her bed, this one a dusty rose, soft from much wear. She sniffed the fabric, breathing in the faint fragrance of cloves. "Packed away in cloves and tissue," she murmured, holding the dress up to her and admiring it in the mirror. "Lady Elizabeth, your taste was impeccable."

She sad on the bed, running her hand lightly over the material, thinking of ladies and officers, battle and bivouac. Such a strange life for a lady, to follow the drum, she considered. I wonder if I could ever love someone enough to give up comfort and ease, to ride a horse, sleep in tents, and abandon my privacy. I think I do not know much about love. She thought of Elizabeth following her father through all of Spain and Portugal, and realized with pain that she would not follow Sir Rodney Hampton across the street. "Why ever should I?" she said suddenly, her words a rebuke in the quiet room. She covered her mouth and looked around; she hadn't meant to be so loud.

Lady Bushnell had also left scissors, needle, and thread on the bed, so Susan removed her dress, put on one of her own simple frocks, and cut the buttons off the dress she had been wearing. "Lady Elizabeth, you had a neater figure than mine," she said as she realigned the buttons to allow herself more room.

Evening came quickly, and she lit a lamp to complete the work, humming to herself and looking out at the snow. It was melting now, exposing dark patches of earth. She willed spring to come, even as she sighed and watched clouds weighed down with snow boil up again from the northwest. She snipped the thread tail off the button and leaned back in her chair, her eyes on the road from Quilling. The room was warm and her eyes closed.

"Susan? Susan?"

She opened her eyes slowly, reluctant to surrender her peace, to see someone of familiar height and bulk standing in the open doorway. It was full dark outside, and the coals in the hearth had settled into a compact glow. She sat up and turned the lamp higher. "Someone wants me? Lady Bushnell?" she asked him.

"No. Just me," the bailiff said, apology at disturbing her evident in his voice. "I knocked, but you were sunk pretty deep." His eyes went to the rose wool dress on the bed. "I remember that dress."

Susan indicated the other chair in the room. Leaving the door open, he crossed to the hearth, squatted down to add some more coal, then sat in the chair.

"Was she pretty?" Susan asked, looking at the dress, too.

He rested casually in the chair, his feet propped on the fireplace fender, making himself entirely at home, to her amusement. "Oh, something like," he said, his voice warm now with reminiscence. "Her hair wasn't as dark as yours, and her eyes were green like her mother's. She was a bit of a flirt, with a quick temper." He folded his hands across his stomach, more completely relaxed than Susan had seen him yet. He looked at her. "You'd probably have found her an ignorant puss—Lady Bushnell could never interest her in books or theorems—but she knew tactics and strategies as well as the rest of us, and much better than the little lordlings with purchased commissions."

I believe I could listen to a Welshman all day, Susan thought, making herself more comfortable. I love the way his voice lifts like a question at the end of his sentences. "Would I have liked her?" she asked, wanting him to speak.

He considered the question a moment. "I doubt it," he said honestly. "She was an imperious baggage, quite proud of her horsemanship and her command over the men of the regiment." He sighed and looked at the fire again.

"Were you in love with her?"

He chuckled, but did not look at her. "We all were," he said softly. "It wasn't so much that she was pretty—offhand, I think you're more attractive than she was—but she was *there*." He spread his hands palms up in his lap, his eyes still on the fire. "You can't have any conception how nice it was to just pass by Lady Elizabeth on the quick march and smell her. By God, we stunk the length and breadth of Spain, but she always smelled so sweet." He reached behind him and fingered the dress on the bed. "Of cloves."

Do you think me attractive? she thought. Too bad one of my own kind never did. "How sad that she died," Susan murmured.

"Yes. Did you know, she was just newly engaged to one of the officers of the regiment?" the bailiff commented, taking his booted feet off the fender and sitting up straighter.

"How tragic!"

He shrugged. "It doesn't matter, not really. Her fiancé died at Waterloo." He looked at her then. "She would just have been a widow like her mother and sister-in-law. My God, there is a whole generation of young widows. Can I tell you how much I hate war?"

His words hung in the air, and she could think of nothing to say. After a moment, she picked up the blue dress again and sewed on another button while the bailiff returned his gaze to the flames. She watched his profile, dark and intent, his shoulders tense, and half rose from her chair, her hand extended to touch him.

Reason prevailed; she put down her hand. But the bailiff had turned slightly when she rose, so she could not sit down like an idiot, with no explanation of her sudden movement. She remembered the package on the bureau and crossed in front of him, her skirts brushing his legs. She handed it to him. "Forgive my manners. Did you come for this package? I don't know why I didn't just leave it on the kitchen table."

He looked at her in surprise, as if wondering why he had come at all. "Why, yes, I did," he said smoothly, then laughed. "What a bumbler I am!" He opened the package and pulled out two letters. "One to you and one to me."

"To me?" she asked, accepting the folded sheet with her name clearly written on it.

He nodded and then laughed again, less self-consciously, as he pulled a glove from the package. "And a present from our friend Joel Steinman."

Susan put down her letter unread and pulled her chair up before the fire and beside the bailiff. "What kind of joke is this?" she asked, grateful that his mood had changed.

He laid the glove across his leg and opened his letter. "No joke, Susan. My chief shepherd lost his left hand in a shearing accident a few years back. I wrote to Joel about it, and now he sends the right glove that he has no use for, every time he buys a new pair."

"The two of you are so clever," Susan commented, picking up the glove.

"It's a small thing, but just what old Ben Rich needed to get himself over the melancholy of it all," the bailiff explained. He smiled again in that oblique way that she was beginning to recognize as shyness. "I don't think any old Waterloo shades would rise and haunt me if I fibbed and told the old fellow that Steinman was a war hero. It seemed to help."

"I think you were all heroes," she said softly, shy herself now as she returned the glove to his leg.

"Not all," he said, his voice intense again, with no lilt to it. "Not all," he repeated, leaning back again. "I could tell you . . ."

He paused. "Except that I won't." He picked up the note from the employment agent, and his face relaxed as he continued reading. "Oh, this is good, Susan. 'David, here is another glove for Ben Rich from his Jewish Waterloo hero, Steinman the Magnificent.'" He looked at Susan, then back at the letter. "Except that I don't understand this part," he commented, holding the paper closer to the fire. "'Remember the debt I said I could never pay? Have I paid it now? Let me know what you think. Your Waterloo albatross, Joel.'" he crumpled the letter and overhanded it into the fireplace. "Joel is, at times, inscrutable."

"Waterloo albatross?" Susan asked. She hitched her chair closer. "I have been wondering how you know Mr. Steinman. And what is this debt? And I wish I knew why he was so keen to send me here, considering that Lady Bushnell is a bit of an ogre," she grumbled, folding the blue dress and putting it on the bureau.

The bailiff looked up from the little blaze from the burning paper and gave her his full attention. His frown turned into a modest smile, and then a grin that went all the way to his eyes. She gazed back at him, pleased that he was gone from gloomy to elated in so short a time, and unable to resist smiling at him, too. What a good thing that my social class makes me impervious to bailiffs with shady backgrounds, she told herself. All of a sudden she didn't know what to do with her hands. As David Wiggins continued to smile at her, she put them behind her back. Welshmen are so changeable, she thought. I wonder what is on his mind?

"I'm glad you're feeling cheerful again, but I am just nosy enough to want to know how you became friends with a Jewish employment agent, and at Waterloo yet? I would not have thought Mr. Steinman to be soldier material. That is, if you don't mind telling me," she asked, wondering why it was she had a marked tendency to babble in front of the bailiff.

"Oh my word," David said, still regarding her with an expression that was beginning to make her stomach feel warm. "I suppose I saved his life, and he decided to become my burden. He swore he would do me a good deed that would fulfill his obligation."

"And did he?" she asked. "From that letter, he seems to think so. Do you?"

"I think he has," the bailiff replied after another moment of regard in her general direction. He patted the chair she had vacated. "Sit and I'll tell you. It's not a long story."

She did as he said, thinking about Aunt Louisa and propriety, then tucked her feet up under her to be more comfortable. It would be rude for me to tell him that ladies did not listen to war stories, but who is to say that I am still a lady, anyway. There was nothing proper about having this man in her room, and so late at night, except that it felt right. Somehow, I must learn to trust my own judgment, she told herself.

"It's a tame enough story, Susan. Joel Steinman was a purchasing agent with the army at Ostend, on the coast," David began.

"You knew him then?"

He shook his head. "No. Our acquaintance was one of those sudden war things. He and others in the commissary went to Mont St. Jean to witness the battle from its height, so he told me later. The Fifth formed one of the squares on the battle line above the farmhouse called La Haye Sainte."

"Wheat fields?"

"Yeah," he said simply, and for a moment his eyes saw something far away. "By late afternoon it was not much of a square, what with Boney's lovely daughters pounding away, and the *chasseurs* riding at us when the guns were silent." He looked at her. "Have you ever been in a situation that you thought would never end?"

She decided it would be fatuous to compare endlessly waiting for her London Season to something as desperate as that battle, so she shook her head.

"It was the longest day of my life, and the shortest," he said simply. "Time passed so strangely. It was during one of those intervals when the *chasseurs* were retiring down the hill and our own gunners were running from the protection of our squares back into the firing lines, when someone in the rear decided that we might—just might—be low on ordnance. Some of the noncombatants watching the fight were pressed into service. Joel was one of them." The bailiff closed his eyes as if to aid his memory. "He leaped off the cart and tugged out two or three boxes of cartridges before we noticed that the *chasseurs* were returning, and the cart and driver had fled the front lines."

"So there he stayed and fought?" Susan asked when the bailiff's silence continued.

He opened his eyes. "No. There he stayed in time for a shell to crash into his arm. It must have been one of the last shells, before the cavalry was on us again. I was the closest man to him not otherwise occupied, or not wounded too seriously, so I ran to help."

"No wonder he feels under obligation to you. How good that you were quick enough."

To her surprise, he shook his head. "I was one of two sergeants still alive, and I left my position beside Lord Bushnell." His voice shook, and his hand knotted into a fist as it rested in the arm of the chair. He looked at her again, as if asking for judgment. "What could I do? My duty was to stay by my commander, and here was this man screaming in agony. I went to him, jerked on a tourniquet, but after the next charge, Lord Bushnell was dead."

Susan rested her hand on his arm. "What could you have done differently?"

She removed her hand when he looked at it. "I should have let Joel die, and stayed by my commander, as I had done in all battles since Talavera, serving both father and son."

She watched his face in the gentle glow of the fireplace and lamp. He seemed not so much troubled by what he was saying, as thoughtful. I suppose you have had years to revisit this strange weird landscape over and over in your mind, she considered. "I'm sure the men of the regiment who survived do not blame you for what happened. How could anyone be everywhere?" she asked.

He touched her hand. "I don't know why I am telling you this. Susan, as soon as I left Lord Bushnell's side, he was shot by one of his own men. I had been protecting a coward from his own regiment."

Chapter Nine

ℭ

Susan stared at him as his words sank in. "But . . . but I thought he was a hero. I mean . . . everyone thinks so!"

The bailiff nodded. "It's what I chose to tell because I couldn't bear to break Lady Bushnell's heart a third time." He took her hand and pressed it against his chest, and she did not remove it this time. He made an eloquent face. "Think of it, Susan. I lied and stole all my life, until I was stripped naked and facing three-hundred or death. Lying, conniving, and stealing is how you survive in a workhouse, and it was how I lived in that first regiment after I fled Wales."

"I wouldn't know," she said softly, wondering why she had ever complained about the course of her life.

"No, you wouldn't," he agreed, matching her for calm. " 'No, governor, I would'na steal a bowl of gruel. 'Tmust h'been Owen there,' " he mimicked, aping his own Welsh accent. " 'Lor' love ya, sir, it's my turn for the blanket,' or the extra mutton gristle, or a spot closer to the fire. That's how I survived, Susan. And then Lord and Lady Bushnell saved my life, and in exchange I promised never to lie or steal again."

He released her hand, but she moved it no farther than the arm of his chair as he leaned forward, chin on hands, to stare into the fire. "And now I am living the biggest lie of all, because I cannot bring myself to tell an old lady the truth."

Susan pulled the thought around in her mind, then leaned forward, too, unable to mask the intensity in her voice. "And so you protect her from the truth in this little valley? You see to it that no one new ever comes in, on the odd chance that someone will let drop the truth? And why do I think that the lady's companions don't stay around mainly because of you, and not her?"

"It's true." He grunted at the irony of his choice of words, then turned to look at her with some apology in his dark eyes. "Lady B rubs along for a week or so with a lady's companion—and I tell you she's liked some of them—then she asks me what I think. I tell her the woman won't do, and she's gone like that." He snapped his fingers and Susan jumped. "I'll do anything to keep Lady Bushnell's heart from breaking." He hesitated.

"If you have something more to tell, you might as well," she said, her voice low as she spoke almost in his ear. Although why you are telling me, I cannot understand, particularly if you are planning to dismiss me soon, like the others.

"Old Lord Bushnell knew the failings of his son," the bailiff said, leaning back again, as though the conversation was beginning to exhaust him. "When I crawled down that gorge to see what was left, after he and Lady Elizabeth tumbled off, he was still alive."

"Poor man," Susan said, taking the bailiff's hand this time.

He nodded. "Elizabeth was already dead. I don't know where he got the strength, but he pulled me almost on top of him and made me promise to stick very close to his son. 'He's no soldier, but his mama thinks he is. I'm depending on you,' were his last words to me before he ordered me to shoot him." He turned bleak eyes on her. "And so I owe everyone a lie."

"Except me," she said, tightening her grip when she knew she should be letting go.

"Except you," he echoed, then flexed his fingers in her grasp. "Have a care there, lady, or you'll squash my milking fingers." Before she could protest, he brought her hand to his lips, kissed it, then released it. He stood up and stretched. "I only came for my package," he said with some amazement in his voice. He stood in front of her chair then, his hands on the arm rests, leaning over her. "Do other people confide in you?"

"No," she replied simply. "No one has ever cared enough to tell me anything beyond the commonplace." Her face hardened. "My father has never trusted me with the truth."

He touched her cheek, then stood away from her. "Then he is a fool." Her expression did not change, and he picked up Steinman's glove from the chair, went to the open door, and nodded to her. "I think I'll go check my Waterloo wheat now."

She glanced at the clock. "It's past midnight! Don't you ever sleep?"

"Of course I do," he said, amused, his voice ordinary again. "But as it is, tonight I would only dream of Waterloo, or of you, and neither topic is productive, especially since you have turned down my wonderful offer of marriage. Wise woman." He chuckled, then closed the door behind them. She listened for his foot-steps on the stairs, but heard nothing. He knows how to go down these stairs quietly, she thought.

"If those are your only choices, sir, then dream of me," she said softly. She picked up Joel Steinman's unread letter and lay down on her bed. Mrs. Skerlong would have it that my class and up-bringing make me impervious to the bailiff, she thought. I am sure this is true.

She held the letter up to the lamplight. "'Miss Hampton, I may have found a solution to your problem,'" she read out loud. "'I am negotiating now with a recently widowed woman with two young daughters who is searching for just the right governess. If things aren't working out (and perhaps I made a mistake), let me know, and I will keep you abreast of this posting. Regards, etc., Joel Steinman.'"

I will write you in the morning, Mr. Steinman, she told herself. As much as David Wiggins seems to relish late-night confiden-tialities, I think the cold light of morning turns him into a realist again, she reminded herself. I do not think I am long for this posi-tion. And yet, something tells me that I am the first lady's com-panion he has confided in.

She went to the window, restless suddenly with the size of the room, and stood there until she saw the pinpoints of light in the succession house. The wheat came again to her mind's eye, and she thought of it growing steadily through the long winter, care-fully nurtured by someone who had watched it mowed down by artillery and stomped by cavalry into red mud on the deadly slopes of Mont St. Jean. The bailiff said he would be planting this Waterloo strain in the spring, the amalgamation of seeds he had created from totally different backgrounds. She stepped out of her dress and still stood at the window, watching the light as she was sure he watched the wheat. When she got in bed finally, she rested for a long time on her elbow, half sitting up to look at the chair the bailiff had drawn up to the fireplace. How pleasant it must be to share a room and a bed with a man, she thought, not drawing back from the topic as she would have in Aunt Louisa's house. How pleasant it would be to know that when she took a candle from the downstairs hall table and started up the stairs, someone would follow her, or take her hand and lead the way. I would like to share a bed with a man, she decided, and while there would be lovemaking and whatever that might entail that Aunt Louisa never told me, I would like to relax in bed and talk with someone besides myself, someone who loves me enough to listen.

It was a cheerful notion, and for the first time in years did not end with the bitter knowledge that her father's improvidence had made a husband so impossible. She held her hands up to the moonlight that streamed in the window, thinking of the Waterloo strain, that bit of green born of war and the worst that men could do to each other. David, am I getting some tiny glimmer of what that wheat means to you? she asked herself. That brave stand of wheat in the succession house was spring in winter; the quiet after the guns were silent; the low voices of husband and wife talking and laughing with each other when the house was still. Does it represent peace, and every good thing for someone whose life has been hard, to say the least? She sighed and wrapped her arms around her pillow, content for the first time in years. And all from silly old wheat, she told herself as her eyes closed.

The bailiff was gone in the morning, off to a cattle auction in Chipping Norton, Mrs. Skerlong said as she dished up a great bowl of porridge for Susan. "Middle of February, regular as clockwork since the Conquest, I suppose," the housekeeper said, sitting down with Susan. She touched Susan's hand. "I think all the cattle buyers try to cheat each other, and see who can drink and wench the most without their wives finding out," she said. "But the lads must have their week of fun."

Susan laughed and dipped into her breakfast. "Does *anyone* actually go there to buy cattle?" she asked.

The housekeeper shrugged. "Somehow it all happens. Tim the cow man got back this morning from spending the winter with his mother in Bristol, so at least we do not have to do the milking while David is gone."

And thank goodness for that, Susan thought, sprinkling more sugar on her porridge. The only thing I have ever done with milk is drink it. I could learn, though, and make myself useful, she told herself, thinking how little Lady Bushnell wanted her presence.

"Something more, and this for you," Mrs. Skerlong said, pulling a scrap of paper from her apron pocket.

Susan read the note, then looked at the housekeeper. "It seems I am to weed the plants in the succession house, and check for ripe strawberries while David is gone," she said.

"You've proven to be a useful body to our bailiff," Mrs. Skerlong said, amusement in her eyes.

Susan nodded, reading no more into the statement than she

hoped the housekeeper intended. "Now if only Lady Bushnell would undergo a metamorphosis and discover how useful I could be to her . . ."

There was no metamorphosis. After a morning of more silver polish in the kitchen, spiced with Mrs. Skerlong's pungent comments about the locals, Susan took her book to Lady Bushnell's private sitting room for an afternoon of *Emma*. And each day during the bailiff's absence, Lady Bushnell listened politely, and even went so far once or twice to smile in those places where Susan laughed out loud. There seemed to be no unbending, no softening of Lady Bushnell's resolve to see this lady's companion gone like the others. Perhaps she likes me, but knows that her bailiff will only dismiss me after a suitable probation, Susan considered after one interminable afternoon. Liking someone can be so complicated, especially if that someone will be gone with the crocuses. She told herself not to hope too much, even if the bailiff had taken her into his confidence. He could just as easily see that she left.

Despite the uncertainty, Susan did not write to Joel Steinman. She told herself each morning that she would answer his letter, but she did not. Instead, she plagued Mrs. Skerlong for housework to keep her occupied in the morning, spent a frosty afternoon reading to a silent woman, and in the evening weeded plants in the succession house. Tim the cow man—he must have a last name, but Susan could never get him to own to one—saw that the room was kept warm and well lit. His chief topic each evening before he retreated to his quarters attached to the cattle byre was to admonish her to put out the lamps when she finished. And each evening Susan patiently promised until he was satisfied. He would hand her a pail with a little milk for the cat, remind her again of the lamps, as though she had the attention span of a tulip, then stalk off, muttering to himself.

"This holding employs its share of eccentrics," Susan told the cat as she pushed up her sleeves and weeded the Waterloo strain. The little animal, rounder each day with kittens in the making, followed her down one row and up the other, rubbing against her ankles if she happened to pause long enough for that much feline fellowship.

When she finished the wheat, she turned to the other plants, humming as she weeded, and content to do as the bailiff asked. She wondered what Aunt Louisa would think if she could see her with dirt under her fingernails and strawberry stains around her mouth, but she didn't let it occupy too much of her mind. She breathed in the wonderful fragrance of loam, fortified earth, and green things growing, and understood why the bailiff spent so much of his time where she was now. When she finished, she hitched herself onto David's tall stool, leaned on the drafting table, rested her chin on her arms, and looked over her green domain. She dreamed that she could watch the wheat grow.

At the end of each evening, she reminded herself to write to Joel Steinman, but the intention never got much beyond the first-floor landing when she returned, pleasantly tired, from the succession house. She would sit in her armchair before the fire, her stockinged feet on the fender, her dress pulled up around her knees, totally satisfied with herself and grateful to David Wiggins for the homely task he had sent her.

Lady Bushnell was another matter. I am determined that some afternoon you will unbend and offer me tea, she resolved every time she smiled at the old woman, opened the book, and began to read. It never happened. She would read five or six chapters—they were in volume II now—ask if there was anything else she could do, and grit her teeth at Lady Bushnell's peremptory dismissal. She would smile her brightest smile, the one that Mama always said could coax eggs out of roosters, and leave the room.

"I have never been so determined to drink tea," she told the housekeeper the next morning. She made a face. "You would think I had a controlling interest in the East India Company!"

"Well, we will continue to put that extra cup and saucer on that tray for ballast," Mrs. Skerlong assured her. She looked at Susan. "David Wiggins returned late last night," she said.

"Oh, excellent!" Susan declared as she picked up her polishing cloth and yet another candlestick. "Was he sober?" she asked, her eyes merry. She began to rub the candlestick, then put down the cloth with a shake of her head. "Mrs. Skerlong, I cannot face another morning of silver paste! Could you commission me with something else to do?"

"I think the books in the library needs dusting," Mrs. Skerlong said with a smile of understanding. "And here is some furniture polish . . ."

"Oh, don't say that word!" Susan interrupted with a sigh.

". . . for the pianoforte," Mrs. Skerlong continued. "Lady Bushnell and David are in the bookroom."

I will polish first, and get it over with, Susan decided as she closed the door to the library and opened the draperies. She coughed from the dust off the curtains, wiped her eyes with her apron, and looked around her with some pleasure.

The mullioned windows let in only a moderate amount of sunlight, but it was enough to put a golden glow on the oak wainscoting. Again she was struck with the permanence of the manor and its graceful endurance through one more winter in several centuries of changing seasons. I love this house, she decided as she set the polish carefully on the window ledge and raised the piano lid. She played a tentative chord, pleased with the resonance of the instrument. A person could curl up quite comfortably on that sofa over there, she thought, while someone more proficient than I played this piano.

She considered Joel Steinman's letter, and the possible governess position, and played another chord. If I can get that job, I had better be able to verify my claim to teach piano to children, she told herself as she ruffled through a stack of music and appropriated a Bach invention that looked promising, if played at a glacier's speed.

"I disremember this many notes," she muttered, her eyes on the music as she poised her fingers over the keys. "Forward and easy does it, Susan. How bad can one person be?"

I could have been worse, but I'm not sure how, she had to admit when she concluded with a chord that while not triumphant, was at least three parts right. Thank goodness I do not have an audience. I'm sure they would be throwing things or making rude noises. She turned the page and poised her hands over the keys again.

"Don't even think it, Miss Hampton!"

Susan gasped and put her hands behind her back as Lady Bushnell uttered each word with emphatic precision. The bailiff laughed from the doorway as the widow, moving slowly but deliberately with the aid of a cane, bore down upon her. After one terrified look around, Susan closed her eyes and sat very still. To her horror, Lady Bushnell ordered the bailiff to pull up a chair. Susan just barely stifled a gasp when the widow thumped down her cane on a spot by the piano stool and the bailiff positioned the chair. He helped her sit down, then stood behind the chair. Susan knew that she did not have the courage to look at either of them, so she kept her eyes resolutely trained upon the Bach.

Her courage fled when Lady Bushnell thumped the music with her cane. "Begin again, Miss Hampton. From the top."

Susan turned back to the previous page, where the notes appeared to have multiplied at an alarming rate. She stared at the page, opened her mouth to beg off, then closed it. I would only babble, she told herself. I wonder if Lady Bushnell can smell fear.

Susan took a deep breath and began to play, wincing at the notes and grateful, at the same time, that Bach would never know what atrocities she was committing on his music.

She struggled to the end, and held her breath after the final chord. Out of the corner of her eye she saw the bailiff go to the window, where he stood, shoulders shaking, and stared out at the snow. She was too afraid to glance at Lady Bushnell. The widow cleared her throat and Susan winced again.

"Miss Hampton, if my pianoforte were a living thing, we would have to shoot it to put it out of its misery."

David Wiggins exploded into laughter, which he quickly stifled when the dowager glared at him. "You, sir, are less than useful at moments like these," Lady Bushnell pronounced. "Surely you can find something to do!"

"Without question, ma'am," he replied promptly, his voice a trifle unsteady. "Do be kind to Miss Hampton, my lady. After all, she did weed the Waterloo strain to perfection while I was gone."

"I suspected as much," rejoined the widow, clearing her throat in a decisive manner that must have terrified a generation of her husband's lieutenants. "I can still see dirt under her nails! Really, Miss Hampton!"

Susan blushed and stared at her hands as though they were someone else's picked up by mistake. "It was late last night, my lady," she mumbled, "and some of it must surely be silver polish."

"Miss Hampton, you are a ragamuffin! I wonder that Hamptons ever had any pretensions to society, if you are a representative sample! Begin at the top, Miss Hampton, and take it more slowly this time. David, busy yourself!"

Two hours later, Susan was still beginning at the top. I will remember these two lines when I am old and gumming my porridge, she thought as perspiration trickled down her back in the cool room. But she was playing those two lines better, she knew she was, even if the tempo was as lugubrious as Lady Bushnell's demeanor was glacial. She sighed and stopped at the end of the second line when the widow began the ominous tapping of her cane on the floor, the signal to pause and face the music. She looked at her employer.

You are so impeccable, she thought in grudging admiration, knowing that the pins were coming out of her hair as she nodded in time with the music. Of course, I am doing the work here, Susan considered as she dragged her eyes to the top of the page again and poised her fingers—nicely arched now, thanks to Lady B's admonition—over the keys.

"That will do for now, Miss Hampton," Lady Bushnell said.

Susan winced at the "for now," but closed the music book with relief. She glanced at the furniture polish on the windowsill and wondered why she had ever thought polishing silver in the kitchen was a chore. Her stomach growled and she blushed.

"I will release you now, Miss Hampton," Lady Bushnell said as she began to rise from the chair.

Susan leaped to her feet to assist her, marveling at the lightness of the old woman's bones. "You have taught me a great deal this morning, my lady," she said as she stood with her hands at the widow's elbow.

"It is only the beginning, Miss Hampton," came the reply, and Susan tried not to make a face.

"Oh, Lady Bushnell, I do not mean to take up so much of your time! Surely you have oodles of things more valuable . . ." she began, and was silenced by an emphatic tap of the cane as the widow stopped her stately progression to the door and turned to stare at her companion.

"Don't babble, child! My dear Miss Hampton, it is I who should thank you!" she said, and Susan dreaded the glitter in her magnificent green eyes.

"Wh . . . whatever for, my lady?" Susan stammered.

"Of all that endless parade of lady's companions, you and you alone have given me something to do!" she continued in triumph. "When you are not helping David in the succession house—although why he needs such assistance I cannot imagine. He's managed well enough alone before—I expect you to be in here, practicing diligently."

"Y . . . yes, ma'am," Susan replied.

They continued to the door, where Lady Bushnell stopped when Susan opened it. "Tell Mrs. Skerlong to bring my luncheon into the breakfast room this time, instead of my room. I feel positively energized, Miss Hampton. And I expect you in my room for another four or five chapters this afternoon. Emma Woodhouse is such a flibbertigibbet, that I wonder what Jane Austen was thinking! Spare me from maiden ladies in parsonages! Modern writers are such a trial."

"Yes, ma'am," Susan said. She dropped a curtsy and stepped into the hall. I have been sentenced to hard labor at the piano, she thought. Joel Steinman, perhaps I will consider your latest offer.

"Oh, and, Miss Hampton . . ."

"Yes, Lady Bushnell?"

"That rose pink becomes you better than it did my daughter."

My goodness, Susan thought as she smiled at Lady Bushnell and escaped to the safety of the kitchen. The Skerlongs and David looked up from the table, where they were eating. She delivered Lady Bushnell's luncheon request, and the housekeeper's eyes widened in surprise.

"She never eats in the breakfast room anymore," Mrs. Skerlong said, getting up to prepare Lady Bushnell's luncheon.

Susan sank down at the table, leaning on her elbows in a way that would have sent Aunt Louisa up into the boughs. "She says I have positively energized her," she confided in a mournful tone. "We are to practice every morning." She remembered herself then and straightened up, smoothing her hair back into its customary lines and replacing the pins. "David, Lady Bushnell has made me her project!" she wailed.

He laughed and pushed a bowl of stew in front of her. "Whatever possessed you to start playing in the first place?" he asked, handing her a spoon.

"The silliest thing!" she admitted. "My letter from Mr. Steinman told me of a possible opening as a governess to young girls that he thought I might be suited for, if it should develop. I thought to practice to see if I had enough proficiency to teach children." She ate a few bites then put down the spoon. "I am an idiot."

"No, you're not," David disagreed, his smile replaced by a frown. "A new position, eh?"

She nodded. "He said it may come to nothing, but he wanted to see if I was interested. And I am, of course, considering how little headway I have been making with Lady Bushnell. Until now!" She sighed and began to eat again.

"You've written him?" David asked after Mrs. Skerlong left with the luncheon tray and Cora followed with a teapot. His tone was casual, with just enough of an edge to it to make her look at him in surprise, and then hope he hadn't noticed.

"Actually, no, I haven't," she replied, surprised at herself all over again. "And I really don't know why not. Perhaps I would miss the Waterloo strain too much, and dirt under my nails." Impulsively, she reached out to touch his arm as it lay on the table, but stopped herself in time. "I think your succession house is the sanest place in England."

He nodded, his eyes bright. "It is. I sit there at the drafting table and dream about covering England with the Waterloo strain, and other seed improvements of my engineering." He looked embarrassed. "Pretty ambitious for a lying Welsh sneak thief."

She thought of her own moments at the drafting table, watching the wheat in parallel rows in front of her. "Anything's possible, I think, if one sits at that table long enough," she said mildly, then frowned at him. "See here, sir, you are not a sneak thief! Those days are long over."

"But I am a liar, eh, Susan?" he murmured.

She returned his steady gaze, and thought, unaccountably, of her father. "I wonder if anyone really ever tells the truth, sir," she said, matching his calmness.

"I am sure I would not dare," he said enigmatically. He stood up, then reached across the table suddenly to touch her cheek. "Come with me this afternoon to choir practice, Susan," he said, and it didn't sound like a mere suggestion. "We'll deliver Joel's glove afterward and you'll see me in action again." He grinned. "Joel is such a war hero in this part of the Cotswolds!"

And you, sir, what are you? she asked herself as he picked up his coat from the rack and left the kitchen. And most of all, she thought as her hand went to her cheek, why do I care what the bailiff does?

Chapter Ten

"You probably think I am missish in the extreme to be mournful about no tea again with Lady Bushnell this afternoon," she told the bailiff after he handed her into the gig, climbed in after her, and settled a blanket around them.

He spoke to the horse in Welsh, and they started in the direction of Quilling. "She's never offered me tea, and I've known her over twelve years," he observed, amusement evident in the crinkles around his eyes. "Of course, I am not a gentleman, and never expected such attention." He stared straight ahead at the road between the horse's ears. "It couldn't be that you worry too much about inconsequentials, could it, Miss Hampton?" His expression was blank, his tone neutral, and she wondered suspiciously just how much experience he had around women.

She let out an unladylike protest. "Oh, worse and worse! Now I am Miss Hampton again!" She tucked her hands under the blanket. "Perhaps I do borrow Monday's trouble from Tuesday," she admitted grudgingly, then hesitated until he glanced at her. "I am being bold, indeed, Mr. Wiggins, but have you ever been married? You remind me of my Aunt Louisa's husband, rest his soul, with that placating tone that could only come from the hard usage of experience," she accused, humor high in her voice. "I know when I am being condescended to."

He chuckled and made himself more comfortable as he overlapped into her space on the narrow seat. "I thought you would. And the answer is yes, or sort of, I suppose. I had a woman in Spain."

He did not say anything for a considerable distance. "Oh," Susan said finally. "I'm prying, aren't I?" she asked when the silence stretched some more.

"Not really," he replied. "I opened the subject, I think, in a sideways kind of fashion. Sometimes I forget that you have quite excellent powers of observation, Susan."

"Where is she?" Susan asked.

"She died giving birth to our son during the withdrawal from Burgos. We couldn't stop for anything. Our son died, too."

"I'm so sorry," she said, contrite right down to her toes. "I wish I had not asked in such a flippant way."

"No matter. It was a long time ago," he said, his voice wistful for a moment. "Sometimes it seems to have happened to someone I hardly know anymore. But to the case in point: Jesusa didn't speak any English, or not much, and I have discovered that women are mostly the same in any language." The subject didn't seem to make him sad, and she wondered at his resilience. "I learned pretty early that a bland tone in Spanish let me get away with any amount of reproof."

"And so you reprove me about my worries?"

"A little," he agreed, "but only a little. Are you so sure that your aunt or your father wouldn't have exerted themselves to find you a husband, had you remained in London?"

"I have no money," she reminded him simply. "What man would be tempted?"

He stared straight ahead again. "I cannot imagine that there was no one of your class who wouldn't rejoice in a wife with high looks and some considerable intelligence, even if she were as poor as Job's turkey."

I am at least smart enough to know when I am being complimented, Susan thought, and, sir, you take my breath away. "I think that's the nicest thing anyone ever said to me," she told him frankly, also staring straight ahead.

"Well, then, tell me 'thank you' prettily," he said, amused. "The problem is your father, then, that man you won't write to," he surmised, nudging her shoulder. "I gather he is a walking debt machine and scares off sensible suitors. I remember little lords like that in Wellington's army."

She nodded, too embarrassed to speak, and marveled, as the village came gradually into view, at just how many emotions she could feel in such a short drive.

"Then if you can't find a rich man with sense, you'll have to marry a poor man, after all," he concluded, turning the gig into the churchyard. He gestured toward the church. "And since you won't marry me, let me introduce you to our poor *and* single curate." He grinned at her.

"Are you so determined to find me a husband?" she whispered, blushing fiercely and surprised to find herself balanced so delicately between irritation and high good humor. "And must you bring up that proposal? I thought we agreed you were impulsive and feeling sorry for me."

"Did we?" he asked, his face bland again. "If you say so, it must be true. I forgot."

She let him help her from the gig. "Did Jesusa find you exasperating?" she asked.

"Of course she did," he replied with equanimity. "She loved me."

I think I have just learned an interesting lesson, if I am to believe the bailiff, Susan told herself as she walked beside him into the vestry. The man who exasperates me even more than the bailiff is my father, but I do not feel inclined to forgive him, and I am certain I do not love him. In this, as in other matters I could tell, I suspect I am very much the bailiff's inferior, she considered honestly. And yet Lady Bushnell, who knows David Wiggins well, will never offer him tea because he is not a gentleman, and Aunt Louisa would lock me up for a lunatic if I brought him home to dinner. Not that I ever would, she amended hastily. It's the idea that counts here. Perhaps it's time I stopped being a snob, considering that I have little to be arrogant about these days.

"We're redding up some special music for the Easter service," he explained as he showed her to a pew at the back of the church.

"Heavens, Lent hasn't even begun yet!" she said with a smile.

"We need all the practice we can get," David said. "And I am late. Well, if we become too much of a torment to ears accustomed to better singing in London churches, wander out among the gravestones, or count daffodils. We won't be much above an hour."

She was content to listen, and agree with the bailiff's assessment of the choir's abilities. Still, she reasoned, what they lack in competence, they make up for in enthusiasm. And it was hard to overlook the magic of a Welsh bass among the underendowed English. She decided that a few more Welshmen in the lower registers would make this a choir worth listening to. I imagine the curate longs to recruit beyond these borders, she thought, but I doubt that recruitment was a subject addressed during his study for holy orders.

And speaking of the curate, that could only be he, leading the music. Susan watched with amusement at first, and then interest, as the curate in his rusty black led his little choir through a somewhat labyrinthine Bach cantata. From her viewpoint, she could only regard his shoulders, which were rather narrow, and the back of his head, which at least contained abundant hair of an auburn shade. Come to think of it, he appeared to be all narrow planes and elbows. She was forcibly reminded of a marsh bird.

But an earnest one, she had to allow as the curate sang along with his choir, his enthusiasm wholehearted. How intently they follow him, she observed. Well, almost all, she amended, turning her attention to Cora Skerlong in the contralto section, who was trading lingering glances with a tenor. Susan smiled at the bailiff, who intercepted her glance at the young lovers, and returned a grin between rests. Good for you, Cora, she thought. It looks as though our bailiff will be casting about for another milkmaid and girl of all work before long. She sighed. Perhaps I should volunteer. I don't seem to be doing Lady Bushnell much good as a lady's companion, beyond affording her some amusement with my execrable piano playing.

I wonder that no one gives the bailiff looks like that, she thought idly, not that it's a concern of mine. He isn't beyond his early thirties, and so what if he lived a little harder during those years than most men? Heaven knows it makes him an interesting conversationalist, and after all, one cannot make love all the time. She sat up a little straighter. Susan, mind your thoughts.

She noticed a mouse scooting from the wall to the pew in front of her and hurriedly raised her feet to the prayer bench. He has all his hair—such a rich, dark color—and appears to have all his teeth, which is more than Cora's tenor can boast, from the look of him. And while the bailiff is only a little taller than many Welshmen, he does not have that lightness of frame, she considered. He's built to stay, and perhaps that does not appeal to some. Of course, if a young woman, or even one his age could sit with him before a fire, or watch him measure and regard his precious wheat, she might be inclined . . .

The mouse moved again and Susan tucked her feet under her. And I had better stop worrying about tea and bailiffs and diligently apply myself to the pianoforte. A letter to Joel Steinman would be in order, too, although I have been threatening that for a week. Why didn't I just give up and stay in London? Perhaps the bailiff is right about someone wanting me; stranger things have happened.

She turned her attention to the choir, willing the mouse away by ignoring it, and resolving to suggest that the bailiff offer the curate a kitten when they were born. One cat could do the job. It wasn't a large church, such as she was used to in London. Sheepfold, manor, church, or inn, it is all the same in the Cotswolds, Susan decided after a thoughtful look around. The centuries sit lightly on stone. These buildings will be here long after I have

stuck my spoon in the wall. She smiled, intrigued that while mor-
bid, the thought was far from unpleasant. The bailiff could be
right; maybe what I consider large issues really aren't so important. I must remember to ask him sometime if he felt that way before Waterloo, or only after. Or it could be that I am a slow
learner in the school of life.

Choir practice was over. She looked up in surprise at the silence, and then the voices blended now in idle chatter as singers
hunted for cloaks, scarves, and mittens, and considered dinner
and chores. Sitting in this chapel, one could become a philoso-
pher, she thought as the bailiff came down the aisle with the curate. She looked around for the mouse, decided it was gone, and
put her feet on the stone floor again.

"Miss Hampton, this is our curate, Mr. Hepworth," David Wiggins said.

She held out her hand to the cleric, discovering to her amusement
that his front was all planes and angles, too. He had a kind face,
though, and light eyes that held a welcome, even while his face
blushed a fiery red. Only the charitable would call him handsome.

"Pleased to meet you, sir," she said as they shook hands. She
twinkled her eyes at the bailiff for a brief moment. "Mr. Hepworth, perhaps the bailiff will give you a kitten in a few weeks.
Your church mice could use a challenge, I think."

The curate blushed more vividly, then recovered himself, even as
he still clung to her fingers. "I trust it will be a benevolent kitten,
Mr. Wiggins." He released her hand. "This is a sobering considera-
tion, Miss Hampton. Here I had been thinking that the various
squeals and exclamations from the congregation during my sermons
were raptures over my scholarly doctrine and sophisticated wit."

She laughed, delighted to know that somewhere far down in the
church's hierarchy there was a curate with a sense of humor.
"You know them better than I, sir," she replied, giving him the
full benefit of her eyes. "But I do recommend a mouser."

"Anything you wish, Miss Hampton," Hepworth replied, his
voice fervent. He extended his arm to her as the three of them
walked toward the door.

She took it, and caught a glance from the bailiff just before he
looked away for one of his oblique smiles. You are a matchmaker, sir, she thought as she walked into the late-afternoon sun
with the curate. He handed her into the gig as though she were
made of cobwebs and eggshells, then took her hand again as the
bailiff walked around the horse and climbed up beside her.

"Please give my regards to Lady Bushnell and tell her that I will pay her a parish call next week. It's long overdue, more shame to me," he said as he released her hand a finger at a time.

"I will, sir," she said.

She could feel the bailiff chuckling beside her as they turned toward Quilling Manor again. "I wonder why the sudden clerical interest in Lady Bushnell?" he mused. "Lady B won't have anything to do with him. I think she's irritated with God and His staff of well-wishers and do-gooders."

Susan laughed. "That relieves my mind, sir! Here I had thought I was the only thorn in her side. If she doesn't care much for the Almighty, either, then at least I am rubbing along in good company!" She leaned toward the bailiff. "Who *does* she like?"

He inclined his head her way. "Keep this under your bonnet, Susan, but I doubt that any of us measure up."

She looked at him then up close, admiring his brown eyes and grateful that she was in no danger from the power of them, or the comfort of his presence alone. "Then it will fall to me to offer the curate tea and address some innocuous conversation his way?"

"I am certain of it, Susan." He straightened up, assuming that bland tone that made her giggle. "Mr. Hepworth has a nice parsonage, with a housekeeper and a maid, I believe. He is a third son with two livings that I know of, so you could probably afford new shoes every year," he teased.

"More than you could have offered me?" she teased back.

He smiled. "Jesusa went barefoot. It's a good thing you already turned me down."

They laughed together at the absurdity of it, but the bailiff offered no more suggestions as he turned off the main road to the manor and toward the stone buildings in the shelter of the low hills. "Ben Rich," he said when she looked at him. He pulled out Joel Steinman's glove. "You can present it to him."

She took the glove, enjoying the buttery feel of the tanned kidskin as she removed her mitten and ran her finger across it. "My father used to spend more on gloves than I am to earn from a year with Lady Bushnell," she said as she replaced her mitten. "I think that is one of the reasons I am so out of sorts with him."

The bailiff whistled. "That *is* a lot," he agreed, then put his head close to hers again and whispered. "Maybe you should hate him for ever and ever for that, and then some. Silly blighter. What is his excuse for living?"

"Wait, now, you're speaking of my . . ." she began, then stopped. "You're making fun of me," she said firmly.

"Only a little," he said. "Did he ever read to you, too, or brush your hair, or scold you when you needed it?"

"Yes," she admitted. "But David, he's ruined my life!"

The bailiff only smiled and pulled to a stop in the neat half circle in front of a stone building with three sides. "Ruined your life?" he repeated. "Come now, Susan. Do Hamptons run much to high drama?"

"You don't understand," she began as he held out his hand to help her down.

"I'm sure I do not, Susan, if you say so," he agreed, all complacence.

"Only an idiot would argue with you!" she said with some feeling, then put her lips firmly together. *And I am fast showing myself to be an idiot. I shall change the subject.* "What is this place?"

"A good place to change the subject," he replied promptly, then held up both hands to ward off her expression. "It's the shearing floor," he said with only a slight tremor in his voice. He led the horse and gig more within the shelter of the building and blanketed the animal. "We'll be in there working our arses off when it's almost summer."

"You or the sheep?" she asked, and was rewarded with a laugh.

"Both, Miss Hampton, both," he smiled fervently. He led her toward the pens, where the sheep milled about and expressed considerable dissatisfaction. "Ben keeps the ewes with lamb close by, and the rams farther out, but not too far." He raised his voice to be heard above the sheep. "We try to birth as many of the lambs here, and then release them to the far pasturage when it's warmer." He took her hand as the wind picked up, and she followed him to a separate stone cottage where smoke poured from the chimney. "Ben knows his weather."

She found herself occupied with anchoring her skirt and petticoat against the sudden wind and let him lead her along. As she looked toward the cottage, the door opened and a small boy tugged her inside. He was as dark as David Wiggins, but slim of frame, with that silent watchfulness of shy children. The bailiff nodded to him and spoke in Welsh. The boy's face lit up and he answered at length, gesturing toward the sheepfold. The bailiff returned another comment, and the boy hunched himself against the wind and ran to the fold.

The single room was cluttered, and Susan was prepared to think ill of its tenants, except that there was no dirt or bad odor. She sniffed the air, breathing in the pungent aroma of wool and lanolin. She sat on one of the two benches, admiring with her eyes a pile of sheepskins in one corner that must be the communal bed, and a border collie nursing a litter of pups and keeping one eye open on the visitors.

"Is he Ben Rich's son?" she asked when David sat beside her.

"None of that. I took him out of a Welsh workhouse when Ben reconciled himself to living a few more years without a hand. He was six then, and the workhouse governor had never bothered to give him a name, only a number."

"Surely not!" Susan said, shocked.

The bailiff shrugged. "That's what they do when they get little mites who don't look strong enough to survive." He managed a short laugh, with no humor. "And they feed 'em watered gruel to make sure they don't live long, and bury them three or four to a plasterboard coffin." He looked with satisfaction in the direction that the boy had gone. "Number Three July fooled them and had lived to six years when I came looking for a shepherd's left hand. I named him Owen Thrice, and Ben Rich can testify that he's worth his weight in gold."

You are an amazing man, she thought as he went to the door, alert for sounds she could only strain to hear. "They didn't recognize you when you returned?" she asked on a hunch.

He grinned at her. "You're a hard one to surprise, Susan," he said. "No, they didn't. A lot of water has tumbled under this bridge." He sighed. "The old governor was gone, damn his eyes, but they're still just numbering the babies. Sometimes I think nothing ever changes, but once in a while . . ."

He opened the door then, and the shepherd came in, his hand held tight in the boy's two hands. "Wind's picking up, Davey," he commented. "What's so important that it can't wait until snow's gone from the air?" He nodded to Susan. "You got married at last," he surmised, a smile creasing his face.

"No, no luck there, even though I tried," David said cheerfully while Susan writhed inside with embarrassment. "She turned me down. This is Miss Hampton, Lady Bushnell's newest companion."

"You might want to reconsider, lass, so don't burn that bridge entirely," Ben told her, his voice mild. He held out his only hand to her. "Pleased to meet you, miss."

She took his hand, determined not to be embarrassed if no one else was. "Your hand, sir!" she exclaimed, forgetting whatever poise she was attemtping. "Oh, my! It's so soft!"

"Comes from working with sheep, lass." He winked at her and grinned, and she found it imposible not to do the same back.

She held out Joel Steinman's glove to the shepherd. "Actually, sir, Mr. Steinman sent this to the bailiff and asked me to present it to you."

The shepherd took the glove and rubbed it against his cheek. "You mean Colonel Steinman, lass," he corrected, a smile on his face, "hero of the Fighting Fifth Foot, Regular Army."

"Oh, no! Yes! I'm sure I do," she amended as the bailiff trod upon her foot. "He . . . he wanted to make sure that you wore it in good health," she said as she moved away from David Wiggins and his boots.

"Well I do," said the shepherd, pulling on the glove with his teeth and flexing his fingers. "I don't mind telling you that it still gives me a boost on bad days to know that I'm sharing gloves with a genuine Waterloo hero."

"You know, of course, that you ought to be shot for telling such stretchers," she scolded the bailiff as he helped her back into the gig an hour later, after mutton stew and coffee strong enough to choose its own path into her stomach. A fat lot of good it does me to admonish you, she considered, taking into account the mild look on his face.

"Who's hurt by such a lie?" he asked as he reached over her to make sure the blanket was tucked in around her hip. "Joel approved when I told him what I was doing and sent me two more gloves, and it kept a good shepherd out of the boneyard." He touched her shoulder. "Besides all that, I earned the right to use Waterloo any way I want, and that's why I lie to Ben Rich and Lady Bushnell, too."

"Well, it isn't right."

"You weren't there," he shot back. "I've earned my lies."

An uncomfortable silence settled between them. Amazing, isn't it, she thought after a long silence, that two people can sit rump to rump and feel so far apart. "I'm sorry," she said simply. "Forgive me."

"Forgiven," he said as he turned the gig onto the main road to Quilling Manor. "Just promise me that if I ever get caught in one of my benevolent lies, that you will have the good grace not to laugh."

"I'll promise no such thing," she declared. "And I'll not extricate you from webs of your own weaving."

"That's an answer worthy of Jesusa," the bailiff said. He looked round at her. "Now I suppose I may ask if *you've* been married before!"

This conversation could become a trial, she thought, at a loss as to how to answer him. Of course he knew she had not been married before, but she wondered what he was implying, and then sighed. It would be easy to remain impervious to bailiffs, if they did not make it difficult. I do not know what to say.

She was spared the bailiff's further scrutiny by the approach of Cora's tenor from the direction of the manor. "Here comes Cora Skerlong's constant lover," David said, indicating the gig with his whip. He nodded as the man passed, and continued on slowly, even though it was nearly full dark. "He sits once a week with Cora in Mrs. Skerlong's parlor. I do not think he has ever kissed her," the bailiff mused.

"One mustn't rush into these things," Susan said.

"But he's been courting her for five years, Susan!" the bailiff replied with a laugh. "Five years," he repeated, his voice full of wonder. "I should have wedded, bedded, and been a father several times over in the same space that our tenor the lover has worked up to holding Cora's hand."

"Then why have you not, sir?" she asked, before she thought.

He shrugged and then winked at her as he reined into the barnyard. "I can't get anyone to say yes to a proposal, Miss Hampton!" he teased. "Women are more picky in England than ever they were in Spain. Let me help you."

If I keep my mouth shut, I may get out of this with no more embarrassment than I deserve, she told herself as she let the bailiff assist her from the gig. "Perhaps you should not persist in asking the wrong women," she blurted, ignoring all her own good advice.

"I do not ask the wrong women," he insisted.

"You asked me," she pointed out. It seemed perfectly logical to her, particularly since he had admitted his proposal had been impulsive. *And why does he persist in referring to that silly incident?* She had started to follow him into the stable, but she stopped. *And why do I keep remembering such a harmless offer?* She turned and started for the house, giving herself a mental shake.

"I could offer some pointers to Cora's tenor," the bailiff said, falling in step beside her.

Susan laughed.

"I could!" he protested, the humor high in his voice. "Jesusa used to say I could *besar* and *coger* with the best of them, and she ought to have known. Tell me what you think."

As she thought about it later, in a lukewarm attempt at justification, Susan decided that there really wasn't anything she could have done to prevent what happened. He didn't exert any force, so she couldn't blame his larger size. What he did do was adroitly maneuver her against the stable wall and kiss her with some considerable thoroughness. Even then, she couldn't blame tactics. His were sound enough, but she didn't have to stay there and let him put his hands on each side of her face and kiss her. And yet, once he had begun, she noticed a disturbing tendency on her part to let him do what he wanted.

It had troubled her before on awkward occasions that she never seemed to know where to put her hands, so she bowed to her own inadequacies and just put them around him. It turned out to be as good an idea as any, considering that her mind was turning into cotton wadding, and after all, she reasoned later, she needed something to hold on to when her knees started to melt a little. This must be a Hampton deficiency, she decided, brought about through too many years of inbreeding within the peerage and landed gentry. The bailiff's knees seemed quite steady, so that piece of logic was sound enough. Even more to the point, he had a certain single-mindedness that she probably would have admired in another setting.

It took a mental leap later, but she decided that even when he pressed against her so tightly, his intentions were benevolent. Not only was he holding her up, he was certainly keeping her warm. She had to admit, however, that it was a strange kind of warmth, one that plonked rather forcefully into her loins and stubbornly stayed there throughout the duration of that kiss.

But later, in the solitude of her bedroom, no amount of mental cartwheels could dance around the realization that she had been kissing him back as thoroughly as he was kissing her. I hope he will overlook it, she thought. Oh, my goodness, did I really do all that exertion with my *tongue*? What could I possibly have been thinking?

At the time, it seemed so reasonable. Their lips came away from each other with a homely little smack that made him smile, even as she was beginning to wonder if her eyes would ever focus again in this life.

"That was, um, *besar*," he explained. "I think maybe Cora's tenor hasn't tried that yet."

She attempted to pull her jumbled brain back together again as he released her and continued toward the house again, as though he had only stopped to admire the evening sky. "Then what is *coger*?" she asked. Conversation is in order here.

He grinned bigger than any man had a right to, and shook his head. "That's what comes later when good girls say yes to proposals. Sorry, Susan. Good night, now. Sleep tight."

Chapter Eleven

Ꞇ

Sleep tight, my Aunt Matilda's blue garters! Susan thought irritably as the sky began to lighten. She sat up and glared at her pillow, turning it over to look for a cool spot. There wasn't one; they had all been used up in a night of tossing about in indignation, embarrassment, and finally, the acutest sort of misery that the bailiff wasn't there in bed with her, *besar*ing and *coger*ing.

It had taken most of the night to get to that much truth-telling, and she had to wonder at the pointlessness of lying to herself for all those idiotic hours. In the time between dark and dawn, she reviewed all of Aunt Louisa's rigid, patient little conversations about men, and what they wanted from women, and how they went about getting it. She recalled the book (How could I forget Professor Fowler and that endless title? *Creative and Sexual Science; Manhood, Womanhood, and Their Mutual Interrelations*), that was passed quickly from aunt to cousin to cousin and then to herself, and the accompanying blushes and titterings. She remembered Aunt Louisa's stiff question, "Well, do you need to know anything else?", and the tone that dared any of them to say yes.

In particular, after her night of chewing goosedown, Susan remembered that little section called "The Sleep of Love." She rested her chin on her knees, and couldn't resist a bleary-eyed smile as she quoted from memory, "'The disappointed lie awake hour after hour,'" But I'm sure Professor Fowler, the old prude, did not mean what I am thinking, she admitted honestly. His disappointed maiden feels chagrin because she flirted out of turn. My disappointment comes from the fact that I did not go far enough to suit myself.

"Both-er-a-tion!" Susan said. She leaned against the headboard, plumped her pillow behind her head, and drew her knees up to her chin. She wished with all her heart that Mama had been alive to administer the sexual lecture that Aunt Louisa delivered as her duty to her niece. As much as she disliked thinking about her father, Susan remembered the fun that he and Mama had had together. She wished she had a shilling for every time she found Mama sitting on Papa's lap, or just watched them with their arms around each other, doing something as prosaic as observing the geese cross the lawn at the estate.

Sitting there grumpy and displeased with herself, she knew she could have asked Mama anything. And what would I have asked, she considered as the sun came over the hills. If I could have one question answered now, what would it be? She transferred herself to the window seat and scolded herself for not moving there hours ago. The windowpanes were cold and felt good to lean against.

"I would like to know one thing, Mama," she said softly. "Just one thing only, and I can carry on from there. Professor Fowler's tedious book spoke of duty, and creating children, and Aunt Louisa assured us that men take what they want and women weep. But, Mama, is sexual congress *fun*?"

Her heart told her it was. When she worked past all the embarrassment and confusion she had felt last night after the bailiff's thorough kiss and her equally fervent response, one overriding emotion remained. "Mama, I enjoyed that immensely. I didn't want it to stop, and if I had even held out my hand to the bailiff, he would be lying in that bed right now, taking up space."

It was power she had never imagined before, and it frightened her even more than the actual act of love for the first time. To exert that kind of authority over another human being awed her, humbled her, and took her breath away. She leaned against the window, wondering how many glittering diamonds each season flirted and danced and teased while fathers and lawyers drew up documents and transferred funds, all in the name of love. It was the way the *ton*—her *ton*—did things, but sitting there watching the immensity of the morning come, and examining her own raw feelings, she knew suddenly how wrong it was.

I worried so much about no dowry and no comeout, she thought, shaking her head over her own stupidity. Even if I had possessed those things, those proud badges of my class, there was never any guarantee that I would be happy with my husband, in bed or anywhere else. Quite the contrary. It's not called the Marriage Mart for nothing. Well, I am far away from the marketplace here, and I must trust myself to do what will make me happy.

"How frightening," she murmured and drew her name on the windowpane. "I wonder that anyone makes right decisions."

It can't be easy, she thought, reminding herself of the way her brain dissolved into mush last night from nothing more than a kiss. How can rational judgment withstand a kiss from David Wiggins? Well, I do suspect that in the annals of kissing, it was quite a kiss, she told herself. If there were contests for such things, the bailiff would at least be eligible to compete. Oh, my word, he would win, was her next fervent thought.

She had no experience to base that on, beyond the certitude that no woman had ever been so thoroughly entertained in such a brief space of time. She smiled at her own silliness and drew a circle around her name. "Susan, it's not as if you're the only female on the planet who ever felt this way." She drew an exclamation point after her name. "It just seems like it."

She took her time dressing, choosing a dark green wool with a white collar she had crocheted. For all this, she hoped the bailiff would not be in the kitchen when she came downstairs. I must compose myself, she told herself as she tucked in hairpins here and there to anchor her braids. I must remember that I am a lady.

She sighed and rested her hands in her lap. And that is part of the problem, she reflected. I suppose the bailiff had no business kissing someone of my class, and here I go again, putting that between us like a partition. Aunt Louisa would say that we all have our place in life and that the classes have no business mingling. Susan looked at her name on the window, with its hopeful exclamation mark melting as the sun hit the glass. Oh, I hope she is wrong. I hope I have enough wisdom to do the right thing, as soon as I figure out what that is.

Whatever glee, joy, and luck she had felt in David Wiggins' embrace last night was gone at breakfast, replaced by the most exquisite sort of confusion. The bailiff was finishing his porridge when she came into the kitchen. If it was any consolation, he stared into his bowl in thoughtful fashion, and his eyes didn't look any livelier than her own. She watched him quietly from the doorway, shy beyond words and wondering what to do with him.

I mean, do I just sit down and chat about the weather, or the sheep, or that your lips ought to be bronzed and preserved under glass. What am I thinking? she asked herself from the doorway. Calm, Susan. You still have to eat and perform the functions of life, even though you are intrigued with the possibility of all this, and feeling friskier than a spring colt.

She must have made some sound from the doorway (Am I whining and don't know it? she wondered), because the bailiff looked around and smiled at her. "Good morning, Susan," he said. She hunted for some sign of shyness on his part, but he looked the same as usual. His calmness deflated her. Either you are not as involved in this as I am, or you are a master at hiding your feelings. I will pretend it is the latter, she told herself.

"Ready to face the lion again?" he asked.

I wonder which lion you are referring to, she considered as she nodded, too bashful to speak, and sat in the chair he patted. She accepted the porridge from Mrs. Skerlong and began to eat. She stopped soon enough, looking down at the bowl in surprise, curious to know why the housekeeper would feed her wood pulp. But no, it was the same porridge; she was different. She applied herself to breakfast again, and Mrs. Skerlong went to her chair by the stove, where the cat was waiting to leap into her lap.

The bailiff shifted his chair a little so he could look at her. "Do I owe you a rather large apology?" he asked in a low voice.

It was a good question, and she was struck all over again how different this situation was from any she had ever encountered before. She considered him thoughtfully, mindful of his nearness, but less fearful of it than if he were a marquess, impeccably dressed and bearing down on her from across a ballroom. The bailiff was so comfortable-looking. She met his eyes briefly, then blushed and looked away. And yet you have the power to disturb me profoundly. I do not remember that quality about any of the viscounts, marquesses, or baronets I pined over, she marveled. Sir, you take my breath from me.

"No, you owe me no apology, large or small," she said honestly, and set down her spoon. She turned to face him; a man used to plain-dealing deserved more than her profile. "Now if you had held me down against my will and forced such a kiss on me, I would demand one." She looked at her hands in her lap, uneasily aware of the warm glow that was spreading throughout her body again. "But as I offered no objection then, I could not expect to make one now. No, you owe me no apology."

It was the bailiff's turn for confusion, and it relieved her to know that his air of assurance did not go all the way to the bone. This is not a case-hardened rascal, she thought, and I am so glad. His sudden bewilderment pleased her as nothing else could have.

"Well, I . . . I don't go around kissing like that on a . . . well, a regular basis," he managed finally, backing up his chair slightly as though some of her own warmth were reaching him, too.

Or perhaps Mrs. Skerlong was adding a ton or two of coal to the Rumford. She glanced toward the stove, but there were no stokers around it, shoveling in coal. This is an odd kind of warmth, she thought. I like it, but it could make me peevish.

She reached out to touch his arm, to reassure him that she did not mind, but she stopped at such a prosaic gesture. How odd this is, she considered, as shyness took over again. After last night, I am amazingly familiar with this man's lips, his teeth, his tongue, and yet I won't be so forward as to touch his arm. This is strange, indeed.

She sighed and looked him in the eye. "David, I don't want to talk about what happened last night."

"I can't wonder at that," he murmured and started to get up.

"No!" She did put her hand on his arm to detain him then, and he sat down quickly. "No," she repeated, her voice softer. "But I do want to think about it. There's a difference." His shoulders lowered, as though in vast relief, and she was touched to the heart.

"Maybe tonight in the succession house we should talk about it? I won't have you thinking me a scoundrel." He shook his head at his own words. "A bastard, a liar, a poacher, and a thief maybe, but not a scoundrel," he said with some humor evident.

"Perhaps we'll talk tonight," she said, smiling, too, at the absurdity of what he was really saying. "And I do not think you are a scoundrel," she assured him. "The circumstance of birth was out of your control, and maybe you poached and thieved, and you're one of the most accomplished liars in the realm, but you're not a scoundrel."

"Thank you!" he exclaimed with a laugh. He pulled his watch out and looked at her over the edge of it. "All joking aside, are you avoiding your incarceration in the library with Lady Bushnell and the dread piano?"

He turned the watch around and she gasped and rose hurriedly to her feet. It's interesting, she thought as she carried her dishes to the sink, but somehow I am not so frightened by Lady Bushnell now. I have other matters to concern myself with.

Or so she thought, until she stood outside the library door and steeled herself to open it. She reminded herself that this was what she wanted. Lady Bushnell needed something to take an interest in, and if it turned out to be an interest in the shortcomings of Susan Hampton, so be it.

"Need a little push, Susan?" said the bailiff.

She jumped. Why did he persist in sneaking up on her? Before she could scold him, he had opened the door, applied enough pressure to the small of her back to propel her in, and closed the door gently behind her.

"Miss Hampton, so kind of you to come!"

Lady Bushnell sat next to the piano. She motioned Susan closer and indicated the piano stool. "Make sure it is at the right height for you," she said. "You will be spending much of your time perched upon it, and while I will have you learn discipline, I will not have you uncomfortable. Ready, Miss Hampton? Of course you are. Let us begin with a C-major scale. What could be simpler?"

Susan adjusted the stool, then squared her shoulders and positioned her hands over the keys. She played the scale once, twice, three times and then realized the futility of keeping count as Lady Bushnell tapped her ankles with the cane each time she faltered or abandoned the rhythm. Papa, you would perish if you ever worked so hard for thirty pounds, she thought in desperation each time she neared the end of the scale and the widow took a tighter grip on her cane.

I will still be playing this C-major scale when I am old and arthritic and unable to eat without drooling, Susan thought an hour later. She paused and tried to shift her legs out of the range of Lady Bushnell's relentless cane. I have played this silly scale in triplets, quarter notes, sixteenths, dotted eighths and sixteenths, and still she hammers at my ankles.

"I don't seem to be much improved," she said dubiously to Lady Bushnell, leaning down to rub the ankle closest to the cane.

The widow sat with her eyes closed. "How excellent that we have plenty of mornings to correct your deficiencies," she murmured.

"I doubt I will ever be much good," Susan temporized.

Lady Bushnell opened her eyes and glared at Susan. "And that is the trouble with Hamptons! You flit from undertaking to undertaking, and as a result, never accomplish anything." She raised her cane to point it at Susan. "I intend for you to improve."

Susan paused, her hands in her lap. I suppose I could take great offense at what this woman is saying about the Hamptons, she considered. I could be like Papa, and pout and frown, or Aunt Louisa, and gobble and snarl. She smiled at Lady Bushnell instead. Or I could grit my teeth and practice and learn from what she is trying to teach me, whatever her motives (indeed, I do not trust my own!). I am trying to run away from the Hamptons, but rather, perhaps I should make the name an honorable one in these parts.

"And so I shall, Lady Bushnell," she replied. "From the top again?"

Without even looking at the widow, she could tell that her response had startled her. There was a sharp intake of breath, and then a chuckle so low as to be almost unheard. It might have been imagined; it probably was, in fact, as her own stomach was beginning to growl. Take that and that, Lady B, she thought grimly as she slowly crawled up the scale, and then down again. She felt so good about it that she played a C-major chord with all the aplomb of a pianist finishing a concerto. She looked at Lady Bushnell and could not resist the laughter inside her. To her amazement, the widow began to laugh, too. It did not last long, but at least she did not attempt to hide her amusement this time.

"You are a scamp, Miss Hampton! I would say that you have done everything that could possibly be done to a C-major scale except turn the page sideways and dump the notes on the floor. Tomorrow it will be G-major. Now, wipe that smirk off your face and go away for a while!"

Only a day ago, Susan would have cringed at her words. Instead, she smiled at her employer, and realized, with a twinge close to pleasure, that she was beginning to understand Lady Bushnell. "Very well, Lady Bushnell. I will hobble off and soak my ankles," she said. She paused and leaned against the open door. "You won't object if I practice in here again right after lunch?"

"I recommend it!" she replied. "However, you should practice on the harpsichord instead. Our good vicar Mr. Hepworth wrote me that he is making an afternoon call. I will, of course, receive him in the best sitting room, but the piano, I fear, would be too noisy, even this far away. We cannot have him thinking that I am doing injury to caged wildlife or recalcitrant servants! He is less likely to hear the pain you might inflict upon a harpsichord."

It was all said with a faint twinkle in Lady Bushnell's green eyes, one that invited comment. "He will never know I am there, punishing piano or harpsichord, my lady," Susan agreed.

"Then we understand each other," Lady Bushnell replied. "I must admit I wonder why he is coming. He already knows what I think about God, and I rather thought that would discourage him." She seemed to be almost speaking to herself as she rose and went to the window. She turned back to glare at Susan. "I informed Mr. Hepworth several years ago that God is an untidy ditherer who leaves too many loose ends, and he has not bothered me since. Neither Mr. Hepworth nor the Lord."

"My lady, you didn't!" Susan burst out, her eyes wide.

"I did!" she said, coming toward Susan now. "I also told him that if Regent and Parliament oversaw the realm the way God looks after the universe, Napoleon would be scratching his ass in the House of Lords right now."

She spoke with conviction and a firmness of spirit that belied her years, a fearless woman completely sure of herself. I could see you leaping off your horse and throwing yourself in front of a whip and a dying man, Susan thought as she watched her employer's slow but graceful passage to the door. You were meant for a much wider stage than this.

Lady Bushnell stood close to Susan now, and from her height advantage looked down on her. "Correct me if I am wrong, but do I have *you* to blame for this sudden clerical interest in Quilling Manor, Miss Hampton?"

"Oh, surely no . . . Well, perhaps," Susan amended, deeply aware of the silliness of attempting to argue with Lady Bushnell. "The bailiff did introduce us yesterday. But I am sure it is you he is interested in, my lady."

They regarded each other, eye to eye, and neither looked away. "That may be the largest pile of verbal horse manure you have ever uttered, Miss Hampton," Lady Bushnell said finally. "Who will be next? Our bachelor landowners? The physician? The constable? Every widower between here and the Bristol Channel?"

"I haven't met them yet!" Susan protested, unable to keep the laughter from her voice. "It is only the vicar."

Lady Bushnell nodded, her eyes still bright. "Lord Bushnell always said I was prone to vast exaggeration, but wouldn't you agree, Miss Hampton, that the vicar looks rather like a marsh bird?"

My thoughts precisely, Susan reflected as she nodded. "He does appear to be all elbows and angles, my lady."

"We are agreed upon that, then," Lady Bushnell said as she stood aside for Susan to open the door wider. "I should think a young woman would prefer a man with more substance to him. Miss Hampton, do you have an opinion on the subject?"

"No, my lady," she said and blushed.

"Then why do you blush?" Lady Bushnell demanded. "I should hope a woman your age would have some opinion on what pleases her in a man!"

"It's not really a subject that ladies today speak about, Lady Bushnell," she said, mentally kicking herself for her condescension. But I am thinking about it, and it is making me decidedly warm again. I am wondering quite a lot what the bailiff would be likely to attempt after such a kiss. I am wondering how it would feel, and whether I would like it. And I stand here, the world's biggest hypocrite, and assure you that I have no interest in such things.

"And that is one of the reasons I was happy to incarcerate myself here, Miss Hampton," Lady Bushnell continued. "After-dinner conversation among women is not nearly so entertaining as it used to be." She banged her cane on the parquet floor for emphasis. "Now we speak of dresses, colic, and mustard plasters. Would it embarrass you to know that fifty-five years ago my sisters and I used to listen at our parent's bedchamber door when they thought we were asleep? Miss Hampton, ladies live in a dull world today!"

As she watched Lady Bushnell make her stately way down the hall toward the stairs, it suddenly occurred to her that here was someone who could talk to her about the bailiff. *If only I dared,* she thought. *And I do not.*

After a thoughtful luncheon in which she only uttered monosyllables to Mrs. Skerlong, and at least had the good sense not to look about in expectation of the absent bailiff, Susan returned to the library and the harpsichord. She found the instrument much more to her size and taste, the tinkling of the plucked strings soothing and orderly. She heard the vicar's voice in the hallway, and smiled to herself. *I wonder if he will make some excuse to visit the library,* she thought, and played even more softly.

Looking at the mantel clock, she timed the vicar, allowing him half an hour for the socially correct visit. She found one of Haydn's music box pieces and set it before her. "A long-suffering man is the vicar, Mr. Haydn," she said, her eyes on the notes. "A half hour closeted with a woman who thinks God is a flibbertigibbet must seem an eternity." Still, she was pleased that he would come, and flattered herself that it was because of her that he came to soften up Lady Bushnell. And there was the bailiff, playing matchmaker in the church. *Oh, what* is *your game, David Wiggins?*

She played a few notes, but the bailiff remained on her mind like a tune heard before breakfast and then hummed all day. *If he was ever all elbows or angles, it was a long time ago.* She wondered why he had not been present for lunch, then decided that he was feeling shy, too, or at least reconsidering his late-night attentions. She played a few more notes. *I believe I will write to Mr.*

Steinman tonight, she told herself. He will eventually find me another position, and that will be that.

She waited until a respectable time had passed for the vicar to have taken his leave, then picked up *Emma* and went to the best sitting room. She knocked and entered, then stepped back in dismay. The vicar was still there, and looking at her with something close to devotion in his eyes.

"I didn't mean . . . I thought . . ." she stammered. "I can come back later."

Lady Bushnell shook her head. "You are just in time, Miss Hampton. Won't you join us for tea?"

"Tea? You want me to join you for tea?" she gasped.

"I believe it is a common practice in the afternoon, Miss Hampton," the widow said, her voice serene but her eyes wicked. "We would like you to pour."

This must be a dream, she thought as she sat down at the tea table. I am having tea with Lady Bushnell. She deftly poured a cup for the widow, then turned her attention to the vicar. "Mr. Hepworth, will you have sugar and cream? Isn't this lovely weather we are having? Do tell me when the birds come back to this valley. Spring is my favorite time of year."

Chapter Twelve

I am babbling, she thought desperately. I hope no one notices. She managed a glance at the vicar, and saw, to her amazement, that he was regarding her seriously, as though she were speaking the greatest wisdom since Solomon. The bailiff would be laughing to my face, she thought as she smiled at Mr. Hepworth.

Her store of idle chatter seemed endless, and she could only thank generations of Hamptons who had probably small-talked their way from Hastings to the present. What's bred in the bone will come out of the mouth, she decided grimly as she gave the vicar the advantage of her dimple, tried not to catch Lady Bushnell's much-too-observant eyes, and spouted magnificent nonsensicals worthy even of Sir Rodney.

So help me, Mr. Hepworth, you could toss in the idle comment here and there, she thought later as the visit wore on and she found herself reaching an end to her store of trivia. To her dismay, the vicar appeared to bask in her prattle as he ate one macaroon after another and held out his cup for more tea. There was no help from Lady Bushnell, who sipped her tea, and seemed content to gaze out the window, particularly at such times when her shoulders began to shake.

Susan was considering prayer for divine intervention when she glanced at the clock. She set down her cup. "Mr. Hepworth, haven't you Evensong in an hour?" she asked, grateful as never before for the practices of her church.

"Oh, my!" he exclaimed, setting down his cup with a click that made her wince. He scrambled to his feet and looked about in confusion for his hat, reminding Susan more than ever of a marsh bird. Lady Bushnell had by now devoted her entire attention to the view outside the window, and was making small sounds vaguely incompatible with her customary dignity.

It was a small matter to see him to the door, accept his profoundest farewells, and focus her attention on the chandelier when he nearly tripped over the design in the carpet. Only when the vicar was on his horse and galloping toward Quilling as though pursued by revenue men did Susan dare return to the sitting room and Lady Bushnell.

The widow sat with her hands folded quietly in her lap, but her eyes gave her away. In another moment her hand went to her mouth as she motioned to Susan to shut the door. She began to laugh first, a hearty, come-from-the-toes, infectious kind of laugh that Susan was powerless to resist, even had she wanted to. She joined in, laughing until she had to wipe her eyes and clutch her middle, complaining of too-vigorous lacing.

"Lady Bushnell, I had no idea that taking tea with you would be so perilous to my sorry store of clever chitchat," she said finally, when she could speak.

"And *I* had no idea that one man could drink so much tea, eat so many macaroons, and gaze with such adoration," Lady Bushnell retorted. "I daresay Evensong will be brief, considering all that tea he consumed," she said and started to laugh again. "Oh, dear!" she exclaimed finally as she accepted a handkerchief from Susan. "Miss Hampton, our vicar is profoundly lovestruck. Does this mean more such visits? Can it be that my peace was less disturbed when my lady's companions were stealing apostle spoons, pressing Bible tracts on me, and attempting to roger my bailiff?"

If it bothered Lady Bushnell, the agitation didn't show, Susan considered. And why on earth wouldn't any redblooded woman want to roger him? she thought, and didn't bother to blush this time. "I don't mean to be trouble, my lady," she said, her voice light. "Blame the bailiff for introducing Mr. Hepworth yesterday."

"I could hardly blame the bailiff for dark eyes, and a pretty face," Lady Bushnell insisted. "Miss Hampton, you are going to be a great deal of trouble for me, I suspect. Not only must I teach you to play the piano, and attempt to eradicate your more regrettable Hamptonisms, but now I suppose I must chaperon the vicar, and any other stray bachelor that David Wiggins drags home! My own daughter was less exertion, and I did not employ her!"

"I shall warn the bailiff not to introduce any more single gentlemen to me," Susan replied, matching Lady Bushnell's teasing tone. She watched Lady Bushnell, noting how bright the color was in her cheeks, and how young the voice. If any of this silliness keeps you from dismay at your own solitude, or worry about your independence, I think I shall create lots of trouble just for you, she thought.

The daily reading of *Emma* lasted only through one chapter, as one or the other or both of them would think of the vicar and begin to laugh all over again. "Tomorrow, Miss Hampton, tomorrow," said the widow as she dabbed at her eyes. "Miss Austen deserves our undivided attention. That will do for now." She looked at Susan over the handkerchief and her expression turned thoughtful. "Miss Hampton, if I had not already discerned that you were as clear as glass, I would begin to suspect that you were planning all these diversions."

"I would never!" Susan replied, smiling as she replaced the bookmark and rose to leave. "If you need me . . ."

"I do not," Lady Bushnell replied, but without that brusque tone of yesterday. "Remember, Miss Hampton, the G-major scale tomorrow. And I will sharpen my cane."

She was laughing as Susan closed the door. No, I am not clever enough to plan diversions for you, Lady Bushnell, she considered, but I know someone who is, someone who knows you much better than I.

She deliberated the merits of accosting the bailiff, and decided honestly that there were none. I simply must not be shy to meet him, she decided. After all, we have agreed that this whole kissing business was just something that happened. At least, I think that is what we decided, although I cannot recall the precise conversation.

In the long run, it did not matter. The bailiff was away from the manor, and so Mrs. Skerlong told Susan, without any subterfuge to find out on her part. "He has gone to the sheepfold," the housekeeper explained as she set places for three instead of four. "I can always depend upon Ben Rich to occupy him through the supper hour," she said.

"The sheepfold?" Susan asked, striving for a certain vague disinterest that signaled nothing more than idle curiosity. "We were there only yesterday."

"Aye, and he'll be spending more and more time there, until the lambing is done. And soon they'll be letting the rams and yearlings out to more distant meadows. A busy time of year is spring, Susan."

"And then the bailiff will plant his Waterloo wheat?" she asked, taking the plates and cups from the housekeeper and arranging them on the table.

Mrs. Skerlong nodded, then directed her attention to the Rumford again. "He's been planning that crop of wheat for five years now, I'm thinking." She shrugged. "What the good of it is, I don't know. Everyone else just saves wheat back from the harvest and plants that the next year. Why this is better, I couldn't say." She removed a pot from the stove and dipped soup into their bowls.

"He thinks his strain will produce better wheat," Susan said, thinking of the wheat in the succession house, force-grown and lovely as it swayed in the artificial breeze of the furnaces.

The housekeeper cut off several slices of roast beef from the pan warming on the hob and put them on a platter. She called Cora from the laundry room and the three of them sat down to dinner. "I wondered why he did all that," commented the housekeeper as she swabbed at the meat juice with a chunk of bread. "Then one day I was redding up his funny stand-up desk in the succession house, and there was a piece of paper with 'Quilling Seed Farm, David Wiggins, Proprietor,' written as fancy as you please on a scrap of paper!" The Skerlongs looked at each other and laughed, as though it was an old joke.

"You think he can't do that?" Susan asked, ready to spring to the bailiff's defense.

"It seems a broad dream for a poacher on the run from Wales who knew more about the end of a gun than a stalk of wheat when he came here," she said, chewing placidly, her words a mild reproof of Susan's quick statement.

Susan nodded, for form's sake, and addressed herself to the roast in front of her. People change, she thought. I have changed since the wind and snow blew me into Mr. Steinman's agency. Others can change, too. She thought of Lady Bushnell and her fierce desire to maintain her independence, and sighed. Sometimes we have to change, even when we don't want to.

Mrs. Skerlong looked at her with a smile in her eyes. "That sigh came from your toes, I'm thinking." She leaned forward across the table. "Don't worry; David Wiggins always finds his way home."

Susan regarded the housekeeper with amusement. A month ago, I would have taken such affront at your presumption, she thought, but no longer. "Actually, Mrs. Skerlong, I was thinking of Lady Bushnell," she replied, leaning forward, grateful that it was the truth. "What happens if Lady B becomes ill and her daughter-in-law really does step in?"

There was a long pause. "None of us like to think of it."

"But she's sixty-five."

"And she's spent years and years marching with regiments, following the drum from India to Spain," Cora chimed in softly. "I think it would kill her to be forced to leave her independence behind and go to her daughter-in-law."

Susan nodded again. "And all in the name of kindness. How sad."

The three of them sat quietly for long minutes, with only the sound of soup bubbling on the stove to compete with the silence. Finally the housekeeper heaved herself up from the table. "Well, we are glum gussies," she said, "and why borrow trouble from tomorrow?" She looked at Cora, then Susan. "Cora, did we forget to mention to Susan about tonight?"

"It's the third Wesnesday," Cora said, as if that explained it all. She must have observed Susan's blank look. "Mum and I go to Quilling to listen to the bell ringers." She blushed and looked at her mother. "Timothy Rudge plays the bells," she said, as if that explained everything.

It did. "And he also sings tenor?" Susan asked.

Cora nodded, quite rosy now. "We stays overnight with Mum's sister and comes back by early morning."

"But how do you get there?"

Mrs. Skerlong rose and gathered the dishes toward her. "We take the gig. David rode the saddle horse to the sheepfold. And now if you won't mind helping with the dishes, I can get Lady B's dinner ready and in front of her and still be on time."

She saw them off from the back steps, two women well bundled against the night air clamping down cold and hard, with warming boxes at their feet and bell ringers on Cora's mind, at least. Susan stayed where she was for a long moment, hugging her arms close to her body, admiring the brittle sunset. How beautiful this will be in summer, she thought as the cold defeated her and she stepped inside. I wonder where he will plant the wheat? She remembered the perfection of summer nights on Papa's estate when they still owned it, and the pleasure of rustling her way through the rye and the barley before it was too tall.

She stood by the window in the kitchen, trying to imagine the sight of wheat in June fields on a long, sloping hillside in Belgium, just before it all turned into mud and blood. "I think it would be a sight not soon forgotten," she said, writing "David Wiggins, Sergeant" on the frosty pane this time. "It must have been the last good memory for many."

With the cat in her lap, she dozed in front of the stove until she heard Lady Bushnell's bell. She hurried to the breakfast room to retrieve the remains of dinner, arranging cup and plate on the tray in the empty room. Lady Bushnell had already left; Susan heard the sitting room door close quietly as she picked up the tray and started for the kitchen.

She stopped in the hall. Setting the tray on a side table, she went quietly to the sitting room door and knocked. "Lady Bushnell?" she asked. "May I come in?"

"Yes."

She entered the room, cheery now with the light of several lamps and a fire which Mrs. Skerlong must have nurtured before she left. Susan drew the curtains closed and hesitated at the window. Lady Bushnell sat in her usual chair, the yellowing letters on her lap and beside her on a small table. Several had fallen to the floor.

"Let me help you." Susan knelt and gathered up the pages, the ink pale with age now. She placed them on the table, wishing she had an excuse to stay. "Is there anything I can do for you?" she asked, knowing those were hated words to her employer, but unsure of what else to say.

"I have already told you that I can manage," Lady Bushnell said, her voice firm, as though she spoke to a slow child. She indicated the letters in her lap. "I like to read these in the evenings."

How can you manage? Susan wanted to ask. I can hardly read them, with the ink so faded. "Very well," she replied, when the widow said nothing more. "But if you need me . . ."

"I won't."

"If you do," Susan continued, "I am close by. Good night, Lady Bushnell."

She washed the dishes in the kitchen, feeling heavy as the solitude of the manor descended on her shoulders. At home I would be playing whist with Aunt Louisa and my cousins, she thought. And perhaps Papa would return from a successful turn at the tables and favor me with idle chat about his plans. She set her lips firmly together. But I am *not* homesick, and Papa's plans are my ruination.

With a sigh of exasperation, she took Mrs. Skerlong's shawl from the peg by the door and swung it around her shoulders. I will weed strawberries in the succession house, she told herself with an impatient twitch of her shoulders. It ought to remind me that there is no going back to London and Aunt Louisa's house.

Tim the cowman must have lit the lamps and stoked the furnaces, because the room was bright and warm enough for moisture to condense on the glass. She sniffed the air, appreciating the fragrance of leaves and loam when all outside was still patchy with snow and suspicious of more. "This is more like it," she announced, sitting at the drafting table to admire the wheat.

She soaked in the sight before her and was acutely mindful of its calming effect. I wonder if it is the wheat, or the man who tends it so faithfully, she thought, feeling at peace with herself again. I should leave him a little note and tell him that Lady B asked me to take tea today, she thought as she looked about on the ledge under the table for paper.

She pulled out a letter instead, which she would have returned without reading, except that the title in bold lettering caught her attention. "Waterloo Seed Farm," she read. I like that better than "Quilling Seed Farm," David. She read the letter to herself, noting the misspellings and shaky grammar, but impressed with the message. "So you would volunteer some of your wheat to others for trial, sir?" she murmured. "That is a good idea." She folded her hands on the drafting table, looking at the list of names running down one side of the letter. "And I suppose these are all local landowners within easy riding distance, so you can check on your experimental wheat."

She put away the letter and got down off the stool, curious to know if the bailiff would allow her to help him with the spelling and grammar. I hope he will not be too proud, she reflected. I would be, she thought honestly. Let us hope that the bailiff is a better person than I am.

The strawberries claimed her notice then. She weeded them and ate a few that interested her, thinking of berries sugared and fed to attentive gentlemen sharing alfresco luncheons. At least, her cousin Fanny had embellished that tale after one event of her London Season and passed it on to a cousin chafing at home. Susan tried to imagine feeding a sugared strawberry to David Wiggins, and could only laugh, shake her head, and weed a little faster.

Even the succession house felt lonely, and she looked about for the cat, who should have been shamelessly toadying about her ankles and nudging her for pets and ear rubs. Kittens, is it? she thought. She wiped her hands on some burlap sacking and walked around the succession house, peering into dark corners where David had pointed out beds he had made of toweling in the hope that the cat would pick a comfortable spot for "the blessed event," as he put it. No luck. Of course, reasoned Susan as she made another circuit, what cat ever did the convenient thing?

She found the cat and kitten on the third circuit, lying on the bailiff's uniform jacket, which had been rolled up and stuffed inside a box next to the bags of seed wheat. The cat was vigorously licking the slimy, unfinished-looking kitten curled up beside her, mouth open in a soundless meow. Then as Susan watched, the cat stopped, and with inward preoccupation, purred louder and expelled a second kitten in a gush of fluid onto Wiggins' jacket.

"I hope your master had no plans for that coat," Susan murmured as she watched in fascination. She was still sitting there an hour later, watching the last of four kittens arrive, when the bailiff returned. At least she assumed it was the bailiff. Seated on the floor between the aisles, she could not see him. She stayed where she was, comfortably seated with her legs crossed Indian style and the scrap of a blanket tucked around her. She knew better than to touch the kittens, but she continued to admire them, tiny, hairless, utterly dependent. It's not that I am shy about getting up, she rationalized. It's just that I do not wish to startle Mama Cat.

"All right, Susan, someone else is breathing in here besides me, and I don't think Tim the cowman dabs . . . lily of the valley is it . . . ? behind his ears. Although he should."

Susan smiled but did not get up. "Your cat had kittens, and I have been observing."

After lighting another lamp, he came toward the sound of her voice. "You really shouldn't sit there on the cold floor," he scolded mildly as he draped his coat around her shoulders and sat down beside her, leaning his back against the counter. He tickled the cat under her chin, smiling as she stretched her neck up. "And good job to you, my dear. You managed to miss all my clever birthing locations and wedge yourself onto my jacket. Why am I not surprised?"

"I hope the coat wasn't a valuable memento," Susan said when the silence threatened to extend beyond her comfort.

"No. I'm not one to gather memories that way." He took up a corner of the coat that he had put around her shoulders and pulled it behind his back, drawing them closer together. "Thanks for weeding the strawberries," he said. "Now, where are the ones you should have picked?"

They weren't exactly touching shoulders, but Aunt Louisa would not have approved. "I ate them," she said, feeling not even slightly repentant. "They were excellent."

"I'm so glad," he replied dryly. "Now suppose Lady B asks for strawberries tomorrow morning, and I have to tell her that her lady's companion ate them?"

Susan couldn't help herself. She nudged his shoulder with her own. "Oh, you know she will not!"

The bailiff chuckled and settled himself a little closer. "I know," he agreed, and was silent then.

She could think of nothing to say. I have babbled enough today in front of the vicar, she thought. I feel just as uncomfortable as I did then in Lady Bushnell's sitting room, but I refuse to blather on this time. Someone else can fill the gap this time.

But the bailiff did not. He sat close beside her, their hips touching now, with his legs drawn up. He watched the kittens through the space in his legs, every now and then reaching out to touch the cat. In a few more moments, she had organized the little morsels of life beside her and they were nursing. The cat heaved a sigh of her own and rested her head on the coat's hatch marks.

"That's a good use for an old relic," Wiggins commented finally. "Five years ago I wrapped Lord Bushnell in it after he was hit. Ah, well."

There wasn't anything in his tone of voice to indicate that he needed comfort, but Susan had to resist the urge to move even closer and rest her head on his shoulder. She had heard stories about men and battle, and how some dreamed and suffered for years, but the bailiff did not appear to be one of them.

"It was just one more incident in your life, wasn't it?" she asked.

He nodded, understanding her perfectly. "It was," he agreed. "Of course, Waterloo was Waterloo, and nothing will ever compare to it, but I suppose you're right. It was just one more thing. I suppose nothing really had the capacity to surprise me, after Lady B retrieved me from death."

She turned a little to look at him then, impressed with his solidity and the calmness of his nature. *Someday, if I am very lucky, I will be so wise,* she thought.

He looked at her, a question in his eyes. "What is it you want to say, Susan?" he asked.

"I don't think I could put it into words," she said frankly.

"Try."

She looked at the cat then, and the kittens kneading to suck at her belly. "You impress me with your courage. I . . . I suppose I wish I were that brave."

"You are," he said simply. "You're braver than all the Hamptons who ever lived."

She laughed then. "That would not be difficult!" He was so close that she could smell soap, so she knew it was time to change the subject. "Actually, I came to tell you that Lady Bushnell let me drink tea with her."

Immediately, she wished she had not said anything. The bailiff moved away slightly. She did not pretend that he was merely resettling himself. Their shoulders still touched, but he had shifted his hip out of her range. *What did I say?* she asked herself. *Whatever it was, it was the wrong thing.*

"Good for you," the bailiff said finally. His voice was the same as ever, but it was different, too, in a way that baffled her. "But why should we be surprised? After all, Susan, you are one of them."

"One of them," she repeated. "I don't understand."

Wiggins got up then in one swift motion, holding out his hand to her. She let him pull her to her feet and take the coat from around her shoulders. He walked down the aisle, tossed his coat toward the peg, and sat on the stool at the drafting table.

"You're too much of a lady to remark on how well I speak English," he commented, resting his elbows on the slanting table.

If I can change the subject, I suppose you can, too, she thought, puzzled. "I guess I never considered it," wishing her words did not sound so lame, but curious where he was going.

"When the elder Lord Bushnell made me one of his regimental sergeants, I started to study the officers," he explained, not taking his eyes from her face. "I decided it would be well to imitate their diction, and labor over my faulty grammar." He smiled to himself, but it was a deprecating expression. "I don't regret that particularly, but one of those little lords with a purchased captaincy took me aside before the battle of Salamanca. I'll never forget his words. 'You may sound like a gentleman, Sergeant Wiggins, but you'll never be one of us.'" He grinned at her in genuine amusement. "He was right, of course, bless his blue blood, which, by the way, looked quite as red as everyone else's when spread all over the Spanish plain. 'One of us,'" he repeated, then took out his ledger, effectively dismissing her.

She watched him a moment more, but he was reaching for a pencil, and then looking for his ruler. One of us, she thought, amusement mingled with equal parts of exasperation. You propose to me, then tell me it was just a silly impulse. You almost tip the vicar into my lap. You set me up for Lady Bushnell to order about. You kiss me and trouble my mind and body. And myth and rumor have it that *women* are difficult to comprehend? I am so far removed from my sphere right now that I will do the only intelligent thing.

"Good night, sir," she said. It was so easy to smile at him, and considerably smarter than tears or remonstrations.

"Good night, Susan," he said, returning her smile with one of his own.

She could have passed him without the necessity of another word, and she did, but not before she reached out and touched his arm lightly as it lay on the desk. Figure that one out, Mr. Wiggins, she thought as she left the succession house and saved her laughter for the kitchen.

Before she prepared for bed in the silent house, she sat down to write to Joel Steinman. It was a cautious letter. She had never written to a man before, even if it was to the employment agent who had gotten her this job, and she hesitated a long time, redipping her quill into the ink any number of times. She told about the glove and Ben Rich, and his Welsh shepherd boy, and the kindness of the Skerlongs, and her own determination to be a lady's companion to a lady with twice her own backbone, and miles more character and courage. She described that first disastrous piano encounter, and the bliss of finally drinking tea with the widow. She was careful not to mention the bailiff. After all, she reasoned as the ink dried on the quill again, Joel Steinman knows something about propriety. I must not let him think I am interested in the bailiff. I will add casually that I am interested in the governess position, but not that I am overly anxious, she thought, and put pen to paper again. In the main, this is true. I think I am well enough off here, if only I will concentrate on my duties and not try to figure out what the bailiff is up to, if anything beyond a mild flirtation. Aunt Louisa would have it that all men are rogues and flirts.

Perhaps she is right, Susan decided as she pulled on her nightgown, tied her sleeping cap under her chin, danced about because the floor was cold, and hopped into bed. Papa cannot resist a gaming table; perhaps the bailiff cannot resist lily of the valley and trim ankles. I wonder what else he cannot resist, she considered as she closed her eyes.

She was asleep then and dreaming of marsh birds looking for their hats, and tea pouring endlessly from a pot as high as the roof into a tiny cup far below while Lady Bushnell hanged on her ankles and tried to scoot her off the piano stool.

"Susan! Wake up!"

It wasn't Lady Bushnell but the bailiff, and he was sitting on her bed, nudging her sideways with his hip to gain a little space for himself as he shook her shoulders. She snapped her eyes open, somewhere still between dreaming and waking, and put her hands on his face. Suddenly, in that curious semisleep, it was the loveliest moment of her life. He was warm, and he was close. Her fingers went to his lips. "Hush!" she said as he kissed her fingers. It seemed to be the most automatic of gestures to the bailiff, because he kept shaking her, and the lovely moment ended. She took her hand away, her mind still fuddled with sleep and the sharpest desire she had ever felt.

"Susan, you've got to wake up! I saw a light on late in Lady Bushnell's room, but her door is locked and she doesn't answer. You have to help me!"

Chapter Thirteen

𝒞

She sat up, fully awake. Without another word, the bailiff pulled her from the bed and into the hall, hurrying with her to Lady Bushnell's room. He paused outside the door, still gripping Susan's arm.

"I was late in the succession house. When I was walking back to my place, I noticed Lady Bushnell's light on. She's never up that late." He spoke rapidly. "I came upstairs and tried the door, but it's locked, and she didn't answer when I called." He released her arm. "I want you to go in first."

She nodded, understanding his position, and stood back against the wall as the bailiff tried to shoulder his way in. "Damn!" he muttered under his breath when the door would not give. He stepped back then, and kicked the door, which crashed open, the lock sprung.

Susan hurried inside, her heart in her throat, but Lady Bushnell was not in sight. She ran to the other side of the bed and stared down at the widow, who lay there looking up at her, her hand on her chest, her eyes huge with fright.

"Oh, Lady Bushnell," Susan exclaimed in a soft voice. She quickly pulled down the widow's nightgown, which had ridden up around her knees and nodded to the bailiff, who stood on the other side of the bed. "You'll have to help me, David," she said.

The bailiff came around the bed, knelt down beside the widow, and picked her up gently. With a sob of relief, she turned her face into his chest and tightened her arm around his neck. "I knew you would come," she said, her voice scarcely louder than a breath.

Susan felt tears start in her eyes as the bailiff swallowed, then held the widow close for a brief moment before lowering her carefully to the bed. Susan hurried forward to pull up the blankets and smooth down the pillow, then stepped back as the bailiff sat on the bed, holding tight to the widow's hands. "Get her some water," he ordered Susan over his shoulder.

Surprised at the steadiness of her hands, Susan poured the widow a drink, and handed the cup to the bailiff. She rested her hand on his shoulder for the smallest moment, and felt her own fear dwindling. "Just a sip now, Lady Bushnell," said the bailiff in a tone that allowed for no argument. Your sergeant's voice? Susan thought as she sat in the chair next to the bed. "Very good," he said when the old woman obliged him. "Can you tell us what happened?"

Never taking her eyes from his face, the widow nodded. She gestured weakly to the pile of old letters strewn by the bed. "I was going to . . . to read these before I turned out the light." She paused, as though the sentence had worn her out, and pressed her hand to her heart again. Tears of frustration welled up in her eyes.

The bailiff raised her other hand to his chest and held it there. "No hurry, Lady Bushnell. Take your time, please."

She smiled at him and closed her eyes for a moment. The bailiff looked at Susan and she could see his jaw working from the tension he was trying so hard to hide from the widow. Impulsively she leaned forward and touched his leg, the only part of him she could reach without getting up.

"My heart . . . I felt like I was suffocating, and all the time, my heart was racing," the widow continued, her eyes, large now with amazement, on the bailiff again. "I got up to get a drink of water and I fell." She closed her eyes again. "It was like that other time."

The bailiff frowned and was silent for several moments, absorbing what she had said. "Do you mean this is what happened before, when you told me you tripped on the stairs?" he asked, his voice firm.

She sighed like a child caught in mischief and forced to confess. "It was. I told you I tripped on a loose rug. I didn't tell you it was because my heart was racing and startled me."

"Lady Bushnell . . ." he began, then stopped. "Oh, never mind," he concluded, resignation evident in his tone.

"It's happened a few other times," the widow admitted. "I was . . . afraid . . ."

". . . I would tell your daughter-in-law," he concluded with some asperity. "Lady Bushnell, you are a scamp and a rascal and old Lord Bushnell would scold you up one side and down the other, if he were here!"

She nodded, smiling now. "Yes, he would, wouldn't he?" Her voice grew serious again. "But he's not here, none of them are.

And neither is the army, and the battles are over, and they have all left me behind! How dare they do that?"

She was silent then, the tears spilling onto her cheeks. Chilled to the bone by Lady Bushnell's anguish, Susan knelt by the bed and wiped her eyes with the edge of the sheet. She rested her head against Lady Bushnell's arm. "David has to go for the doctor, my lady. I'll stay here with you," she murmured.

"Sergeant, I insist that you do nothing of the kind. And that is an order!" she said, her voice weak but determined. "I'll have you court-martialed!" she added, clutching his hand tighter.

"I wouldn't care, madam," he replied gently. "I'm still going for the doctor. You can dismiss me tomorrow."

"And I will," she insisted, but there wasn't any fervor behind the threat. "You can be sure of it."

David chuckled and leaned forward to kiss Lady Bushnell's cheek. She stared at him. "Sergeant, you're taking liberties," she warned, but made no move to release his hand.

"I am for sure, but if you're letting me go tomorrow, it doesn't matter! Now hush and let Susan give you another sip of water. I'll be back with the doctor." Gently he loosened her grip on him and got up. He went to the door and with the slightest gesture, indicated that Susan follow him.

She got up quietly, rested her hand for a moment on Lady Bushnell's cheek, then joined the bailiff at the door. He took her hand and tugged her into the hall.

"Just keep her quiet," he whispered, his lips close to her ear.

She nodded, then turned toward him. "What if she dies? I'm afraid."

He grabbed her in a quick hug then. "You'll do, Susan. Take care of her for me."

"I will," she promised as he released her, "but I'm still afraid."

He was backing away from her down the hall. "Think on this then, Susan. You look really lovely in flannel, but I don't care much for sleeping caps."

You are a rascal, she thought as she went back into the bedroom, took a deep breath to fortify herself, and sat in the spot the bailiff had vacated. Lady Bushnell was crying now, and Susan wanted to cry, too. She wanted to run back to her room, barricade the door, and wallow in her own fear. Instead, she took a firm grip on Lady Bushnell's hand and wiped her eyes again.

"Is your heart still racing?" she asked, dreading whatever answer was coming.

Lady Bushnell nodded, the fright in her eyes unmistakable.

"Then let me help you sit up," Susan said. "I'll put this pillow behind your head. There. Is that better?" Please let it be better, she thought.

To her relief, Lady Bushnell nodded. "I could use another sip of water."

Susan gave her another drink, dabbing at the corners of the widow's mouth when half of it dribbled out. She tucked Lady Bushnell's hair into her sleeping cap again and retied the strings. "The doctor will be here soon, and then we'll see," she said.

To her dismay, the widow began to cry again, noisy tears of childlike frustration layered over with equal parts of resignation and misery. Alarmed, Susan wiped her eyes again, murmuring soothing sounds that had no words as the widow clutched at her heart and gasped for breath. Casting aside the proprieties, Susan hugged the woman close to her own heart, as though willing its steady beat to communicate its regularity to the afflicted one. With a sob and a strength Susan would not have credited, the widow's arms went around her and they rocked together on the bed.

In a few minutes, the tears turned into hiccups, and then silence. Susan held the woman close, running her hands over her back and feeling the delicacy of her bones, the fragility that age distilled. "That's better now," she soothed, letting the widow rest against the mounded pillows again.

Lady Bushnell closed her eyes for a moment, her hands tight around Susan's. "Whatever happens, you must not tell my daughter-in-law," she insisted, her voice weak but charged with fervor that came from a reservoir deep within.

"I do not know that the matter will be in my hands," Susan whispered honestly, unconsciously matching the tone of her voice to the widow's as though they shared a great secret.

"It must be!" Lady Bushnell said, her eyes wide open and fierce, " 'else she will use this as the final excuse to pull me into Bushnell and keep me there."

"My lady, it may be that you need more attention than either David or I are capable of," Susan tried to explain. "How wonderful, really, that she cares so much." At least she will not look at you like Aunt Louisa, measuring your worth and value and begrudging food in your mouth.

"I will be an exhibit!" the widow hissed. "I will be a national relic!" She took Susan by the ties of her nightgown and pulled her closer. "Miss Hampton, I do not think you can understand this, but I have ridden with giants and I do not intend to be fed pabulum or turned into a shrine to be visited and tiptoed around!"

She lay back then among the pillows, exhausted by her exertion. She closed her eyes again, and spoke with the greatest effort. "My daughter-in-law will coddle me and cosset me and talk baby talk." She seemed to sink into the pillow. "It is not a warrior's end." Eyes still closed, she turned her head restlessly toward the door. "Sergeant Wiggins would understand. He knows what it meant to be part of that adventure." She slapped her hand feebly against the bedclothes. "I wish that you had gone for the doctor instead of him. He understands."

So do I, Lady Bushnell, Susan thought. Oh, you don't know. I feel all the cowardice of the Hamptons welling up inside me. Papa would blench and run, offering a thousand excuses with a charming smile. Aunt Louisa would bluster and gobble, and then before you know it, would have backed out of the room. But I must sit here because David told me to.

And I want to, she discovered with a shock as she went to the basin for a washcloth, squeezed out the moisture and added a drop of lavender. She wiped Lady Bushnell's face, humming to herself something she remembered from Mama. The tune went back beyond her memory, before there were even words.

"Lullabies, Miss Hampton?" Lady Bushnell said finally, her voice more calm now.

"Is that it?" Susan asked, smiling in spite of herself. The lavender calmed her. "See now, if the sergeant were here, all you would get would be military tunes."

To her gratification, Lady Bushnell smiled and opened her eyes. Her hand relaxed over her heart, but her eyes went to the door again. "I would like to hear his footsteps about now, wouldn't you?" she asked. "He has a nice stride."

"I've noticed."

Lady Bushnell chuckled, then tightened her hand over her heart again. "Susan, imagine watching a whole army with that certain swing to their walk. Is it any wonder we did not so much mind riding in the rear?"

Susan laughed out loud, leaning forward to touch her forehead to Lady Bushnell's. "Now you confess what kept you following the drum!" she teased gently.

The widow smiled back, her eyes dreamy now, the hurt and pain lessened. "Miss Hampton, do you know what it is like to be loved?"

Susan shook her head. "I wish I did," she replied frankly, then grinned at Lady Bushnell. "Of course, there is the vicar . . ."

"No, not him," the widow said almost impatiently. "He would probably think he had to ask permission to hold your hand, and then only after sitting in my parlor for a year or two."

It was too many words at once. Susan brought the glass to her lips again for another sip. Silence followed, a silence so long that Susan thought she slept. *The bailiff did not ask my permission to kiss me,* she thought as she rested her hand lightly on Lady Bushnell's arm. *I think he could have done anything he wanted without a word to show for it.* "Maybe I could guess," she ventured, her voice soft even to her own ears.

"In that case, get my letters," ordered the widow, just the hint of command back again. "After all, if I am determined to die tonight, I want you to read them to me first. It has been so long."

"But every day I see you with them in your lap," Susan said. She knelt by the bed to pick up the letters closest to them, put them within Lady Bushnell's reach, then went to the desk by the window, where she remembered others.

"Susan, let me give you some advice for when you are old."

There was something so serious in Lady Bushnell's voice that Susan returned to the bed and sat on the edge of it, the letters in her hand. "I like to think that I will appreciate useful advice," she said. "No other Hampton does, so it must be a good thing."

Lady Bushnell gathered the letters closer to her as a mother would gather her children. "When you are old, my dear, you may be surrounded by people who love you. Your children may be there, your husband, too—and don't look at me like that! I am certain you will find a husband." She held the letters close to her face for a moment, then rested them on the coverlet. "Or it may be that you will be alone, as I am, and relying on the help of paid employees."

"Oh, but . . ." Susan began.

"Hush! I know David Wiggins cares about me; he always has. I am beginning to think that you do, too. But you are both in my employ, and that is not the same as family."

"No, it is not," Susan agreed simply.

"My advice is this, and perhaps it's advice that you can use now: don't ever be too proud to ask for help." Lady Bushnell looked at her with a steady gaze as little spots of color blazed out from her cheeks, replacing her pallor. "So I am asking your help now. If this is to be my last night, I want you to read my letters to me. They are all I have left of my loves, and it has been so long."

Susan returned her gaze, confused at first, and then let out her breath in a sigh that came up from her bare toes, as she began to understand. "I did not realize . . . we all thought . . . the letters on your lap," she stammered, the words spilling out of her. "Oh, my lady, a little trouble like this comes with age. We didn't know it was so serious! Were you afraid that if David knew your eyes were this diminished, he would tell your daughter-in-law?"

The widow nodded, averting her eyes in embarrassment. "I wanted you all to think that I was in control of things." She looked at Susan again, reaching for her. "The ink is too faded now! I have sat with those letters for a year now, and I must hear them! I have no other family around me except these ghosts . . ." Her voice trailed off as she gestured weakly at the letters on the bed.

Moved to tears, Susan grasped Lady Bushnell's hands and stared down at them until she felt controlled enough to speak. "It will be my delight to read them to you." She looked at the widow then, her voice more firm. "And not only tonight, but any time you wish." She glanced at the letters. The writing was faded, but she knew it was not beyond her capacity. "Only let me get a shawl and bring another lamp close to the bed. And perhaps some shoes; my feet are cold."

"No wonder! Did he yank you out of bed?" Lady Bushnell said as she arranged the letters, some right side up, some not.

Susan nodded and laughed. "It's a good thing I don't sleep in just a chemise!"

"Or less!" Lady Bushnell said, joining the fun. "I have an idea. My daughter and I used to read together in bed." She made a move to pull back the coverlet.

"Then we shall, too, if that is your wish," Susan declared. "But first, a lamp." She brought the lamps from the desk and dressing table and put them on Lady Bushnell's nightstand. "Very good." She added more coal to the fire in the hearth, then climbed in bed with Lady Bushnell, wondering what David Wiggins would think if he could see them. And where are you, David? she asked herself. Please hurry with the doctor.

The widow lay still, her eyes closed, exhausted by the double exertion of speech and confession. She opened them when Susan slid into the bed beside her, then settled herself lower, and closed her eyes again.

Susan looked at the letters in her lap, righting the upside-down ones, reading the salutations. "These are mainly letters to your daughter?" she asked in surprise.

"Yes, this batch," the widow said, her voice scarcely more than a whisper. "For a while, she lived in a convent school in Lisbon. There are some letters from my husband, when he served in India with Wellington and I was left to chafe in Calcutta with a baby while he took to the field. Charles was born in India."

"I would like to travel someday," Susan said.

"No, you wouldn't, my dear," said the widow, amused. "You'll be a wonderful homebody."

Susan smiled, and pulled out another letter. "And here is one from your son." She squinted at the date and title. "Louisiana? My goodness."

"Wretched place, wretched battle," Lady Bushnell muttered. "Trust Americans to hide behind cotton bales! Can you imagine?" She sighed, and shook her head. "Don't read that one. I think that too little cannot be said about the Battle of New Orleans." She make a dismissing gesture. "I want to hear of Spain."

"Very well, my lady," Susan said, tucking the letter from Louisiana at the bottom of the pile. "Here is one. 'Retreat from Burgos, somewhere west and south of Salamanca, November, 1812,'" she read.

"That one, yes, that one," Lady Bushnell murmured.

Susan edged the lamp closer to the letter, cleared her throat and began. "'My Darling Lizzie, How happy I am that you are well and safe in Lisbon, even if you are not intrigued by Pythagoras and profess that Latin is a humbug and you cannot tell the verbs from the objects.'" She looked at Lady Bushnell. "I gather she was in school then?"

The widow nodded, her eyes still closed, a slight smile on her face. "And loathing every moment of it! After the third time she ran away to join us on campaign, Edward relented and let her stay. Please continue."

Amused, Susan read on. "'We have been retreating and retreating. For all that Hookey says that a good general knows when to retreat and to dare to do it, I am heartily weary of it. It is a sad business, too. We leave so much behind to lighten the load. It is everlasting hardtack, acorns mashed, boiled, sautéed and stewed, and endless pork barely cooked enough to stop the squeal. The rains damp out the fire before anything is well done.'" Susan looked up from the page. "Acorns?"

"They taste surprisingly like roasted chestnuts."

"'We have blown each bridge we crossed, the last one a Roman structure at Valladolid. Think how that would have both-

ered your grandfather, Latin scholar that he was!' Not Lady Elizabeth, however," Susan said to Lady Bushnell.

"No! That child was only happy in the saddle," the widow said,
her features more relaxed now. "Excuse me, Susan, but Edward
once wondered if we could have conceived her on horseback. I
told him he was dreaming, of course! But she was a daughter of
the regiment. If only Charles . . ." she began, then stopped.

Susan thought of the bailiff and his remarks about young Lord
Bushnell. So Lizzie had the heart for combat, and Charles did
not? she reflected, looking at the letter again.

"Here I am. 'It is wine country; between Burgos and Salamanca we have passed any number of vats full of the harvest. Finally, one Dragoon could stand no more. He and his comrades
fired their pistols into a vat. You should have seen the men break
ranks and line up at the bullet holes like pigs to teats! Your father
brought me a drink in his hat.'"

"It was so good that I could overlook the hair tonic," Lady
Bushnell said, her voice dreamy now. "I wanted more, and
Sergeant Wiggins gave me half of his. In a tin cup," she added,
chuckling. "He always had a better sense of what was proper."

Susan turned over the letter. "'I will send this from Salamanca,
if it is possible. Do study harder, my love, and try not to chafe the
nuns so much. Love and kisses, Mama.'"

"I sent it on with Wellington's dispatches from Salamanca,"
Lady Bushnell explained, her voice more energetic now, as if she
gathered strength from the letters. She struggled to sit up, and
Susan fluffed the pillows behind her. "Then we started the worse
part of the journey, Susan. The French were everywhere, trying to
beat us to Ciudad Rodrigo and the border. Look for that letter. I
believe it is dated December 10, 1812."

Susan shuffled through the letters. "Here it is. 'Dearest Lizzie,
It is mud all day and all night. We sleep in it, the men march in it,
we drink it. We are hounded by chasseurs, who cause such trouble in the rear. We were cut off yesterday and forced to hide in
the woods until dark. Corporal Frasier even gave me a loaded pistol. We moved faster after that, stopping for nothing. Sergeant
Wiggins' woman was in labor then, and we dared not halt. I think
I will hear her in my sleep, screaming and screaming in that
springless baggage cart.'"

Susan stopped and put down the letter. I was seventeen years
old that winter, she thought, living warm and safe and still hopeful of a comeout. My biggest worry was whether I would get a
blue dress or a pink one at Christmas. "What happened?" she

asked, not caring if Lady Bushnell heard the ragged edge to her voice.

"She labored for three days and could not deliver that baby. They died," Lady Bushnell said simply. "All the men tried to help Sergeant Wiggins dig their grave, but he said he would do it by himself, and he did." The widow took hold of Susan's hand. "In the rain. Every now and then he would stop and just wail. I wonder if it was a Welsh thing," she said.

Or a lover teetering on the raw ledge of grief, Susan considered. What a life you have led, sir. No wonder you crave the peace and solitude of your wheat. "It is so sad," she said, then surprised herself by bursting into tears.

Lady Bushnell let her cry, then with a slight smile, held up a corner of the sheet. "We can wash these tomorrow," she said as Susan blew her nose fiercely, then scrubbed at her cheeks.

"Tomorrow? You've decided you don't want to die tonight?" Susan asked.

"No, I don't," Lady Bushnell agreed. "We have too many letters to read."

Susan continued reading, following the retreat to Ciudad Rodrigo, then to safety over the Portuguese border and behind the works at Lisbon. She forgot to worry about David and the doctor, or whether Lady Bushnell would survive the night. They curled close to each other, the widow's feet on her legs for warmth as she read the letters. The hours passed, the clock ticked on serenely, and Lady Bushnell seemed at peace, absorbed in the letters, breathing evenly. Susan felt as though someone had taken out her eyeballs, dipped them in sand, and replaced them. She read on, jumping from year to continent as Lady Bushnell rode with her beloved army again.

The clock chimed two. Susan looked up, thinking she heard footsteps, but it was just rain scouring the windowpanes behind the drawn draperies. "'Poor Colonel Whitehead, Lizzie,'" she read, raising her voice a little to be heard over the rain. "'He went to vast trouble to procure such a beefsteak most of us could only dream about. It was hissing merrily in the pan when a six-pound shell dropped down from nowhere and sent the steak into a better world.'" She smiled. "It seems to me, Lady Bushnell, that soldiers worry mainly about battle and food, and I am not sure which is more significant. What say you, my lady? My lady?"

She was almost afraid to look down at the woman curled beside her, but then she heard the reassurance of even breathing, and just the hint of a snore. Thank God, she thought as she pulled the coverlet higher around the frail shoulders and sank herself lower in the bed, exhausted with reading and worry. She gathered the letters quietly together, careful not to rustle the paper.

The letter from Louisiana was at the top of the pile now. She looked at it, then glanced at Lady Bushnell. "January 22, 1815, aboard the Statira," she read silently, the fading page close to her face. "Dear Mama, I have supervised the stowing of Generals Pakenham and Gibbs in rum casks, sealed against the return to London and grieving families. On, Mama! We could get no closer than five hundred yards to the Americans behind those damned cotton bales. Where did they learn to shoot like that? I cannot tell you what happened to the men, but they began to fire in column. Column! Even poor Lizzie would have known not to do that! I could not rally them after General Gibbs was killed, and they ran. You have never seen such murderous fire. *I do not ever wish to hear of New Orleans again.* And now you write in your letter of November 15 that I am to command Papa's dear Fighting Fifth, now that he is gone? Mama, I cannot. Please, may we talk about this when I see you next at home? Yrs. in haste and sorrow, Charles."

The anguish in the words leaped off the page at her. Susan hastily pushed the letter to the bottom of the pile again and looked at the sleeping widow, her eyes troubled now less with exhaustion than great unease. What did you tell him, Lady Bushnell, you who have the heart and spirit of a soldier? Did you remind him of his duty? Did you flog him with words from room to room until he caved in? Did you dare to assume that just because he was your dead husband's son, he was fit to command his regiment? Lady Bushnell, how could you?

Chapter Fourteen

The bailiff woke her again, but this time his hand was gentle on her back as she snuggled close to Lady Bushnell. She thought his lips just touched her cheek, but she could have been mistaken, because she was dreaming about soldiers.

"Susan, wake up," he whispered, his hand warm on her back. "I've brought the doctor, and the Skerlongs will be here soon."

She reached up and touched his face to let him know that she heard, then carefully disentangled herself from Lady Bushnell. "She was cold and wanted me to get in bed and read her letters," she explained to the doctor, who was peering close at the sleeping widow. "She said she felt more calm when I was lying close by."

She thought she heard the bailiff say, "I am sure I would not," as he turned away, but her mind was still fuzzy with sleep. She got up slowly, careful to tug down her nightgown and acutely aware of her undecorous appearance. What seemed perfectly necessary during last night's emergency struck her as almost ludicrous now, especially with Lady Bushnell slumbering so peacefully, the picture of old age propriety.

Wishing earnestly for a robe or shawl now, Susan stood beside the bed and watched the physician. "She really frightened us last night," she offered, aware of how lame it sounded.

To her relief the doctor nodded. "I do not doubt that for a minute," he replied. He looked at the bailiff. "I had my suspicions when you summoned me after her fall." He sighed and rubbed his eyes. "Long night, Wiggins, long night. Now if you will excuse me, I will see if I can do Lady Bushnell any good."

Susan started to leave, but he touched her arm. "I would rather you remained."

"Let me get a robe," she said. "Mr. Wiggins, could you build up the fire? I'll be back in a moment." She hurried down the hall, took a moment to refresh herself, then stood by her window in robe and slippers, watching the dawn make its early false attempt. Against her own will, she thought of the Battle of New Orleans, with its smoke and fog and terrifying accuracy of frontiersmen's muskets and frightened men marching in columns and firing long before they should have. And there was Charles Bushnell, no leader of men, his own deficiencies uncovered by the death of his commander, with no idea what to do. "It is too bad," she said as she drew Charles' name on the icy pane and circled it, before leaving the room.

David waited for her outside Lady Bushnell's door. "I'm tired," he said as he leaned against the wall. "Used to be I was fresh for forty-eight hours, but now . . ." He shrugged. "Peace makes me soft."

She looked at him, her mind and heart still on poor Charles, and tears welled in her eyes. "Oh, David, the things I have learned this night," she began. "Charles . . . Young Lord Bushnell . . . was no leader of men."

"I've already told you that. And knowing that, I wonder why he took command that spring before Waterloo."

"I think I can tell you, but it will have to wait." She opened the door, then looked back at him. "Where did you find the doctor?"

"Delivering a crofter's baby far away from here. That child didn't particularly want to make an appearance, so I had to wait."

He turned bleak eyes on her and she was reminded of his sad part in Lady Bushnell's letter. How hard was it to cool your heels in the crofter's and listen to a woman in travail? No matter; she knew she never needed to ask. The answer was in his eyes. Impulsively, she held his hand for a moment, whispered, "I know," then went inside and closed the door behind her.

Lady Bushnell was awake now, resting demurely in the center of the bed, her letters still scattered around her. "I am feeling fine," she assured the doctor with a glance of determined defiance directed at Susan when the man began to rummage in his bag. "Never better. It must have been a touch of indigestion last night, Dr. Pym."

The doctor gave a noncommittal "H'mmm" practiced in its neutrality, and removed a slender tube from his bag. The widow's eyes widened. "I am fine," she insisted. "I have seldom been better."

"Lady Bushnell, you are a prevaricator of the first water, and I do not scruple to tell you," Dr. Pym said smoothly. "Miss Hampton, do me the honor of pulling aside Lady Bushnell's frills just slightly and positioning this tube where her heart is. I will, of course, not look, Lady Bushnell!"

"You were right to call me," the doctor said to Susan and David as they stood in the hall later. He moved aside for Mrs.

Skerlong to hurry in with breakfast on a tray and good cheer on
her lips almost before she entered the room. "Although she is not
in obvious distress right now, there is still some irregularity to her
heartbeat. It is certainly angina pectoris, and would indicate other
cardiac maladies incidental to advancing years, and less easy to
diagnose." He rubbed his bloodshot eyes. "You must inform
young Lady Bushnell at once."

"Oh, but surely . . ." Susan began.

"At once," he repeated, then fixed the bailiff with a stare. "Perhaps I was unwise to listen to you after her slip on the stairs. I
should have insisted then that Lady Bushnell make that final move
to the family estate, where she can be watched over day and night."

"It will kill her to sacrifice her independence!" Susan burst out.

"It will kill her to stay here!" Dr. Pym argued, exasperated, out
of sorts, and looking for the world like a man who wanted his
bed. "My dear Miss Hampton, I'll give you and Mr. Wiggins
three days . . ."

Susan burst into tears and threw herself on his chest, sobbing,
crowding so close to the doctor that he had no choice but to put
his arm around her or topple over. And once his arm was around
her, suddenly it became his problem.

"Now, see here, Miss Hampton . . . oh, do not cry . . . !" He cast
a desperate glance in the bailiff's direction, but it was a wasted effort, because the bailiff was minutely examining the wallpaper as
though it were a new discovery, and humming to himself. "This
unmans me, Miss Hampton! Oh very well, one week!"

Susan managed to detach herself from the physician. "Oh,
thank you, Dr. Pym!" she exclaimed, careful to keep her dry eyes
averted. "I can't tell you what this means!"

The doctor took her by the shoulder and shook his finger at her.
"And if a week from today I do not receive a missive from you or
Mr. Wiggins, stating that you have done as I said, I will personally go to London and deal with young Lady Bushnell!" He nodded to the bailiff, who was standing closer now. "Sir, if you
would send someone to the apothecary in Quilling, I will have a
compound stirred up for Lady Bushnell that will ease her angina.
Good day now."

With a nod and one last uneasy glance at Susan, who was still
sniffing dangerously, he trotted the length of the hall and clam-
bered down the stairs with a velocity surprising in one of his
years. When she heard the front door close, Susan began her own
inspection of the wallpaper.

She was appalled at her behavior; she had never done anything so blatant before. Perhaps some men are simple, she considered. I wouldn't dare attempt such a stratagem with the bailiff.

He seemed to read her mind, which further disconcerted her, because it was not the first time. She was beginning to think that was the problem of dealing with a man who knew women as well as the bailiff did. Now someone like the vicar would be forever in the dark if she attempted subterfuge. But the bailiff was speaking.

"Susan, that was the most . . . the most . . ." Words failed him for a moment. "Don't ever try that on me."

"Why would I do that?" she asked. It was an innocent enough question, and she wondered why her cheeks burned from the asking of it. Can it be that I think it is a useful tool, or is it that something tells me I'll find much better ways of getting what I want out of the bailiff? she considered as her face flamed and he laughed.

She was spared fumbling around any more conversation when Mrs. Skerlong opened the door, her face serious. "Lady Bushnell is this close to sleep now, thanks to that draft from the doctor, but she wants to see you two for a moment." She opened the door wider.

Lady Bushnell's eyes were closed and her face relaxed and calm, likely the result of the sleeping potion. She opened her eyes, patted the bed, and Susan sat down. She held Susan's hand.

"My dear, thank you for putting up with my crotchets this night," she said, her voice low and dreamy.

"I didn't mind a minute of it," Susan said, and meant every word.

Lady Bushnell held up her hand to the bailiff, who grasped it, a half smile on his face. "But now you'll sleep, my lady, and we promise to tiptoe around and not disturb you."

She nodded and closed her eyes. Susan got up to go, then sat down again when Lady Bushnell tightened her grip.

"My dears, I have two favors to ask of you," she said. "Simple things, really." She opened her eyes, as close as she could come to a look of mischief, with the doctor's sleeping powders doing their work.

"Say on, my lady," said the bailiff.

"You and Tim the cowman can get my harpsichord up here sometime tomorrow, and Susan and I will resume our lessons as soon as we have rested a little. Susan, don't sigh and bite your lip like a baby! I wish Hamptons had some backbone!"

The bailiff laughed. "I am certain we can do that. And the other thing, my lady?"

"I want to go to Waterloo," she said in the same conversational tone, but drowsy now, her words elongated. "Do you realize I have been on every major battlefield the army has fought over for the last two decades, except that one? Arrange it, Sergeant Wiggins. I want to see where Charles died."

"Well . . ." He hesitated and she tightened her lips into a straight line and looked daggers at him. "Perhaps when you're better, Lady Bushnell."

"Arrange it," she repeated, then closed her eyes in sleep. Her hand relaxed, and released Susan's fingers.

David closed the door behind them and walked slowly beside Susan. "She is planning a bolt across the Channel to Waterloo, and *we* have to tell her that she's about to be incarcerated at the family estate?" he asked no one in particular as they strolled along as though it were the middle of the afternoon. "Oh, Susan."

Oh, Susan indeed, she thought, her mind foggy with sleep. "And I have bought us a week's time for what? David, she will be so disappointed in us, so betrayed when she ends up on a golden chain of young Lady Bushnell's forging! And all this done out of kindness. Oh, I am provoked." She sniffed back her tears and glared at him. "But I am not going to waste my tears on you, sir! It would be quite useless."

"Quite," he agreed. He steered her to her room and followed her inside. It should have surprised her, but at the sight of her bed she felt her bones start to melt and she forgot about him.

"I am so tired," she said, looking at her pillow almost lovingly.

"So am I," he agreed. "Go to bed, Susan. I'm sure Kate Skerlong will hold our porridge until the noon hour."

She nodded, shucked off her robe, and crawled into bed, too tired to object when the bailiff tucked the covers around her and then sat on the bed. "You need to know something," she began as her eyes closed.

"H'mm?"

He sounded so close, and then she realized that he had flopped back on her bed and was lying draped across it, his feet dangling over the edge. She was so fuddled that it seemed perfectly logical. She wiggled her toes down until they met the resistance of his body outside the covers, then stopped.

"She can't read anymore. She's been fooling us with those letters on her lap," Susan said as she turned onto her side and tucked her legs closer to her, since she couldn't stretch out with the bailiff lying there.

"What?" The bed jiggled as he turned over. She could feel him flop back again, and his voice sounded disgusted. "And here I think I am so clever and take care of her so well! I had no idea."

She opened her eyes and raised up on her elbow so she could see him in the faint light of earliest dawn. "She had me read some of her letters to her while we waited for you to return with Dr. Pym. Oh, David, her son's letter from New Orleans is a study in anguish! Charles was so desperate to not ever command men again, and I know she forced him into it."

"And that is why we got Charles at Waterloo, I suppose," he finished. He reached out and rested his hand on her ankle as it lay outlined by the covers. "She was the warrior and he was not." He patted her ankle.

"I don't want to be alone like that when I am her age, with nothing to comfort me but letters I cannot read," she said, offering no objection when his fingers remained on her ankle. He didn't really need to rub it that way, but it would take too many words to object.

"Well, you could have accepted my offer," he said.

"But I didn't," she reminded him as she closed her eyes. "I read about Jesusa on the withdrawal from Burgos. Oh, David."

His fingers were still then, but remained resting on her ankle. His sigh was so huge she felt it through the mattress.

"I'm sorry," she whispered. "I shouldn't have said anything."

He was silent so long she thought he had fallen asleep, except that his fingers were massaging her ankle again. "Never mind. It was a long time ago."

"Not so long," she said, drowsy again with the rhythm of his fingers.

"Long enough. Jesusa was a wonderful part of my life."

She knew he was near sleep, too, because his voice was slow and heavy. She shifted her foot, wondering if he would let go. He did, but she discovered that she missed his fingers. "Did you love her?" she asked.

He nodded, scooting himself farther onto the bed and raising up on his elbow. "She could love me cross-eyed, Susan," he said frankly. "I cannot begin to express what a relief she was to me after the terror of a battle. I could forget everything but reveille in her arms."

My blushes, she thought. Why is this man so blunt? The gentlemen she was acquainted with would perish with mortification before they would describe a relationship with a woman in such terms. Then again, a woman would never have to wonder what was on David Wiggins' mind. She thought of her own kind—the bows, the simpering, the smirks, the quizzing, the games—and smiled. I could ask this man anything, and he would tell me. He

would even tell me if he loved me, if I asked him. I do not know
if I am that honest. Or that brave.

"Was she pretty?" she asked instead.

Ha lay down again, but he did not touch her. "No, not really," he
said finally, having given the matter some thought. "She was a bit
full-blown to be English-pretty, like you, but her eyes were simply
matchless." He laughed softly. "It is enough to say that I loved her."

"But you did not marry her," Susan pointed out, wondering
where her boldness came from. It was as though I have a stake in
this, she thought, even though I know it cannot be so.

"No." He sat up then and rested himself against the footboard
of her bed, crossing his legs and watching her. "I wanted to. I
even asked little Charlie Bushnell for permission—he was his father's adjutant then—but he only laughed."

His voice sounded hard to her ears. She sat up, too. "How mean
of him!"

The bailiff shrugged. "Maybe not, Susan." He sighed again and
got up, stretching, then went to the window to peer out at the
coming dawn. "Soldiers and camp followers—older than time.
When wars end, they go away to other bivouacs."

"But you have come here," she pointed out, lying down again,
this time on her back, so she could watch him at the window.

"I have." He sat by her again and looked into her eyes so long
that she wanted to squirm, except that they were hip to hip and he
would have felt her nervousness. If nerves it is, she considered.
Nerves never gave me a warm feeling. "And I have made so
many promises to so many Bushnells that here I remain." His
eyes went to the window. "And I am tied by my own wheat. And
now you are here. I cannot leave."

She knew he would kiss her then, and he did, but it was only
the briefest of kisses. "Go to sleep, Susan," he murmured when
his lips were just a little above hers. "And if you think of anything," he said at the door, "share it, please. I'm fresh out of
ideas, and I think the doctor has us over a barrel."

Susan did not see the bailiff again for three days, and she wondered what kept him away. She went quietly about her own duties, practicing on the harpsichord in Lady Bushnell's room as the
widow kept time with her cane on the floor by the bed. She listened to Lady Bushnell's advice, whispered softer now, and took
it, practicing downstairs in the evenings when she wanted to run
to the succession house and watch the bailiff measure, weed, and
record the wheat's progress.

Or it could be that he has no more ideas than I do and cannot bear to see his defeat mirrored in my own eyes, she considered one night over dinner. I could ask Mrs. Skerlong right plainly where he is, she thought, and try not to blush if she winks at me.

"Mrs. Skerlong, where is David?" she asked point-blank, putting down her fork, which had been shifting food from one side of the plate to the other, in imitation of eating. "Sometimes I see a light very late at night in the succession house, and I think I heard him walking to Lady Bushnell's room this morning, but I do not see him."

Mrs. Skerlong, bless her, did not wink or blink or make any remark to tease. She pushed a mugful of tea in front of Susan. "Oh, my dear, 'tis the lambing. Since he will not pension off Ben Rich, and the Welsh lad is but a child, he must be there, too." She smiled at Susan over the rim of her own mug and took a cautious sip. "In the Cotswolds, no farmer's time is his own until March is over." She leaned closer across the table, looking around as though to make sure that Cora was not within earshot. "We women have a joke in the Cotswolds: 'No virtuous farm wife has December babies,'" she said, and laughed at Susan's blank stare. "My dear, it's the rare farmer that gets between his sheets or his wife's legs during March. He belongs to the lambs."

Susan gulped the scalding tea and coughed. "Oh!" she exclaimed as she reached for the water pot and took a healthy swallow. "You must think me such a dunce."

Mrs. Skerlong only smiled. "I am thinking you are learning our ways here. But then comes April, and January babies, if there's time between plowing and plastering fields for fertilizer, and sowing and dipping and shearing come June." She shook her head. "It's a wonder farmers ever plow their own fields, lass."

And this is the life he chooses, Susan thought after Mrs. Skerlong had patted her shoulders and taken up her customary spot by the stove. It is all work, and rhythm of the seasons, and it could be that I feel its pull, too. But right now, I wish I knew what to do about Lady Bushnell.

They finished *Emma* that first afternoon, and then her time was devoted to the letters, putting them in order back to the days in India and on to the final entries as the army moved in triumph over the Pyrenees toward France. She began to copy the letters in a large hand, showing each to the widow until the woman nodded and said. "I can read these. Oh, pray continue."

She was no closer to a solution as the end of the week approached. The vicar, all blushes and fumbling for words, had paid a visit, and she had spent some time closeted with him in the sitting room, seeking his advice. He had none to offer beyond what she feared. "Miss Hampton, I do not see that you or the bailiff have any recourse but to tell young Lady Bushnell how the wind blows here." He almost took her hand, but shied off at the last minute. "She needs the care of relatives."

He was right, of course. She knew it, and surely the bailiff knew it. After an evening of reading to Lady Bushnell, she administered her medicine, stayed to make sure that she took it all, saw her tucked in bed, and went to her own room. She almost went downstairs again, because she knew that all she would do would be to stare at the calendar and cross off another day without an idea. It was worry at its fruitless worst, and she hated it.

She opened the door and stepped back in fright. Someone sat in one of the chairs before the fire. She looked closer. It was the bailiff, and he was asleep, his head nodding forward; he even snored a little. She smiled to herself and closed the door quickly so the light from the hall would not disturb him. Taking off her shoes, she tiptoed across the floor, took up a throw from the foot of her bed and draped it lightly over him as he slept.

She could not go to bed with the bailiff there, so she put a few more coals on the fire, then quietly eased herself into the other chair. With a quick glance at the man, she rested her stockinged feet on the grate and relaxed in the chair, feeling a strange relief at nothing more than his company. He smelled of wool and sweat, and she wondered when he had shaved last. If I had charge of you, she thought as she leaned back and made herself comfortable, at least you would change your linen every day and take time to wash.

She slept in peace and comfort, waking up only when the bailiff covered her with the throw. She jerked awake, then settled quickly as he rested his hand on her arm. She looked at his arm and tried not to gasp, but it escaped her anyway.

"Your arm! And the other one!" she said in dismay, seeing even in the dim firelight the chap, fissures, and cracks running all the way to his elbows. He had pushed up his sleeves, obviously to keep the rough fabric from brushing against what must be painful.

"It comes with lambing," he said, "and washing my arms over and over in cold water and wind. The cure is lanolin, which I will apply after I am in my own bed and not touching anything." He grinned at her expression. "Of course, if I turn over too fast, I slide right out of bed. Don't stare like that! They'll be better in a month or so when the lambs are bonking around in the pasture."

She settled lower in the chair and stared into the fire again. "Do you come to tell me that you have no solution, either?"

He was a long time answering. "I come to tell you that I wrote to young Lady Bushnell and requested an audience Friday morning in London." He sighed heavily. "And I wrote Dr. Pym. My underbailiff and his new bride have returned, and I can leave him in charge while I take the mail coach."

"Then I am coming, too," she said.

"To resign?"

She glared at him, hot words on her lips, but she could not deliver them because the bailiff looked so tired. "Of course not, David," she said softly. "Perhaps if she sees that the two of us could take care of her mother-in-law, she would be content to let well enough alone. Mrs. Skerlong says that young Lady Bushnell is about to remarry. Surely she does not need the added distraction of a frail mother-in-law."

The bailiff nodded. "I'd like your company. Two may be better than one in this matter." He smiled at her. "Actually, that was why I came here—to ask you just that. And here I was, snoring away and smelling up your room."

"Never mind," she said, sleepy now, relieved to be in the bailiff's presence, and not overly troubled by the odor of hard work. "Yes. Let us go to London and attempt this."

"Good then. I will take the news to Lady Bushnell first thing in the morning, and tell her what we have to do and why. I think she will bear it well enough, if she knows that we are doing our best to keep her here. Then we can catch the midmorning mail coach."

Susan shook her head. "The first thing you will do is wash, and then visit Lady Bushnell."

"Am I pretty rank?" he said and grinned at her.

"You are disgusting," she assured him. "If this is how a whole army of you smelled in Spain, I wonder that you even needed muskets to mow down the enemy."

"They smelled worse, plus garlic," he said as he rose and went to the door. "Good night, Susan dear. Pack a bag and be ready to go to London in the morning. I do not know that we will succeed, but it won't be said that we didn't try."

Chapter Fifteen

 ℰ

Not until Susan sat herself on the mail coach and rested her traveling boots on the straw underfoot did she really believe that they were actually on their way to plead Lady Bushnell's cause. The bailiff sat close beside her, wedged in so tight that he had to turn a little sideways and put his arm around her to steady himself.

She couldn't notice any discomfort on his face, but she was almost too shy to look at him. It was one thing to enjoy his presence from a chair by the fire, and quite another to have him so close that his breath was warm on her neck. They were like whelks in a basket.

Come now, Susan, what is your objection? she asked herself as the coach picked up speed. You know that you care for him, even though it is not the wisest thing you ever did, and hopefully will soon pass. You know how hungry you were for the sight of him during the past few days, and here he is now, practically sitting on you.

She looked at the bailiff then, and discovered that he was watching her, too, his gaze steady and quite calm. His eyes are so brown, she thought, and I did not notice that many freckles before. I wonder if he burns in the summer. She suddenly wanted to kiss him as he had kissed her that one time on the way across the stable yard, and decide for herself if that was merely beginner's luck on her part.

And that is my objection to this situation, she thought, permitting honesty to shoulder out artifice, as it did more and more these days. I want to kiss him and do much more that I've never done, and there are all these dratted passengers who refuse to go away and let me get at my ruin. She permitted herself a little sigh. As my descent into vulgarity does not yet include exhibitions, I will change my thoughts and hope that this irritating warmth will recede and let me breathe.

Her return to normality was aided by the bailiff, or so she thought. He winced when the toddler hugged tight in his mother's arms, kicked out and caught him in the small of the back, forcing him even closer to her. "I trust that you can tell I bathed," he whispered, hardly lover's talk.

She could tell, right down to the carbolic soap he used and the scent of lanolin on his arms. He was so close she thought she could even smell the singe marking the flatiron tip printed on his shirt beside his neckcloth.

"See there, you've singed your shirt," she scolded, her words as prosaic as his.

He shrugged, which made her even more aware of his well-muscled arm around her shoulders and slipping down her back a bit as he grasped the handgrip beside her. "I'm not much of a housewife," he said. He looked around at the other inmates of the mail coach, and she wondered for the smallest moment if he wanted them gone, too.

"Well, I could have done it for you," she whispered back, leaning toward him slightly as the toddler aimed another kick into the bailiff which propelled his chest into her face.

"Sorry, Susan," he said with a frown over his shoulder and a slight shift away from her. "Didn't mean for you to eat my buttons." He tried again. "You've added ironing to your catalog of skills now?"

She nodded, deciding silently that even with a blindfold on her eyes, she would probably be able to pick out that certain odor of carbolic, singe, and David in a roomful of bailiffs. "Cora is even now teaching me how to do ruffles."

"Which I will never require," he added.

"Thank God for that," she said quickly, without thinking how intimate it sounded, how permanent. "I am not doing at all well with ruffles."

He chuckled, and the look on his face changed enough for her to wonder what it was she said that seemed to be settling his countenance into such great contentment. He raised his hand up behind her back and twirled one of her loosening curls into a corkscrew on his finger. "I think your pins are coming out."

"Drat!" she exclaimed, unable to move to do anything about it. "Perhaps it would help if you did not play with my hair," she said, sharper than she intended. The bailiff promptly slid the curl from his finger and settled his arm more comfortably on her shoulder. He leaned back as far as he could, closed his eyes, and was soon asleep.

A man must be tired to sleep in a mail coach, she decided an hour later as the bailiff showed no signs of waking. When the coach stopped to let off a passenger, he settled his head against her breast and slumbered on. I suppose you can sleep anywhere, she thought, remembering Lady Bushnell's letters and the dreadful campaign from Burgos to Lisbon. Did you dream of Jesusa then, and what are you dreaming now? She decided it was a pleasant dream, because his free arm came around her waist and rested in her lap. She looked at the clergyman seated across from them, but he only nodded at her. Oh, dear, I am certain he thinks we are married, she thought.

Well, what of it? she told herself as her eyes began to close, too. I am tired, and I have worried enough for ten lady's companions this past week. She closed her eyes and rested her cheek against the bailiff's hair. He murmured something into her breast and his arm tightened around her waist.

She dreamt then, and it was a naughty dream, with the bailiff figuring prominently in it in considerably more detail than the evasive Professor Fowler ever discussed in his silly book. She was feeling much too dreadfully warm again for it to be a dream, so she opened her eyes and looked down. The bailiff still slept—she could tell by his even breathing—but he had worked his hand inside her cloak and it was cupping her breast in a most alarming fashion that she did not wish to stop. And what are you dreaming, sir? she asked herself, and was hard put to feel anything but a most curious mixture of amusement and incredible desire.

It was such a wonderful, drowsy feeling, especially when he began to run his thumb lightly across her bodice front. My goodness, she thought as the warmth spread, but I don't suppose I ever considered my nipples as anything more exciting than items to be carefully covered when wearing light frocks. This puts a new light on matters.

It won't do, she told herself at last. If he continues this, the other passengers will be vastly distracted when I unbutton my bodice, raise my skirts and throw myself on the mail coach floor. The thought made her giggle, and the bailiff woke up, removed his hand, and had the good grace to blush a shade somewhere between crimson and bonfire red.

"Susan, I do beg your pardon," he whispered, his hand at his side now. He straightened up and moved away, careful to keep his army overcoat tight about him.

She thought he wasn't going to look at her, but after a few minutes, he relaxed, shook his head, and glanced in her direction.

"Well, if you ever had any doubts, I like women," he whispered. "Heartiest apologies."

"Accepted," she whispered back.

He didn't say anything else, and understanding his embarrassment, Susan did not press him. She was content enough to gaze out the window at the growing dark and wonder at herself. *I cannot blame Mama or Aunt Louisa,* she admitted, considering her upbringing. *I was raised to be a pattern card of propriety.* She reflected further; *that had not changed. Each time the vicar visited her, she had no urge to kiss him, or even rest her hand on his shoulder. And now here is the bailiff, a man decidedly unacceptable, and I want to kiss him and do something—anything—to relieve this edgy feeling I have. Strange, indeed. I will watch for Wambley and think of dinner, instead.*

At Wambley, which appeared about as soon as full dark, Susan had good cause to think well again of the bailiff. She remembered Wambley from the nooning stop on her way to the Cotswolds, and as they all left the mail coach in a rush for dinner, she girded her loins for another struggle in the Sword and Shield. *I will plead for nothing more than soup and tea,* she told herself, remembering her complete inability to summon even that much from the overworked public room staff at the busy coach stop.

In the taproom crowded with ravenous travelers, David Wiggins compensated entirely for his naptime lapse on the coach. As Susan prepared to jump up and down if she had to, to attract attention over much taller heads, the bailiff nodded, gestured, and then ushered her to a table that appeared almost miraculously as the crowd parted like the Red Sea.

"However did you do that?" she whispered as a potboy scurried toward them, wiping his hands on his apron.

The bailiff smiled and leaned closer. "You could do it, too, if you were a foot taller and a former sergeant major. Bring us some soup, bread, cheese, and tea," he ordered the potboy. "If you're really quick, there'll be some extra coins just between you and me." The boy grinned at the bailiff and hurried toward the kitchen, oblivious to the calls of the other mail coach riders.

They ate and even had time for a brief stroll about the inn yard before the other passengers emerged from the taproom. It was a quiet walk, neither of them saying anything, until Susan stopped and looked up at the bailiff's outline in the moonlit darkness.

"I can't help it," she said, the words tumbling out. "I must worry. Suppose we are unsuccessful? Suppose young Lady Bush-

nell insists that her mother-in-law come to the home estate?" She
tucked her arm more snugly into the crook of the bailiff's elbow.

"Well, then, you will be looking for another position, and I will
have to take my Waterloo wheat somewhere else that needs a
bailiff," he replied. He sighed. "I can't see the Bushnells keeping
anyone at Quilling Manor, once the old lady is forced to capitu-
late. I'd love to buy it, to be sure, but I have no money for that
kind of purchase."

Somehow, in all her worrying about Lady Bushnell, she hadn't
considered the full effect on the bailiff. "And you'll have to *leave*
Quilling Manor?" she asked, but it was more of a statement.

He nodded. "I've received an offer of a similar position near
Gloucester, but there's no succession house, and I don't think the
owner is inclined toward experimentation." He patted her hand.
"We just have to convince young Lady B." He released his grip
on her. "Of course, any year now, our good parson might get up
the nerve to make you an offer on a leaky vicarage and all the
church mice you could catch, which would assure you a future."

She laughed. "I can't count on that happening in this century,"
she said. "He still isn't brave enough to look in my direction for
more than ten seconds at a time!" And heaven knows he's never
kissed me as you have, or sat in my bedroom chatting, or put his
hands anywhere they don't belong. I don't think it would ever
occur to him, and more's the pity. She looked at the bailiff, and
the smile that made his brown eyes dance, even in the half light of
the inn yard. "And don't remind me of your proposal!"

"I wouldn't dream of it," he assured her. "It would have been a
bad idea, anyway, considering that there would be both of us with
no income." He looked then at the coachman, who was gesturing
toward the mail coach like a hen after chickens. "Come on,
Susan. We'd hate to miss a minute of our excursion to London."

The mail coach was much emptier after Wambley, with other
passengers remaining behind to make connections further south.
They had the entire seat to themselves, and the same parson
seated opposite who continued to smile benignly at them. He
burped quietly several times—a natural consequence of a rushed
meal at the Sword and Shield—then sighed himself to sleep like
an old dog before a winter hearth.

"Put your head on my lap, Susan," the bailiff said as they
started off. "No telling how long before we are sandwiched in
here again."

"I shouldn't," she protested, even as she swung her legs up on
the seat and did as he said.

"If we're going to talk about *shouldn'ts*, you should still be in London under your father's care," he said mildly, resting his hand on her shoulder.

In a few minutes his hand felt heavier and heavier, and she knew he slept again. I wish I could sleep anywhere, she grumbled to herself as she unfastened one hook on her skirt and settled her cloak around her. Perhaps I shall count sheep.

Sheep proved to be unprofitable, because they only reminded her of Ben Rich, and the Welsh boy, and then lanolin, and then David Wiggins, and then back to the problem of Lady Bushnell. You are all so complicated, she thought as she ordered her eyes to stay shut. David, you promise good behavior to Lady Bushnell for ever and ever; you promise Lord Bushnell that you will always keep an eye on her. And young Laby B surely promised her husband, the unfortunate Charles, that she would always take good care of his mother, even if good care is too much care.

But I have promised nobody anything, she considered, and surprised herself by beginning to cry. I'm not bound to anyone by any promises, she told herself through her tears and sniffles. I could leave tomorrow and no one could claim me, or hold me to a mark. She sniffed back the rest of her tears, determined not to wallow in self-pity.

"Oh, Susan, don't cry," the bailiff whispered as he handed her a handkerchief. It smelled of lanolin, and she sobbed harder. "You're a silly widget, did you know?"

"I thought you were asleep," she whispered back and then blew her nose. "I'm feeling sorry for myself, that's all," she explained in hushed tones, her eyes on the parson as she gathered her dignity about her.

She felt him chuckle. "Well, go ahead and cry then, Suzie. My overcoat's had worse on it than tears, I assure you."

He was still then, resting his hand in the warmth of her neck this time. She felt herself relaxing by degrees, until she heard the parson stir as he leaned forward.

"Is she all right?" he whispered to the bailiff.

"She'll do," he replied. "She gets this way sometimes."

I do not! she wanted to protest, but she had the good sense to lie quiet.

"In the family way?" the parson inquired.

She stiffened, felt herself blush from head to toe, then turned her face against the bailiff's thigh so she wouldn't laugh out loud.

"No, I don't think so," the bailiff said, his voice remarkably steady, considering how stiff his own leg was just then. "You know the ladies, sir, and how they are sometimes."

That satisfied the parson. In another moment he snored. Susan rested her cheek against the bailiff's leg again. " 'You know the ladies,' " she mimicked. "No, how *are* we sometimes, Mr. Wiggins?"

"Shut up, Suzie," he whispered, and she could hear the laughter in his voice. Amazingly reassured by his unloverlike endearment, she slept.

London at two in the morning in front of a public house was different from London at two in the morning after a ball in the Mayfair district, she decided as she stood beside David Wiggins and waited for the coachman to hand down her bandbox. The inn yard was busy with farmers rattling in from the country, their wagons filled with produce and poultry for the great London markets. A yawning crofter's lad maneuvered a hog past her as she leaped closer to the bailiff. There by the edge of the lamplight sat a beggar with no legs, his army overcoat bunched tight around him against the chill that rose like the tenth plague off the docks. A prostitute stood closer to the inn door, her hair wild and matted from a night's hard work. She eyed the bailiff and started in his direction until Susan grabbed his arm and glared at her.

"I think I can protect myself," David assured her, a smile in his eyes. "Not exactly your part of London, is it?"

Susan shook her head, and did not relinquish her grip on the bailiff. "I wonder how many diseases she has?"

"More than you could ever imagine," he whispered back. "Now be nice. Everyone has to earn a living, some by their wits, some on their back."

How true that is, she thought as she waited for him to find a hackney. His presence seemed to command less respect in the London inn yard than it had at Wambley. He was shouldered away from the first two hackneys to come along by a drunken company of beau-nasties, who told him to stand back from his betters. The third hackney driver to happen along a half hour later insisted on seeing the inside of David's wallet before he would take them anywhere farther than three or four blocks. "Ye cant's be too careful-like in this neighborhood," the jehu assured them as he motioned them in. He looked significantly at the veteran begging by the inn. "I sees plenty of sorry heroes and scaggy hoors. Beggin' your pardon, miss."

They rode in silence through streets, which grew less crowded the farther they went from the unrefined, earnest heart of the city. The streets looked familiar now. My goodness, she thought as she learned against the bailiff in her exhaustion, was it only two months ago that I braved ice and snow on this street to find an employment agency?

They stopped then in front of the Steinman Agency, dark now except for a lamp glowing in an upstairs window. "We'll stay the night here," David said as he helped her down, then paid the driver. "Joel's expecting us." He smiled at the look of surprise she knew was on her face. "I wrote him, too. My dear, remember this piece of advice: if you're ever lucky enough to save someone's life, you can always use him in outrageous ways!"

So she was smiling, too, when the door opened on Joel Steinman in nightshirt, robe, and cap. He was followed closely by his mother, who took her by the arm and tugged her inside, whisking her upstairs while the men chatted below.

"A little mulled wine will be just the thing," Mrs. Steinman said as she helped Susan from her clothes and into her nightgown. "You get in bed, and I'll hand it to you. Can you feel the warming pan?"

She could, and between the warmth in her toes and the wine that mellowed its way down her throat, she could have purred with contentment. In a stupefying trance of huge comfort, she handed back the goblet, rested her feet on the towel-covered warming pan and closed her eyes.

Susan had scarcely shut her eyes before it was time to open them again, this time at the gentle insistence of Mrs. Steinman, who called her *leibchen* and *bubeleh* and offered the further enticement of hot chocolate passed several times under her nose. She sat up slowly in the feather bed that threatened to pull her under again, gripping the brass bars to prevent a return to the horizontal state. The chocolate was followed by a forced feeding of enough little pastry puffs to get her on her feet and washing herself with wonderful hot water and lavender soap so creamy it was almost sinful. She was humming as she followed a servant to the breakfast room.

"Ah, excellent!" Joel Steinman said as he dabbed at his mouth with a napkin and rose to his feet. "You certainly look better early in the morning than David Wiggins does!"

The bailiff turned around from his perusal of food at the side table and nodded to her. "Smells better, too." He looked at the clock on the mantel. "We're promised at Lady Bushnell's in an hour, Susan."

She nodded and joined him at the sideboard, searching for more of those same little pastries that had revived her in bed. David had the last three on his plate, so she took one of his without any compunction, winked at him, and sat down.

"I thrashed a man once for stealing from my plate," the bailiff commented as he sat beside her.

She responded by popping the pastry in her mouth. "You would never do me an injury," she said, her mouth full.

"No, never an injury," he agreed, smiled at some secret thought of his own, then tackled his own breakfast. He glanced at her sideways. "Although I might be tempted to . . ."

"To what?" she asked.

He smiled that slow smile that was starting to bother her on a regular basis. "Oh, just that I might be tempted to. Eat your breakfast, Suzie."

I should worry when men smile like that, Susan thought. She looked at her own plate, but was distracted by Joel Steinman, who stood beside her chair, then with a flourish, set a present on the table before her.

"Oh, my!" she said, dropping her fork and picking up the package. "Is it in my contract that I am to expect presents from my employment agent? Perhaps I should have read the small words at the bottom. Who knows what else I have promised?" she teased as she opened the package. She stared dubiously at the rectangular object in her hand. "I would like to be delighted, but please tell me what it is, sir."

Steinman took the object from her hand and set it on the table. With the casual air of someone who had been practicing, he rested his palm on top, and reached down with his fingers to wind the back. He released the object, detached the metal spindle and sat back in triumph over his one-handed efforts. "This, Miss Hampton, is a metronome. They are new from Germany and Mamele found it for you."

As the spindle ticked back and forth in strict rhythm, Steinman jiggled a little weight and it ticked faster. "It is to regulate your piano playing," he explained when she continued to stare at it. As he leaned closer to her, Susan was amused to observe that the bailiff suddenly leaned closer, too, in a manner that she could only consider proprietary. "Your letter about Lady Bushnell's tyranny at the piano was so anguished that I knew I had to make amends," Steinman told her. "Perhaps I feel I owe you an apology for foisting that job upon you."

"You owe me no apologies, Mr. Steinman," she said quietly. "It's turning out to be the best thing that ever happened to me."

"Even if we lose it all after our interview this morning?" the bailiff asked, and he sounded peevish.

Are you jealous, sir? she thought in wicked delight. The thought was followed immediately by a most monumental surge of love for the bailiff that went beyond any emotion she had ever experienced before in her life. It left her limp inside; she could only stare at the metronome, because she knew that if she turned her head to even look at David Wiggins, she would cry, or kiss him, or crawl into his lap, or maybe do all three at once. She forced herself to concentrate on what Steinman was saying.

"If it comes to that, Miss Hampton, I must tell you that I have obtained that job for you with the widow and her two daughters. It only waits an interview, and let me assure you that I have told her you walk on water."

"What? What?" she asked. "Oh, yes! Well . . . my goodness."

Steinman grinned at her and stopped the metronome. "You are supposed to tell me 'thank you' prettily for my exertions on your behalf, and not bumble about."

"Thank you," she said, feeling as miserable now as she had felt exhilarated only seconds before. If we do not succeed this morning, I will have no choice but to accept Mr. Steinman's dratted job. I will never see David Wiggins again. She rose to her feet so quickly that both men on either side of her sat back in surprise. "Hurry up, David! We can't be late!"

As they walked to the Bushnell town house, Susan knew she should have engaged in some of that light patter for which the Hamptons were so famous, but for the life of her, she couldn't think of a thing to say. In silence she berated herself for considering for even a moment that just because he was a bailiff, she was proof against him, no matter what Mrs. Skerlong said. I have fallen in love with a bastard Welshman who was a poacher and a sneak thief and a sergeant and now a bailiff. He is of a social class so far removed from my own that I could grow dizzy contemplating the chasm between us, if I allowed myself to. She hurried along, telling herself that the feeling just had to pass, and the sooner the better. I might as well wish away the moon and the tide, she thought, limp again with the anguish of loving the bailiff.

I have been feeling this all along, she thought, without even knowing what the feeling was. Something in the way he had leaned toward her so protectively—so instinctively!—when Joel Steinman made her an innocent gift, must have been the spark that finally lit the tinder. It was as though she knew at that moment that David Wiggins would always protect her, and take care of her, and love her more than himself. The reality of it took her breath away and she stopped and stared at him on the crowded sidewalk.

"Susan?" he asked, looking down at her in alarm. "Are you all right?"

I will never be the same again, she thought. I feel empty and full at the same time, and you ask me if I am all right? "I'm fine," she lied, and continued at her brisk pace.

It still chafed her to take those steps down to the servants' entrance, but she swallowed her pride and followed the bailiff. I wonder if I can find anything sensible to say to young Lady Bushnell, she considered as she stood behind the bailiff in the narrow passageway and admired the broadness of his shoulders. My concern for old Lady B pales beside what I am feeling now about me and David.

After time for a cup of tea that tasted to her like gall and wormwood, the butler showed them into the bookroom. She spent the time in silence, staring at her hands and looking up only once or twice to see the bailiff standing before the cold hearth, his back to her. What are you thinking, sir? she asked herself. Are you wondering at my sudden strangeness, or are you thinking what you will say to Lady Bushnell?

"Don't worry, Susan," he said quietly, and she wondered again at his ability to read her.

Her unprofitable meanderings were relieved by the appearance of Lady Bushnell, who swept into the room, looking almost as disordered as Susan felt, followed by a thin woman in black with a tape measure around her neck, and a man with a sheaf of papers that threatened to spill from his grasp.

"Stop!" Lady Bushnell commanded, raising her hand to the people who almost trampled on her heels. The bailiff turned around in surprise, startled by the circus behind her. Perhaps you were not thinking of Lady Bushnell, Susan considered as she watched him. Then what, sir?

"Madam, how can I finish fitting your wedding gown if you dart about like a minnow?"

"Madam, I must know if you want hothouse plants or spring blossoms for the ballroom. Colonel March says he is allergic to pussy willows, phlox, and lilies. I really must know! The suspense is killing me!" He waved the papers to cool himself, and they fluttered down like leaves from an autumn tree.

With a sigh, Lady Bushnell sat down and glared at the modiste and florist. "Take yourselves off for five minutes!" she said through clenched teeth. The modiste glared right back, but the florist took her arm and pulled her from the room, closing the door behind him with an audible click.

"Colonel March doesn't much care for daisies, either," David said from his place by the hearth. "Lady Bushnell, I had no idea that you were marrying *my* Colonel March. Congratulations!"

Oh, but you have a way with women, Susan thought as she watched Lady Bushnell visibly collect herself and relax ever so slightly.

"He is the best, isn't he?" she said quietly as she patted the chair beside her. "Sergeant Wiggins, you remind me how lucky I am." She smiled. "Can you not stay around here for two weeks and organize this . . . this . . . balloon ascension I seem to find myself trapped in the middle of?"

He grinned back and relaxed in that casual way of his that seemed to fill Susan's entire vision. "You'll manage, Lady Bushnell. Just tell them all to go to hell like your mother-in-law would, and suit yourself."

She nodded, the picture of peace again. "Perhaps I shall. What brings the two of you here? Please tell me it is good news for I need some."

It was not good news, and the bailiff minced no words in telling her. He was still describing Lady Bushnell's lapse when the door opened and Colonel March came in. The bailiff leaped to his feet from force of habit, and Susan thought for a second that he was going to salute the slender little man dressed impeccably in black. No uniform was necessary; this was a man used to leading armies.

He smiled at the bailiff, and to David's momentary confusion, extended his hand. "Come, Sergeant, and let us shake. You are a civilian now, and I am soon to become one."

The men shook hands. "Best of good wishes to you, sir," David said.

The colonel sat beside his fiancée, took her hand in his own and kissed it. "My dear, it is done." He patted his breast pocket. "A special license. What do you say we abandon all these preparations that seem to be taking on a life of their own and elope?"

She turned shocked eyes on the colonel. "I could never, Edwin!" she exclaimed, then allowed herself a squeeze of his hand. "I own that it is tempting." She indicated the bailiff. "And now David Wiggins brings us glum tidings of Mother. Tell Edwin what you have told me, Sergeant," she said.

Patiently David repeated the catalog of Lady Bushnell's troubles for the benefit of the colonel. "The doctor insisted that I tell you, 'else he would." He hesitated, less sure of himself. "And he insisted that it was time now to gather Lady Bushnell to the home estate. He feels this is the beginning of her final illness."

There was a long silence. "Then we must," said young Lady Bushnell finally with a sigh. "I promised poor Charlie."

David cleared his throat. "My lady, Miss Hampton and I have come here to plead the case that she be allowed to maintain her independence at Quilling."

The widow shook her head. "You know it cannot be, Sergeant. She is practically a national treasure, and people would say that I had neglected my duty to all Waterloo heroes and the Peninsula army, too! No, Sergeant. You were right to come and tell us. We need only make arrangements to move her to Bushnell, where she can be watched night and day." She paused and her expression grew petulant. "Why is it that troubles always come bounding after one another like jugglers? We had so hoped for two weeks in Paris . . ." Her voice trailed off and she looked at her fiancé. "Edwin, I am provoked, but I will do my duty."

"My lady, Miss Hampton and I are here to request that we be allowed to continue her care at Quilling," David said. "You, of all people, know how independent she is. It would drive her downhill even faster to give up her self-reliance. Miss Hampton and I will . . ."

"Mr. Wiggins, please," Lady Bushnell interrupted. "You know you have not time for the kind of work she will require." Her eyes were kind as she regarded him. "I was raised in the Cotswolds myself, Sergeant, and I see in you that spring exhaustion that all bailiffs have. And landowners. I think of my own father." She glanced at his hands. "I look at your hands, and I know that if the colonel demanded that you remove your coat and roll up your sleeves, we would see your chapped arms. You're spending your days and nights with the sheep and I know it. Suppose Mother really needed you. Where would you be?"

David got to his feet and walked to the window and back. "Madam, that is where Miss Hampton comes in. She has proven to be a highly reliable lady's companion—better than we had any reason to hope for, considering her age . . ."

The colonel interrupted this time. "And there's her problem, Sergeant, I am sure."

"Oh, I am reliable," Susan interrupted, speaking up for the first time.

The colonel smiled at her, but shook his head. "My dear Miss Hampton, I do not question your reliability, but your pretty face! How long before some young man snatches you away?" He paused a moment, as though wondering if to continue, but forged ahead anyway. "For all that your father is Sir Rodney Hampton, I feel certain you will not remain above another month or two in that place!"

"We've already heard that the vicar is interested," Lady Bushnell interjected. "No, Miss Hampton, we need two people who would never leave the place and disrupt my mother's continuity yet again. The bailiff is far too busy, and I fear you will not stick, no matter how earnest your good intentions." She looked at the bailiff again. "Sergeant, we must make arrangements. Colonel March and I have already discussed this eventuality, and he is willing to offer you a place. Of course, you will not be a bailiff right away, but in time, you can work up to it."

David said nothing, but only looked at Susan, as though he wanted her to solve his problem. I have no solution, she thought as she stared back, her mind in turmoil. We have failed. You must start over, and what will become of your Waterloo wheat?

"Miss Hampton, you need not fear unemployment," Lady Bushnell was saying. "I was talking to Mr. Steinman only this week about hiring some more servants, and he told me of a wonderful offer for your services with a widow and two daughters." She paused, and her tone became more discreet. "Of course, I am certain that you might wish at any time to return to the protection of your father." She hesitated. "Such as it is."

"Or there is always the vicar," teased the colonel, patting the marriage license in his pocket.

In desperation, Susan leaped to her feet, too, and went to stand beside the bailiff. Precious little good this has done, she thought as she glanced at him. We have lost, and a grand old lady is to be ripped from her independence and sent to a certain, smothering death. "You do not understand my constancy," she murmured. "I want to do this for Lady Bushnell, and I know that I can."

"My dear, all we have are your good intentions!" said Lady Bushnell, her voice rising now. "To end this pointless discussion, I don't scruple to add that Hamptons are not known for constancy!"

It was an ugly phrase and it hung in the air like a bad smell. Susan took a step back under the pressure of it, but could only acknowledge the truth of what Lady Bushnell was saying. *Again my father's reputation has ruined my good efforts,* she thought. *Well, I will not have it anymore.*

The solution came to her as she stood there beside the bailiff. She didn't know why it hadn't occurred to her sooner, and she permitted herself a smile—the only one in the room just then. *I will be thought three parts lunatic by everyone who knows me,* she considered as she quickly and coolly weighed the advantages and disadvantages. *Here I go,* she thought as she put her arm through David's suddenly. He tensed, but to her relief, did not back away from her. She took a deep breath.

"David, we have not been entirely honest with Lady Bushnell, have we?" she asked, striving for just that certain coquettish modesty she remembered as a fixture with her husband-hunting cousins.

"We haven't?" he asked, his eyes wide for only a moment. To her infinite relief, she discovered that she had not underestimated David Wiggins. His former careers of felony, poachery, and varying degrees of larceny had fully developed his quickness of mind in chancey situations. Her toes almost curled with pleasure as he sighed, and tightened his grip on her arm. "No, we have not, Lady Bushnell," he said with a sorrowful shake of his head. He looked at her then, almost as expectant as the others, but only she could see his face, so it didn't matter.

"No, we have not," she declared firmly, with what she hoped was just the right touch of embarrassment. "Lady Bushnell, I think I know what will change your mind, and we have been a little shy to admit it. I will most assuredly be constant about Quilling. You see, David Wiggins proposed to me, and I have decided to accept him."

Chapter Sixteen

Susan could not help wincing at the intake of breath from three people in the room. The bailiff staggered back a few steps, but did not relinquish his grip upon her. His face turned amazingly white and she thought for one desperate moment that she was going to have to guide him to a chair and push his head down between his knees. She was almost afraid to look at Lady Bushnell and Colonel March and speculate what they were making of the bailiff's reaction, but to her relief, they were staring at each other.

"I . . . I guess I was just a little shy about mentioning it," David said after several deep breaths of his own.

His words came out in an adolescent squeak that almost made her giggle, but she recovered quickly enough when the bailiff released her hand and put his arm around her waist instead, gripping her so tight that she feared for her ribs.

"My lady, when we're married, we'll be quite able to maintain our care of Lady Bushnell," the bailiff continued, his voice in its normal register now. "I have a house there, of course, but it's just as easy for me to move into the manor with Suzie. She's only a few doors down from Lady Bushnell."

Uncertain of what to make of Lady Bushnell's silence, Susan braved another look in that direction. Colonel March was grinning from ear to ear, but the widow was as white as the bailiff. "We . . . we think it's an admirable solution to your problem, my lady," Susan stammered.

"I think you have lost your mind, Miss Hampton, and I don't mind telling you!" snapped Lady Bushnell.

"Oh, see here now, Eliza!" exclaimed Colonel March. "Miss Hampton seems a sensible chit, and I can personally testify that Sergeant Wiggins is the very man I'd want at my back in good times or crises."

"Edwin, we are talking about marriage, not war!"

"Funny, so was I, my dear," the colonel said, unruffled by his lady love's high-pitched agitation. "Miss Hampton appears to know her mind."

But Lady Bushnell would not be placated. "Miss Hampton, I cannot imagine you so dead to propriety that you would even for the tiniest moment consider a marriage to a man so socially beneath you! Do you *know* his background?"

"He has told me," Susan said quietly. "I have no doubts that despite our very different circumstances, we are quite well suited to each other. And didn't you just say something about my ramshackle father?" she added, trying, but just not quite concealing, the edge to her words. "Perhaps I will be coming up in the world with this marriage, my lady."

"Miss Hampton, don't try me! I suppose you have told your father about this?" she asked, the sarcasm unmistakable in her voice. "Even Sir Rodney must have his limits."

"I have not told him yet," Susan murmured. "His reaction does not interest me one way or the other, my lady. I am over twenty-one and I love David Wiggins, and I think that's about all there is to it. And I believe the issue here is continuity of care for your mother, which we are quite able to provide, especially now."

Lady Bushnell opened her mouth for more argument, but the bookroom door banged open just then and the housekeeper burst in.

"My lady, this will not wait another minute! The invitations have arrived with an error in your name! Your secretary cannot find the invoice for the champagne and the vintner is threatening to take it all back! The chef tells me that unless the pastry cook stops humming the same nasty little song over and over again, he will resign! And there are twelve for dinner! Twelve!" she concluded, drawing out the word and giving it the worth of three syllables.

The door opened wider to reveal the florist fanning himself more vigorously with his few sheets of remaining paper and the modiste coming at him with the tape measure looped ominously. And jumping up and down behind them all was a little man who spoke only French.

The bailiff released his grip on Susan, crossed the room with some long strides, and said a few pithy words to the mob outside before he shut the door on them. He turned to Lady Bushnell. "My lady, you have too much on your plate right now to have to worry about your mother-in-law, as well," he said firmly, in what Susan was beginning to recognize as his official sergeant major's voice. "Suzie and I will manage fine with her, and while it may not be a marriage made in an aristocrat's heaven, we have every intention of being most successful at it."

Colonel March nodded and gathered his sweetheart to his bosom again, where she began to sob. "My love, she'll be in excellent hands, and it's one less matter to concern yourself with right now." He winked at the bailiff. "We can depend upon these two, especially if Miss Hampton marries the bailiff. How steady can you get?"

After another moment's melancholy and a series of deep sniffles, and a good blow into her fiancé's handkerchief, Lady Bushnell looked at the bailiff. "For this summer only," she said, "and then we will see!"

"We'll begin the banns next Sunday," David said.

"Not good enough," Lady Bushnell said, alert again. "That will take almost a month, and suppose something happens to my mother-in-law before then while March and I are cavorting in France?"

"Really, Eliza," the colonel protested, his face pink. "We are hardly cavorters!"

"Speak for yourself, Edwin," she said. "I will not have busybodies in England saying I was romping about while my mother-in-law—a national treasure, I will remind you—was under the dubious care of a sergeant and a . . . a Hampton! No, you will marry at once, or this is off."

The bailiff blinked. "I can purchase a license in our parish after we return, and . . ."

"No, not soon enough," the woman insisted. "I want to see you two leg-shackled before another day passes!"

It was the bailiff's turn to blush. "My lady, I cannot begin to afford a special license. We'll return to Quilling and get a regular license. It'll just be a matter of a week . . ."

"No," she said, sounding remarkably like her mother-in-law.

The colonel coughed to attract her attention. "My dear, I think we could make a wedding present of a special license to these two." He touched his pocket again. "I know all about getting these things now, and if the sergeant will come with me, I am certain we can accomplish this. Of course, as it is already nearly noon, we will have to defer the actual event until tomorrow morning. What do you say, Sergeant?" he asked, turning to the bailiff.

If you're going to back out, now is the time, Susan thought. I know I am not. Let us see if you really meant that proposal two months ago.

"Very well, sir," the bailiff said. "I'll do it on the condition that we can be allowed to pay you back someday when we can afford it."

"Agreed," the colonel said. "Wait here while I steer my dear Lady Bushnell past the hornet's nest outside this door."

The door closed behind them. There was a momentary increase in the volume of misery in the hall, which was stopped by a few emphatic words from the colonel. The voices ceased, and the room was quiet again.

The bailiff remained with his back to her for a few moments. "Collecting our thoughts, are we?" Susan asked finally when the humor of the whole thing grew too piquant to resist.

He laughed then, turned around, his eyes bright, and came toward her. She thought he would kiss her, but instead, he took her by the elbow and walked her to the window, where they both stood, looking out. His arm went around her waist, and he tucked his hand familiarly into her waistband, as though afraid she would try to get away.

"You must tell me something, Susan," he said after a longish time regarding a gardener pruning an elm across the street.

"Anything, David," she said, putting her arm around him. "There's nothing you can't ask me."

"I know, and that's the beauty of it," he said. "Did you do this because you want to help Lady Bushnell to an extreme degree unimaginable, or because you really mean it?"

She let go of him and stepped away, and he was forced to relinquish his grip on her waistband. Pushing against his arms, she backed him up to the wall as he grinned and let her lead him around. "You are dense, David, so dense. Lady Bushnell has only recently reminded me that I am a Hampton," she said, her touch gentle on his arms. "I will remind *you* that Hamptons only do things to suit themselves, and not to smooth the path for others."

He considered her words. "So I take it to mean that you have every intention of marrying me for yourself and no one else?"

"I do."

"When did you decide on this somewhat surprising course?" he asked, then put his forehead against hers. "I've been on battlefields all over Europe, and I swear I never came as close to fainting as I did five minutes ago!"

She laughed and cupped his face in her hands. "Oh, I wish I had a painting of your expression! How I would love to show it to our children in twenty years or so."

His arms went around her then, and he held her as close as he could, with a sigh that made her heart flop. "I think I first admitted it to myself this morning," she whispered into his ear, "when Mr. Steinman gave me that silly metronome."

"Well, it made me jealous," he grumbled. "I mean, I'd like to be able to give you things."

"You will." She kissed his ear. "Now tell me truthfully how long you've been really serious about that proposal."

He held her off from him then, with another look of real surprise, then pulled her against him again so firmly that she knew she should be blushing. "Ever since right before I asked, Suzie, and don't ask me how I knew I loved you. I just did."

It would have been a much longer kiss—her brains were starting to sauté—except that Colonel March came back into the room and harrumphed a few times to get their attention.

"David, I am even now fighting a rear guard action with the housekeeper and the pastry chef, plus an irritating fellow who speaks only French," he said. "Save that for tomorrow and accompany me to Doctors' Commons."

"Yes, sir," the bailiff said, releasing his grip on her. "Can we drop Suzie off at the Steinman Employment Agency on the way?"

"Certainly, lad, but only if you're sure she won't accept another position while you're gone," the colonel joked. "I'm depending on you two to marry and put my fiancée out of her misery."

Susan smiled weakly at him. My stars, Colonel, she thought, I can't even get my lips to work right now. How could I manage a coherent interview? She nodded to the colonel and searched about the room for her cloak, which was draped over a chair in plain sight. And now my eyes aren't even working, she thought as she accepted the cloak from David, who was looking much too self-satisfied for her own peace of mind.

"Doctors' Commons, is it, sir?" the bailiff asked.

The colonel nodded. "Where you will speak up promptly and tell them what you want, so they won't think it is I seeking another license and looking like a bigamist. We'll stop at St. Andrews afterwards, and make arrangements for tomorrow morning, so you will have time to catch the mail coach back to Quilling."

They dropped her off at the Steinman Agency, where she was accosted by both Steinmans, plied with tea and Viennese pastry, and obliged to divulge all. Her narrative was interrupted by Mrs. Steinman's "I knew it, I knew its," and Steinman's grin that grew wider and wider and threatened to split his face.

"See here, sir," she said, putting down her teacup in the face of his relentless good humor, "how long am I to believe you have been plotting this?"

"Since I laid eyes on you, Miss Hampton," he admitted promptly.

"Even if you were fully aware how socially mismatched David and I are?" she accused, amused at his enthusiasm.

He shook his head at another pastry from his mother, who dropped it on Susan's plate instead, with the admonition, "To keep your strength up, dearie." He picked up the metronome still on the breakfast table, and set it in slow motion. "Susan, we live in a new age, an industrial age, one where a Jew can run a company without fear of windows broken, or business ruined by rumor or bigotry." He moved the weight down and the pendulum swung faster. "It is a modern age; consider yourself a pioneer in it, you and your good bailiff. What else is there to explain?" He looked at her, as if asking himself if he should continue. "And I do owe him."

"I do not understand," she said.

"Perhaps you will someday," he replied, "when you've had a little more experience with your bailiff."

She could think of nothing to add to Steinman's artless remark, even if he had looked like he wanted to say more, which he did not. She knew she had greater explanations ahead of her. Susan nodded to Mrs. Steinman and left the room thoughtfully.

This will not be so easily explained to my father, she considered later in the solitude of her room. She took off her shoes and lay down on the bed, struck suddenly by the thought that she would not have many more days or nights of lying in bed by herself. "I hope you are ready for this, Susan Hampton," she told the ceiling. She knew she was; making love to the bailiff, although a new experience, would not be a difficult task. The difficulty lay in the preliminaries; Sir Rodney would have to know their plans. "I am certain your father will not be ready for such glad tidings," she said sternly, "and we aren't even discussing Aunt Louisa!"

For a long moment, she thought about not saying anything to her father, but knew, in the deepest part of her heart, that such an action would never do. He was sure to find out, and then he would think she was too ashamed to tell him. She turned on her side and rested her cheek on her hands. How sad that I meet the man I love and want to marry and have children by, and I have to worry about what others think. The strange thing is, I do not know if I am trying to protect myself, or him.

It was a sobering thought, and she took it to sleep with her, dreaming of her father searching for her long-gone pearl necklace, and settling for the pence on Lady Bushnell's eyelids as she lay dead on top of a cotton bale in New Orleans. And there was poor Charlie, tugging at her sleeve, pleading with her not to send him into battle again.

"Suzie, wake up."

She opened he eyes with a gasp to see the bailiff seated beside her, his hand on her arm. She stared at him, thinking for one terrible moment that he was Charles Bushnell, then she touched his arm to let him know she was awake.

"It looked like a bad dream," the bailiff murmured, kissing her forehead. "I thought to wake you easy from it." He must have noticed the question in her eyes. "My dear, I have a lot of experience in bad dreams. Imagine, if you will, a whole regiment twitching and mumbling."

"It is bad enough that I was dreaming of my father," she said, drawing up her knees and tucking her skirts about her legs. "I don't know what to do about him."

"May I suggest a course of action?" David asked. He leaned his head on her knees. "I think we need to see him and tell him what we are doing tomorrow morning."

She sighed, and reached up to touch his hair. "I suppose we must."

"We must."

After a frustratingly brief interlude involving buttons, hooks, and eyes, the bailiff thought it best for him to retreat to his room and put away the special license before it was too wrinkled to read. Susan replaced the pins in her hair, looked in the mirror to note that she would probably never need artificial coloring for her cheeks, and went downstairs to wait for him. Mrs. Steinman kept her company in the sitting room and found time to offer her three kinds of pastries and tea better than she was used to. Susan ate to oblige her, smiling inwardly with amusement as Mrs. Steinman reached over every now and then just to touch her knee and say something low and endearing in a language much like German.

"Mrs. Steinman, how is it that *everyone* in this household knew my business before I did?" she asked finally, when the pastries were consumed.

"Simple, my dear. You never mentioned the bailiff once in your letter," the woman replied. "Now, if you did not like him, we would have heard about it. Isn't it reasonable to suppose that since you said nothing, it was because you didn't want anyone to think you were interested?"

I learn new things every day, Susan thought as she left the agency with the bailiff. Here I thought I was so clever. She tucked her arm through David's and looked up at him. "Mr. Wiggins, if, in future, I ever get to thinking I am terribly smart, will you just remind me that everyone at the Steinman Employment Agency, and you, too, I think, knew my own mind before I did?"

"Mrs. Skerlong, as well," he said, kissing her cheek quickly as they hurried through the after work crowds. "She muttered something to me about quality not knowing their place anymore, and what did I think of that?"

"And what did you think of it?" she asked, her eyes merry.

He only smiled. "There I have the advantage of knowing something about women, Suzie. I just mumbled something around my oatmeal and kept eating. That usually satisfies women, I've discovered. Some want verification more than real answers."

"I suppose that means that I won't be able to get away with anything," she said, softening her words by holding rather tighter to his arm as they hurried to cross Hyde Park.

"What it means is that you'll be even more creative than most women in getting what you want, which you will get, I have no doubt." He smiled down at her. "What I don't have is any illusions about superiority."

She was still smiling as they arrived at Aunt Lousia's and the bailiff knocked on the door. The butler opened it, and she thought she saw just a glimmer of surprise and pleasure in his eyes. She couldn't be sure, of course; this was, after all, a butler.

"Ames, is my father about?"

He opened the door wider to let them in. "He is, Miss Hampton, and may I add I am sure he will be pleased when I tell him you've come back. Follow me." He led them to the door of the sitting room, then stopped and looked at the bailiff, as if puzzled to see him following Susan. "Is there something you need?" He permitted himself the smallest of smiles. "Miss Hampton, I beg your pardon. Are you owing the jarvey?"

Susan looked at him in surprise. "Why, no, Ames."

The butler appeared not to have heard her. He took a coin from his waistcoat and flipped it at the bailiff. "For your troubles, good man. If Miss Hampton owes you more, follow me belowstairs."

The bailiff caught the coin, bit it, grinned, then tossed it back to the butler. "Mr. Ames, I'm here with Suzie and *we* want to speak to her father."

What happened then was something Susan never expected to see in her life. To her utter astonishment, the butler took a step back, his mouth open in dumbfounded amazement, his eyes wide and staring. "You couldn't possibly!" he gasped.

She stared at him and then at David, who had no smile on his face anymore. With a start that almost made her shudder, she realized that she had never seen a butler with any expression before. I am so ashamed, she thought, unable to look at either man. In all my years, have I ever thought of butlers as humans capable of expression? And come to think of it, what about bailiffs, and shopkeepers and others who do the work of my class? It was a disturbing realization and it shook her to her marrow.

"Ames, where is my father?" she asked.

With monumental effort, the butler gathered himself together and nodded to her. "If you will wait in here, Miss Hampton, and uh . . . you, there." He indicated the sitting room, then started down the hall, picking up speed as he approached the stairs.

"Can I tell you what will be the topic over dinner in the servants' hall tonight?" the bailiff murmured, more to himself than to her as they went inside.

She said nothing, but walked to the window and stood looking out upon nothing, still ashamed of herself. Joel Steinman is right, she reflected. This is an age of industry, and everything must change, except that I did not believe that the changes would have to begin with me. There will be many who cannot comprehend the changes.

"Suzie?" the bailiff asked, and he sounded uncharacteristically doubtful.

Before she could respond, the door opened and her father came into the room. To her sudden relief, his smile was genuine and brilliant, a brightness to it that she remembered from years ago, when he would return to them on the estate after business in London. "My dear," he began, holding his hands out to her, "I knew you did not mean to stay away forever. Welcome home."

He took her hands and kissed her before he noticed the bailiff standing by the fireplace. As Susan watched in shame, Sir Rodney took in the bailiff's casual stance, clothes, and demeanor, and replaced his genuine smile with the vague one reserved for inferiors. He looked back at Susan with a question in his eyes. "A rustic from the Cotswolds to see you home to London?" he asked her. "That was kind of him, but hardly necessary."

"No, Papa," she began, realizing that there was no good way to say this. "May I introduce David Wiggins to you? He is Lady

Bushnell's bailiff at Quilling Manor, where I am working. He and I . . . we . . ." She couldn't get the words out, no matter how she tried.

"Actually, Sir Rodney, Susan wants to tell you that she has consented to be my wife, and we are to be married tomorrow. We wanted you to know."

Susan winced. Even the music of David's Welsh accent could not disguise the plain-spoken words, and the bald fact that there was no other way to make such an announcement, no flowery phrases to make it palatable. She tried to look at him as her father was doing even now, and saw a man in travel-worn clothes, his shoes a little rundown, his hair in need of a good combing. You cannot see him as I see him, she thought with sorrow.

Sir Rodney sat himself down, almost missing the sofa. He opened and closed his mouth several times, then turned on her the patient, wistful look that made her draw her hands into tight fists. "My dear Susan, is it wise to carry a fit of pique to such an extreme? I have won your pearls back, and I feel in my bones that by next Season, you can have a brilliant comeout, perhaps even a presentation at court."

She put up a hand to stop him. "Papa, that's all right. I am glad about the pearl necklace, because I would like to wear it tomorrow, and take it with me."

It was Sir Rodney's turn to look away in embarrassment. "When I say I have the pearls, well, I have, only I do not have them right now precisely," he temporized. "They are as good as won back, depend upon it."

"How many times have they changed hands since January?" she asked, her voice quiet, even as she burned with shame.

"Only three times, daughter," he said proudly. "And I always get them back. You'll see." He turned his kindly, patient gaze on the bailiff. "You'll see how well I can take care of her, once I win them back again. You may go, sir. I'm sure we don't need you."

"I think Susan does," said the bailiff gently, as if he were speaking to a child. "We wanted to let you know about the wedding tomorrow morning at eight in St. Andrews."

There was a long pause. Susan looked hard at the bailiff, willing him to end the interview so she could tug up what remained of her dignity and tow it after her from the room. Sir Rodney came closer to the bailiff, peering at him with curiosity, as though he were another species.

"See here, sir. I could call you out for offering such an insult to my daughter."

"I would never accept such a challenge because there has been no insult," David said evenly. "I love your daughter, and I will provide for her."

Sir Rodney shook his head helplessly. "I seem to have loaned my dueling pistols to someone, anyway." He looked at his daughter, and she cringed at his desperate expression. "Susan, did we lose those with the house to that Lancastershire weaver?"

"Oh, please, Papa, that's enough," she begged. "David, I . . ."

"Brother, shall I send for the Watch?"

Susan gasped and turned around. Her aunt stood in the doorway, Ames at her shoulder looking wooden in a righteous sort of way.

"That won't be necessary," the bailiff said. "Susan and I are leaving."

"It can't be soon enough!" she snapped, turning on her heel.

In another moment, Susan heard her moving quickly up the stairs. Sir Rodney cocked his head to one side and listened, alert for trouble from the look of apprehension in his eyes. He sighed with the relief of a child when a door slammed, and then regarded them again, his expression perplexed, as if wondering what to do with them.

The bailiff nodded to Sir Rodney. "Grand to meet you, sir. For my part, you may keep the pearls, if you ever get them again. Your need sounds greater than ours. Come, Susan, or we'll be late for dinner." He held out his hand to her, and she took it gladly, even if she was unable to meet his eyes. "Excuse us, please."

He tugged her into the hall, then stopped suddenly as he took her face in his hands. "Save your tears for outside, Susan," he said softly and kissed her forehead.

By great force of will, she made it to the steps outside, then burst into tears. David kissed her again and stood there a moment with his arm tight around her shoulders.

"Let's go, my dear," he said finally as she rummaged for a handkerchief in her reticule. "At least they can never accuse us of not telling them."

She wiped her eyes, blew her nose, and was about to speak when the second-story window above them opened. She looked up instinctively at the sound and saw Aunt Louisa lean out, a dress box in her hands.

"Don't leave without all your clothes, Susan," she said. "You'll need something in sarcenet and satin for mucking out stables and paying calls on milkmaids!"

"Oh, Aunt, no!" Susan exclaimed as the woman dumped out

the evening dresses she had carefully packed away, and her mother's wedding dress. She stood in dumbfounded, amazed misery as the beautiful fabrics rained around her, some impaled and torn on the iron railings by the sidewalk, and others to catch the breeze, to drift and sink into the standng water of the gutter. Caught by a particularly malicious gust of wind, Maria Hampton's wedding dress sailed into the street and fell under a carter's muddy-wheeled wagon. The fabric caught in the spokes, ripped, and dragged behind the wagon as it rumbled down the street.

She felt David tense beside her, and despite her own shame, and the deepest pain she had ever felt, she looked at him. His face was a study in rage, a mirror of the greatest fury she had ever seen before. Her terror increased as he grabbed a silk shawl that drifted past him, twisted it into a rope and turned to go back into the house.

"No!" she shrieked, grabbing his arm and throwing all her weight against him. The window slammed shut, even as she heard the click of the lock on the front door. "No, David," she repeated, her voice low now, pleading. "No."

The bailiff looked down at the shawl in his hands and threw it away from him as if it had a disgusting smell. Without a word he took her hand and pulled her down the steps and away from the house. She hurried to keep up with him, heedless of the pedestrians who stepped aside for them, startled by the cold rage on his face.

He stopped finally to catch his breath, sitting on the stoop of a darkened house. She stood a little away from him, not fearful of him, but in such agony over her relatives that if the Lord had seen fit to advertise the opening of a chasm, she would have been the first in line for the drop. The bailiff had the good grace not to look at her, which did more for her immediate peace of mind than anything else could have.

"Susan, come here," he said finally. "Oh, come on, I won't bite." He held out his hand.

In another moment she was sitting beside him, his arm around her again. "Forgive me, Susan," he apologized. "I sent a man to hospital once for less provocation than that woman provided."

She rested her head against his shoulder. "It is I who should ask your pardon, David. I'm sorry my relatives are so appalling."

He chuckled, and drew her closer. "I'll say this only once, Suzie: I was raised better in a workhouse." He kissed her cheek. "How in God's name did you turn out so well?"

She thought she was too numb to cry, but she surprised herself.

When she finished, she straightened her bonnet and smoothed her skirts about her. I wonder if I will dream about Mama's dress dragged behind that cart, she thought as she stared into the street, then blew her nose vigorously. "I hope that you have not changed your mind about marrying me," she said, putting the image of the dress from her mind, even though she knew it was etched on her heart forever.

The bailiff was silent so long that she reached for her handkerchief again, stopping her hand only when he put his cheek against hers. "Your relatives would probably say I have few virtues, Suzie my love," he said finally, "but I am constant and I know my mind." He stood up and tugged her to her feet after him, then smiled at her. "And haven't we just assured Colonel March and Lady Bushnell how dependable we are?"

She nodded, suddenly shy, thinking of tomorrow.

"Then depend upon me, Susan."

Chapter Seventeen

𝒞

She spent a perfectly sleepless night, moving from the bed to the chair, to the window seat, and back to the chair again. She had never been in love before, but knew she loved the bailiff. She knew she would never be comfortable until she was married to him, but the initial effort of making love to a man gave her room for thought and some misgivings.

Mrs. Steinman had taken away her traveling dress to give it a good brushing and pressing, and she had indulged herself with a good soak in the tin tub, contemplating her bare knees and wishing that everyone in the world would go away except the bailiff. As the water turned cold, she decided that while she was not precisely frightened by the prospect of acquiring a husband, she wished there had been better sources of information than Professor Fowler's profoundly silly book, and Aunt Louisa's admonitions. There has to be considerable pleasure in the married state, or people wouldn't have been indulging in the practice since Adam and Eve, she decided as she dried off, got in her nightgown, and waited for sleep to come.

That it did not came as no surprise. First she indulged in a hearty round of castigating her relatives and wishing them all to hell or Australia—whichever was worse—and followed that with a few more tears and a fervent desire to remember the Hamptons no more. She devoted the remainder of the night to the bailiff. She considered all his virtues, and found herself quite unable to recall any defects, beyond a certain single-mindedness regarding wheat, and a regrettable tendency to forget about washing when he got really busy.

She knew she could deal promptly with the latter, so it was not an issue. I will even volunteer to scrub his back, she thought, then quickly put the idea from her mind as she felt herself growing uncomfortably warm for March. As for the wheat, she found it al-

most as fascinating as he did, so it could not be a defect. I have
lived much of my life around idle fritterers, which David is not,
she told herself. If he likes to spend his spare time rearranging the
characteristics of grain, at least I will always know where I can
find him. Grain—at least in this form—does not drive men to distraction, or ruin them, or spend their money, or make their wives
and children weep and mourn. She smiled to herself and thought
of Lady Bushnell. I will devote myself to my employer and become proficient at the piano if it kills me. I intend to be a very
good Wiggins, even if it is a borrowed name from an English village. If it was good enough for the King and his shillings, it will
do for me.

After midnight, she heard David and Joel come up the stairs,
laughing and then shushing each other outside her door until she
had to cover her mouth to keep from betraying her own amusement. David's room was next to hers and the walls were thin
enough for her to hear him whistling. The ropes creaked, so she
knew when he got into bed. To her additional amusement and
frustration, she heard him begin to snore. The sleep of the innocent or the thoroughly experienced? she asked herself, while I
toss and writhe about and contemplate what mysterious tomorrow
night will uncover.

She was dressed and downstairs for breakfast before the men.
Mrs. Steinman worked in the kitchen with her scullery maid, and
Susan joined her, happy to finish the recipe for plum cake while
the other woman prepared eggs for baking.

"You couldn't sleep?" Mrs. Steinman asked.

Susan shook her head and peered closer at the recipe, hoping to
hide what she knew was a red face.

Mrs. Steinman sat at the table, her eyes focused on distant
scenes, the eggs forgotten. "I remember my wedding day. I had
never laid eyes on my husband before."

"Never?" Susan asked, stopping the dough in midstroke.

"It was not our custom, little one," she replied. "And when I
first saw him, it was through a thick veil." She turned her attention to the eggs again. "I didn't get a really good look at him until
after the ceremony." She chuckled. "And then a much better
look."

Susan brought the bowl to the table and sat down. "You must
have been terrified," she said as she continued stirring.

"Why?" Mrs. Steinman asked, surprised. She touched Susan's
hand. "You see, my dear, I trusted that my father would arrange
well for me, and he did."

How fortunate you are, Susan thought. My father's ideas of arrangement generally involve telling stories only he can believe, and smiling big enough to cover the worst shortcomings. She looked down at the bowl, sighed, and redoubled her efforts.

"My dear, it is plum cake, not whipping cream," Mrs. Steinman said, her voice gentle. "Perhaps your father will come to the wedding and make amends."

I do not think there are words enough in this entire universe to apologize for last night's display of family love, she thought, even as she smiled and nodded. "Perhaps he will. Here, Mrs. Steinman, is the oven ready?"

She thought that breakfast would taste like ashes and bonemeal, but she surprised herself by consuming the largest share of baked eggs and looking around for more, to the bailiff's amusement. Perhaps it is not so surprising, she thought as she went to the sideboard for warm plum cake. I didn't have the heart for dinner last night.

The bailiff joined her there. "I don't know, Susan," he began, shaking his head. "I don't remember your eating so much before for breakfast." He winked at Steinman. "Joel, didn't you assure me that two can live as cheaply as one, but only half as long?"

They ate quickly, with an eye on the clock. "I suppose we will not see you after the ceremony?" Joel asked as he pushed himself away from the table.

"No. We leave immediately for Quilling," David replied. He glanced at Susan. "We leave it to you to tell that nice widow who wants a governess that the incomparable Susan decided instead to marry a Welsh thief, poacher, veteran, and . . ."

". . . future proprietor of Waterloo Seed Farm," she interrupted, dabbing at her lips with the napkin. "While I do not expect us to be rich someday, we will be adequately respectable. Come on, David. Let us get married."

The wedding was quickly performed at St. Andrews Church. She clutched the bailiff's hand, whispered her responses in a terrified voice, and only stopped shaking when he clamped his hand around her wrist to hold it still and slide on the wedding band. She couldn't remember a word the priest said; she might as well have been married in Hindustani. She stood and shook, and knelt and shook, and barely recognized her signature after she signed the registry. Mrs. Steinman cried, Joel grinned, and Colonel March looked as relieved as when General Blucher arrived in the eleventh hour on Waterloo's field. Beyond a somewhat bemused drunk in a back pew and an old lady who talked to herself, there were no other wedding guests.

Well, I did not expect more, Susan thought as she raised her cheek for Colonel March to kiss, and followed it with the warmth of Mrs. Steinman's embrace. "May you be as happy as I was," the woman said, then whispered. "From my mouth to God's ears."

Then there was only time to say good-bye to everyone, laugh at Joel waving his empty sleeve again, and catch the mail coach at its nearest location. She sat close to her husband and admired the ring. "When did you find time to get this?" she asked as the mail coach started.

He took her hand and ran his fingers over the ring. "When I went to Chipping Norton for the cattle fair."

She gaped at him. "David, I had turned you down only days before! You were so confident?"

"I was so confident," he replied simply.

She slept most of the way to Oxford, her hand resting on his thigh, his arm about her shoulders. After Oxford, she stayed awake for the rest of the trip, too shy to speak, but content to tuck herself close to him and watch the mile posts come and go. The bailiff didn't seem to mind her silence. He dozed, resting his head on her shoulder and relaxing completely. When he woke, he told her his plans for the Waterloo Seed Company, and then maintained a conversation with the farmer seated on his other side. Susan listened to traded experiences of *scours, joint ill,* and whether to sow barley in the full moon or the new moon, and wondered what her former friends would make of such talk. I have much to learn, she thought, and it goes so far beyond what I will discover tonight. My genteel upbringing has prepared me for nothing.

"You have a quizzical look on your face," the bailiff commented after the farmer left the coach at a crossroads and they started again.

She smiled at him. "I am thinking how ill-prepared I am for life with you." It was so honest that she blushed.

The bailiff glanced around to see if the other passengers were sleeping, and kissed her quickly. "You only have to remember two things, Suzie," he murmured, his lips close to hers.

"Just two?" she whispered, wanting him to kiss her again.

"I like my meals on time and I'll be putting my cold feet on your legs when I come in late at night after a lambing or a calving." He kissed her again. "I think everything else will revolve pretty much around those two matters," he concluded, his words teasing her. "What about you?"

She chose her words carefully. "I could tell you that I don't ever want to be shouted at, or made to feel little, but you would never do that anyway," she said as she traced the outline of his jaw with her finger. "I know you will not beat me, or use me unkindly, because it is not in your nature. No one told me; I just know."

"Oh, Suzie," he said, and it was more a sigh than words. "You do me honor."

"All you have to remember is that I love you, David," she whispered.

"Done, Mrs. Wiggins."

They arrived in Quilling at the end of the long spring day, when the sun was gone, but the sky was not yet dark. While Susan waited in the public room, the bailiff paid the innkeep for stabling the horse and gig and went to claim them. Susan sat quietly, drinking tea and remembering her first visit there. You are right, sir, she thought as she watched the keep pour ale for a customer. This is a friendly village. I have found a husband in this place, and our children will likely go to school here.

David came back then and motioned to her. She rose to go when the innkeep called to the bailiff. "David, Ben Rich's little Owen stopped in this morning. He told me to tell you to please stop at the sheepfold on your way to the manor." He took a few swipes at the counter with his damp rag. "He appeared agitated, but acted like he didn't want me to know, the little beggar."

"Oh?" the bailiff said, the concern evident in his eyes.

"Told him I could send some men, if he was having trouble, but the little ragged muffin puffed up like a lord and said he was perfectly capable. Lord save us, David, but what's in the water in Wales to make all men from there think they are kings?"

They rode in silence to the sheepfold, David alert for trouble, but nothing appeared out of the ordinary. "Ben? Owen?" he called when the gig rolled to a stop in front of the stone building.

The door burst open and Owen Thrice ran out. The bailiff leaped from the gig in time for the lad to grab him around the waist. "Mr. Rich is sick," he sobbed. "I've been doing the best I could."

David knelt by the boy and wiped his face. "I'm sure you have, Owen," he said. "Let's go inside and you can tell me everything."

He rose and helped Susan from the gig, shrugging at her while the boy tugged him along by the hand.

The crofter's cot looked much the same, except that Ben Rich was lying in bed, faintly snoring. Two lambs negotiated the room on the stiff legs of newborns, gradually picking up speed while a ewe paced back and forth.

"Owen Thrice, what on earth!" the bailiff exclaimed. "Watch your step, Suzie."

Owen sat beside Ben Rich, who continued to slumber through the baaing. The air was redolent with sheep manure. Susan felt her eyes beginning to water from the fumes, and she longed to open the door, but that would only lead to the exodus of the lambs and an increase in the young boy's misery, which was already amply evident on his face.

"Mr. Rich is sick and I've been taking care of him," Owen said.

"The sheep, lad? We have pens for them outside, last time I looked," David said.

Owen Thrice burst into tears, adding his noise to the confusion about them. " 'Twas Ben's idea, Mr. Wiggins. He thought to help me from his bed. I tried and tried to help one of the ewes, but she died anyway, and then one of that ewe's twins died, and I tried to get the orphan lamb to suck her but the ewe wouldn't let him, and now I don't know what to do, because Ben sleeps and sleeps," he said in one breathless sentence, the words tumbling out of him.

Without any comment, the bailiff handed Owen his handkerchief. When he had collected himself, the boy hunkered down in front of the hearth like the bailiff, looking up at him as though he knew David could solve all problems.

"Where's the dead lamb, lad?"

Owen indicated with his head. "Beside the shearing shed. I . . . I didn't know what to do with it."

"Then go get it."

Susan blinked in surprise, but didn't say anything. She went to the bed and put her hand on Ben Rich's forehead. He was cool now, but the stiffness of his nightshirt and the sour odor about the bed, obvious even in the ripe-smelling room, told Susan a tale of high fever and sweats. "He appears to be only sleeping, and he is not hot," she told the bailiff, who nodded and sidestepped the lambs, who continued their rapid circumference of the room.

Owen struggled in with the lamb carcass, which he flopped down in front of the bailiff. Immediately, the ewe took an interest and came closer, nosing her dead lamb and making anxious purring sounds.

"Watch, lad, and you can do this next time," David said as he picked up a knife from the table. Deftly he made several slits around the carcass and skinned it so fast that Susan blinked in surprise. "Catch me the orphan," he ordered Owen, who leaped up and wrestled the lamb to a standstill. Just as quickly as he had skinned the animal, he slid the skin onto the orphan and sat back. "Watch this, lad," he said.

The ewe nosed the orphan wearing her twin's carcass. In another moment, the rejected lamb was nursing successfully. The ewe's other baby soon joined the adopted orphan, and Susan laughed out loud to watch them nurse, their tails twirling ecstatically.

"Works every time," David commented, then looked at Susan, apology in his eyes. "I'm going to stay here and see what else needs to be done. Take the gig, Suzie. Tom will unhitch it for you." He wiped his hands, then put them around her waist. "You'll have to tell Lady Bushnell the glad tidings."

"But when . . ."

"As soon as I can, love." With a look to make sure that Owen was staring at the lambs, he kissed her with all the fervor of that first kiss in the barnyard. "Make me a warm spot in bed."

Cora Skerlong's stodgy suitor had taken her and Mrs. Skerlong to the village, so there was only Lady Bushnell to tell, and she took the news with equanimity and obvious pleasure, once she had satisfied herself that Susan had made no sacrifice. She patted the side of her bed and took Susan's hands in hers.

"I imagine that all the Hamptons have risen as one to tell you what a goose you are."

Susan nodded, feeling wary.

"Then you don't need that from me, too, my dear," Lady Bushnell said briskly. "I am most grateful that you have convinced my daughter-in-law that I am not suffering from any neglect that will reflect on her. She can be positively frightful, at times."

"You should really thank Colonel March," Susan said. "It was he who convinced Lady Bushnell and paid for the special license."

"A man of sense," she agreed, her eyes merry. "Charlie once told me that he thought Edwin March should have commanded the regiment."

And so he should have, Susan thought, remembering with a chill the desperate letter from New Orleans. "In a married state, the colonel and Lady Bushnell deem us worthy to keep you from the cocoon of the family estate," she assured the widow. She looked down at her hands then, suddenly shy. "David thinks it best that he move into the house with me."

"So do I," Lady Bushnell said. She patted Susan's hand. "Only think how convenient this will make our trip to Waterloo this summer! I own I was wondering how we were going to do it."

"Oh, Lady Bushnell, I don't think . . ." Susan began.

Lady Bushnell put her finger to Susan's lips. "Hush, child! This will appear altogether more sanguine to you in the morning, after a good night with the bailiff."

"As to that, I believe the sheep have his attention tonight," Susan said in an agony of embarrassment.

"I doubt it," the widow replied briskly. "Get yourself ready for bed, then bring us some tea." She smiled at Susan, shedding the years. "It appears to me that you could use some advice."

What I need is courage, Susan thought as she poured hot water from the Rumford, took it to the laundry room, and washed herself thoroughly. She smiled. And someone to scrub *my* back. She reached for the cold water bucket to douse her warmth, gasping at the change in temperature, wondering at her own eagerness for the bailiff, felt even through her nervousness. The wretched Professor Fowler says that all maidens are reticent, and only surrender—oh, what nonsensical phrase did he use—ah, "that pristine prize most precious"—silly twaddle—with the greatest reluctance. She dried herself until she tingled, then put on nightgown and robe. "I think, Professor Fowler, that your wife is to be pitied," she said out loud as she prepared the tea tray and went back upstairs, her bare feet quiet on the stairs.

Lady Bushnell was dozing, and Susan almost set down the tray and left the room. No, I need some advice, she decided as she clattered the cups in their saucers and was rewarded with one eye, then two, staring at her.

"Well, pour it and sit down," said the dowager. "First I suppose you should get me those dratted medicaments from the bureau that the doctor insists on dosing me with. I assure him I have never felt better, and he becomes almost rude in reply."

"You cannot fool him, Lady Bushnell."

She handed Lady Bushnell the glass of water with powders dissolved in it. She drank it and made a face. "I pay him enough to overlook my occasional nastiness, if I will overlook his," she retorted. "Sit down now, and tell me what you need to know."

Susan was silent, not knowing where to begin.

"Do you need to know *everything*?" Lady Bushnell asked finally. "What is the matter with modern youth?"

"Oh, no!" Susan assured her. "What I mean is, I understand the . . . the fundamentals. What I don't understand . . . what I want to know . . . oh, Lady Bushnell, is it *fun*?"

Lady Bushnell smiled, and motioned for Susan to fluff her pillows. "Trust your Aunt Louisa to scare you to death! No wonder her own daughters are so pasty-looking." She snorted and settled herself lower in the pillows. "I don't suppose any of their husbands will ever see them even by candlelight with their clothes off!" She reflected on that a moment. "Not that anyone would want to, I think."

"That's all right then?" Susan asked. "I mean, I was wondering how . . ."

Lady Bushnell reached up and touched Susan's cheek. "My dear, it is vastly fun and impossible to overrate. If you're scared silly now, that will change."

"Well, not precisely scared silly, my lady," Susan argued.

"Then you are more sensible than I was!" The widow laughed out loud. "On our wedding night, I locked myself in the dressing room and refused to come out."

"I don't think I will go that far," Susan said.

"I didn't think so! And there was my husband, pounding on the door and saying, 'Lydia, I am a major!' over and over!" She laughed, then wiped her eyes. "Dear me, but that is a memory."

"You came out finally?" Susan asked.

"No, actually," Lady Bushnell continued, the merriment welling up in her again. "He took the door off the hinges and then just sat there on the floor and laughed until I thought he would perish from want of breath. I cried a little more, got the hiccups, and he held my nose and made me sip porter by the teaspoon until they stopped."

"And then?" Susan prompted.

Lady Bushnell regarded her with bright eyes. "He consoled me most successfully."

"I suppose you will not tell me any more now," Susan teased. She gently took out one of the pillows behind Lady Bushnell's head, and smoothed her hair back until it was tucked under her sleeping cap again. "You will tell me I must find out for myself."

"Of course, my dear," the widow said as her eyes closed. "You will have your own stories to tuck away in your memory." She opened her eyes. "Do you know, Susan, I think you and I should write down my life story."

"Including the major, hiccups and hinges?" she asked.

"Perhaps not everything," she said, her voice drowsy now as the powders took effect.

"Tell me one thing, Lady Bushnell, and then I will know enough," Susan said after a moment's hesitation. "The first time, does it . . ."

"Hurt, my dear?" Lady Bushnell opened her eyes and motioned for Susan to sit beside her on the bed again. "Let me answer you this way by telling you something about David Wiggins."

She did as Lady Bushnell directed. "I suppose you will tell me now that Sergeant Wiggins was the regimental Don Juan."

"Far from it! As far as I knew, he was completely loyal to Jesusa." Lady Bushnell took Susan by the hand. "What I am telling you has nothing to do with his conjugal abilities. How would I know? But I do know this about him: I cannot recall a time, except just before or after battle, when he did not help Jesusa draw water, or gather wood. He was a sergeant! He could have delegated such homely tasks, or left them to her entirely, as other men, but he did not."

Susan looked down at her wedding ring and turned it thoughtfully on her finger. "I think I understand what you are telling me." She looked at Lady Bushnell, done with reticence. "He will use me kindly."

"I am certain of it. I must say that it gives me some satisfaction to think that, all Hamptons aside, you just might be the luckiest woman in England." She patted Susan's hand, then released it. "Go get some sleep now! When the sergeant decides that the sheep will keep, you'll be busy enough."

It was food for thought, and consoling enough to suit her. She went thoughtfully to her room after hearing the Skerlongs return home, and going downstairs to tell them of her marriage. She finished her commentary in a room absolutely silent, asked the dumbstruck housekeeper to leave the back door unlocked for the bailiff, and hurried upstairs with a grin on her face.

Lady Bushnell was right; Susan found it much easier to sleep this time. After a night of no sleep, and the discomforts of the mail coach, she gave herself up to the mattress without a qualm. She woke up once in the early hours, and patted the space beside her, but there was still no bailiff. "Damn the sheep, anyway," she murmured before closing her eyes again.

He came to bed when the sun was making preliminary motions to rise, and the room was just lightly pinked with early dawn.

Sunk down as deep in sleep as she was, he did not startle her. He sat in the chair by the cold hearth, regarding her as he eased his feet out of his boots with a sigh. She came to life gradually, her drowsy eyes moving from his stockinged feet to his stubbled face, to his lively eyes.

"Good morning," he said.

"Mmmm," she replied. Some fussbudget in the back of her brain was telling her to pull down her nightgown, because, after all, who was this strange man with morning stubble? The more alert section of her brain—the one that seemed to be speeding up her heartbeat and breathing—was reminding her that she was married now, and wasn't that a fortunate thing, especially since she was pulling back the covers to welcome him into her warmth?

"Mrs. Wiggins, you are a sight to behold."

Still webbed in the fuddle of sleep, she looked over her shoulder for Mrs. Wiggins, then reddened and came more awake. "Oh . . . me," she said, feeling stupid and randy at the same time.

He grinned and took off his clothes. Her eyes widened, but she gulped and made room for him in the bed. He sank down with a sigh, putting his arm out to gather her in. He smelled quite strongly of sheep, but the odor, she was discovering, was far from unpleasant. After the tiniest hesitation, she moved into the space he created, so close to his heart, resting her head in the hollow of his shoulder and her hand on his bare chest.

He was content to stretch out and let go of the long night, quiet, peaceful—boneless, almost—beside her. His feet were cold on her bare legs, but not for long. Gradually her own warmth took off his chill and he moved his feet away.

If she had thought to be afraid of the bailiff, there wasn't any reason. He took her hand, kissed her fingers, and moved it lower until her eyes grew wide again. "My stars," she breathed. "I didn't think you would be so . . ." she paused, her fingers gentle.

"Large?" he asked, grinning at her.

"No. Soft. But not precisely soft," she amended, discovering trouble forming words as he allowed her to explore him. She gave up the attempt at speech and kissed him instead. She thought to protest his whiskers as he kissed her, then as he nuzzled her neck and breasts she couldn't think why it had mattered, and then she couldn't think at all, beyond the fact that she was on her back now, and she didn't want to be anywhere else in the galaxy.

She followed his advice, softly whispered in a voice not really like his own, trusting him with all her heart. She relaxed as much as she could, wincing only slightly, hoping he wouldn't notice, then devoting herself to his rhythm, which became hers, too. If there was anyone or anything else in the world except the two of them, she didn't know of it. The joy she felt was beyond any contentment a hundred Lady Bushnells could have explained. Finally his whole body relaxed on hers, and no matter how heavy he felt, she knew she could sustain him forever.

He raised up finally to look at her out of focus, eye to eye, nose to nose, completely part of her. When he lay beside her again with another sigh, she felt a loss all out of proportion to her previous fears. She couldn't explain why, but she had wanted him to continue his motions.

He stretched out his arm to pull her in close again, and she moved without hesitation this time, resting her legs on his. "I had all the fun this time," he said into her ear, tugging on the lobe with his teeth, which caused her eyes to roll back in her head, an anatomical response she had never been aware of before. "We'll remedy that with practice." He kissed her cheek and caressed her breast, then stopped and whispered, "All this lanolin, Suzie, and your chest will be so oily you'll slide right out of your shift."

"I think I already did," she whispered back, smiling when he laughed and continued his efforts. In a few moments, his hand stopped, and he slept, warm and heavy and totally to her liking. She dozed a few more minutes herself, then carefully eased herself out from under his hand.

She hunted around on hands and knees until she found her nightgown by the door, where the bailiff had tossed it. She put it on again and thought about adding coal to the fire, but it was more exertion than she wanted, just then. She sat in the chair instead, surrounded by the clothes he had dropped, wondering idly if he was inclined ordinarily to pick up his clothes or leave them strewn about. She drew her legs up close to her body, pleased to know there was no pain at all, only a little tightening of muscles unused to a husband.

She watched the bailiff, certain there was no handsomer slumbering man in all the British Isles. The prominent lines of his face, so firmly Welsh, seemed to loosen as he abandoned himself without a struggle to sleep. No matter how minuscule her experience in these matters, she knew she had some function in furnishing the depth of the rest he now enjoyed. *I suppose I share that honor with sheep,* she thought with a smile, *and a late night's work.* She stood up and stretched. *But he will not be looking for sheep when he wakes up,* she considered, flexing her fingers over her head. *I think I will find some warm water. I wonder if Lady Bushnell will mind terribly if I am late to piano practice this morning?*

Chapter Eighteen

❦

Lady Bushnell did not seem to mind that Susan missed piano practice entirely that morning when she rushed in, breathless, to apologize, and dashed out again. Likewise, Mrs. Skerlong made no comment at Susan's tiptoed trips to the Rumford for warm water. She merely looked up from her knitting and managed a long, slow wink that set Susan giggling like a schoolroom miss. On Susan's last trip to the kitchen before lunch, the housekeeper went so far as to suggest to her that tomorrow would be a fine day to wash sheets, if she wished to bring hers down. When Susan blushed and nodded, she offered some whispered advice on how to deal with sheets in future that seemed practical. Susan went back upstairs thoughtfully, serene in the confederacy of women.

With some reluctance, the bailiff left for the sheepfold after lunch. She decided it would be easier to send him on his way sooner if she could quickly break him of the habit of pulling her up close in such a tight embrace and keeping her there until she started to feel peevish, and put her hands places Professor Fowler would have gasped over. It's your fault this time, she thought as she contemplated another trip downstairs and resolved to get a larger water can for their room. He surprised her by going for water himself, and coming back, his face red.

"Mrs. Skerlong has a way of looking at me," he complained. He smiled to himself as he squeezed out the cloth and tossed it to her. "Wash yourself this time. That may be part of my problem."

And so it was later in the afternoon before she sidled into Lady Bushnell's room and seated herself to continue her enlargement of the letters. She wrote in silence, deeply aware of Lady Bushnell's eyes on her as the widow rested in her chair close by. When she finally looked up, their eyes met and they both burst into laughter.

"Mrs. Wiggins, I take it that no one had to remove any hinges this morning?" the widow said as she dabbed at her eyes.

"Not even one, Lady Bushnell," Susan said. She reached out impulsively and touched the woman's face. "You were quite right about David."

"I thought so," she returned her gaze to the window. She leaned forward, her attention on the view as she motioned Susan over. "My far vision is better, Susan, but still I wonder: is that your bailiff on the near slope?"

Susan stood behind the widow's chair. "Yes," she said. Oh, Lady Bushnell, I could spot him two counties over, I know I could, she thought. She felt peevish again, and restless, even though he was at least a hectare away. "Oh, and look, I think he is going to direct the plowing."

The widow watched, her lips twitching with amusement. "A busy man is our bailiff. He plows all morning *and* all afternoon!"

They laughed together, Susan's hand on Lady Bushnell's shoulder. "I think it is the Waterloo wheat, my lady," she said, her voice soft. "I think he is going to plant it where you can see it from your window." I did not think it was possible to love you any more, my dear bailiff, she thought, but I do now. "He's going to share it with us."

"He is also going to take us to Belgium this summer," Lady Bushnell said briskly. "Help me up, Susan."

She did, knowing she should say something about Lady Bushnell's dreams, but was unable to comment beyond, "Oh, Lady Bushnell," which only earned her a sour look.

Lady Bushnell directed her to the bureau, where she leaned against her and rummaged in the top drawer. "Susan, there is another, older packet of letters there. To the left. Under those handkerchiefs, I think. Ah, yes. Take them out. You can transcribe them later. And beside them, that little box. Help me to bed now."

She did as she was asked, shocked but silent at the pain on Lady Bushnell's face from so little exertion, and the way her hands trembled as she guided her carefully to the bed. She helped her into bed, cringing almost at the tremendous effort Lady Bushnell made to stop the trembling, and then chagrined at the disgust on the widow's face at her own weakness. She held up her shaking hands to Susan, staring at them as though they were not her own.

"Susan, I have wrestled with army horses and sawed on more reins than your bailiff ever will, and look how they tremble now! I despise old age."

She closed her eyes in exhaustion, and Susan hurried back to the bureau for the doctor's powders. Lady Bushnell offered no objection this time as Susan raised her head so she could drink the potion. She lay silent, visibly gathering her strength about her as Susan knelt by the bed and leaned her cheek on the woman's hand.

She moved her hand finally, and patted Susan, her touch, in its own way, as gentle as the bailiff's. "There, pet, did I worry you?"

Susan nodded, deeply moved at the endearment. She put her forehead against the coverlet for a moment, overwhelmed at the love she felt for Lady Bushnell, too. I wonder if it is possible to die from as much love as I have had this day, she thought. I sincerely hope not.

She opened her eyes on the velvet box by Lady Bushnell's hand. Around the clasp, the nap of the green fabric was worn with much opening and closing. She rested her elbows on the bed and picked up the slender box, looking at Lady Bushnell with a question in her eyes.

"Open it, my dear. I think your bailiff has one of these, too."

She did as she was bid, to look upon a circle of silver elegant in its austerity, with the profile of the Regent. She pushed the token around with her finger, turning it over to see seated Victory, Waterloo and the date. She looked at Lady Bushnell again.

"It is a Waterloo medal, Susan, given to all participants, officers and men alike," said the widow, her eyes still faded from heart pain, but less so than only a moment ago.

"Whose is this?" she asked, fingering the dark red ribbon the color of blood, edged in blue.

"This is Charles's medal," she said softly. "His widow was in Ireland, visiting her grandparents' estate, when it was sent to Bushnell, and then forwarded to me here by mistake. I should have returned it, of course, but I did not." She took the medal from its case and held it close to her eyes. "I like to look at it, but, Susan, I also wonder if Charles deserves it."

Susan felt the familiar chill again. She got up off her knees and sat beside Lady Bushnell. "Perhaps you could return it now to your daughter-in-law?"

"I could," she agreed. "Mostly I want to go to Belgium, look the bailiff in the eye, and finally get the truth from him about that day at Waterloo. I do not believe he is telling me everything."

"I've told her all I'm ever going to tell anyone about Charlie and Waterloo," the bailiff commented that evening as he weighed out the Waterloo wheat in the succession house and she sat at his drafting table, watching him.

"Are you being fair?" she asked, soaking in the beauty of his face. "She is used to honest dealing, and didn't you promise her you would never lie again?"

He sat back on his heels, stroking the mother cat who wove herself around him. "I also promised a broken hulk of a man at the bottom of a gorge that I would take care of her, no matter what, my love. I don't think he meant for me to break her heart again. Now you tell me what to do."

She was silent, looking down the row of boxes in front of her. The bailiff had uprooted the experimental wheat, and only the bare soil remained, ready to receive the next strain. We tried so hard not to let her daughter-in-law kill her with kindness, but I wonder, are we being any fairer? she reflected.

The bailiff set down the cat and came to the drafting table, draping his arm over her shoulder. "What? I know you mean to say something. Say it, please."

She leaned back against him. "Perhaps Lady Bushnell is the best judge of what she should know. He was her son, after all."

It was his turn for long silence. He kissed her neck finally with a peremptory smack then went back to the wheat in the sack. "We'll have to differ in our opinion, then, Suzie. I choose not to tell her, and I hope that you will respect my wishes."

"Of course I will," Susan replied, getting off the stool to rescue a kitten determined to explore a grain bucket. She saved the baby teetering on the edge and returned him, squeaking, to his mother. "As a woman, and I hope, a mother someday, I will always want to know the minds and hearts of those I love," she said, her hand on the bailiff's head as he knelt by the sack again. "But I respect your wishes in this matter."

He smiled up at her and poured a careful handful of the experimental grain in the leather sowing sack. When he finished, he sat back on his heels and regarded her with such animation in his eyes that she blushed and looked away, feeling again the tension so little understood yesterday, but a permanent part of her emotions today.

"I sent Tom the cowman to stay with Ben and Owen tonight," he said as he stood up and hung the sowing sack on a hook out of the reach of any mice. "That means I have to get up early and milk, and begin the sowing."

"And? And?" she teased.

"And I thought you wouldn't mind if I sowed a little tonight," he concluded, taking her by the hand and leading her from the succession house. "Or a lot." He kissed her then, and she wondered if they would even make it as far as the first-floor landing, if they even got as far as the house.

"Mrs. Skerlong told me once that farmers don't really have time for this sort of thing in spring," she murmured as he hurried her up the stairs.

He pulled her into their bedroom and started on his buttons. "I'll have you know that old Lord Bushnell himself once complimented me on my organizational skills. Don't just stand there laughing at me, Suzie. Take off something!"

She decided in May that Mrs. Skerlong, estimable woman in so many ways, was certainly wrong about farmers and wives in spring. She also discovered that the odor of lanolin had the curious effect of making her look about for the bailiff, or start counting the hours until they could decently excuse themselves for bed. It was knowledge she chose not to pass on to the bailiff. He already has enough power over me, she told herself as she rested on him after one particularly passionate interlude. I would have to be stupid to tell a sheep farmer that lanolin makes me randy.

She discovered that other things did, too, even some of the letters she was copying over now for Lady Bushnell, the little packet she had hidden away in the bureau with Charles' Waterloo medal. They were love letters the old colonel had sent to Calcutta from Lucknow, when he was engaged in the field and she was awaiting the birth of their son from the safety of the city. While Lady Bushnell dozed in her bed—as she did more and more now— Susan sat at the desk by the open window, fanned herself, and told herself she was ridiculous to squirm over the colonel's frank expressions of longings for his wife. Just copy it, Susan, she told herself.

She finished two letters in her large, careful printing, made sure Lady Bushnell was soundly asleep, and went in search of the bailiff. He was never hard to find, and never too difficult to distract, either. Other than a simple admonition to lock the door of the succession house, and then the calm observation, twenty minutes later, that they must have scared the kittens, he was eager to let her have her way. "Just as long as you leave me to worry over the major decisions, Suzie, I am ever so obliging," he told her as he helped her back into her dress and did up the buttons.

"And what constitutes a major decision?" she asked, contented enough now to return to the copying of letters.

"Oh, whether we go to war with the United States over tariffs, or, let me think, whether I'll make a profit on this year's wool clip. I leave the rest to you."

He didn't, of course. There were times when he came in search of her, giving Lady Bushnell such flimsy excuses that Susan could only roll her eyes and look everywhere but at her employer. Lady Bushnell's earlier comments to the contrary, he was never gentle with her then. She couldn't have cared less. Her own fervor amazed her, and she had to agree with the bailiff when he had said after their first night together that all they needed was practice, and lots of it.

She discovered that she also treasured those times when they just strolled the hillside in the evening to stand among the Waterloo wheat. Being with the bailiff, in bed or out of it, was its own reward. If she could have taken out her heart and handed it to him, she would have.

"Why did you plant the wheat on a slope?" she asked one evening before the sun went down as they stood in their usual spot on the hillside.

"It's how I remember it, Suzie, sloping like that to Hougoumont and La Haye Sainte," he said, squatting in the field to run a practiced hand over the grain, measuring its height. "Only after that first night when we dug in, and it rained so hard the field was a trampled mess." He shook his head as though trying to clear his brain of the memory. "Then at the end of that endless day, it didn't look like a field at all, but a cemetery where the ground had been turned over and all the corpses flung out on top." He smiled up at her, something of embarrassment in his expression. "I guess I want to see it this way, and not muddy and bloody." He shrugged and looked over the field toward the manor house. "I think every soldier has his way of dealing with battle; this is mine."

Tears came to her eyes, and she sniffed them back.

"Don't cry, Suzie. If it'll make you feel better, I also look at this field and think how lucky I am to be a steward over my Waterloo wheat. It's good grain, and it will make us a seed farm, someday," he said as he tugged her down to sit beside him. She leaned against his shoulder, secure in the knowledge that she was the most fortunate woman in the British Isles.

It was easy then to tell him of her increasing fears for Lady Bushnell. She had never been around someone dying before, but she knew in her heart that Lady Bushnell was facing death, and soon. Dr. Pym never told her. He came three times a week, full of town gossip and good cheer, and more potions that Lady Bushnell only shook her head over. "My lady, we'll see you well and hearty before harvest," he said, concluding his most recent visit.

When he closed the door behind him, all bay rum and bluff humor, Lady Bushnell only looked at Susan, and they both knew.

"Promise me you will never lie to me, Susan," was all she said. "Let me know straight up what is going on."

"I cannot fool her," she told the bailiff on the hillside as May slipped into June.

He massaged her knee thoughtfully. "Has she asked you about Charlie?"

"No, thank God. I pray she will not." She took his hand and pressed it to her cheek. "But she does ask me all the time now when we are going to Belgium. She talks of Brussels, and Mont St. Jean, and stopping at the chateau at Hougoumont. Oh, David, is there any way we could take her there?"

"It would mean our jobs and no character references, Suzie, if the Marches found out," he said. "No. The answer's no. It's what I tell her when she asks me."

"But she keeps asking!"

"And we keep telling her no, Susan. It just can't be."

It was easy enough to agree with him, sitting there in the wheat, his hand on her leg, but harder all the time as she finished copying the letters, then began to write Lady Bushnell's army experiences in the Peninsula, as the widow dictated them. After wrangling half a day over the title, they decided they would call it "A Lady's Reminiscence in the Army of Wellington."

"I like that," the bailiff said one night when they were lying in bed, pleasantly pleased with each other. He kissed her hand and draped it over his chest. "Where do you start?"

"Well, you usually don't object if I touch you here and here," she mentioned, moving her hand and putting her leg across his.

"Silly! You know what I mean. Does she begin at Vimeiro?"

"Yes. And we've already covered that part where she rescued that wretched Welshman from three hundred lashes. Let's discuss this later, David."

"He was a wretch," the bailiff murmured, rolling over and giving her his undivided attention.

Later, when he slept, his arms protective around her, as usual, she lay awake, thinking of Lady Bushnell. *Every day now, you ask me about Waterloo, and I feel your urgency, and all I can do is shake my head and tell you no. You tell me of Busaco, and Ciudad Rodrigo, and horrible Badajoz, and I write it all down, but behind it all, like a blaze behind a fire screen, is Waterloo and Charles.* She sighed and burrowed closer into the bailiff's warmth. *Your mother's heart has to know.*

She knew better than to pester the bailiff anymore about it. "Susan, that's enough," he had said firmly one night on the hill. The wheat was almost up to her waist now, and she ran her hands across it as he did, enjoying the prickle of the forming kernel in the hull against her palms.

She stopped, embarrassed. "I know you have other things on your mind," she apologized. Only last week the bailiff and his crofters had washed the sheep in the dip beside the shearing floor. He had come home so tired from picking up sheep and tossing them into the narrow trough of water that she had to sit on his back and rub his arms and shoulders so he could sleep. The shearing would begin tomorrow.

"I shouldn't pester you," she said as she looked at the manor beyond the wheat. "It's just that she wants it so badly and . . ."

"Sometimes we don't get what we want," he interrupted, his voice short.

She looked at him then, really looked at him, admiring the fineness of his face. "You did," she said softly. "So did I."

"Susan!" he protested. He took her hands in his, turned up the palms, and kissed them. "Susan." He smiled at her, his irritation gone already. "I suppose we will have the most stubborn children."

"Of course," she agreed as she watched the storm leave his face as quickly as it had come. "There's nothing weak about this Hampton."

Later on, much later, when she had time to contemplate the many-stranded weaving that is fate, she asked herself as if saying Hampton brought on what followed. It didn't seem likely, and she was not superstitious, but there was something in the saying; she knew it.

The shearing went without a hitch, all noise, and heat, and smell and excitement, and crofters' children running about beside the shearing floor where the itinerant shearers did their rapid trade. The bailiff even tried one sheep, grinning at her as he wrestled the sheep between his legs and clipped away, stripping it naked. The odor of lanolin rose and filled the stone hall, and she had to turn away, smiling to herself and thinking naughty thoughts for the bailiff to satisfy later.

Lady Bushnell had insisted on coming along for the shearing. "I am always at the shearing, Susan, so save your breath to cool your porridge," the woman insisted. She sat ramrod straight like royalty, taking in the business of the day, accepting a glass of ale from an awed Owen Thrice.

"Is she a queen?" he whispered to Susan.

"I think so," Susan whispered back. Most of all you are a colonel's wife, she thought, her arms around Owen's shoulders, a follower of the drum who did not flinch from guns, or hunger, or siege, or betrayal, or the fickleness of fortune, that tawdry slut. I wonder what you would do if I told you I loved you, she considered. She had no answer, so she kissed the top of Owen's head instead, sending him into the worst paroxysm of mingled pleasure and embarrassment. He released himself from the burden of affection by teasing a crofter's child and making her cry.

It was a long day, and she was glad, for Lady Bushnell's sake, to see the end of it. The widow was much too tired to read any of her army letters, or eat anything beyond a few bites of gruel, which came with Mrs. Skerlong's loving admonitions about overdoing it, and "forgetting that we're not as young as we think we are, Lady B."

The bailiff dragged himself in later, reeking of wool, exhausted beyond food and single-minded only about his bed. He offered no objections when Susan helped him from his clothes, and was asleep before she extinguished the lamp. If he even moved all night, she was unaware of it.

In wordless conspiracy, Susan and Mrs. Skerlong let them sleep the next morning. They ate porridge and milk in the kitchen, listening to the thunder rumble and then fade. "I wish it would rain," Mrs. Skerlong said as she took the dishes to the sink. "Have you seen such weather?"

She had not. The sky was gray-green and seemed to loom over the earth like a blanket, casting an eerie shadow on the Waterloo wheat. She sniffed the air, shading her eyes with her hand to watch the thundercloud rise up and up like a genie out of a lamp. It was quiet, too, with no barnyard fowl complaining; even the birds were silent.

How good that I am not given to megrims over the weather, she thought, even as she frowned at the sky and wandered from room to room, dissatisfied without being able to explain why. She looked in on the bailiff, who slept bare on top of the sheets now, sweating from the strange, wet heat. Lady Bushnell stayed decorously under the covers in her room, but she seemed troubled by dreams.

When Susan came downstairs, she noticed the letters on the small table by the entrance. They must have come yesterday while we were at the shearing, she thought, picking them up to read the directions, then dropping them with a gasp, as though they burned.

It was her father's handwriting and the letters were addressed to Lady Bushnell and David Wiggins. Her first thought was to fling them into the fireplace, but there was no fire in the hearth. She was still sitting on the staircase steps when the bailiff came downstairs. He sat beside her obligingly, questioning her with his eyes.

"Love, if the weather saps your energy, go back to bed," he told her. "I doubt that anything won't keep until later in the day, except the harpsichord." He smiled at her. It was already an old joke in their young marriage. Nothing deterred Lady Bushnell from Susan's daily piano practice, not female complaints, or outside duties, or even the bailiff's needs, after that first week of fervid marriage.

She nodded in the direction of the table. "Letters."

A puzzled look on his face, he picked them from the silver basket and sat beside her again. "One to me," he said. "Well, don't be so blue about it, Suzie. I don't have a secret wife, and I'm not owing taxes."

"It's my father's handwriting," she said, her words clipped and shorter than she meant them to be.

"Don't bite me now," he said mildly.

Mrs. Skerlong came into the hall with Lady Bushnell's breakfast tray. "She's pulling her bell, Susan," the housekeeper said as she edged up the stairs between them. The bailiff handed her the other letter. "Thank you, David."

He borrowed one of her hairpins, slit the letter open, then replaced the pin. She felt him stiffen beside her as he read the letter, and read it again. "By damn," he said finally when he finished the second reading. "By damn." He looked at her, and it seemed to her, nerves on edge, that he scooted slightly away from her. "What a parent you have, Suzie. Thank God I'm a bastard."

Her fingers almost numb, she snatched the letter from his outstretched hand. Her eyes filled with tears almost before she began, so on the first reading she saw only snatches of "Newgate," and "debts," and "no help from any source," and "I'm relying on you." Shocked down to her toenails, she swiped at her eyes with the hem of her dress before she turned the page over.

"You'll like the back page even more," her husband said. "Don't miss a word of it."

She glared at him, angry at his unexpected sarcasm, but she calmed herself enough to read every word. She read it again, even as her husband had done, nausea rising in her throat. "No," she whispered. "How can he think . . ."

The bailiff took it from her and opened his mouth to speak, but stopped at the sound of Lady Bushnell's cane beating on the floor. They looked at each other, and Susan saw her own reflection in the depths of his eyes. It did not please her, any more than the frown on his face. He stood up and helped her to her feet, then hurried ahead of her up the stairs.

"Susan, your father is a monster," met her at the door like a lead wall. Lady Bushnell glared at her and thrust the letter at the bailiff, who read it, then stared at her, too. She leaned against the wall, afraid to come any further into the room.

"Oh, this is good, Lady B," the bailiff said. He looked at her then. "Suzie, he asks . . . no, no, he demands that your employer pay him enough money to keep his sorry hide out of Newgate." He looked down at the letter. " 'Knowing how you feel about my daughter, I am sure you would not wish to see her suffer with the knowledge of my incarceration. Yours, sincerely, etc. etc.' "

"Someone should have shot him in a duel years ago," Lady Bushnell said.

"Wait until you hear mine. Me, the lucky husband," he said.

Susan flinched at his angry words, swallowing her nausea with the greatest difficulty. "Please don't use that tone," she pleaded.

"Maybe you can suggest a better one, after you hear this?" he snapped back. "Lady Bushnell, he asks me to doctor the estate books and send him two hundred pounds!"

"God!" Susan gasped. She sank to the floor, but no one noticed.

"Hear this, Lady B. 'My own steward cheated me regularly, I am sure, so I know it can be done, depend upon it,' " he read, each word more clipped than the one before. With an oath that made her ears hum, he balled both letters, strode to the window, and threw them as far as he could. When he turned around, staring at her, his face was as hard as stone. She could not meet his eyes, even as a voice inside her pleading "It's not me," tried to scratch its way out of her throat.

To her ineffable relief, the expression passed. In another moment, he gave her a hand up from the floor and helped her to sit on Lady Bushnell's bed. "I'm sorry, Suzie."

For me, or for you, she wanted to whisper. His hand was heavy on her shoulder, and she felt weighed down, instead of buoyed up, as usual, by his touch. She couldn't see his face, but she could see Lady Bushnell's, and her pain reached full circle.

The widow lay back against her propped-up pillows, looking every minute of her years. She groped for Susan's hand. "Dismiss it, Susan. He's not worthy of a tenth part of you." Her eyes seemed to fade and dim as she looked at the bailiff then, and Susan understood the source of her agony, even before she spoke of it. Oh don't speak it, dear lady, she wanted to say.

"Sergeant Wiggins, do you understand what damage parents can do to children?" She made a fierce gesture with her hands that had nothing to do with old age about it. "We've just flayed Susan with our anger, and it's not her fault."

"I don't mind," she managed to whisper. "You didn't mean it."

Her hand tightened around Susan's. "My dear, I am trying to point out to your lug-brained husband that parents can do some terrible things. I wonder if I am any better, but you will not tell me. Should I have forced Charles to take command of the regiment? Did *I* send a coward son to a living hell? Am I no better than Sir Rodney Hampton?"

Her voice was as loud as the bailiff's had been a moment ago. Susan covered her ears with her hands. I cannot bear it if you lie *or* tell the truth, husband, she thought.

"He was no coward," the bailiff lied.

"I don't believe you," the widow said.

"Then ask Susan and take her word over mine." His fingers bit into her shoulder like an auger.

"He was no coward," she lied. "David told me everything."

She knew if Lady Bushnell was to believe her, she had to look her in the eyes, so she did, raising her own ravaged face to the widow's. Her gaze was steady, dishonest as the day was long, and entirely fitting for a Hampton. She knew from the bottom of her heart that Lady Bushnell believed her, and the knowledge was bitter beyond belief.

Lady Bushnell relaxed against the pillows with a great sigh. She squeezed Susan's hand, then released it. "Very well, Susan," she murmured, closing her eyes.

I must get out of here, Susan thought, wondering if there were enough hours left in the day to get her to that door that seemed miles away. "Excuse me, please," she said, and hurried from the room.

Her husband followed her. She looked back at him, but did not stop as she moved toward the stairs. She paused halfway down, and looked up at him. "You can still tell her the truth," she pleaded.

"I don't have to now, Susan, and you know I can lie with the best of them."

She didn't know why she said what she did then, even before the words were entirely out of her mouth. It was illogical, and nonsensical, and totally without merit, and meaningless. It was the kind of thing that she would never sling at him, even on her worst day, because she knew, as only his wife could, how false an accusation it was.

"Did you lie about loving me, just to keep her cocooned here from the truth?"

She knew, if she lived to be older than everyone in England, Scotland, and Wales combined, she would never forget the shock on his face. He reeled back as though she had slapped him, then retaliated without a thought, even as she had.

"I consider that remark worthy of a . . . Hampton," he snapped, the word coming out like every dirty thing imaginable.

With a sob she turned and fled down the stairs and out the door.

Chapter Nineteen

I cannot believe I married such an idiot, she thought as she walked fast down the lane past the Waterloo wheat, and over the brow of the slope. I think if I had a sharp object in my hand, I would do him damage if he followed me. And he had better not follow me.

She looked over her shoulder then, wishing that he was behind her, even as she had wished him to hell only seconds before. You numbskull, she fumed at the top of the rise. You haven't even the good sense to follow me! Why was a woman ever plagued with such a husband? Well, never mind.

She took off her apron and stuffed it in the crotch of a tree beside the main road to Quilling. I will walk until I cool off, then I will go back and apologize, she thought. Of course, I don't know that I can apologize for being a Hampton, she reasoned as she walked along, scuffing at the pebbles in the road. But I can ask your forgiveness for doubting for even one moment that you loved me.

"That's the only thing I am really sure of right now," she said out loud, and felt immeasurably better. She stood still a moment, thinking about turning around, then decided against it as embarrassment washed over her again like a cold bucket of water. How could I be so hateful? she asked herself. And how could you say such a mean thing back?

All love and moans and groans aside, it's hard to be married, she decided as she walked thoughtfully into Quilling an hour later. She wasn't wearing a bonnet, and her face felt uncomfortably warm. She looked away from the sun, feeling the odd puffs of wind that blew here and there, as if as confused as she felt. The sky had a greenish cast to it and she felt a moment's uneasiness. I should go right home, she considered.

But she was tired from the walk and the exertion of all that anger. With another frown at the sky, she went inside the public house. It was cool and dark, as she had hoped it would be. She sighed and sat down at a table, grateful there was no mail coach stopped now, with travelers clambering for attention. *I shall sit here and feel sorry for myself for a few minutes, then go home and apologize to my dear husband.* She smiled to herself. *And he had better apologize to me, or I'll . . .*

"Would you like some tea, Mrs. Wiggins?"

It was the innkeep. She smiled at him and shook her head. "I never seem to come here with money for tea!"

He grinned at her, went back to the counter, and returned with tea. "I think I can trust you or David to stop by with a coin, next time you're in Quilling."

She gave him a grateful look and sipped the tea. While the cares of the world didn't exactly roll off her shoulders, they did loosen up a bit. She looked at the brew in the cup. *I wonder what other people in the world do without tea?* she asked herself. *They can't imagine themselves civilized.* She blushed a deep red. *Not that I was so civilized an hour ago.*

"Mrs. Wiggins . . . is everything all right at the manor?"

She looked up at the innkeep, a question in her eyes. "Sir?" She put her hand to her hair then, realizing how wind-blown and blowsy she must look, she who never let a pin get out of place, except when David, drat him, played with her hair. *And here I am without bonnet or gloves,* she thought in dismay. *No wonder he is worried.*

So much concern deserved a straight answer. "No, no, we're all fine at Quilling Manor," she assured him, then took a deep breath. "It's only that I've had a dreadful quarrel with my husband, and I stormed off the place."

The innkeep chuckled and pulled out a chair. "May I?" he asked.

"Of course."

He seated himself. "A bad fight?"

She rolled her eyes. "It was a brawl! I can't believe how rude we were to each other." *What am I doing saying this to an innkeep?* she asked herself as she took another sip. She glanced at him then, and could see only sympathy, and a lurking good humor that made her glad all over again that she lived near such a friendly village. "It was awful. Ghastly."

He nodded, serious enough, but with that smile playing around his lips. "So ghastly that you cannot go back and make up?"

"Oh, no! It's just . . ."

". . . hard to swallow your pride, Mrs. Wiggins?" he asked, his voice kind.

She nodded. "Hard for him, too, I think," she said in a small voice.

"Oh, Welshmen are a trial, so I hear," he agreed, shaking his head. "And we all know David's past. He was quite a blackguard in his younger days, and you know those army men."

"He's a wonderful man!" she exclaimed, leaping to the bailiff's defense. "And as for the army, there never was a better sergeant major, I am sure! And if you could see him with his wheat, and the sheep, and . . ." She paused and looked at the innkeep, watching his smile grow larger and larger. "Oh, sir! I'm a goose."

He laughed. "Only a little one."

She finished her tea, pushed the cup away, and rested her chin on her hands. "You're married, I know. Do you ever have disagreements with your wife?"

The innkeeper leaned back in his chair. "Oh, ho, so now it's just a disagreement?"

"Well, yes," she admitted. "But I wanted to rip his arms out and beat him with them!" She paused. "For a few minutes." She leaned closer to the innkeeper. "I hope you'll overlook this silliness, sir."

The innkeeper smiled and looked around the room vacantly. "Did someone just say we had a conversation? Funny, I disremember it."

She gave the innkeeper her sunniest smile and rose to go when the whole building shook with a clap of thunder. It was followed by a tumult of rain. She sat back down in surprise.

The innkeeper went to the door and looked out. "This is a relief for us, isn't it? I own I do not like it when the sky turns green and it's hotter than Dutch love. Thank God the storm's broke."

She went to the door and peered out. The street was deserted now, with people seeking shelter in doorways and under awnings. The rain thundered down, breaking the oppression that had hovered all day. She watched it with equanimity. When it stops, I can walk home in the cool now, she thought.

A sudden blast of cold air from the north made her take a step back from the doorway. The innkeeper closed the door against it and went to the window with her. "I don't like that," he muttered, looking intently to the north. "Someone's getting a load of hail right now, I don't doubt."

She nodded in agreement, then sucked in her breath so suddenly that he stared at her in consternation. "The wheat!" she gasped. "Oh, the wheat!"

She wrenched open the door and ran into the street for a better look up to the north, up the road she had just stomped in such anger. The innkeeper followed her into the street and took her arm, but she shook him off. "I have to go home," she shouted, over the wind and rain. "I have to."

"David would want you to wait," he insisted, even as he released her arm.

"No, he wouldn't," she contradicted. "I know him much better than you." And I know what that wheat means to him, she thought as she ducked her head against the worst of the rain and ran up the road. It's every dream he's ever had, and it's his salvation from Waterloo.

She was soaked to the skin before she left the village, but she ran on, stopping only long enough when her shoe strap ripped to fling off both shoes, tug up her skirts and run faster. The lightning frightened her, but it was a fast-moving storm, and left only flickers of light and sullen thunder to accompany the pounding rain. Her side ached as she ran toward the farm, past the turnoff to the sheepfold, and into the barley field to save a few minutes. And then she was over the rise and staring down at the Waterloo wheat, holding her side and trying to catch her breath.

She gasped in horror at the sight before her. The wheat, beautiful and lime green only an hour ago, lay flat and churned into the ground. Hail littered the field like canister shot. If a mighty army had fought over the field before her, she knew it could not have looked worse. Words failed her, even thoughts, as she stared at all that destruction then sank to her knees, utterly devastated. When she caught her breath, she sat back on her heels finally, and smoothed her hair away from her eyes, thinking that if she could see better, maybe it wouldn't be as horrible.

It was worse. Every stalk seemed bent and disfigured from the storm. As she grieved and cried, she saw the bailiff walking slowly up the slope, his hands held out, palm down, as though he could only stare in shock and measure his phantom wheat still. She didn't think he saw her, a muddy little figure toward the top of the slope, so she stood up and started toward him, slipping, but running faster and faster until she threw herself into his arms and nearly bowled him over backward.

"Suzie!" he said, his voice hollow with pain. "Suzie," he repeated, her name a caress this time. "Suzie," he whispered, and her name held the whole world in it.

She could only burrow her face into his shoulder and cry, so he clung to her until she was silent. Unable to look at him, she wiped her eyes on his soaked sleeve. "I am so sorry about the wheat, David. How can you bear it?"

She didn't really think he could hold her any tighter, or closer, but he did. "Wheat? Who cares about the wheat, Suzie? It's you! Can you forgive me for being so rude? Oh, I love you."

Her eyes widened, and then she understood him perfectly. "Oh, David," she whispered. "*I'm* more important than the *wheat* right now?"

"Oh, God!" he exclaimed, hugging her to him again. "I can plant this stuff again. It's you I can't replace, Suzie."

The rain poured down and she felt herself sinking into the mud, but she never felt safer or more secure in her life than at the moment. "I'll gladly forgive you, my love, if you'll forgive me."

"Done, then," he said, "and over and forgotten."

From the comfort of his soggy embrace, she looked at the field. "This is terrible."

"It's not the worst thing I've ever seen," he replied. "Not by half."

"Waterloo?" she murmured.

He kissed the top of her head. "Oh, no, Suzie, no. The worst sight in my whole life was your face on the stairs when I said those rude things."

"But everyone knows how dreadful Waterloo was!"

He took her arm and started down the slope with her. "It was just a battle—granted, a huge ordeal—but still just a battle. I did my job, got my pay, and even a medal, too. But you're my wife, and absolutely bone of my bone and flesh of my flesh." He kissed her muddy hand. "The two don't compare."

She could only sigh and stare at him. "David."

"That's it?" he asked after a longish pause.

"Yes. I can't think of anything else to say."

They moved slowly down the slope. She stopped at the bottom and looked back at the wheat. "Will you plow it under and try again next year?"

He gazed at the destruction, his lips pursed, nodding to himself. "I have a better idea, Suzie. I'm going to leave it alone, and see what happens."

"David, it's dead!"

He turned her around and started her toward the manor again. "Since I swiped that handful of wheat from the granary at La Haye Sainte, I've been tinkering with it, adding strains of strong

wheat from around here, and from Yorkshire and Kent. Let's see
how sturdy it is. Call this my ultimate experiment, if you want."

"It might come back?" she asked, then looked over her shoulder in amazement.

Amused, he turned her head around and kept her pointed toward the house. "Let's give it time, Suzie. Like us."

She tried not to spend too much time looking at the wheat
throughout the month of July, but without much success. She
moved the desk in Lady Bushnell's room so she wasn't facing the
window anymore, and that helped, but evenings found her looking, even though her devotion to that battered field amused the
bailiff.

"I think you're more worried than I am," he said one night
when they were in bed, drowsy from a day of summer work.

She backed herself more firmly into his slack embrace and
tugged his arm over her. "Since you don't seem to consider this
one of your major decisions to worry about—I will remind you of
that conversation—then someone must!"

"Silly," he said, idly massaging her breast, then resting his
cheek on top of hers. "Then here's a matter of major importance
for you: I'm feeling a huge urge to give you my best efforts right
now."

"I can tell," she said mildly. "Well, if you refuse to worry, then
I suppose I should humor a lunatic."

She did, of course, with the greatest of pleasure. When he slept
beside her, warm and heavy, she thought about Lady Bushnell.
Each day took them closer to the end of the reminiscence, and
each day saw her grow weaker, but continue to soldier on. Susan
kissed David's shoulder and wrapped her arms around him as he
stirred and muttered something. Lady Bushnell knows the end is
near, she thought.

The widow had said as much to David only the day before as
the two of them sat beside her bed as she dictated her story to
Susan. They had finished the last battle on Spanish soil, and were
beginning the march through the Pyrenees that would lead to
death and the end of the colonel's story. Susan could see how the
ordeal was exhausting her, but when the woman refused to quit,
Susan pleaded a headache. I'm not lying, either, she thought. I
don't feel so good myself. "Let's stop now, Lady Bushnell, for I
am tired, even if you are not," she murmured.

"Very well, Susan," the widow said. "You can get my powders
now."

Susan did as she was bid, but stood still by the bureau, glass in hand, when the widow motioned her bailiff closer. He sat on her bed then, his hands on either side of her in a gesture so intimate that Susan felt tears in her eyes. Oh, Lady B, are you father and mother to both of us? I have not been much of a lady's companion, but you have been a parent to me . . . and my husband.

The widow put her hand on David's cheek, and he kissed her fingers, while Susan swallowed the lump in her throat. "My dear sergeant," she began, her voice exhausted. "I will not pester you about Waterloo anymore."

"I wish I could have obliged you, my dear," he said.

She patted his cheek. "I know." She turned her head slightly in a glance that took in Susan, too. "I must accept the fact that I could not go everywhere my dear army went."

In the week that followed, they were diverted momentarily by the letter from Aunt Louisa, thanking Lady Bushnell for sending three hundred pounds to keep her wretched brother from Newgate, and assuring them that it would never happen again. "Until the next time," Susan murmured when she folded the letter. "Oh, my lady, thank you for saving him."

She nodded. "You must deal with him next time, Susan, you and your husband, and I fear it will not be easy." She patted Susan's hand, her eyes wistful. "I hope you will learn, in time, to forgive him for . . . for not meeting your expectations." She sighed. "Few of us do, I fear."

"I don't know that I can forgive him," Susan said honestly.

"In time, my dear, in time," the widow murmured.

It was a week of almost superhuman effort for Lady Bushnell. The widow dictated only in short sentences, her hand pressed to her chest most of the time, as if to block out continual pain. She called David sergeant now, and through her own grief, Susan was not sure that she even knew him as bailiff anymore.

"I cannot bear it," she told her husband on the stairs as they went up after dinner to sit with her.

"You must, of course, Suzie," he murmured, his arm around her. "I was so busy with the barley harvest today, I forgot to ask you at dinner: is she almost done with the reminiscence?"

"We finished it this afternoon, David." She began to cry. "It's over now."

He sat with her on the stairs, his arms around her until she could dry her eyes, square her shoulders, and march into the room with him.

To her surprise, Lady Bushnell was sitting in her chair by the window, the mound of letters in her lap, and the green case with the Waterloo medal on top.

"I'm tired of this room," she announced, and to Susan's relief, her voice sounded strong again. "Sergeant, I want you to take me out to that slope. Susan, you go ask Tom the cowman to take the chair. Sergeant, you can carry me." She smiled at him then, and the years seemed to tumble from her shoulders. "I remember that you carried me once, didn't you? After Busaco, when the river was high?"

"I did."

Susan didn't dare look at him. She knew that voice.

They did as she ordered, Tom carrying the chair and putting it where David quietly directed. He nodded to the widow and hurried back down the slope, shaking his head. The bailiff set Lady Bushnell in the chair, still clutching her precious letters and the medal case.

She was silent as she looked over the Waterloo wheat, watching it dance in the early-evening breeze. It had returned, as its engineer had predicted, battered but whole, the grain heads heavy now with the fruit of summer. Here and there were bare patches where the pounding had been too great, but the field stood and waved its own challenge to the elements.

"You were right about the wheat," Lady Bushnell said, reaching up her hand for the bailiff to hold it. "You are not always right, though. I ask one thing more of you, Sergeant Wiggins."

"Pues, le pídame, dama," he said, surprisingly, in his bad Peninsula Spanish.

She flashed him a smile that stripped away more years, until Susan had to turn away to keep her heart from cracking in two. Oh, Lady Bushnell, she thought. I love you so much. You are the bravest of the brave.

"Was I wrong to send Charlie to the regiment? Was he a coward at Waterloo? Be truthful now, you rascal, I beg of you."

Susan bowed her head and looked away from the wheat, across to the field beyond, where the sun was starting to set. Please, David, do the right thing.

"Yes, you were wrong. He was a coward and unfit to command us at Waterloo," David said, his voice low and wrenched out of his body by the roots. "A lesser engagement he could have handled, but not Waterloo. We stayed alive because of Colonel March."

"And you?"

"And me. And the other sergeants who didn't make it out."

It was a lot to digest, and Susan was not surprised at the silence from the chair. She turned around and rested herself against David's back. "Thank you a thousand times," she murmured against his shirt. When she felt him tense, she knew Lady Bushnell was struggling to speak. She closed her eyes and listened with her heart.

"Do you think Charlie will understand that I only did what I thought was best?" she asked in a voice destroyed with grief. "He was from a family of warriors, so he had to be one, too. The times demanded it. Didn't they, sergeant?"

"*Sì, dama.*"

"But tell me please, was he shot by his own? I have heard it rumored, no matter how you've tried to protect me. I must know all, Sergeant."

"No, my lady. He died in battle. He was not shot by his own."

Lady Bushnell sighed then, a great sound of relief. "Thank God for that." Her voice changed then, taking on its authority then. "Very well, Sergeant, I wish you and your wife would just leave me alone here until the sun goes down. Go away for a while." She managed a chuckle. "Susan, you should have brought a blanket with you, as I have seen from my window what you and the sergeant do, when the mood was on you, and you thought I was sleeping!"

Susan laughed and took her husband's hand, and kissed it. "That only encourages him. Come, Sergeant, let's leave your *dama* alone for a time."

He nodded, and released the widow's hand. He kissed her on the cheek, pausing there a moment until she chuckled. "Sergeant, don't you dare cry. I'll lose all faith in the regular army, if you do! Kiss me, Susan."

She did, determined not to cry.

"You weren't much of a lady's companion," the woman murmured, her hand against Susan's cheek. "You'll never be a pianist, and I'm not sure modern novels are for me."

"True. Actually, I felt more like a daughter, Lady Bushnell." She dug deep within herself. "I love you, you know."

"I know." Lady Bushnell straightened herself. "Thank you for these letters. Now, go on. Take the sergeant somewhere for a stroll."

"Yes, ma'am."

"And you might go ahead and tell him what I've been suspecting, if you haven't already."

"How did you know?" she asked, suddenly shy.

"I've had two of my own, and I know the signs, my love."

Susan led the bailiff away, and to her relief he did not protest. She tugged him farther up the slope and down to the trees beside the road.

"Tell me what?" he asked when she finally allowed him to stop. They leaned against the fence beside the road. "I think I know, but please, let's hear it."

"Well, maybe someday you can write 'Waterloo Seed Farm, Wiggins and Son,' on the top of your order books," she said quietly. "Or maybe 'Daughter.' Women are good at growing things, too."

"Obviously you are," he said after he kissed her. "Thank you."

She rested against the fence, then turned to face him. "Now you owe me the truth, David."

"I already told it. You heard me."

"You did, but not all, I'm thinking. Charlie *was* killed by his own. You told me that before. Even in the end you could not tell her all the truth."

He looked back at the hill as though he could see Lady Bushnell through it. "I do not think an old woman needs that much truth. She had enough information now to square herself with her son—and herself."

Susan placed herself in front of her husband and pulled him close to her, hooking her thumbs into the back of his pants so he could not move away from the fence. "I know you."

"I should think so," he temporized, his expression cautious.

"I know you," she repeated more firmly. "Who are you protecting still? I want to know. Is it . . . is it Colonel March?" She leaned her forehead against him for a brief moment. "Is it you?"

He hesitated, then looked down at her. "I can't lie to you, can I?"

"No, you can't. Your lying, stealing, thieving, poaching days are long gone, Sergeant, and you know it."

He waited, and thought, and she did not press him further. Finally he put his arms around her. "It wasn't anyone in the regiment, so there's no shame there." He sighed. "He had to die, Susan; we all knew it. This wasn't the same regiment that fought in the Peninsula. We had green troops. You could see them weaken with each charge of French cavalry up that slope." He shook his head, as if trying to rid himself of the memory. "And there was poor Charlie, screaming and scurrying around inside the square, trying to burrow under the corpses."

She shuddered, trying to imagine the horror.

"The person who killed him didn't belong to the regiment."

"Who?" she demanded.

"Joel Steinman," he said simply.

"God, no!" she breathed. "But . . . but you said. His arm . . ."

"It wasn't all the way off then. That came later at the field hospital." The bailiff's arms tightened around her. "He watched Charlie through one charge, and how Major March and Sergeant Mabry and I worked like Turks to plug holes here and there, draw the men in, keep them battle ready, tell them to aim and fire. It just happened that I was watching him when he did it."

"How?" she asked, barely breathing out the question.

"After that charge, he took a pistol from Lieutenant Chase's body, propped it on his knee, and drilled Charlie right through the forehead."

He could speak then, and more freely, as if the telling of it released him. His tone became almost conversational. "It was the neatest hole you ever saw, Susan. An engineer couldn't have spaced the thing better, right there between his eyes."

"Joel," she said.

"Joel. I'll never forget the look on his face. He put down that pistol—it was slippery with his blood, dripping in it—and leaned back against that stack of corpses with a serenity I could never even attempt. Susan, I think the army missed out on a great warrior in Joel Steinman."

Quietly, arm in arm, they walked back over the brow of the hill and stood, watching the Waterloo wheat in the last light before the sun set.

"She's asleep, Suzie," the bailiff said as he looked toward the chair.

"No, my love, she's dead," Susan said. "Stay here."

To her relief, he did not follow her. Lady Bushnell sat with her head forward against her chest. Her eyes were closed, but she seemed to be staring at the letters in her slack grasp. As Susan watched in silence, grief, and love, the breeze picked up some of the letters and carried them into the wheat, to lodge fast against the stalks. She watched them go, peace in her heart.

The medal box had fallen to the ground. She knelt beside the chair and picked it up, running her hand over the velvet cover, as Lady Bushnell had done so many times. She opened it, and took out the medal, shaking it to the length of its ribbon, admiring it again.

"For heroes," she whispered as she raised up and put the medal around Lady Bushnell's neck. "For heroes."

Epilogue

She didn't try to force David to go to the funeral at Bushnell, the family estate. It was enough that he prepared the coffin, spending hours at it and coming to bed red-eyed and in need of great solace. She and Mrs. Skerlong dressed the body and tucked the letters around her feet. She kept the reminiscence. The sergeant put the medal around her neck again before he nailed the coffin shut.

"And so it goes," he said as he watched the carter take Lady Bushnell away to the family vault to lie quiet and in peace at last beside husband, daughter, and son. "Suzie, we'd better pack. I can't see any of Lord Bushnell's relatives who inherit keeping us on here to play with wheat and shear sheep." He turned his attention to the slope as he did so often now. "I wish I could have bought it, of course, but Lord Hackingham by Gloucester did promise me a place, if I wanted it. It may take a few years, but we'll do all right." He tightened his grip on her shoulder as the cart moved over the hill and out of sight. "I'll write him in a day or two."

He still hadn't written by the end of the week, but she did not press him. She was content to stay close by him, resting her head against his shoulder during the long evenings when time was painful, and holding him in her arms as he tried to sleep.

By the next week, the bailiff seemed to have turned a page in his own book of life. He woke up one morning to tease her about her familiarity with the washbasin as she retched into it, then glared at him. After a half hour's consolation of a more tender nature, he whistled his way down the stairs, and her heart was glad again.

They were finishing lunch and going back to the inventory that the Bushnell estate had requested when Colonel and Mrs. March pulled up at the front door in a barouche.

"Colonel, how nice to see you," the bailiff said from the front steps. "And Lady Bushne . . . no, no, Mrs. March!"

Susan joined him, and welcomed them in for tea in the sitting room. As they sipped their tea, the Marches spoke of their honeymoon in France and Belgium.

"Sergeant, you wouldn't believe what's happened to the battlefield!" the colonel exclaimed, setting down his cup with a click.

"Oh? What can you do to a battlefield?"

"It chaps my thighs," March said. "You know the tree . . ."

"Who could forget?"

"Gone. Tourists!" He spit out the word like a bad taste. "And damn me if the Belgians—the damned Belgians!—aren't building a monument bigger than Babel! Chaps my thighs," he muttered again.

Susan twinkled her eyes at her husband, and he winked back. "It was just a battle, sir," he said.

Colonel March glared at him. "Sergeant Wiggins, that's almost blasphemy!" He muttered something into his teacup as he drank the last of it. "But I'll overlook it." He smiled at his wife then, and reached into his coat. "Here's what I really came to give you. The Bushnell family—Lord Bushnell had some distant cousins— thought I should give this to you. Here. Read it."

The bailiff took the letter and opened it. He read it through, swallowed several times, and handed it wordlessly to Susan.

She took the letter, feeling light-headed and knowing it had nothing to do with the baby. She sat on the edge of David's chair and he put his arm on her leg, as though in serious need of her presence. She read the letter, then folded it quietly and tucked it in her heart.

"Quilling Manor? And the whole farm?" she asked when she could speak.

The colonel nodded. "And she willed you two an annuity for ten years so you can get the Waterloo Seed Farm into full production. I think you both meant more to her than you knew."

Susan kissed the top of her husband's head. No, Colonel March, she thought, we knew.